The Vilokan Asylum of the Magically and Mentally Deranged (Books 1-3)

ISBN: 9781804675816
Perfect Bound

First published in 2023 by bookvault Publishing, Peterborough, United Kingdom

An Environmentally friendly book printed and bound in England by bookvault, powered by printondemand-worldwide

THE CURSE OF CAIN

THEOPHILUS MONROE

PROLOGUE

Ten Years Ago

IT WAS MY FIRST job interview. You'd think, over the course of my six-thousand years of existence, I'd have interviewed for a job at some point. For the better part of a century, I'd operated a private psychotherapy practice in New York City. Ever since I graduated from the University of Vienna, the prized student of the renowned Sigmund Freud. I didn't need a job. I worked for myself. It was better that way. I'd always had difficulty playing with others. But this was a once in a lifetime opportunity and I needed a change of pace.

I had plenty of experience as a psychotherapist. This was the first time I'd ever considered my "curse" as a qualification.

I glanced at my typewriter-produced resume. I know computers are supposed to be more efficient. I won't say that you can't teach an old dog new tricks, but, well, it certainly doesn't come easy.

I chuckled to myself. The whole old dog thing...

The World's First-Ever Werewolf.

It looked just as absurd on my resume as it sounded when I read it aloud. It wasn't my only "First-Ever." The other one, though, well, the entire world knew it already. Anyone who'd ever bothered to pick up a Bible and read the first handful of chapters. Not to mention, it was hardly a qualification or skill.

So far as I knew, the Voodoo Queen didn't have an official job application. If she did, I hadn't seen it yet. Maybe I'd have to fill one out *if* she offered me the job. The nurse who recommended me, a rather attractive woman who I knew only by the name "Rutherford," suggested that based on my unique background and her recommendation, the interview was little more than a formality.

It isn't everyone who has both professional and supernatural qualifications to serve as the lead psychiatrist at an asylum for the magically and mentally deranged.

I felt out of place as I made my way through the French Quarter. I rarely wore a suit. A nice button-up shirt, a tie if necessary and a decent pair of slacks was my usual get-up. But I was both interviewing for a job and meeting a queen. I needed to dress in my Sunday best. Not that I was a churchgoer, or anything. I wasn't opposed to religion. Many people say they feel "judged" when they go to church. I don't know about that. But when you're renowned in their holy book as the world's first murderer, someone who killed his own brother, well, I suppose "being judged" is baked in to the experience.

I double checked the address on the index card Rutherford gave me when we'd met in New York.

I cocked my head. This couldn't be right.

A head shop in the French Quarter? The name *Marie's*, in a neon glow on the sign above the door, certainly fit. The Voodoo Queen, Marie Laveau, was the one I was supposed to meet.

I pressed open the door. A chime sounded, probably meant to alert one of the place's patrons that a potential customer had arrived. I covered my nose. I don't mind the smell of incense, but in this case, the smörgåsbord of odors was overbearing.

A middle-aged man, a joint in one hand, wearing a Guns 'n Roses t-shirt, pressed his way through a beaded curtain from another room.

"Can I help you, dude?"

I smiled. "I'm here to see Marie."

"The name's Chad."

"Nice to meet you, Chad. But it's a Marie, not a Chad, I'm supposed to come see. She's expecting me."

Chad cocked his head. "Dude. No way. You're... him?"

I sighed. "I am Dr. Cain."

"Holy crap! I mean, you're famous!"

"I'm well aware. Though, I suppose, the word infamous would be more fitting."

"I know, right? It's not everyday you meet a Bible villain. I mean, Batman has the joker. You're like the joker to Abraham or something."

I narrowed my eyes. "I'm not a villain, despite what you've heard about me. Not to mention, Chad, have you even read the book of Genesis? Abraham wasn't even born yet when I appeared in that book."

"Right on. Right on. No judgment, man. You do you. I mean, killing people sucks. But you know, it's the past, right?"

I nodded and narrowed my eyes. "The distant past."

Chad extended his joint toward me. "Want a puff? You know, to chill out, or whatever. I'd hate for you to, you know..."

"I don't kill people regularly, Chad. At least not so long as we aren't under a full moon."

Chad scratched his head. "I don't know what that means. But that's funny. Full moons. Werewolves. Nice joke."

I smiled. "Not a joke. Please, I'd like to speak with Madam Laveau. We had an appointment."

"Right on. Right on. Follow me, dude."

I resisted the urge to sigh out-loud. I knew that Voodoo wasn't exactly conventional. I suppose, though, my experience dealing with monarchs in the past gave a distinct impression of what I should expect when coming to interview with a Voodoo Queen. The last thing I expected was a head shop instead of a castle, or a stoner like Chad acting as the queen's gatekeeper.

"You must be Dr. Cain!" a woman exclaimed as we entered her back room. The odors in the head shop were a mixture of various kinds of incense. In this room, what I presumed to be the queen's chambers, it was frankincense that predominated.

"Your Highness," I said, bowing my head.

"Call me Marie. And have a seat. I have to say, I'm quite thrilled by our potential partnership. We could certainly use someone with your qualifications."

I handed Marie my resume and sat down on an overstuffed couch. My butt sank in about three feet when I plopped down on it.

Marie laughed. "You didn't need a resume, Cain. Your reputation speaks for itself."

I sighed. "My reputation isn't usually what I like to lead with when trying to make an introduction."

"Well, why not? You're the world's first werewolf! You'd have to be a real square to find that as anything less than intriguing."

I snorted. "That wasn't the reputation I was speaking about. Most people don't even know that about me."

Marie raised one eyebrow. "You mean that whole Cain and Abel story?"

I nodded. "That's the problem, isn't it? It's hardly Cain's story. It's not my brother's story, either. What would the story of Romeo and Juliet be if all anyone ever read was the last scene, the tragedy at the end?"

Marie bit her lip. "So, you and Abel were forbidden lovers?"

"Christ, no!" I said, laughing. "That's not what I meant!"

Marie snickered. "No judgment, either way. I mean, there weren't so many people in the world back then. You had to get your jollies somehow, child."

I cocked my head. It wasn't every day that someone called me "child," especially since I was reasonably certain that I was the oldest living person on earth. "I only mean to say that my relationship with my brother was a long story that ended regrettably. And my role in that tragedy, well, it's a regret that I've had to live with ever since."

Marie waved her hand through the air. "Well, I should say your crime certainly falls outside of the statute of limitations."

I smiled. "Right. I'm not exactly worried about being arrested for it."

"Most job applications don't even require you to report a felony if it's been longer than seven years since your conviction. We don't need to speak of that matter any further at all unless you'd like to, Dr. Cain. I'm more interested in your professional credentials."

I smiled. "I was mentored by Sigmund Freud. I've been operating a private practice in New York for the better part of a century, now."

"And as the world's first werewolf, how has that factored into your professional experience?"

"It hasn't. I mean, aside from not taking appointments around a full moon, it doesn't play much of a role. I suppose, you know, since it's the curse I inherited as punishment for killing my brother, though, my experience gives me a unique insight when dealing with troubled patients."

"How so?"

"Well, I clearly have dealt with family issues. You'd be surprised how much one's family dynamics undergird many psychological conditions. And as a werewolf, I know what it's like to come to grips with the worst of myself, the passions I feel, and what can happen if the wolf gets out of the cage, literally or metaphorically."

"Tell me, Dr. Cain. What's it like. As a wolf?"

"Anything you feel as a human, any anxiety or regret buried in the subconscious mind, fuels the wolf. In my case, it's crucial I sort out any issues or resentments. But in my experience, while not everyone literally becomes a werewolf, there is a monster within everyone that can emerge, birthed from the pain of one's past, that must be dealt with before it takes over and destroys lives."

"Tell me, Cain. Have you ever treated any witches, hougans, or mambos?"

I cocked my head. "I've had patients who practice Wicca, if that's what you mean."

Marie smiled. "You've lived long enough, Cain, and seen your share of things others have not, that I presume you know that's not exactly what I mean."

I nodded. "Of course. I've met my share of witches through the years. I can't say my experience with vodouisants is all that extensive. And I can't say I've treated anyone whose practice of their craft goes beyond common, harmless and even benevolent, spells."

"How about vampires? Have you ever treated a vampire, Cain?"

I shook my head. "I can't say that I have. I've met a few through the years. But again, I can't say I've ever had a vampire patient if that's what you mean."

"No worries, Cain. I didn't expect you had. Perhaps a few were-wolves?"

I smiled. "Of course."

Marie grinned. "I think we should make for fantastic partners with what years I have remaining."

I narrowed my eyes. "What years you have remaining? I don't know your entire story, Marie. But I know you've already lived beyond the years most humans might."

"But not nearly so long as you, Cain. Still, I do not intend to live forever. I must choose a successor. One, to take my place as the Voodoo Queen. And, another, who can fill my role at the Vilokan Asylum, someone who can help those with damaged minds. You bring with you qualifications I lack. As a supernatural being of a sort yourself, you have a great foundation, a reason to empathize with our patients. With my guidance, Cain, I hope you will continue my efforts to care for our community after I'm gone."

I took a deep breath. "How much do you know of my condition, the nature of my curse?"

"I understand the risks involved if that's what you're asking."

"I presume that I'd be expected to treat dangerous and powerful supernaturals. You realize, if any of them attempt to kill me..."

"I know all about the seven-fold curse, Dr. Cain. I've done this for a long time. I'm confident that with certain precautions, we can ensure that none of the patients evoke the mark of Cain."

"But if someone ever did, if even one patient tried to kill me, the results would be catastrophic. If Vilokan survived, at all..."

Marie smiled at me kindly as she interrupted my words. "In the Voodoo world, when dealing with a supernatural person of any sort, there are always curses or marks that could lead to equally devastating consequences, Cain. Managing such risks, well, as the Voodoo Queen I suppose you could say that's what I do."

"But you said it yourself. You're looking for a successor. Once you're gone, how can I be sure that I'll have the same protections?"

Marie took my hand in hers. "The successor I choose will be equally capable as I am to do what must be done to preserve the safety of Vilokan. You can trust me, Cain."

I nodded. "In that case, I have a few questions."

"I'm an open book. Ask and I shall answer."

"Do you offer your employees a decent health care plan?"

Marie smiled. "Certainly, though I doubt you'll be using it much given your... condition. Welcome to Vilokan, Dr. Cain."

CHAPTER ONE

Present Day

THE COOL, DECEMBER AIR fluttered through my thick fur, chilling my hide. I leaped from one patch of dry ground to the next, making my way to the old graveyard in the middle of Manchac Swamp. I peered through the canopy above. The blue light of the full moon cast shadows on my beastly form. Perched on my hind legs, I stretched out toward the sky and howled. The rougarou echoed my call. It didn't take long before the pack of five wolves came bounding together through the swamp, splashing their way through the waters.

Donald appeared first, his silver fur catching the moonlight from above even as bits of algae clung to his enormous frame. He was the pack's alpha. Even in human form, he was a large man, nearly six and a half feet tall and eclipsing three hundred pounds. As a wolf, he was twice the size.

Were I a normal wolf, being smaller of stature than Donald, he'd resist my dominance. But I was the first werewolf. I was the alpha of alphas.

I snarled, baring my teeth. Wolves typically exhibited their prowess in any number of ways. Growling, fighting, even mounting one another. I wasn't about to mount Donald. I might have been a werewolf, but I was no animal.

With a whimper, Donald lowered himself to the ground in deference to my authority. I won't say that size doesn't matter when it comes to one's place in a pack's hierarchy, but it's secondary to experience. We'd been through this routine before. It didn't take much to exert control over the pack. I'd been working with them for a while.

This wasn't your average pack. There are two conditions that might cause one who has inherited my curse to shift. The full moon is, of course, the most common reason the wolf might emerge. The second, rarer condition, is if the wolf is in proximity to an infernal object. For more than a century, such a relic bound these wolves: the Witch of Endor's flambeau.

The witch had used it in her necromantic art. She'd formed it from the fat of her own child. She imbued it with infernal power. It was with this very relic that she once evoked the spirit of the Prophet Samuel. Though, in her time, she did much more than that.

So long as the flambeau burned in Manchac Swamp, it enthralled these rougarou. It held them in their wolfish form and ensured they never wandered from the swamps. About a year ago, that changed. The spirit who guarded the infernal item took material form. She left the swamp and took the flambeau with her.

With the hellish relic gone, these wolves now behaved as common werewolves might. Only, living as wolves, never shifting back into human form, for more than a century... well... they had more than a few issues.

They say you can't teach an old dog new tricks. What nonsense! These wolves certainly could learn. They could adjust to their new mode of existence. I intended to help them do exactly that! It might take some time. A century's worth of habit, living constantly as wolves, isn't easy to overcome. But it's certainly possible. After all, it wasn't until I'd met Sigmund Freud, who later trained me in his methods, that I learned to process several thousand years of pent up resentment toward my long-deceased parents, my brother, and even God himself.

I had more than one motive to work with the rougarou. The well-being of the pack was my chief concern. As a psychiatrist, I'm always looking out for the benefit of my patients.

For the better part of the decade, I ran the Vilokan Asylum for the Magically and Mentally Deranged. Treating warped vampires and werewolves, troubled witches or shifters, comes with risks. No matter how brutish or murderous my patients might be, it was my job to ad-vocate for them. I was the world's first murderer—perhaps you've read my regrettable tale in the book of Genesis. I had reason to empathize with my patients. Change was possible. It was for me. I was no longer the same envious, resentful man who'd killed his brother.

With the rougarou in my thrall, we took off across the swamp. There was no better way to spend the night as a werewolf than to run. Over the course of the last six thousand years, I'd spent my share of nights alone. I'd run through the deserts of Nod, to the east of Eden. I traversed the Persian Royal Road and the roads of the old Roman Empire. I climbed the Alps and the Himalayas. Howling at the moon atop Mount Everest was a crowning achievement.

None of these things could have been possible had it not been for this gift—what I once thought to be a curse. And none of these ad-ventures were more satisfying than when I joined another pack, like the rougarou in Manchac Swamp.

We ran, and we ran, from one side of the swamp to the next. Even the gators who swam in the water didn't dare peek above the surface when the rougarou were on the prowl. When a full moon graced the skies, it was as if all of nature bowed to our temporary rule.

We reached the tree line at the edge of the swamp. Before we turned to make another pass across the swamp, we paused, admired the moon in the sky above us, and howled a reverent song of adoration to the force that granted us our power.

A wolf echoed back. I cocked my head as my pointed ears instinctively bent toward the sound. A single, solitary wolf in the distance, mimicking our reverie. It wasn't a common wolf. There was no mistaking a werewolf's cry.

My heart skipped a beat. The wolf was in the city. The sound came from somewhere near the French Quarter.

My first instinct was to take off as fast as I could. But I couldn't leave these rougarou behind. They weren't ready for that. Without my guidance, they'd lose control. Still, a werewolf alone in the city was a recipe for disaster. There was only one option. We had to pursue the solitary wolf *together*. If we didn't, the creature wouldn't only leave a body count behind, but its presence would attract hunters to the region. The *last* thing I had the time to deal with, now, were werewolf hunters.

I growled. We didn't speak when we were in wolf form. Not in human language. But there was no mistaking my intentions. The rougarou knew what we had to do. I darted headlong toward the city. They followed me at a brisk pace. I was faster than the rest. I made myself slow down just enough to ensure they could keep up. If I got too far away, my thrall over them would falter. And if that happened... you don't want to know.

It's not that I lacked faith in the pack. These wolves were well on their way. They'd progressed far in our group therapy sessions at the Vilokan Asylum for the Magically and Mentally Deranged. But they weren't ready to be left alone.

If a single wolf broke from the pack, or their natural alpha claimed control, there was no telling how they'd respond. After all, there was one cardinal rule that I'd insisted they follow. That they never leave the swamp. If they saw me break that rule myself, they'd follow suit. If they entered the city without my lead, there was no telling what horrors might ensue. Not only would it likely lead to human casualties, but it would probably undo all the progress we'd made over the last couple of years.

I had to be careful. Werewolves are fast. Not the speediest super-natural species out there. Vampires and certain elementals are quicker. And, of course, there are those who can teleport, who negate the need for speed entirely. Still, being faster than most mammals, and even some automobiles, it wouldn't take long for us to reach the city.

Yes, werewolves have many gifts. Strength and speed are chief among them. Subtlety, however, was not something that suited us. Werewolf 007 was likely never to become a thing.

Still, we were as discreet as we could be. If anyone saw us, word would travel fast. In ages past, it wasn't such a risk. In the age of smart phones and instant communication, however, if even a single human spotted us and dared to speak of what he witnessed, it wouldn't be long before werewolf hunters would descend on the region.

Once we hit the city limits, we slowed down. In this shape, my keen sense of smell and acute hearing were invaluable as we bounded from building to building, opting for the less-traveled streets and alleys on our way to the French Quarter.

The night was young. Even in the winter, since the temperatures were always tolerable in the deep south, there'd be a lot of activity in the always-popular French Quarter. The lone wolf's howl had probably already garnered a lot of attention. Howling again would have been the easiest way to lure the wolf into our pack. It also would have risked causing a panic. Not to mention, while a single howl might not cause enough ruckus to alert any hunters, it was too risky to howl back and forth.

I sniffed at the air. I'd have to track the wolf that way. If we were lucky, particularly since there were so many of us, the lone wolf would do the same and find us first. The situation was too dire, though, to rely on luck.

Acting as the alpha, the rest of the rougarou followed my lead. We were enormous beasts. Even on all fours, the shortest of us was six feet tall. I was eight. I hunched over and lurked through an alley near St. Anne Street on the north side of the French Quarter. I picked up the wolf's scent. He wasn't far.

I was grateful for that. If we had to cross Bourbon Street, our chances of not being seen were slim to none. He was to the west of our position, heading north. Another stroke of luck. They say you shouldn't look a gift horse in the mouth. The saying is even truer for werewolves.

We pursued him all the way to St. Louis Cemetery No. 1. It was a newly turned wolf. I could tell by its scent. His pheromones told me he was afraid. It was likely the first time he'd ever turned. That was a good thing. While younger wolves are more susceptible to violence, acting out their urges in typically gruesome ways, apprehension tempered their fury.

We found the wolf clawing at the ground beside one of the many above-ground tombs in the cemetery. I approached him, nuzzling the top of my head against his shoulder.

He stopped digging, turned, took two steps back, and whimpered. Accepting an alpha's control, not to mention the prospect of joining a pack, was difficult for new wolves. He didn't know what he was. He didn't know what I was, or that there were packs of our kind at all. My job was to convince him I was safe. That *we* were safe.

With older wolves, even lone wolves without a pack, intimidation was usually the best way to exert control and show my dominance. A new wolf like this one wouldn't respond well to the usual displays. No growls or snarls. I lowered my hind quarters and sat. He needed to know I would not attack. I was a friend. The pack mimicked my posture.

The young wolf stood on all fours and cocked his head. He took one step toward me. Then another. He sniffed at my body. My face, my arms, and, as I lifted my legs again, my butt. Of course, he had to sniff my butt. That's what wolves do. Unless you've been a wolf before, you wouldn't understand.

After he examined me, he lowered his head. A clear sign of submission. It was done. He'd follow me as one of the pack.

It was a minor victory. We still had to make it back to the swamp unseen. For this young wolf, his journey, his challenge, was only beginning.

Chapter Two

THE ROUGAROU HAD SEVERAL large footlockers stored in a small cabin in the swamp. It was where they kept their clothes. Thankfully, I had a spare set of pants and a few t-shirts there just in case. It was always a good idea to have a few extra clothes on hand. Sometimes the shift comes on suddenly, before a wolf can fully undress. I'd ruined my share of shirts and slacks through the years.

The other wolves were getting dressed. The plan was to regroup at the Vilokan Asylum where we could process the night's events. At the moment, though, I focused my attentions on the new wolf we'd found and assimilated into the pack.

Back in his human form, he was curled up in the fetal position on a patch of grass. He was a young man, probably a year or two shy of twenty. A college-aged boy, I imagined. We had more than a few of those who made regular trips to the French Quarter. New Orleans is known for a lot of things. A party hub for recently come-of-age young folk was not the least of them. I rested my hand on his back.

"I'm Cain," I said. "What's your name, son?"

"M-m-my name is Ryan."

"I have some clothes for you," I said. "Why don't you put something on? It's awfully cold out here."

"Th-thank you, s-s-sir."

I handed the boy my spare pants and shirt and turned my back to give him a little privacy as he dressed. His stutter wasn't unexpected. Most wolves, after their first shift, awaken in a state of shock. Add to that the fact that it was cold outside, and it was no wonder the poor lad was shivering.

"Do you understand what happened last night?" I asked.

"I don't know. My mind is spinning right now. It feels like a dream. I mean, am I really a werewolf? And you... you're one too?"

"Yes," I said. "I know how terrified you must be right now. But I suspect you knew, already, that werewolves were real."

"I don't know. I mean, a couple of weeks ago, something bit me. The thing moved so fast I didn't even know what it was. I was out camping. It jumped out of the woods. A few seconds later, three men followed it. I heard gunshots. I went to look but no one was there. I knew something big was out there, something that attacked me. But a werewolf? Sort of hard to believe."

I sighed. It wasn't surprising at all that Ryan had encountered a werewolf before. If it was fleeing hunters, it made sense that whoever bit him fled the scene before it ate out his heart. Yes, that's what wolves typically go for. As disgusting as it sounds—and to me, it's still gross whenever I think about it while in human form—the heart is the most delicious part of the body. Wolves rarely bite and flee. I imagine of every hundred werewolf victims out there, only one or two of them survive to become werewolves themselves. Ryan was lucky.

"Where did this happen?" I asked.

"In southern Missouri," Ryan said. "I'm not from around here. I just came down here with some of my frat brothers on winter break."

I released a breath that I didn't even realize I'd been holding on to. If the hunters were in Missouri—which, oddly enough, is a hotbed for supernatural activity—they weren't in New Orleans. It relieved me

I wouldn't have to deal with *that* now. Still, if there were hunters in Missouri, and Ryan was a werewolf now, it probably wouldn't be safe for him to return home. Certainly not until the next few nights had passed and, even then, it would be better to keep him close until he learned to tame the wolf.

"Did any of your friends see what happened?" I asked.

Ryan shook his head. "I don't think so. We were all drinking at a club. I felt ill, so I went out for some air. That's when it happened..."

"Did anyone else see you? After you changed into a wolf?"

"I really don't know. I mean, I was so freaked out by what was happening. What were the chances no one saw me at all?"

I shrugged my shoulders. "Better than you might think. Very few wolves go for a kill on their first shift. Most of them are too afraid, too shocked by what happened, and find a place to hide until they turn back. But next time, you'll be much bolder in wolf form."

"Can you help me? Is there any way to stop this?"

I shook my head. "There is no way to undo what you've become. But there are ways to manage your condition. If you'd be willing to accept it, I'd like to offer my help."

"This is going to happen to me again?"

"Unfortunately, it will. Every full moon."

Ryan chuckled nervously, shaking his head. "I can't believe this is happening. How do you think you can help, anyway? You'll... change... with me again?"

I nodded. "I will. But that's only a temporary solution. It's a small part of my program. You need to learn to handle your cravings as a wolf even if I'm not there."

"How can I do that?" Ryan asked. "Oh, my god! Dude, I don't want to kill anyone. Why is this happening to me?"

"I run a place, a facility, for people just like us. People who've become something more than human. My job is to help them adapt. To prevent them from harming themselves or others."

"And you want to lock me up there?" Ryan asked. "I can't just disappear like that... I have a family back home. They're expecting I'll be back for Christmas."

"And you can be," I said. "Some of my patients require long-term in-patient care. That's not the case for werewolves. Though, certainly, you'd benefit from it. There is much you can do once this full moon wanes before the next one rises to prepare."

"I don't know," Ryan said. "My classes start again in a couple weeks..."

"I know this is difficult to accept, but this has to be your priority now. Even above school, above family. You can still have a normal life, Ryan. But that requires you to handle this transition responsibly."

"But I can go home for Christmas?" Ryan asked.

I smiled. "Of course you can. The full moon will pass before the holiday. Still, I'd recommend you return after it's over. I want to help you adjust."

"But... how much does it cost? I don't know if my insurance covers this kind of thing."

I laughed. "We don't work with insurance companies, Ryan. But at the Vilokan Asylum, we don't accept payment from our patients, either. Other interested, wealthy, benefactors fund our operation."

Ryan scratched his head and stared off into the trees. "I can't believe this is happening."

I placed my right hand on Ryan's shoulder. "None of us choose this life, son. But you are at a crossroads. Do nothing, and the wolf will consume you. It will take over your life and, given that hunters are already on the prowl in Missouri, it will probably be a short life. Or, you can come with me. I can help you. You can have a normal life. If you'd like to finish college, you can do that. Have a career if you'd like. Even start a family. You'll still need to manage this change every full moon, but that's not as daunting a prospect as I'm sure it feels right now."

Ryan huffed. "That's not really much of a choice, is it?"

"It may be the most important choice you ever make. And I'm not the only one who wants to help. This pack, they've all been through what you're going through. You aren't alone."

"What is this? This treatment? Is it some kind of rehab?"

I chuckled. "Not exactly. You don't have a problem, or an addiction, rooted in your psyche that needs to be overcome. Do you have experience with something like that?"

Ryan nodded. "Yeah... it's a long story. I mean, I just got in with the wrong crowd for a while. I tried things... I was hooked."

"We can talk about that later," I said. "But if you've overcome an addiction, son, this won't be nearly as big a challenge. So long as you fully give yourself to the process. I promise, I can help you."

Ryan nodded. "Alright. I'll do it. Thank you, sir. I'm really scared."

"That's a good sign, you know."

"That I'm afraid?"

"Of course it is," I said. "It's those who have no fear of being the wolf, who are hooked on the power and thrill of the change, that are least likely to succeed. I have a lot of hope for you, son. I've seen many young wolves, just like you, live full and satisfying lives."

"That gives me some hope," Ryan said.

"That's all it takes," I added. "Hope is a powerful thing. Even stronger than the wolf. Come with us. Welcome to Vilokan Asylum of the Magically and Mentally Deranged. I'm Dr. Cain. I'll be supervising your treatment plan. This isn't the end of your life, son. It's just the beginning."

CHAPTER THREE

Most of my patients are well-seasoned in the world of the supernatural before they ever walk through the doors at the Vilokan Asylum. With younglings, be they new wolves or vampires, it's a unique experience. It can be overwhelming. Not only must they come to grips with what they've become, but they have to process an entire world of magic and monsters that they never knew existed. In my experience, that's every bit as much of a challenge for younglings to accept as it is for them to embrace their own changes.

I watched Ryan's face as we approached the magical doorway on the side of St. Louis Cathedral in Pere Antoine Alley. His jaw nearly hit the pavement when I touched the wall of the cathedral and a door appeared that hadn't been there before.

Vilokan was what you might call a voodoo underworld. The Voodoo Queen governed the place. For a long time, that was Marie Laveau. She's quite famous. Particularly in these parts. Perhaps you've heard of her. She was there, in fact, when Vilokan was first established. The history of the underground city went back to America's slave holding past. It was a place established by voodoo hougans and mambos as a refuge for the oppressed. It was a place where slaves could practice their religion without interference. In those days, it was also a place where slaves could engage in other illicit activities like to learn to read and receive a basic education.

A magical firmament prevented Vilokan from flooding. Since New Orleans is at or below sea level, it was essential. Even common basements are uncommon in the region. The cemeteries, like the one where we'd found Ryan before, are also different from most. The dead are buried in above-ground tombs and mausoleums. Even a shallow grave in New Orleans is impossible. Thus, the whole notion of an underground city was beyond belief for most.

A new queen had recently taken charge in Vilokan. Annabelle Mulledy wasn't your typical mambo. In fact, she was born to a slave-holding family. An irony that wasn't lost on many of Vilokan's citizens. If she hadn't sacrificed so much to save Vilokan from several supernatural threats in recent years, they'd never have accepted her. All things considered, though, she'd made a brilliant partner in service to my efforts at the Vilokan Asylum.

Like the newly crowned Voodoo Queen, I also hadn't come from the voodoo world. I didn't practice the arts. Still, I served their purposes well. The former Queen Laveau established the Vilokan Asylum to treat hougans and mambos whose misguided attempts to summon the Loa warped their minds. Evoking a Loa wasn't at all irregular for vodouisants. In fact, it is at the heart of their craft. Still, there are some Loa who one should never evoke. What are the Loa? Call them demigods, if you like. Some view the Loa as something closer to angels than gods. No matter, they are powerful entities that, when mounting or possessing a practitioner, can grant many blessings or curses. Appeal to a Loa in the wrong way, or bid for the services of the wrong Loa, and you were likely to end up at my Vilokan Asylum.

The Voodoo Queen granted citizens of Vilokan admittance to the asylum without qualification. Through the years, though, New Orleans had attracted a broader swath of supernaturals and those who engaged in paranormal or supernatural arts. The Voodoo Queen of the Twenty-First century had interests beyond those of her own community. She was the steward of any supernatural activity in the region. For those not born into voodoo families or already connected to Vilokan, admittance to the asylum required a special dispensation by the Voodoo Queen.

Annabelle Mulledy was quite progressive in such matters. Since she'd become queen, we'd accepted a wide variety of supernaturals into our treatment program. For obvious reasons, I had a particular interest in ensuring that werewolves had every opportunity to receive my help at the asylum. So far, Annabelle had been willing to sign off on anyone I'd petitioned to her for admittance.

Annabelle trusted my judgment. Anyone I brought into Vilokan, technically, represented a potential threat. Not only because they were largely in need of mental and magical health services, but because if they weren't already aware of the place's existence, they risked exposing Vilokan's existence to outsiders.

Based on Ryan's reaction, as we traversed several flights of steep stairs leading into the city, and more, when he saw the magical firmament above, he was exactly the sort of outsider that Annabelle worried about. I didn't have any reason to suspect that Ryan, in particular, was a risk. He needed and genuinely wanted help. Still, he was an outsider. I'd need to pay her a quick visit before I could formally begin his treatment program.

In the worst-case scenario, well, there was a Loa, Maman Brigitte, who could erase someone's memories. I wasn't a fan of that process, for obvious reasons. Erased memories are suppressed memories. Such things are the fodder for many psychological conditions that might develop later. Still, I knew it was a possibility if, for whatever reason, Annabelle might reject my petition.

The magical firmament above Vilokan cast a blue hue over the entire city.

The power that flowed above us clearly transfixed Ryan.

"It's really something, isn't it?" I asked.

"It's incredible," Ryan said. "What is it?"

I smiled. "It's a peculiar magic. It keeps us safe down here."

Ryan released a nervous chuckle. "It's a real trip, dude."

I nodded. "You could say that. I need to stop and see someone. It will only take a few minutes. Follow the rest of the pack to the asylum. I'll be with you shortly."

Ryan was still staring at the firmament. "Yeah. Sure. Alright."

I buttoned the collar on my shirt and straightened my tie. I rarely wore it so formally. I liked my tie and collar loose. It wasn't a style choice so much as a sense of duty. Seeking an audience with a queen, in my experience over the course of the last several thousand years, usually demanded a lot of ritual.

It varied, of course, depending on the culture of the kingdom the monarch ruled. In some kingdoms, it was required to stand in the presence of a king or queen. In others, they expected you to kneel or prostrate yourself before your ruler as an expression of submission, reverence, or even worship.

I've met King David of Israel and Nebuchadnezzar of Babylon. I was a tutor, briefly, to the young Alexander the Great. I've consulted with Pharoahs like Tutankhamen. I once appeared before the so-called Divine Augustus and, later, the certifiably insane Emperor Caligula. Yes, it's true, Caligula once appointed one of his horses to the Senate. Believing himself to be a god, he once waged a war against Neptune. Rome, for all its might, was never an adept naval power. He thought if he could plunder the treasures of Neptune, he could compel the sea-god to calm the seas in service of Rome's interests. Caligula literally led legions into the sea to collect millions of seashells. He demanded a Roman Triumph when he returned, a parade reserved for those emperors who returned from splendid victories in battle. It was no wonder his own Praetorian guard saw him assassinated. As I reflected on my time in Caligula's court through the years, it occurred to me it was that time which first sparked my interest in mental illness. I tended to the small flames of such curiosities for centuries. It wasn't until I'd met and studied under Freud that much, if any, of what I'd observed in Caligula's behavior made any sense. He was, after all, in love with his own sister. Caligula, I mean. Not Freud.

I digress. I'd met hundreds of kings, queens, dictators, presidents, and prime Ministers. As different as they were, they all had one thing in common. Approaching them always involved ritual. Some of them required gifts, tokens of sacrifice to honor their authority. Others lavished gifts upon me as a reminder that they were the stewards of every manner of provision. Gracious lords who wished to be revered as such.

Only Annabelle Mulledy, of all the governors or rulers I'd ever met, required no reverence at all. She abhorred formalities. She insisted that I, and everyone else, behave as if we were equals. It was nice, to a point, but also mildly awkward. It's hard to break thousands of years' worth of habit when dealing with queens. Ensuring I looked my best, centering my tie and fastening my top button, was my way of attempting to show due respect to her majesty—a term I'd never dare use when addressing the Voodoo Queen of New Orleans. She wouldn't have my head for it if I did. Though, I suppose, if I ever died, she might shrink it.

Annabelle didn't even have a proper throne room. She had an office. She'd claimed the old headmistress's quarters at that Voodoo Academy. It was a school, of sorts, for hougans and mambos in Vilokan.

Since becoming the Voodoo Queen, Annabelle had prioritized the modernization of Vilokan. While a rickety staircase once led to the office, she now claimed as her quarters, now she had an elevator. She'd even established phone lines in the city. We couldn't use cell phones in Vilokan, of course. Something about being underground and shielded by a magical force-field disrupted cell signals. At least it was possible to contact the Voodoo Queen in a pinch. Her office alone had an external number. Somewhere, I imagined, she'd run a traditional phone line from Vilokan to the surface. Probably along with the lines she'd used to bring electricity to the Voodoo underworld. I wasn't sure how she handled the electric bill, since we were an obscure underground community. I imagine her voodoo had something to do with it.

I bit my lip as I rode the elevator up toward Annabelle's office. She'd likely chastize me for not calling ahead. But I didn't use a smart phone, myself. I spent so much time in Vilokan that it wasn't worthwhile. Besides, such new-fangled technologies befuddled me. As old as I was, change never came easy.

The elevator had doors on both sides. I entered one door to go up. When I exited, after it took me to the level on which Annabelle's office was located, the opposite door would lead me into her office. Of course, she'd have to open the door from her side of it.

I pressed a "call" button on the panel in the elevator. A few seconds later, the sound of static sounded from a speaker. Then she spoke.

"Can I help you, Cain?" Annabelle asked, clearly having identified me on her monitor. There was a small camera in the elevator, too.

"I need to file a petition for a new patient."

I heard a click through the speaker. Then a ding as the door opened.

Annabelle was a pretty girl. Much younger, in fact, than one might think for someone in charge of the Voodoo world. Especially considering the fact that her predecessor had held the title of Voodoo Queen for more than a century.

Annabelle brushed a stray strand of long black hair from in front of her face as she slid a white sheet of paper across her desk. "Well, why don't you come on in? Make yourself at home."

I nodded. "Of course."

I pulled out a chair on the opposite side of Annabelle's desk, grabbed a pen from a jar on the edge of her desk, and started filling it out.

"So, who are you hoping to bring to the asylum, Cain."

"His name is Ryan," I said. "He's a new werewolf. He won't be staying for more than a few days. But he'll be back after the holiday."

"I see," Annabelle said, twirling a pen of her own in her hand. "You realize that the Vilokan Asylum is nearly at capacity."

I nodded. "I do. But this is an urgent case."

Annabelle sighed. "Every case is urgent for the magically and mentally deranged, Dr. Cain. Until now, I've signed off on all your requests. I fear, though, that I might soon have to exercise more discretion. We simply must ensure that the asylum accommodates the needs of our community."

I sighed. "If you don't sign off on this boy, he'll return to Missouri. There are hunters there. Suppose they catch him the next full moon, which they likely will, they'll execute him."

Annabelle nodded. "I'll sign off on your petition, Cain. I trust your judgment. But there are pressing matters, more serious cases, that are piling up."

"We have four rooms open," I said. "He'll only be using one for a couple of nights. Until this full moon passes. As you know, it is possible that a wolf might shift more than a single concurrent night so long as the moon appears near its apex. Especially around the solstice."

"Correction," Annabelle said, examining the print-out of a spreadsheet on her desk before she retrieved a folder from one of her drawers. "There are only three rooms available. And for the next few nights, unless you discharge someone, there will only be two."

"A new case?" I asked.

"We brought her in last night. I'd like you to look it over."

I raised one eyebrow. "She's already at the asylum?"

"Nurse Rutherford is processing her as we speak," Annabelle said.

I pushed the form for Ryan's admission to the asylum aside. I'd fill out the rest after I examined the file Annabelle gave me. I opened the manila folder and started to read.

"Annabelle, I'm not opposed to treating witches. Necromancers, though, are notoriously difficult to manage."

"Difficult, but not impossible. I'm not looking for your agreement here, Cain. I've already signed off on it. She's waiting for you at the asylum as we speak."

I shook my head. "Necromancers often work with infernal objects to cast their spells. You realize how risky that can be for me, or for other wolves in my care, I presume."

"Yes," Annabelle said. "But they have searched her. She possesses no such object. She cannot force you to wolf-out if that's your worry."

I flipped through the pages of the file, examining the girl's history. She was twenty-nine years of age. She was raised by a coven of caplatas, Voodoo priestesses who practiced the art with both hands. "Both hands" was voodoo-speak indicating that they used both the light and dark sides of voodoo. For the caplatas and bokors, all magic required balance. To wield the light meant embracing the darkness as well. This girl, I discovered, had briefly attended the Voodoo Academy. She'd been a member of College Samedi, a school in the Academy that specialized in death magic. They expelled her in her second year for animating the corpse of a recently deceased mambo, binding the corpse to her will, and using the zombie slave to do her homework.

I chuckled a little as I read the girls' file. I had to admit that it was quite impressive. Resurrecting and binding zombies wasn't unheard of in the world of voodoo. Raising them with any semblance of their former intelligence, or tasking them to perform mentally taxing activities, wasn't something that any run-of-the mill student from College Samedi could pull off. Frankly, the fact she could do it at all, suggested that she was already advanced far beyond the Voodoo Academy's curriculum. Still, cheating is cheating, I suppose. Heaven forbid that the powers-that-be at the Academy would set aside a few rules in order to nourish a promising student's potential.

Annabelle couldn't be blamed for that. She wasn't Voodoo Queen, yet, when it happened. In fact, she wasn't even aware Vilokan existed when this witch attended the school.

"I don't understand," I said. "The witch resurrected a zombie. Standard magic for those who hold the aspect of a Ghede, correct?"

Annabelle nodded. "It's her cheating that was cause for her expulsion. At least that's what we have in the records. It's curious, though."

"What is?" I asked.

Annabelle reached into a drawer and pulled out another file-folder. She retrieved a sheet of paper and slid it across her desk toward me. It was a photocopy of the original report. Much of it had been blacked out by a Sharpie.

"Why on God's green earth... or beneath it as the case might be... would someone censor a disciplinary report?"

Annabelle shook her head. "I can't say. This report was signed by Hougan Jim Asogwe. When I attended the Voodoo Academy he taught the philosophy of the arts. It's a basic general education requirement for students of all the academy's colleges."

"Does he still teach here?" I asked.

"That would be the problem. I'd ask him about it, but he died when Vilokan flooded a few years back."

I pressed my lips together. The flood was quite the ordeal. I survived. It wasn't the first flood I endured. That whole Noah and the Ark incident was a real pain in my furry ass. Annabelle was just a student at the Voodoo Academy when one of her rivals shattered the firmament. Many people drowned. Annabelle saved a lot of people. It was one of many uncommon feats of heroism that I imagined inspired the former queen, Marie Laveau, to appoint Annabelle as her successor.

"Well, this certainly is ironic, isn't it?"

"What is?" Annabelle asked.

"You said that this witch practices necromancy. If you need to discern the truth behind the deceased Hougan's report, a necromancer would certainly come in handy."

"Well, we clearly can't do that," Annabelle said, shaking her head. "I mean we could. But that would be awfully hypocritical."

"Indeed, it would be. Look, Annabelle, I have my reservations but I will do what I can to treat this patient. I take it I have little choice, anyway."

"Not really," Annabelle said, smiling back at me kindly.

I grinned back. "I'd suggest, then, that you temper your expectations. Necromancy isn't the result of a mental or magical derangement. There's nothing about it that psychoanalysis can correct other than by examining the witch's choices, by trying to discern what draws her to this brand of black magic."

"Just keep reading," Annabelle said. "You'll find that this witch, while originally coming from the Voodoo world, practices very little of our craft. And her brand of necromancy is not like any other I've ever encountered."

"This file is quite thick. I'll read it more thoroughly after my group debriefing with the wolves. Would you care to fill me in on the basic gist of what we're dealing with?"

"Most necromancers do very little other than what anyone who evokes the Ghede Loa in Voodoo might accomplish. They consult the dead as mediums. They raise zombie slaves. But it seems, whatever she did in the Voodoo Academy that got her expelled comes from a power she's since nurtured. She doesn't just raise mindless corpses, Cain. And she doesn't merely consult with ghosts. She raises the dead, with their souls and memories intact. And those she has raised all have one thing in common. They have a score to settle. They rise seeking revenge on those who wronged them in life."

I pressed my lips together. "Annabelle, I know your past. I know your family was attacked by a resurrected caplata when you were a young girl. I know that she also raised zombies and assaulted your family. That witch, too, sought to punish you and your family for the evils of your ancestors. Are you sure that you aren't going after this witch for personal reasons?"

Annabelle took a deep breath. "I expected you'd pose that exact question. You aren't wrong, to a point. I know how dangerous it can be when people are raised from the grave. Even more so when they have a vendetta from their past life that they hope to settle. But my experience regarding this matter is, in this case wholly academic and professional, not personal. I only insist that you prioritize this case because I know how dangerous such a necromancer might be."

"My apologies, Annabelle. I didn't mean to imply you didn't have good reason to be concerned. I simply wanted to remind you that in such cases, when they hit close to home, we might find ourselves acting less objectively than we wish."

Annabelle nodded. She signed the form I'd given her to petition for Ryan's admittance to my treatment program. I hadn't even finished filling it out. Most of the blanks remaining weren't things I knew anyway. I didn't know a thing about his medical history, his allergies, or who his emergency contact might be.

"Thanks for that," I said.

"I suspect I'm not the only one who struggles with objectivity, Cain. You have reasons of your own to prioritize the admittance of young werewolves to the asylum. Your bias, though, is not at all misguided. You advocate for those such as this werewolf precisely because your experience tells you it is crucial to intervene. That is all I am doing now.

I realize that unwilling subjects, no matter their condition, are difficult to treat. I know, further, that necromancers are challenging to work with at the asylum. I would not insist that you take this case if it was not important. If the necromancer did not pose a significant threat. If she cannot be treated, Cain, there's only one option."

"Banishment," I said.

Annabelle nodded. "And I do not relish in the necessity to cast human beings, even if they're evil necromancers, into the void."

I nodded. "Understood. And you aren't wrong. I'll see what I can do. I have one question, though."

"You wish to know why the witch's name is not included in the referral I've given you."

"You practically read my mind, Annabelle."

"Her name is on this disciplinary report from Hougan Jim, however. Take a look."

I looked more closely at the sheet of paper Annabelle handed me before. My eyes widened instinctively when I saw the name. Cassidy Brown. "She's not the first 'Brown' I've treated. There's Mercy Brown, the vampire witch. Then, Julie Brown, the materialized ghost who once guarded the witch of Endor's flambeau."

Annabelle nodded. "And Mercy and Julie are sisters. The latter the product of an affair between Mercy's father and a slave."

"Unfortunately, no one has seen Julie since she used the witch's flambeau to thwart an incursion into Vilokan by the Order of the Morning Dawn."

"I have not forgotten. She saved all of us. If the Order had their way, they'd have used their celestial power to destroy every witch and vampire in all existence. Werewolves, too, most likely. Surely our entire voodoo community."

I nodded. "I believe when Julie used the flambeau it also consumed her material form. She's a ghost again. But where she's gone, I cannot say."

"It is perplexing," Anabelle admitted. "I've inquired with the Ghede, but neither Maman Brigitte nor Baron Samedi have knowledge of her whereabouts. Nor do we know what happened to the flambeau."

"Perhaps its power was spent and the relic is no more. Still, we should operate as if it is still out there, somewhere. It's the only item I've ever encountered that could call forth a spirit in the way that Cassidy appears to be able to do."

"But if she had the flambeau, if she acquired it somehow after Julie disappeared, it wouldn't explain why she could do something similar when she was a student at the Voodoo Academy. So far as anyone knows, Julie still possessed the flambeau at that time. Still, something tells me that the answer to this riddle is in the text redacted from her disciplinary report."

"My gut tells me the same," I said. "And I'll make sure that Miss Brown receives the best care I can provide."

Annabelle nodded. "Make sure you read the rest of her file. It regards the incident that brought the witch's activities to my attention."

"Of course I will read it as soon as possible," I said. "But would you care to give me the Cliff Notes version of what happened?"

"We received an anonymous tip that Cassidy Brown was preparing to resurrect Delphine LaLaurie."

I scratched the back of my head. "The serial killer known for torturing and executing slaves in the nineteenth century?"

Annabelle cringed. "The same."

"Why would anyone with connections to the Voodoo world want to raise her?"

"I believe that LaLaurie only tortured and killed slaves because they were vulnerable. They provided a woman with sadistic tendencies an opportunity to exercise her proclivities. But an angry mob later ran LaLaurie out of the city. I believe that Cassidy Brown hopes that if the resurrected Delphine LaLaurie were to exact vengeance on the families of those who belonged to that mob, it might coincide with the witch's own interests."

"What interests, specifically?" I asked.

Annabelle shrugged her shoulders. "Consider that one of your tasks as you treat the girl. If there's someone she hoped LaLaurie might wish to kill, it may give us a better clue as to the necromancer's motives."

CHAPTER FOUR

I MADE MY WAY down the hallway toward my office. Trig moon-walked his way past me, serenading no one in particular to the tune of "Billie Jean." Trig was an ogre. He insisted he was the reincarnation of Michael Jackson. I had to admit, his voice wasn't half-bad. He was no Michael Jackson, but he could have probably passed for a young Tito. Based on his voice, not his appearance.

He was about thirty years old, which is young in ogre years, but hardly what Michael called a PYT. Given the ogre's age, since he was born before the King of Pop died, reincarnation wasn't possible. Possession, perhaps. But even that was unlikely. If you could come back and possess someone, would an ogre be your choice of host?

Trig wasn't all that unusual, though, given the average temperament of the patients at the Vilokan Asylum. In cases like his, I found that cognitive-behavioral therapy was most effective. I'd lead the patient to challenge his own cognitive distortions, whatever messed up thinking under-girded his delusions. It usually worked well. In Trig's case, well, considering a smooth criminal just glided past me backwards in the hallway, his progress had been slow going. Sometimes a delusion must run its course. He couldn't stop until he'd had enough.

The Vilokan Asylum was a single-floored facility. It was also one of the newer buildings in Vilokan, given that most of the buildings were constructed prior to abolition. The asylum had been built in the late nineteen sixties. It had that sort of unusual, modern architecture that makes buildings of such vintage stick out like a sore thumb. Painting over the burnt orange and olive green was one of the first changes I made when I accepted the job as the facility's chief psychiatrist. The newer paint job was less distracting—whites, creams, and light browns. There wasn't much that could be done about the floor plan. All things considered, though, it was efficient. The hallways were arranged sort of like spikes on a wheel with the nurses' station at the hub. My office, and the exit to reception, were down one hall along with the visitor's room. Nurse Rutherford typically covered reception. While the bulk of our resources served the in-patient population, I also had a fairly extensive out-patient practice. Rutherford scheduled my appointments.

It would be remiss of me if I didn't admit that Rutherford and I had a complicated, personal relationship. Nothing improper. Everyone knew about it. And we didn't engage in anything less than professional inside the asylum itself.

Not usually, at least. Despite what people might think from their exposure to prime-time medical dramas, most hospitals or asylums aren't the best places in the world to hook up. I will not say that nurses and doctors didn't have their trysts from time to time. But certainly not in patient rooms. At least they didn't in my institution. I can't say the patients didn't engage in extracurricular activities from time to time. Such is par for the course in an asylum. But I discouraged it as much as possible.

I say all that to say this. I'm not exactly sure what Rutherford and I were. Despite being a psychotherapist, helping patients come to terms with their emotions, I was notoriously bad at deciphering my own feelings in matters of the heart.

Still, Rutherford was a spunky woman. Not quite forty, which meant, relative to me, she was just a spring chicken. When you are thousands of years old, dating younger is the only option.

I dropped off Cassidy's file at my office before I made my way down one of the other hallways to the group therapy room. I preferred not to use the common area for group sessions. Especially not with the wolves. Their condition wasn't like anyone else's at the asylum. And, in a place like Vilokan Asylum, the common area, as you might expect, was ripe with distractions. There was no telling what kind of chaos might ensue at any moment.

Our session wouldn't take long. Presumably, I'd have my first session with Cassidy afterwards. There was an entire process that new patients went through when brought into the asylum. A basic medical profile had to be established. We needed to know if there were any dietary considerations to accommodate. Vampires needed a supply of blood. Some elementals needed other kinds of sustenance beyond common food. And some folks were simply gluten or lactose intolerant.

I stepped into the designated group therapy room at the end of the hall, the opposite side of the "wheel" from the hallway that led to the group common room. The rougarou sat around a long, rectangular table. Ryan was among them. He almost jumped when I stepped through the door. I'd like to say I remembered what it was like. I did, but I didn't. The first time I shifted, I went on a regular tear across the land of Nod. In those days, no one really knew what much of anything in the world was. But I knew what I'd done. I remember shaking my fist at the heavens.

"Is this how you'd curse me for killing my brother? To make me a killer, again, and again?"

God didn't respond. He couldn't be bothered. Little did I know, though, that I'd also created about a dozen more werewolves that night.

After that, short of a world-wide flood, there wasn't any containing the spread of my curse. Perhaps that was why the flood happened.

Still, those memories were so distant, so remote in my mind, I wasn't sure what of them was true and how many of my recollections were actually embellishments I'd convinced myself through the years were true. It's not like I'd intentionally altered my recollections. But when it's been so long, well, it's hard to know what's true about one's memories. Did I remember things as they were? Or was I remembering my own memory of it all? Like playing a game of telephone, every time I recalled the past, I set up a fresh memory that became the baseline for my next recollection—with a few new embellishments.

As much as I questioned the facts of what might have happened in those days, particularly since I wasn't sound of mind, I remember even less about how it felt. The only emotion I could recall was anger. I remembered the fury. But was that what I felt after I'd shifted... or only *while* I was the wolf? Aside from having a slightly larger frame, sharper teeth, and a lot more back hair, my human existence wasn't that much different from what it was when I became the wolf. I was volatile. I couldn't be trusted. I didn't trust anyone else. I was a bitter person. I was a husband and a father. I established a great city. An ancient metropolis rivaling some of the most marvelous cities in history. But all that business was little more than a distraction from the pain, the insecurity, the fear, and the rage that kept me up at night.

If Ryan was at all like me, I could remember this much—as terrifying as the wolf was, its nature resonated with something primal in the human spirit. I'd know. I was a part of only the second generation of humans, ever. And despite all of humanity's advancements, discoveries, technologies, and philosophies, it was striking how little the species had changed. People were taller now than they used to be. They had bigger feet. But other than that, the core of the human creature was the same. The emotions, the motives, the drive that I'd experienced the day I grabbed that stone and slaughtered my brother, when I took the shape of the wolf for the first time and terrorized Nod, all of that was still a part of me. There weren't too many people, human or otherwise, that I'd met who didn't reflect the same traits.

"How are you doing today, Ryan?" I asked.

Ryan shook his head. "I'm afraid."

I pressed my lips together. "But you enjoyed it, too, didn't you?"

The rest of the rougarou were smiling. They'd been through this routine themselves. Only when I'd done this with them, it was after they'd been stuck in wolf form for a century and the better part of another one.

"No, I... I mean, I was a monster..."

"It's okay, Ryan. If you ever wish to tame the beast, you must first accept the truth."

"What truth is that?" Ryan asked.

"That the beast is nothing more than an unrestrained version of what you already are. You enjoyed the sensation, though you're terrified to admit it, because the beast is everything you'd be if you had no limitation, no restraint, no qualms about what you might do if unleashed from your conscience."

Ryan shook his head. "I would do worse. I spent most of the night terrified."

"As most do their first shift," I said. "But you also felt it, didn't you? The strength and power of your form. The hunger and desire to hunt, to kill, to rule."

Ryan snorted. "To rule?"

"Common wolves do not share that urge. They are content to find their role in the pack. But the werewolf is man as much as he is wolf. It is the very temptation that once befell my parents, to become like god themselves. This urge, this craving, is common to all men. It lingers deep within, usually suppressed by the conscious mind. But when the wolf emerges, when we become werewolves, the collar that restrains our corrupted soul is removed. Yes, the werewolf wishes to rule. Not because he is a wolf. But because he is a man."

Ryan cocked his head. "Look, Doc. I appreciate the insight and all. But I just want to get this thing under control and move on with my life."

I smiled. "And to do that, son, you must recognize what your nature tells you. What are those urges? Where do they come from? What is the driving force unique to you, to your life, that reinforces what is unsavory in all of us? Once you recognize those things, you are better suited to counter your urges when the wolf takes over."

"It was different in my case," Donald said. "I didn't know how to behave as a human after the flambeau left, after we'd been wolves for so long."

Christopher, a mohawked thinner member of the pack, snickered. "You should have seen him. Donald was roaming all around the French Quarter sniffing people's butts."

"At least I didn't hump their legs!" Donald snapped back.

Evie, Christopher's girlfriend, giggled. "Man-wolves. So uncivilized. They went around peeing on everything, too."

I laughed. "None of this is behavior at all uncommon in the French Quarter. Even outside of Mardi Gras."

Ryan smiled wide. "I can't imagine what that must've been like. How was it after you turned again the first time? After you'd become human again, I mean."

Donald folded his hands. "Cain was with us. He's been with us every turn since. We'd never have survived without him. And more than that, we wouldn't have the lives we've built for ourselves now."

"So it's true?" Ryan asked. "I can have a normal life?"

"Define normal," Andrew, another of the rougarou added. "I mean, is anyone really normal?"

Yvette, a taller woman with long, red, hair, who was typically shyer and more reserved than the rest, raised her hand.

"Yvette," I said. "You may speak."

"I'm still not comfortable in my own skin. But a lot of people aren't. I think the key is to realizing that even as humans, we still have normal human problems to deal with, too. We can't blame everything on the wolf."

"Very wise," I said. "Using the wolf as an excuse is the surest way to delay your progress. No matter what happens when you turn, you must process it later. The more work we do, now, between shifts, the less likely it is that we'll do anything we regret as wolves."

"So, what do your lives look like now?" Ryan asked. "Your human lives, I mean."

"I'm married to a woman," Donald said. "Carol didn't know about my condition until recently."

Ryan cocked his head. "What did she think you used to go do every full moon?"

"She thought I was bowling."

Ryan laughed. "All night long?"

Donald shrugged. "It wasn't the best excuse, I admit. She saw through it eventually. She assumed I was having an affair. I was afraid to tell her the truth. In the end, it was the only option if I wanted to be happy."

"And how did she take it?" Ryan asked.

"She thought I was full of shit," Donald said, chuckling. "Can you blame her? It made things worse at first. Until I could prove that what I was telling her was true."

"How did you convince her that you were actually a werewolf?" Ryan asked.

"He took a freaking video of himself changing!" Christopher piped up, shaking his head.

"Smart," Ryan said. "But it sounds like you weren't happy about that."

"I wasn't," Christopher said. "None of us were. If that video got out, if anyone else saw it..."

"Even if Donald's wife, Carol, reacted the wrong way, our secret might have been exposed," Evie added.

"One of the rules of our pack," I said, "is that we must respect our anonymity. In this instance, I cannot commend Donald's method. But it is important that we be truthful with the people we allow into our lives. If you decide to get into a relationship with a human, my advice is to consult the pack."

Ryan sighed. "I don't know. My whole life is back in Missouri. I don't know if I can leave everything behind."

I smiled. "You could always transfer to LSU. If you'd like, I have connections at the University. I could get you admitted."

Ryan sighed. "I don't think I could afford out-of-state tuition."

"We can help you pay for that," Donald said. "We are like a family, Ryan. We'll all pool our resources to help."

Ryan wiped a tear from his eyes. "I don't know what to say..."

"If you'd like I can make the call. You could start as soon as next semester. What is your major, Ryan?"

Ryan shook his head. "I'm still undecided. But I think I might like to study psychology."

I smiled wide. "In that case, Ryan, you've come to the right place! I'll tutor you myself, if you'd like!"

"That sounds great, Dr. Cain!"

"Consider it done. Welcome to the pack, Ryan."

CHAPTER FIVE

RUTHERFORD WAS WAITING FOR me outside my office.

"The necromancer is here. She hasn't exactly been cooperative."

I nodded. "I suspect not. She's not exactly here by choice. I trust we've installed all the usual wards?"

Rutherford nodded. "They're up. So far, she hasn't so much as tried to cast any spells. She's hardly spoken at all. She won't even answer my questions. It's awfully hard to get a medical profile for a patient who won't speak."

It wasn't uncommon that new patients might give the nurses trouble. Especially those committed here by force. It's universally true, in the world of psychiatric health, that those who desire help are more likely to succeed. In the Vilokan Asylum, well, we have a greater share of uncooperative patients than most human institutions. It comes with the territory.

Magic can warp minds, especially for those who practice it experimentally. With the increasing popularity of hedge witchery as of late, it was a frequent problem I often treated. Certainly, there are responsible hedge witches out there. But practicing any sort of magical craft apart from a coven of any sort is, by nature... experimental. Spells have a way of backfiring. Witches who train in a coven have the benefit of learning from the mistakes of others. Usually, those mistakes occurred over centuries. The "lore" of the coven helps new witches avoid the most grievous errors. Of course, some of the most powerful witches I'd ever dealt with were hedge witches. As hazardous as experimental spellcraft can be, it also leads many hedge witches to discover new powers and spells unknown to others. With this necromancer, if she was indeed practicing solo, from the hedge, there was no telling what power she'd stumbled upon that gave her the power described in her file—she animated not only corpses, she raised souls.

I stepped into my office. Cassidy Brown sat reclined on my red velvet chaise. She was a pretty girl, likely in her late twenties or early thirties. Her skin was a shade or two lighter than mine. Her complexion was flawless. Her eyes were black as night. I'd seen it before. Those who dabbled with necromancy exhibited that peculiar trait. Something about gazing into the beyond, connecting with the dead, darkened the irises. Her hair was short, trimmed just above her ears. She was wearing a Snoopy gown. Not by choice. She'd already been processed and her usual clothes were in storage, awaiting her discharge. Anyone in residence at Vilokan Asylum wore a similar gown. Not all of them featured the dog from the The Peanuts cartoons, but quite a few of them had cartoon patterns.

Over the years, I'd received two complaints in patient exit interviews more than any other. The first had to do with the food served at the Asylum. The second concerned the gowns. Jumpsuits might have been more comfortable. But I wasn't a fan. Jumpsuits suggest that my patients are inmates, as if they were at my asylum to be punished rather than treated. Hospital gowns suggest healing. It may be subtle, but the smallest thing that taps into the subconscious mind can have profound effects on treatment success. I was supposed to be an ally to my patients, a doctor, not a warden. The last thing I wanted to do was give the impression that I was an adversary. I was an advocate for my patients. If it came down to it, I'd even challenge the Voodoo Queen if it was for the good of my patients.

"I'm Doctor Cain," I said, wheeling my chair out from behind my desk and sitting down in front of Cassidy as she laid across my chaise. I'd learned, a long time ago, that sitting behind my desk presented an authoritarian posture. Something so subtle as sitting beside the patient communicates an alliance. I was on her side. When dealing with patients who didn't want to be there, it was essential. Before I could help anyone, no matter their problem, patients needed to trust me.

Cassidy, though, hardly acknowledged me as I sat next to her. She stared straight at the ceiling as if she were looking right through it to something on the other side.

"Why don't you tell me how you're feeling," I said. "I realize you aren't here of your own accord. But since you're here, why not make the best of it?"

Cassidy continued staring at my ceiling. I knew she could hear me. She just wasn't talking. It wasn't the first time I'd encountered patients who used this strategy. If they didn't want to be here, well, they figured they'd just give me the silent treatment. If they don't talk, well, talk-therapy wouldn't do them much good. They figured that would mean we'd discharge them. That might be the case in some human institutions. But when you're dealing with the magically and mentally deranged, there's more at stake than the patient's mental health.

Think of it like this. Would you feel comfortable if a mentally unstable person had constant access to a firearm? Magic was like a weapon. At least, potentially so. And most of the time, we couldn't disarm practitioners. Our wards protected us *most of the time* in Vilokan Asylum. Still, wards have loopholes and limitations. Not to mention, warding a facility, or a building, was one thing. Warding or silencing an actual person, a witch, was counterproductive. Silencing a witch warped the mind. It wasn't a viable option. Whatever derangement a witch might possess, muting her abilities would only exacerbate the problem.

I rested my clasped hands over my crossed legs. "So you don't want to talk. I can understand that. I'd probably keep my lips sealed, too, if they dragged me into some underground hospital without my consent."

Cassidy didn't respond. Empathizing with the patient was one of my many strategies. It was no masquerade. I felt for her, as I did for any of my patients who were there unwillingly. My empathy was genuine. As a werewolf, those who feared me had restrained me more than once over the years. Before I'd gained a semblance of control of my more beastly nature. Slavers captured me another time, though not on account of being a werewolf. It was during the height of the transatlantic slave trade. They threw me on a ship bound for the Americas. Unfortunately, for them, a full moon rose during the journey. I'll just say that few of them completed their voyage.

After that, since I more closely resembled the people of the African continent than Europeans, I often got myself captured intentionally. I saved many good people that way. I also took a lot of lives. It was a mixed bag. I hated killing—even if by doing so I was saving the innocent and punishing the oppressor. Every time I killed, even if I did so as a wolf, I could swear I saw my brother's face on my victim's countenance as they took their last breath.

I grabbed Cassidy's file from my desk. "So, I see you used to be a student at the Voodoo Academy. College Samedi, right?"

Cassidy took a deep breath but, again, refused to respond.

"Someone redacted your file. Blacked out everything. Seems to me that someone was trying to hide something. Why would they do that?"

I let my question hang in the air for a few seconds before continuing.

"The way I see it, whoever did it was trying to protect you, to prevent others from learning about what happened. Or, I suppose they were so threatened by whatever happened they didn't want the truth to get out."

Cassidy clenched her fists. I was striking a nerve, even if she still refused to speak.

"I'd like to help you, Cassidy. I wasn't the one who put you here, you realize. But I have a job to do. If you help me out here, I can help you. But you need to talk to me."

Cassidy turned her face toward me and looked at me intently. I don't think she blinked her eyes once. Then she opened a hand and held it out to me.

I grabbed her hand. It was cold. More chilling than even a vampire's touch. The moment her skin touched mine, her black irises expanded until each of her eyes was completely black.

"Cain..."

Cassidy's mouth was open as she spoke, but her lips didn't move. She was a either fantastic ventriloquist, or the voice wasn't her own.

"Who am I speaking to?" I asked. I'd learned through the years, treating supernatural creatures and those adept with magic that I couldn't assume conventional DSM diagnoses. This very well might have been a case of multiple personalities, but there was nothing I'd seen from her file when I perused it before that suggested this was the case.

The voice within Cassidy billowed a laugh. If she were laughing herself, her chest would have risen. To laugh like that would require a deep inhale. Instead, her body remained still and calm. Still, all of this could easily be a ruse. Witches have many methods whereby they might produce sounds, or even voices, that sound different from their own. I couldn't rule anything out.

"How long has it been? How many years have passed?"

I cocked my head. "I don't know what you're talking about. Tell me your name."

"You know my name, brother."

I bit my lip. Cassidy likely knew who I was. She knew my past and my story. Was she trying to scare me now? I wouldn't bite.

"You aren't Abel. Tell me, who are you, really?"

Again, the voice within Cassidy laughed. "But I am, brother. And you know what they say..."

"Tell me," I said. "What do they say?"

Again, the voice laughed. "An eye for an eye, brother."

I yanked my hand away from Cassidy. Her eyes returned to normal, and she sat up in the chaise. A grin split her face from ear-to-ear.

"Cassidy," I said. "We're here to talk about you."

Cassidy narrowed her eyes. "Release me, Cain. Or I will release him. And trust me, he has only one thing in mind. Abel will not rest, again, until he's had his vengeance."

CHAPTER SIX

I LAUGHED A LITTLE under my breath as I left my office. It wasn't the first time someone had tried to leverage my past against me. Cassidy wasn't even the first patient to try it. When they record your worst mistake in the first few pages of history's all-time number one bestseller, it comes with the territory. Fortune accompanies fame. Misfortune follows infamy.

I couldn't release Cassidy into the general population until she was at least willing to play ball with her treatment program. Any attempt to threaten any Vilokan Asylum personnel earned a one-way ticket to solitary. When a patient threatened me, no matter how indirectly, it was a particularity sensitive matter. After all, if her threats escalated to action, she'd afflict herself with the seven-fold curse. The last thing I needed was a necromancer, trapped in werewolf form, terrorizing the asylum. There have been a handful of occasions when werewolves were loosed upon the asylum. There wasn't a good way to deal with the problem. In every instance, people died. Annabelle already made it clear—if something like that happened again, well, she'd have no choice but to exclude werewolves from the asylum.

Still, I had my methods if push came to shove. An injection of colloidal silver could down a wolf fairly quickly. It was like poison to our systems. The younger the wolf, the less likely one was to survive. If someone injected Ryan, for instance, it would end him almost instantly. If someone injected me with colloidal silver, or shot me with a silver bullet, it might take as long as a week before the poison spread. But say someone shoots me. They become a werewolf themselves, intent on turning seven more.

As you may have read in the book of Genesis:

□□□ □□□□□□ □□□ □□□ □□

Anyone who slayeth Cain, vengeance shall be taken on him sevenfold...

That's how King James translated it into the English tongue. To "slayeth," though in no way means that one need to kill to inherit this sevenfold curse. A better translation would be, "to smite with deadly intent." Yes, even an attempted murder upon my person could turn one into a werewolf.

The rougarou of Manchac Swamp had become werewolves in the common manner. Other wolves had bitten them, descended from someone else who'd probably attempted to kill me ages ago. Unfortunately, the Mormon library didn't have records of werewolf ancestry. There was no way to trace their lineage back to me.

Those who had attempted to kill me through the years, under the seven-fold curse, were bound to the wolf's form no matter the condition of the moon until they'd turned seven more wolves in kind. That meant, in almost every instance that once one intended to kill me, the problem escalated. Usually, the one who wanted me dead still did even after he changed. Add to that a new pack of similarly untamed wolves and it was quite the challenge. My only recourse, in such an instance, was to exert control. To force them into submission. To pacify their murderous intent as their alpha.

Meanwhile, say someone shot me with a silver bullet, I'd have the challenge of not only a growing pack of newly turned werewolves, but I'd have to remove the bullet. Depending on how far the silver spread in my system, I may need a witch and a healing spell to recover. If someone injected me with colloidal silver, well, it's obviously more difficult to remove from my body. I'd fall ill more quickly. The first thing to go, based on my observation of its effects on other older werewolves, would be my mind.

I'd have a few hours, at most, to find a witch who could heal me before I'd go into a rage. If I was in werewolf form, well, it could be quite problematic. Though, even if it happened while in human form, I could be a handful. My curse gave me enhanced strength. My senses were especially acute.

I say all that to say this—when a patient exhibits even the slightest threat against my person, extreme measures have to be taken. We'd have to place Cassidy not only in solitary, but in a wing of the asylum built and reinforced to contain a werewolf. Just in case she assumed my curse.

That Cassidy didn't wolf-out on the spot likely meant her threats were disingenuous. Of course, suppose she truly could raise my brother. What if she were to unleash him on the world, filled with something in the neighborhood of six thousand years of resentment directed toward me? It wouldn't be Cassidy who directly attempted to kill me. Her threat was more subtle. She only threatened to resurrect someone who she presumed might want me dead.

It was difficult to predict how such indirect threats might manifest relative to the seven-fold curse.

A king once sent a guard to kill me. It wasn't the guard who was afflicted, in that instance, but the king. He knew who I was. He knew about the curse. He mistakenly assumed if he merely commanded someone else to carry out his murderous intentions that the guard would be the one afflicted. The guard, however, was only carrying out an order. He did not know who I was. For all he knew, I was a murderer. Well, I mean, I was. But not recently. No matter, it was not the guard's job to judge my innocence or guilt. He was simply carrying out a directive. It was the king who was responsible. The guard was no different than an executioner acting on the authority of a judge.

The key is that it's deadly intent that triggers the the seven-fold curse. The guard's intention was only to carry out an order. The *deadly* intent belonged to the king. Had the king merely asked the guard to arrest me, and the guard decided on his own to kill me, it would have been the guard who inherited the curse.

Who was that king, you might ask, who became a wolf? Lycaon, King of Arcadia. It's a long story. Homer told a partial version of the tale in his *Ovid*. The king had killed his own child, offered him up as burn offering, a meal, to one of his Greek deities. You'd think, after the whole situation with Abel, I'd know better than to interfere with and get involved in someone's sacrifices. I called out the king for his horrible crime. I hailed the king's rival, King Cecrops of Attica, as a virtuous leader who offered a whole burnt offering of barley to the gods.

I know what you're thinking. Abel sacrificed from his flocks, a blood offering. I offered the Lord a burnt offering of grain and wheat. In my case, God rejected my sacrifice. I was the one cursed.

In Lycaon's case, he cursed himself by his offering. He murdered his own child to pull it off. He sent his guard after me and merited the seven-fold curse. Lycaon became a werewolf. He soon turned seven others. Legend credits Zeus with his curse. I don't know if Zeus ever existed. What I know is that it was Lycaon, not the guard, who intended to kill me. He feared I might expose his villainy.

I tell that tale for several reasons. If Cassidy resurrected Abel, all that would matter was who had deadly intent. Was Cassidy threatening to resurrect Abel because she wanted me dead? Not at all. She made the threat in hopes I'd release her. That would still be her motive, presuming she followed through. If Abel wanted me dead, well, who could blame him? Still more, he died before I was cursed. Say the necromancer raised him. Would he know the consequences of exacting his vengeance? What would happen to him if he followed through?

I furrowed my brow as I flipped through the rest of Cassidy's file, the parts I hadn't read before now. I'd only perused the file casually in Annabelle's office. Now, I wished I'd examined it in more detail *before* I conducted Cassidy's initial session.

Cassidy's father's name was Everett Brown. He was the great-great grandson of Julie Brown. When I was counseling the now-disappeared ghost of Julie Brown we'd spent quite a bit of time diving into her lineage. From a Freudian perspective, examining one's ancestral background is important. From my perspective, applying Freud's theories within the rules that govern the supernatural realm, examining one's descendants can be just as important when considering a person's magical derangements. It was as true for me as anyone else. Living with the recognition of what my wolfish offspring have done, the horror they've caused throughout history, is a guilt I'm sometimes inclined to internalize.

Julie never gave me any reason to believe she'd met Cassidy or even knew about her. It wasn't entirely surprising. Julie Brown had lived in the same swamp, guarding the flambeau of the Witch of Endor along with the rougarou, for more than a century. But when we looked into her descendants, nothing about Cassidy ever turned up.

Cassidy's father made sense. It was her mother's name, printed nowhere in her file except on her birth certificate, that gave me pause.

Deborah Benton.

It was the maiden name of Deborah Freeman, the mother of Niccolo Freeman. Cassidy wasn't just a descendant of Julie Brown. She was the half-sister of the world's first vampire.

CHAPTER SEVEN

I ONLY EVER ENCOUNTERED Niccolo Freeman a few times. Annabelle knew him far better than I ever did, though she had a complicated relationship with the ancient vampire. How could an *ancient* vampire be the brother of this relatively young necromancer who was now sitting in solitary at the Vilokan Asylum of the Magically and Mentally Deranged?

Niccolo and Annabelle were classmates at the Voodoo Academy. He was a young but ambitious student. He wasn't a vampire—yet. To make a long story short, while battling a nasty Loa, Kalfu, Annabelle evoked Baron Samedi. He was the chief Loa of the Ghede—one family, or nanchon of Loa. The Ghede govern the realm of the dead and the boundary between life and death itself. The Rada Loa, like Erzulie Freda, Papa Legba, and others are mostly peace loving, benevolent Loa. The Petro can be more aggressive. Loa like Marinette, or Kalfu. Some Loa, like Ogoun, the Loa of War, belong to both the Petro and Rada nanchons.

As an aside, Ogoun and Annabelle were an item—another long story that, perhaps, I'll tell at another time. I tried to stay out of such affairs provided it was irrelevant to my treatment goals with a patient.

To digress, in their effort to combat the Loa Kalfu, Niccolo and Baron Samedi ended up trapped together in Guinee. It was a place I knew well. My parents did, at least. They were born there; lived there for some time before they screwed it up, ate the wrong apple, and got kicked out of the only place they'd ever known. To prevent them from ever returning, God severed the realm from the earth and set it on another plane outside of space and time. The Voodoo world called the place Guinee. For my parents, for Adam and Eve, it was Eden.

Only when the Baron was sent there he emerged in his "red" or warped nature. He and Niccolo engaged in a struggle that endured for some time. In the end, Niccolo entered a bargain with the Baron. One that sent him to the earth with a peculiar aspect of the Baron cohering in his flesh. One that gave him a craving for the souls that cohered in human blood. In exchange, the Baron freed him and sent him to earth—several thousand years ago, when the native tribes still thrived free of European influence in North America. In time, Niccolo made his way to Europe. Many of his progeny reproduced, creating other vampires, and the rest was history. In the last few years, however, when Niccolo finally had lived long enough to catch up to his earthly life, he reacquired his human soul and gave up his life. He'd grown weary of existence. When I was working under Marie Laveau, she tried to convince me to intervene. To help the ancient vampire adjust. He was less than inclined to take part in my program.

From my many conversations with Annabelle, I knew the whole affair troubled her. She felt responsible for what happened to Nico and, therefore, the existence of the vampires. I couldn't counsel Annabelle at the Vilokan Asylum. Checking herself in, even enrolling in my out-patient program, could lead some to question her already tenuous authority as the Voodoo Queen. I'll say, rather, we conducted our sessions on a more informal basis. I couldn't call Annabelle a patient—but that was a semantic distinction, only.

I could relate to Annabelle's burden. As the first werewolf, who by a single act unleashed a horror on humanity that had plagued most of mankind's history, I knew what it was like to feel the weight of so many lives on my shoulders. Annabelle bit no one. She never drank blood. She was anything but a vampire. Still, she felt that the role she played in the events that led to Niccolo's vampiric rebirth meant she owned some of the guilt for those who the vampires born from Niccolo's bite killed and turned.

I left the asylum and made my way back to Annabelle's office. This was a coincidence that I couldn't overlook.

The elevator dinged when it reached Annabelle's office. "Annabelle, we need to talk."

Annabelle nodded, waving me in. "I expected as much."

I scratched my head as I sat in one of the two chairs arranged in front of Annabelle's desk. "So, are you aware that Cassidy is Niccolo Freeman's half-sister?"

Annabelle sighed. "I am. But Nico was the vampire, not Cassidy. She's a few years older than Nico. Well, older than he was in his prior human life. I realize how this looks, but I don't think there's any connection between her activities and the vampires."

"But perhaps you have more of an interest in Cassidy's case than you're letting on."

Annabelle shrugged her shoulders. "I don't think so."

I smiled and nodded, resting my elbows on the armrests of the chair and steepling my fingers. "My mentor, Freud, called the process 'undoing.'"

Annabelle snorted. "That means nothing to me."

"It's a defense mechanism, similar to how one might seek to make amends for something that burdens the conscience. We engage in undoing when we take an action that we hope will negate or magically erase our previous error."

"I'm not sure how helping Cassidy could undo my mistake with Nico," Annabelle said.

I folded my hands and rested them on the edge of Annabelle's desk. "It can't. The truth is, we can never completely erase the past. Even if we were to go back in time, which is quite possible, we're bound to find that what has happened must happen. Sometimes, even, a well-intentioned effort to change the past ends up setting the very events into motion that led to our regretted error in the first place."

Annabelle laughed. "Well, I know better than to go back in time, Cain. That's not what I'm doing."

"I agree. But I believe you're still undoing by proxy. If you could not save Nico, if you felt guilty for what happened to him and all that ensued, his sister is an apropos candidate to save in his stead. You couldn't help Nico. If you can save Cassidy, well, you may feel that doing so helps balance out the guilt you feel over your past."

Annabelle shook her head. "So you're implying that this situation has more to do with me than Cassidy?"

"Cassidy needs help. She is a real danger and risk to all of us. Still, I would be amiss not to consider that neutralizing her threat might also be a personal matter for you."

Annabelle bit her lip. "Maybe you're right. Hell if I know. But say you're right. How does that change things?"

"Regarding Cassidy, I hope it won't cause any problems. When we are personally vested, Annabelle, we might act differently than we would under normal circumstances. I need your assurance that you will allow me to oversee her treatment plan accordingly. But I'd be lying if I didn't have personal motives, as well."

Annabelle pinched her chin. "What do you mean, Cain?"

"She's threatened to use her... abilities... to resurrect my dead brother."

Annabelle raised one eyebrow. "Are you shitting me, Cain?"

I squinted. "Am I what? I don't think I could possibly..."

"Not literally, Cain. Good Lord!"

"Apologies. I have a hard time keeping up with youth-speak."

Annabelle giggled. "Understandable! Hell, I'm barely twenty now and the kids are saying things these days even I can't figure out."

"It's always been that way. It's gotten worse since the Internet and Video Games."

"It's not just video games," Annabelle said. "It's YouTube. Did you know that kids now watch other people play video games on YouTube more than they play games themselves?"

I snorted. "That sounds awfully boring."

"You're telling me! Totally ridiculous. And so is the notion that you'd come here lecturing me about being too invested in this case, only to reveal that she's threatened to resurrect the brother you murdered, Cain!"

"That was a long time ago," I said. "But you're right. Some wounds never heal. I did not come here to play the hypocrite, Annabelle. I came so that we might both look out for the other. I will examine your involvement to ensure your objectivity when making decisions regarding Cassidy. I would like you to do the same for me."

"She's hardly the first patient you've had who threw your history in your face, Cain."

"Agreed. It's hard to avoid when the details of the worst moments of your life are in the most widely circulated book in human history. Still, this case is unique."

"Why do you say that?"

"Because I think Cassidy might very well be able to do exactly what she's threatened. And if she brings back Abel, I'm not sure I'll be the best doctor to handle this case."

"So you came here to resign, Cain?"

I sighed. "I'm not sure."

"I won't accept it. You're the only psychiatrist in all the world with experience treating both magical and mental ailments. It may compromise your objectivity, even more than my own. But we have no other choices here. If we can't help her, we won't have many other options beyond banishment. I can't do that. I won't do that."

"Because that's what you did to Nico?" I asked.

"I didn't banish him to the void," Annabelle said, crossing her arms in front of her chest.

"But you left him in another world. And I suspect you're afraid if she's sent to the void she might return more villainous than before."

Annabelle tucked a few strands of stray hair behind her ears. "It's not an irrational worry. People have found their way out of the void before. But that's not all it is, Cain. You know that already."

"You don't want to wrong her the way you wronged Nico."

Annabelle nodded. "I didn't leave Nico in Guinee on purpose. Nevertheless, I was responsible. I brought him there to begin with. I can't do that to his sister. We have to help her. Please, Cain. Do this, if not for me, for Cassidy's sake."

I sighed. "I will see this case through, Annabelle. But I should warn you in advance, if she brings back my brother, I cannot predict how I will respond."

Annabelle huffed. "I thought you worked through all your sibling rivalry issues with Freud."

I scratched the back of my head. "I did. But it's one thing to make amends to a dead man. I've done a lot during my life, thinking it atoned for my sin. But if Abel came back, do you really think he'd accept that as a valid amends?"

Annabelle shook her head. "Probably not. I wouldn't if I were him. I'd be pissed at you, Cain."

I chuckled. "There's a reason you're the queen and I'm the therapist, Annabelle. Your bedside manner sucks."

Annabelle giggled. "Just telling you like it is, buddy!"

I smiled. "In a strange way, I appreciate your forthrightness. I cannot say that you're wrong. If I was Abel, if he was the one who killed me and I was brought back thousands of years later to see my killer living a good life, happy and content, I don't think I'd be particularly pleased."

"We each have our secrets here, Cain. We have our reasons. I'll have your back if you have mine."

I nodded. "It's a deal. I suppose we're a lot more alike than different in this matter. I think I've been engaging in some 'undoing' myself. I know I cannot erase the past and all the damage my curse had led to throughout history. That's why I put so much effort into the wolves. I can, perhaps, mitigate some of the danger my kind presents to the world today."

Annabelle smiled. "If that's the case, well, then we should take on more vampires at the asylum. You know, since I played a role in creating vampires to begin with. That would be how I'd best 'undo' my mistake."

I narrowed my eyes. "Touché. Still, in either case, we have no choice but to expand our operations. We are nearly at full capacity and there's so much more benefit we could do if we had a larger facility."

"We have limited real estate in Vilokan, Cain. I don't know how we'd possibly expand."

"What if we expanded on the surface? An outpost above ground? Think about it, we could treat wolves there without worrying about them escaping and running rampant in Vilokan."

"But also unleashing them on the city."

I shrugged. "If we weren't treating them, they'd be free to wreak havoc on the world anyway. We can take measures to keep them within the facility."

Annabelle took a deep breath. "It's not a horrible idea, Cain. Let me give it some thought and see what resources I can gather to implement something like what you're proposing."

CHAPTER EIGHT

AT THE APEX OF a full moon, every werewolf shifts. Occasionally, especially during the solstices, wolves might shift two or three consecutive nights. It's awfully inconvenient. It's also dangerous. Shifting takes a toll on both the body and the mind.

A wolf's first shift isn't as dangerous as some believe. More often than not, the wolf is afraid, navigating his or her new existence. For a newly turned werewolf, however, the second night is the most dangerous. When it happens on a solstice, and the werewolf is likely to shift on concurrent nights, it's doubly horrific.

I had a lot going on at the asylum, especially with the whole Cassidy Brown situation, but I had to go out with the pack. I couldn't guarantee we'd shift two nights in a row. Of the thousands of years I've been a werewolf, though, I could probably count on my fingers and toes the number of solstices that came and went with only a single shift. Both solstices, the winter and the summer, were associated with full moons. During the winter solstice, the full moon was at its lowest in the sky. During the summer, the highest.

The low moon and high moon had different effects on the wolf's natural temperament. During the low moon the wolf is more irritable, more easily provoked, than during other moons. During the high summer moon, however, the wolf is almost giddy, there's a thrill, almost a high to the whole experience that fuels the wolf's nighttime activities.

Given my choice, I'd take the high moon over the low moon every time. Don't get me wrong, an excited or hyperactive wolf can do a lot of damage. It's nothing, though, compared to the sort of rage that can emerge when someone provokes a werewolf during the low moon, during the winter solstice.

All these factors combined to make this the worst possible time during the yearly lunar cycle to experience one's first or even one's second shift. Ryan would be fine. I'd make sure of that. But I'd also have to stay close to him. Any number of things might distract him, piss him off, or send him into a rage. I needed to be there as alpha to put him back in his place if something like that were to happen.

Typically, I showed up in Manchac Swamp after the transformation was complete, before the pack could get any crazy ideas on their own to do anything they might regret. Given the volatility of Ryan's condition, however, I joined them for the night's preparatory rituals. Donald could lead the pack through the process well enough and, while I could assume control at any moment, eventually Donald would have to lead the pack without me. The more I could allow him to lead, even if only during our pre-shift preparations, the better it prepared him for the future.

"Everyone gather around," Donald said as we all formed a circle atop the hill where the pack began its shift on Manchac Swamp. It was the very hill where the flambeau was once buried. For most of their wolfish existence, the pack spent its days and nights lurking around the hill, which was also an old graveyard, complete with wooden crosses. Most of the remaining markers had missing cross pieces. Still, to the average passerby, if anyone dared to boat this deep into the swamp, it was a jarring sight.

A graveyard in the middle of a swamp is enough to give almost anyone nightmares. If the people knew the true story, why the people buried there had died, it would compound the dreadfulness of the nightmare several times over. Julie Brown, the ghost who guarded these lands, had lived in a logging town nearby at the turn of the twentieth century. While Julie was a benevolent spirit, she was a terror to many during her earthly life. She was a caplata. The people in and around her village knew her well for her charms and her curses. And when the town that she called home turned against her, she pronounced a curse on them all.

As legend has it, she lived in a small cabin in the swamp. She sat on her porch, playing her guitar, as she sang, "One day I'm going to die and take the whole town with me."

Soon thereafter, her cursed prophecy was fulfilled. An opening to the void caused what many believed to be a hurricane in 1915. She died in the storm. Most of the town drowned with her. They were buried on the very hill where we now gathered.

Julie's father, something of a religious zealot, had found the Witch of Endor's flambeau. He gave it to his daughter, born out of wedlock, and bid her to guard it even in death. Thus, the legend of the ghost of Manchac Swamp, and the rougarou who fell under her charm and that of the flambeau, was born.

We stood in a circle on the hill and did as we often did in group therapy. We took our turn sharing our struggles, releasing whatever resentments or troubles we had, lest we seized on those things once the wolf emerged. Since this was the second night in a row, and the pack members discussed whatever was troubling them already the night before, most of what anyone had to share the group already knew. Still, it was important to speak out-loud whatever might be on one's mind.

"Who'd like to go first?" Donald asked.

Evie cleared her throat and glanced at Christopher. "Chris has been jerkin' his gherkin too much. I think he really needs to come clean with the group."

"I have not!" Christopher piped up. "I'm not the one who just bought that toy off of Amazon."

Evie shrugged. "Sometimes a girl needs something a little extra. What can I say?"

I coughed into my hand. "I don't think those are issues that will trigger the wolf."

"I agree," Christopher said. "Doing it doggy comes natural to us, anyway."

Ryan snickered. "You guys do it in wolf form? I mean, not to pry, but..."

Christopher narrowed his eyes. "We lived as werewolves for more than a century. Of course we do! That's an awful long time to be pent up."

"Tell me about it," Yvette said, diverting her eyes to the horizon.

"Wait," Ryan said. "Could you, you know, get knocked up as a werewolf?"

"I wouldn't know," Evie said. "Chris is sterile."

"I am not! Not as a human, anyway!"

Donald took a deep breath. "This is important, guys. Can we please stay on topic? If anyone has anything to get off their chest before we shift, this is the time to do it."

I pressed my lips together, resisting the urge to speak up. Donald had the matter under control, more or less, anyway.

"Wait," Ryan said. "Are werewolves infertile?"

I snorted. "Only when shifted. Don't worry. It won't impact your long-term ability to reproduce."

"Have you had kids, Cain?" Ryan asked.

"It's been a long time, but yes. When you've lived as long as I have, though, and you've seen many children grow up, live their lives, and die, it can be wearisome."

"That's an interesting question, though," Donald added. "We won't die of old age now that we're werewolves. Do you think we shouldn't have children?"

I shook my head. "I have no regrets. I loved every child I ever had. But you must come to grips with the fact that if you have children, you will probably outlive them. It is a hard thing for parents to accept."

Donald snorted. "Well, in that case, I have something to share."

"Go ahead," I said.

"Carol is pregnant."

"Oh my God!" Evie exclaimed. "Congratulations, Donald!"

Donald smiled widely. "I was a little worried, I have to admit, that my baby, you know... might change in the womb."

I shook my head. "Our condition is not genetic. You have no reason to be anxious, Donald."

Donald sighed. "That's a tremendous relief. I've been meaning to ask but, you know, I wasn't really sure how to bring up the topic."

"I had a daughter before," Christopher piped up.

"Before we became wolves?" Evie asked.

Christopher nodded.

Evie backhanded Christopher on the shoulder. "Why haven't you mentioned that before?"

Christopher shrugged. "It's difficult to talk about. But I suppose I should. You know, since it's a regret. After we became wolves, and the flambeau bound us here, I never saw her again. She was only two when the wolf bit me and I turned. And then, the hurricane. Thank God, my wife and daughter weren't here at the time."

"Wait," Evie said. "You were married, too?"

Christopher sighed. "It was a long time ago, Evie. Like I said, I don't enjoy talking about this stuff."

"It's still good that you did," I added. "That kind of loss, if not addressed, could fuel the wolf's rage."

Evie placed her hands on her hips. "You still should have told me, Christopher."

Christopher rolled his eyes. "Don't tell me you're jealous of my dead family, Evie."

"I'm not!" Evie insisted. "I'm just upset you never said a thing about it until now."

I glanced at Donald. "Are you going to address this?"

Donald sighed. "I don't know what to say, Cain. I know I need to handle these things, but I can see both sides to this."

I nodded. "Then help Christopher and Evie see each other's side. You're the alpha, Donald. You cannot allow the moon to rise while tension remains in the air."

Donald cleared his throat. "Christopher lost people who meant the world to him. We all did when we were bitten. Surely you had a family before, Evie."

"Not a spouse and children!" Evie protested.

"But you had people you loved," Donald said.

"Yes," Evie said. "My parents and my sister."

"Then surely you can understand why it might still be difficult for Christopher to talk about this."

Evie sighed. "I suppose I get it. I don't know how I'd feel if I'd had children before all this happened."

Donald pivoted and looked at Christopher. "And surely you can realize why, as you and Evie are trying to build a life together as humans now, she might appreciate knowing more about your past."

Christopher snorted. "Yeah, that makes sense."

I winked at Donald as a way of communicating my pride in how he was handling the matter. "This is substantial progress, everyone. When we discuss these things, it leads to a much calmer, docile wolf."

"I'm afraid of leaving my family behind," Ryan said.

"Tell us about your family, Ryan," Donald said.

Ryan shrugged. "I'm the oldest of three boys. My parents are good people. Hard workers. My dad is a mechanic, my mom is a hairdresser."

"How old are your brothers?" Evie asked.

"Hunter is thirteen. Connor is sixteen. Connor plays quarterback for his High School football team. Hunter plays the piano. I never really found a passion like that. I don't know why not. I mean, I like to draw."

"That's a worthy passion," I said.

Christopher smiled. "I'm not a great artist or anything. But I enjoy it."

"It's important to have hobbies," I said.

"What about you?" Ryan asked. "Do you have any hobbies, Dr. Cain?"

I laughed. "When you've lived as long as I have, I think you dabble in almost everything for a season. I went through a painting phase during the renaissance."

"Were you any good?" Christopher asked.

I laughed. "Not really. You won't find any of my pieces in any museums, if that's what you're asking. But I once spent an evening with Michaelangelo, assisting him as he painted the ceiling of the Sistine Chapel in Rome."

"Holy crap," Ryan said, shaking his head. "That's amazing. I'd give anything to see something like that happen in real time."

I smiled. "There are blessings to this life. Yes, there is heartache. All of us will see those we love grow old and eventually die. But the things we might live to see, if we embrace this life, could be quite remarkable."

Ryan chuckled. "I can imagine, like two hundred years from now, telling someone I once saw Billie Eilish perform live."

"Shut up!" Evie interjected. "I love Billie!"

Christopher snorted. "She plays her songs over and over in our apartment. Don't get me wrong. She's pretty good. But damn, you'd think after the first three hundred times you hear the same song on repeat you'd want to listen to something else."

Evie giggled. "Well, it's a lot better use of Alexa than telling her to fart, Christopher!"

Christopher laughed. "It's hilarious!"

"Wait," Ryan said. "Alexa farts?"

"Totally!" Christopher piped up. "She makes all kinds of them, too. Little poofs. Long, juicy ones. Any kind of fart you could imagine."

Donald rolled his eyes. "Well, our time is running short. And we still have to go through our yoga routine."

Ryan cocked his head. "Excuse me?"

"We do yoga to prepare," Donald said. "It loosens up the body. It makes the transformation less painful. It also helps us clear our minds. It's good for the wolf."

Ryan chuckled. "Alright. Well, I have to warn you. I'm about as flexible as a brick."

"It will come with time," Donald said. "I'm a large man. You wouldn't think I could get my foot behind my head. But now I can!"

Ryan squinted. "A part of me doesn't want to see that. Another part of me has to see it!"

"Watch and learn," Donald said. "Alright everyone. Lets start with a vinyasa and go into downward dog."

Ryan raised one eyebrow. "Downward dog? Ironic."

The entire pack laughed.

"You know," Donald said. "I think that every time we do it. But I try to bite my tongue."

"Don't worry," Ryan said. "You're about to be a father. The dad jokes will come in soon enough."

"But you're not a dad," Donald said.

Ryan shook his head. "You're right. But my dad tells so many lame jokes I think it's rubbed off on me."

"I think you're going to make a great addition to our pack," Donald said, grinning ear to ear. "Just follow along, and do your best."

CHAPTER NINE

THE FULL MOON ROSE on the horizon. It was waning, but to the wolf's eye, it looked as full as it was the night before. My joints popped as my bones expanded. I'd shifted so many times it wasn't at all painful. For these wolves, while the rougarou were more than a century old, they'd spent most of that time not shifting at all. There were more snaps and pops in the air than you might hear eating a bowl of Rice Krispies in a chiropractor's office.

Then there was the fur. The wolf's fur is coarser than human hair. It comes in even as the skin itself is changing. When it does, it presses through the pores in an excruciating fashion. The pain assuages quickly as the human skin gradually adapts, but those first few seconds feel something like a sunburn in a hot shower. Only when you're shifting you can't jerk away from the heat or turn it down. There's no choice but to endure it.

The skin is the most painful part, but it's not the worst. The human heart pumps a certain amount of blood through the body at a particular rate. As the body expands, the heart has to work faster. The heart expands, too, while shifting. But the beat rattles the body like an earthquake. In the ears, it's as loud as the bass might be if you stuck your head into the woofer at a rave.

There was nothing remotely pleasurable about the shift itself. A few female werewolves have told me that the pain is comparable to childbearing, if you were giving birth from every orifice of the body at the same time. I didn't have a barometer to understand at all what childbearing felt like, but I knew how it felt to turn into a werewolf. For the first several centuries, it was unbearable. Now, it was still horribly uncomfortable, but tolerable. These wolves, though, were still enduring the worst of it. The yoga they did to start did nothing for the skin, or the heart, but it lessened the striking pain that accompanied the expansion of the bones and joints. Some packs make a habit of drinking before shifting. Granted, it helps with the pain. While the transformation lowers the blood-alcohol-content slightly, mostly because of the increase in body mass, it doesn't sober the wolf up completely. There are few things in the world more insufferable than drunk werewolves. Take my word for it.

If there's any consolation to it all, it's that once the transformation is complete, the pleasure, the passion, the heightened senses of the wolf are so exhilarating that you almost forget the pain you went through before. Again, if the transformation is akin to the sensation of childbearing, the result is comparable to the exuberance of a mother when it's over and she holds her baby for the first time. A totally different sort of feeling, for sure, but the contrast of the before and after is just as stark.

The wind blowing through our fur wasn't as cold as the night before. It was still refreshing. I'm not sure if it was more being in wolf form or being in nature that awakened my senses to the world around me more. There was something to the fact of running through the wild, being surrounded by lands barely touched by human hands, that invigorated me. Even when I wasn't a werewolf, a walk through the forest, walking barefoot through grass, or staring at a star-filled sky had an effect on me that was almost intoxicating, but with clarity rather than the cloudiness of mind that comes with a strong drink.

I ran as close to Ryan as I could. For a newly turned wolf, he was coming along nicely. But that second turn was always the most dangerous. Most wolves are still a little fearful the second time they shift, but not so frightened that their terror overcomes their other primal urges. And once those passions were loose, not even my thrall could keep him in check.

We raced from one end of the swamp to the other. Ryan was slower than the rest. He was still learning how to run. I lagged behind as the rest bounded ahead. It was an excellent test for the pack. The further the others moved from where Ryan and I ran, the less my influence guided them and the more Donald's leadership took over. Even separated by a few miles, I had *some* influence over the others. Enough that with a howl I could bring them back into my control if necessary. Still, if they could run with Donald entertaining no urge to leave the swamp, it was a win. So far, so good. Ryan was my first concern. He was the only one I wasn't sure Donald could handle without me. Another couple shifts, the more Ryan integrated into the pack, the more comfortable I'd be allowing him to run with the rest. Not to mention, once he found his speed and could keep up with the pack, I'd have less to worry about.

We ran all night. From time to time, Ryan and I would cross paths with the rest of the pack as they blasted through the swamp waters. There was more that Ryan needed to learn than how to run. He needed to learn how to use his other senses, especially his keen sense of smell. He was learning fast. By the end of the night, he was already running at nearly the pace as the rest. We'd practiced picking up the scent of some gators in the swamp, pursued them, and had ourselves a meal. It's never a good idea to overeat as a wolf, especially late in the night. A full wolf's stomach was bound to lead to a case of constipation back in human form if we ever over-indulged. Trying to convince a young wolf to exercise moderation when it came to a feast was difficult, but with my influence Ryan did well, leaving half of the gator we'd hunted behind as he and I together moved toward the edge of the swamp and watched the sun rise. We only had a short time left before the full moon disappeared.

Ryan's head jerked eastward. He smelled something. I sensed it, too. It wasn't another alligator. It wasn't one of the other wolves. It was a human scent.

I growled, halting Ryan as he started toward the figure in the distance. Whoever it was that had wandered to the border of the swamp saw us already.

Ryan stopped in his tracks and turned back toward me.

Bang!

A bullet caught Ryan in the shoulder. He buckled over. A bullet wound wouldn't hurt a werewolf. He'd heal quickly. Provided it wasn't a silver bullet...

I bounded toward Ryan and examined the wound. The black blood that poured out from it told me all I needed to know. Whoever shot him was a hunter. He knew what he was doing. It was silver...

A wound to the shoulder, as opposed to one striking an artery, would take a while to spread. As a young wolf, he'd have a couple hours before it would kill him.

Bang! Bang!

A sharp pain hit my back.

Damn it! I turned, and not six feet from me stood the hunter. He wore all black. A hood pulled over his head obscured his face.

I turned and snarled at the hunter.

Then he pulled back his hood.

I hadn't seen that face for six thousand years. The last time I'd seen him, when I crashed that stone into his skull, he'd looked at me with wide eyes in shock. That look, one that communicated the pain of betrayal, was burned into my mind.

Now, my brother looked back at me with his face contorted, his lip curled in disgust.

My fur started to shed. Clumps of it fell to the ground around my feet. My bones snapped back into their normal shape. My heartbeat usually slowed when I turned back to human form. This time, it continued to pump as hard as ever before.

The pain in my back from the gunshot wounds burned.

For a moment, I stood before Abel naked. My eyes met his.

He smirked. "Long time no see, brother."

No sooner did he speak and his body expanded. A golden colored fur burst from his skin. The clothes he was wearing ripped from his body and fell to the ground. It was the seven-fold curse. He wouldn't turn back again until he'd changed seven more wolves himself.

His eyes were wide, twitching as he changed. He didn't expect this. He was dead before I was cursed. I didn't know how long it had been since he was raised—surely the work of Cassidy Brown—but she hadn't warned him about this.

He could have leaped on me, devoured my heart, and had his vengeance. Instead, overcome by terror and confusion, he took off and ran toward the city.

CHAPTER TEN

I COULD MAKE IT a day, maybe longer, before I'd succumb to the silver. The wounds burned. It wasn't the first time I'd been shot by silver bullets. The anguish would spread throughout my body. It might not kill me so soon, but the delirium from the pain would cloud my mind if I didn't take care of it quickly. Ryan didn't have that much time.

It wasn't long before the rest of the pack joined us, already shifted back and dressed. Donald had a change of clothes draped over one of his arms. Evie held a pair of sweatpants and a t-shirt in her hands.

"Shit!" Donald shouted. "You were both shot!"

"Who the hell shot you, Cain?" Christopher asked.

"It was my brother. Resurrected by a necromancer. And it's already too late. He shifted."

"We can go after him," Donald said. "But if we do..."

"You will not stop him while you're in human form. And we need to get Ryan back to Vilokan first. He doesn't have time to spare."

Donald nodded and tossed me a change of clothes. I slipped into a set of jeans and a t-shirt while Evie and Christopher dressed Ryan. Donald helped Ryan to his feet, but his legs buckled under him.

"We're going to have to carry him to my truck. I'd like you all to join me. It's going to take all of us to get Ryan into Vilokan to see the

Voodoo Queen. She can heal him, but we need to get him to her within the hour."

All our vehicles were parked on a gravel road close to the edge of the swamp. Donald heaved Ryan into the back. He was still breathing, but passed out from the effects of the silver in his system.

I don't think I ever drove so fast in my life. I pushed my truck to its limits, praying we wouldn't get pulled over by the cops on our way back to Vilokan. There wasn't any way we could explain why two of us had gunshot wounds and, worse, if they insisted on taking Ryan to a hospital, he'd die there from his wounds. They wouldn't know how to treat silver poisoning in a werewolf.

I had a habit of counting my blessings, and this was no exception. We made it back without incident. If we weren't werewolves, with our enhanced strength, there wouldn't be any way we could carry Ryan down all the stairs that led from the magical doorway on the side-wall of St. Louis Cathedral into Vilokan.

Donald held Ryan in a fireman's carry the whole way as we made our way to Annabelle's office.

"Can you heal him? Both of us, I mean? We were shot. Silver bullets."

Annabelle stood from behind her desk and ran over to us. "Someone shot you, Cain? That means..."

"I know what it means. We'll have to handle that later. But right now, we have to focus on Ryan. He doesn't have much time. Can you do it?"

Annabelle took a deep breath. "Not alone. Give me a moment."

I nodded as Donald laid Ryan down on the floor. The rest of the rougarou made their way into the office on a second elevator ride behind us.

Annabelle went into a room behind her office. I didn't know what she had back there. I never asked. She returned a few moments later, her eyes glowing green.

"A Loa?" I asked.

Annabelle shook her head. "Not exactly. A friend. You know my story, Cain."

"Isabelle?" I asked.

Annabelle nodded. Isabelle was a ghost who had possessed Annabelle ever since her family was attacked by a caplata when she was only a child. Isabelle gave Annabelle power that she'd drawn directly from the Tree of Life in Eden. I didn't realize that Annabelle still had access to Isabelle. I wasn't about to question it. The power she could wield when united with her formerly soul-bound familiar was exactly what we needed.

Annabelle pressed her hand to the wound in Ryan's shoulder, releasing a torrent of green mana from her hand.

Ryan gasped and his eyes snapped open as the wound healed in seconds.

"Let me see your back, Cain."

I nodded, removed my shirt, and turned my back to Annabelle. She pressed her hands on my two wounds and repeated the spell that already healed Ryan. The pain left my body in an instant.

"Thank God," I said. "Pass my gratitude along to Isabelle."

"We may still need her," Annabelle said. "Do you know who shot you? With Isabelle, we can forge a blade that can cut a portal straight into Guinee. It might be the best way to get rid of the newly cursed wolf."

"It was Abel," I said, shaking my head.

Annabelle looked at me, her eyes wide, still glowing green. "This was Cassidy's doing?"

I sighed. "I believe so. I don't know how she did it. She's still locked away in solitary, so far as I know. And more, how she told Abel how to kill us... or how he got a gun... I mean, he wouldn't even know what a gun is! We didn't even have swords, much less guns!"

Annabelle sighed. "Cassidy must have some way to speak to those she raises. A caplata, who raises zombies, can control them. If she can exert some influence on your brother, that might explain it."

I scratched the back of my head. "It still doesn't make sense. The asylum is warded. Whatever power she's wielding, it must be stronger than our spells."

"Or a brand of magic that cannot be warded against," Annabelle said. "And there aren't a lot of candidates, much less one that might also have the power to raise the dead."

"Infernal magic," I said. "Most likely drawn from an infernal relic."

"And not just any infernal relic, Cain."

I sighed. "The flambeau of the Witch of Endor."

"It must be," Annabelle said, helping Ryan back to his feet with Donald's help.

"But it disappeared with Julie Brown. How could Cassidy have possibly acquired it?"

"She's a necromancer, Cain. And since Julie and she are of the same bloodline, Cassidy could have brought her back more easily than you'd think."

I shook my head. "But that still doesn't answer how she might have the flambeau with her inside the asylum."

"Beli," Annabelle said. When she spoke, a blade formed in her hand. It radiated flashes of pink and green magic. "The same way I can evoke this blade when Isabelle's soul dwells in me."

I stared at Annabelle's blade, transfixed by the power that coursed through it. "Are you saying that Cassidy bound Julie's soul to herself?"

Annabelle nodded. "And when she did, she also acquired the flambeau. We wouldn't have seen it when we searched her because it was hidden within her. And, Cain, if she can evoke the flambeau, it won't be safe for you or the other wolves to return to the asylum."

I shook my head. "I have to talk to her. I can handle myself if she forces me to change."

"Perhaps," Annabelle said. "But the others... I can't risk that."

"I can keep them under control," I said.

"Even under the evocation of the flambeau? I'm not so sure..."

"She's right," Donald piped up. "That thing enthralled us for a century. If she wields it, Cain, she'll usurp your control over the pack. We have to leave."

I shook my head. "I've shifted by the flambeau before. When Julie used it, she didn't control me."

"But you weren't under that thing's spell for nearly so long as we were," Donald added. "And we don't have six thousand years' worth of experience controlling the wolf on our own."

"We can do it," Christopher said. "We will resist it. If we have to. We've been working on taming the wolf. I know how powerful that item is as much as the rest of you. But we're also stronger now than we were before!"

I pressed my lips together. "No, Christopher. Donald is right. You may be able to resist, but if you can't, there's no telling what she might make you do. We're already facing a werewolf under the seven-fold curse. If my brother turns others and forms a pack of his own, we'll already have our hands full worrying about them."

"We can't risk having two packs on the loose in the city," Annabelle said. "We need you all to get as far away from Vilokan as possible."

"What if we shift again tomorrow?" Ryan asked.

I shook my head. "It's not likely to happen. On the solstice, two nights in a row are expected. A third is exceedingly rare."

"Rare, but not out of the question," Christopher added.

"You're right," I said, nodding my head. "If that happens, let me know. I'll do what I can to help. For good measure, though, it might be a good idea to chain yourselves up tonight."

"Where would we do that?" Donald asked.

"I have a place," Annabelle said. "My old home, in fact. It's a former plantation. I was considering giving it to Cain as a satellite location for the Vilokan Asylum."

I cocked my head. "Your home? Are you serious, Annabelle?"

Annabelle nodded. "If there's a lesson to learn at all from this incident, it's that there may be advantages to having an above-ground campus. I'll see to it you have everything you need to restrain yourselves through the night."

"Thank you, Annabelle. That's quite generous of you."

"It's for the wellbeing of all of us, Cain. We need more space, and we can't have any more wolves running loose in Vilokan."

I nodded. "I still need to talk to Cassidy. Her cards are on the table now. If I can get her to talk openly and honestly, I may be able to help her sort out what's motivating all this."

"What's important, Cain, is that we help her. If it means banishment, so be it. Though, if she's really wielding an infernal relic like the flambeau, I'm not sure that talking about her feelings will prevent her from doing whatever she's planning."

I sighed. "We don't know what she's planning, Annabelle. From our perspective, what she's doing looks downright evil. But think about it for a moment. If a ghost could come back from the dead and get revenge on his killer, and if that tale was cast as a Hollywood Blockbuster, who do you think audiences would cheer for?"

"That's not fair, Cain. That's only one half of the story. The things you've done, the agony you've felt for centuries, the way you now help others, is a part of the story, too."

"You prove my point, Annabelle. What I'm trying to say is that everyone has a perspective. Very few of us are pure good or pure evil. Still, we tend to judge one another as if the world were populated by heroes and villains. One person's hero is another's villain. Anyone who has been to war, who has bothered to consider the conflict from the other side's perspective, knows as much. Right now, we've ascertained that Cassidy is using an infernal object, possibly the Witch of Endor's flambeau. We've guessed that she's bound the spirit of Julie Brown, her own ancestor, to herself in order to acquire the relic. And we suspect that she's raised my dead brother and commanded him to kill me. But we must ask what motivates Cassidy to do such things? Do you truly believe that she thinks she's the villain of this story, Annabelle?"

"It doesn't matter what she thinks, Cain. She's using infernal power, she's practicing necromancy, she's using her power to kill. I'm not sure that there's any way you could spin any of that as heroic."

I smiled. "Tell me, Annabelle. Have you ever done something you knew was wrong because you knew you had no other choice? For the sake of the greater good?"

Annabelle bit her lip. "If you're speaking of Nico, how I left him in Guinee..."

"I wasn't talking about him, Annabelle. I was talking generally. You are the one who brought it back to the specific. But since you went there, after that event and in some ways because of it you saved hundreds if not thousands more lives."

"But many people died because I couldn't bring Nico back and he became a vampire."

"That's true. But you didn't enter the bargain with Baron Samedi that made him a vampire, did you?"

"Of course not, but still..."

I raised my hand slightly to silence Annabelle. I knew where she was going. "What if someone made a movie and told you it was about a young witch who created the world's first vampire. Would you think, for a second, that the witch was the heroine of the story?"

"Probably not, but if that movie was about me, that would be a shitty synopsis. It's not the full story."

"And until we know Cassidy's full story, Annabelle, we cannot rush to judgment. I need to talk to her."

Annabelle shook her head. "And what will you do, Cain, if she evokes the flambeau and forces you to change?"

I shrugged my shoulders. "Then, I'll change. She'll find I'm not as easily manipulated, even in wolf form, as the rest of the pack might be. Still, it's not a bad thing that I should allow myself to be vulnerable. I can use that to convince Cassidy to tell me about her plans. Why resurrect Abel? Why did she plan to revive the killer, LaLaurie? What's her real motive and what does she hope to accomplish? Until we know that, until she opens up and speaks to me, we simply cannot banish her to the void. We need her side of the story. Perhaps we'll find lurking behind her less-than savory methods a common belief, or goal, that we might help her achieve in another way."

Annabelle pinched her chin. "Well, Cain, you certainly have a lot of faith in people. More than I do."

"I've lived long enough to see good people do horrible things. I've also seen people you might think to be evil rise to the occasion and do what's right. The scales could tip either direction in almost any situation. I prefer to remain an optimist, particularly with my patients."

Annabelle grinned. "Well, I suppose that's why you're the therapist, Cain. But I still have a responsibility to ensure the safety of the Voodoo community. If push comes to shove, I'll do what's necessary."

"Understood, Annabelle. I'd expect nothing less from you. I simply ask that you expect nothing less from me than to advocate for my patient."

"Even if she's already tried to kill you?"

I chuckled. "Wouldn't be the first time. When you treat the magically and mentally deranged, it's par for the course."

CHAPTER ELEVEN

I BARELY MADE IT through the front doors to the Vilokan Asylum when Rutherford pulled me aside.

Rutherford was her first name. I could relate. I also have a last name as my first. It wasn't always that way, but it had been a few thousand years since the name "Cain" ranked near the top of the world's most popular baby names. You can blame the Genesis tale for that.

Rutherford Rigdon. She'd captured my attention from the day I was hired at the Vilokan Asylum. For a common woman, without interest in voodoo, witchcraft, or possessing any peculiar abilities, it struck me as odd from the start that she'd worked as a nurse at the Vilokan Asylum.

The former queen, Marie Laveau, hired her ages ago. Not every nurse is trained to deal with the mentally ill. Even rarer is one who is adept at working with the magically deranged. Rutherford was a rare gem. As the story goes, apparently she was working in a ward under a prestigious cognitive-behavioral therapist in New York when a vampire got himself committed to her ward. On the surface, it was a brilliant move. He could feed on any of his fellow patients and, given the severity of many of the cases in that particular asylum, most of his victims would either be oblivious to what he did or the therapists wouldn't believe them if anyone tried to report him.

Much to the chagrin of her superiors, however, Rutherford took the reports seriously. She reached out, independently, to the Voodoo Queen. It took a while to find someone who would accept her claims. Marie Laveau hired Rutherford on the spot and maneuvered to see the patient transferred to Vilokan Asylum.

The Asylum was run by hougans and mambos with little more than a cursory knowledge of mental illness. The former Queen, Marie Laveau, was the closest thing any of them had to a therapist. They hired Rutherford to help bridge that deficiency. It was on her recommendation, after a chance encounter I'd had with Rutherford at a convention for psychotherapists, that they hired me. That, too, is another story that might be told. In short, her former supervisor from New York was also present at the convention. He'd spotted Rutherford, cracked a few jokes about his former nurse who'd believed one of his former patients' delusions that he was a vampire. My interest was piqued. I started a conversation with Rutherford on the topic, and the rest was history.

I'd say it was love at first sight. From my perspective, at least. It took her half a decade or more before she gave me the slightest hint that she might be interested as well. Even now, knowing we had feelings for one another, our relationship was far from conventional. Yes, we enjoyed each other's company on an intimate level frequently. But so much of our time together was at work, within the confines of the Asylum, that she had a hard time opening up to me. Ironic, I know, since I'm supposed to be an expert at that sort of thing. But when the heart is involved, when it's personal rather than professional, I couldn't play the therapist with Rutherford. That's not the kind of "playing doctor" I'd recommend in a relationship.

Rutherford never spoke of her family. They'd been estranged for years. She never told me why. I suspected she could use a therapist of her own, a secular therapist, to help her come to terms with her past. I couldn't be that therapist. It would be a conflict of interest and, frankly, if I even tried, it would likely blow up in my face. If she saw me as her therapist, rather than her lover, it would ruin our romance. I didn't press the issue. She never suggested it. But I knew, from my background, that she had issues that were preventing her from connecting with me fully. Daddy issues, perhaps. But until she talked to me about it, I wouldn't and couldn't push.

"What's the issue?" I asked. "I presume Cassidy has something to do with it?"

Rutherford cocked her head. "Not at all. She's been sitting in her room sleeping, reading a book, doing nothing of note at all since you left."

I furrowed my brow. "She's done *nothing*? Are you certain?"

"Absolutely. I've been at the monitors most of the night."

I scratched my head. "Strange. I was certain she was up to something..."

"What makes you say that?"

I sighed. "Long story. An incident that came up last night with the rougarou. I thought she had something to do with it. I'll fill you in later. What's the issue now?"

"It's Trig," Rutherford smirked. "He's started a flash mob."

I squinted. "What's a flash mob?"

Rutherford giggled. "It would be easier to show you than explain it."

I made my way behind Rutherford's desk in reception. She had a monitor there, streaming a life feed of the rec room. A majority of the patients were gathered, lined up, doing some kind of dance. Trig was in the front leading the show.

"What the hell am I looking at?"

Rutherford grinned. "It's the *Thriller* dance."

I sighed. "Michael Jackson?"

Rutherford nodded. "I'd say it was harmless fun. But they've been doing this for three hours now. I tried to intervene, but it's like they don't even see me. They're in some kind of trance. They finish the dance, then start all over again. What's even weirder, while Trig is singing the songs, there isn't any beat, no music at all playing."

"And they're all moving in sync," I said. "How is that even possible? It looks like a choreographed dance."

"It is," Rutherford said. "Many people know it, but I find it hard to believe that all the patients do."

I scratched my head. "Some kind of mind control?"

"I'm assuming so, but that's not a kind of magic I was aware ogres practiced."

I sighed. "It's not. One of the witches, perhaps a caplata, must be the culprit. My best guess is someone is using Trig's delusion to cause a distraction."

"But all the witches and caplatas in residence are also a part of the flash mob. I'm not sure how effective a distraction it could be if the dance also enthralled the witch responsible."

I pressed my lips together. "Not every caplata here is involved."

"But Cassidy is in solitary. How could she be doing that?"

I shook my head. "I'm not sure. I need to talk to her. I'm not at all optimistic she'll tell me what's happening if she even knows. She's been less than cooperative so far."

Rutherford smiled. "If anyone can get through to her, Cain, it's you."

CHAPTER TWELVE

I TOOK A DEEP breath before walking through the door. I wasn't typically nervous before speaking to a patient. It was my job and in my line of work I'd seen my share of things that would raise the hair on the back of your neck. But this was personal. She'd threatened me before. She spoke to me *as if* she was Abel. Then Abel shot me in the back. Rutherford said she hadn't done squat except literally squat in her room since I left. And while I couldn't pin the whole "flash mob" situation on her, I figured talking to her about it might be less confrontational than asking her if she'd raised my dead brother or intended to raise Delphine LaLaurie. Compared to either of those situations, inspiring an off-the-rocker remix of an old Michael Jackson video was rather tame. Provided, of course, it ended soon. The patients couldn't stop dancing. They were sweating. Dehydration would set in sooner rather than later.

As ridiculous as it sounds, the situation had the potential to become graver than anything else that we'd thought Cassidy might be responsible for so far. For now, though, it was a rather light subject. A great way to break the ice.

I unlocked the door with my janitor-sized set of keys and stepped into Cassidy's room. She looked at me and smiled widely. "Cain! Great to see you!"

I narrowed my eyes. "Nice to see you, too. You certainly seem in a better mood than before"

"We talked before?" Cassidy asked. "I mean, I know who you are. So I suppose we must have."

I pressed my lips together. "What's going on Cassidy? Do you know why you're here?"

Cassidy cocked her head and looked at me with wide eyes. "I... well... I have flashes. I was at the Voodoo Academy. They were concerned that I'd inadvertently used my skills to raise someone dangerous. Then, darkness. Next thing I knew, I was here."

"Cassidy, this is going to sound strange. But can you tell me what year it is?"

Cassidy rolled her eyes. "Of course! It's 2009!"

I sighed. I couldn't tell Cassidy the truth. Not yet. If I did, well, the notion that she'd missed more than a decade of her life would be disturbing and cloud her mind. But this clearly wasn't the same Cassidy I spoke to when she first arrived at the asylum.

"And when did you wake up here? After you blacked out at the Voodoo Academy, I mean?"

"I've been in this room ever since. It's been several hours, less than a day. I don't know. I don't have a clock in here."

I pinched my chin. We covered the whole asylum in basic silencing wards. It prevented most kinds of magic from entering. This room, however, was doubly protected. On the floor was the veve of Papa Legba, a distinct pattern, like a sigil. A veve was used by a hougan or mambo to evoke the Loa associated with its unique pattern. Papa Legba was the Loa primarily responsible for governing the crossroads. At least, he used to be. Before Annabelle's soul-bound familiar, Isabelle, took over most of his work. Legba hadn't been to Vilokan in some time, but, presumably, he still possessed the same power. If Cassidy Brown was possessed by someone, Legba's veve would silence whatever spirit, Loa, or even demon had taken hold of Cassidy's mind.

"I've seen Asogwe Jim's disciplinary report, Cassidy."

Cassidy narrowed her eyes. "Why did Asogwe Jim write the report? He wasn't on the disciplinary committee before..."

"Before what?" I asked.

"Before I blacked out. I guess it must've been nerves. They were talking about kicking me out of the academy."

"You belonged to College Samedi, correct? You worked with the Ghede?"

Cassidy nodded. "I was the head of my class, and Maman Brigitte said I was the most promising student she'd had in years. I can't imagine she'd stand for my expulsion."

I cleared my throat. "Again, Cassidy. How did you know who I was?"

"I'm not sure. A dream, maybe?"

"You can recall your dreams? From the time after you blacked out?"

"When I woke up, I thought I did. I was terrified for a moment. Then, most of what I thought I was dreaming faded in an instant. Still, for some reason, seeing your face jogged my memory. I knew your name. I knew you wanted to help me. Did we talk, before?"

"I talked to someone," I said. "I'm not sure it was you."

Cassidy scratched the back of her head. "Someone else was speaking for me?"

I nodded. "I believe so. Tell me, Cassidy. Who was it they said you'd nearly resurrected? Why were they so concerned about it?"

"It wasn't in my disciplinary report?"

I shook my head. "Someone blacked out parts of your report. There are details about your situation, Cassidy, that I'm not privy to."

"They wouldn't tell me. They said if I heard her name it would awaken her, that she'd gain control over my mind..."

"Cassidy, how do your abilities work? I've seen in your file that you can raise spirits, not just the bodies of the deceased. Is that correct?"

Cassidy nodded. "That's right. But when I do, the spirits dwell within me. Not permanently. It's a temporary bond. It allows me to put them in another body."

I scratched the back of my head. "And when you do that, what happens to the person you bind the spirit to?"

"Well, that's the thing. If I put the spirit into someone who is still alive, they might rattle around in that person's mind, try to gain control. They rarely do. Usually they just leave, go back to where they were. But if I bind the spirit to an animated corpse, the spirit will reform the body to resemble who they were in life."

"So it's almost like a resurrection. Except the body they possess only looks like the one they had in life?"

"That's right. Why do you ask?"

"I'm still trying to piece things together, Cassidy. I'll tell you shortly. If you can answer a few more questions."

"Of course. I'll tell you anything you'd like to know."

"Who were you trying to resurrect? I know you don't know who it was that the disciplinary committee said you actually raised, but you said you were trying to raise someone else."

Cassidy blushed. "It's sort of silly. But you know, he was a gift to humanity. The songs he wrote, I know he wasn't the same artist he used to be. But when he died, I had to try and bring him back! I was his biggest fan!"

I narrowed my eyes. Was it even possible? The date lined up. She thought it was 2009. "Are you talking about Michael Jackson?"

"Obviously! I know I wasn't supposed to use my gift for something like that. But his songs were so important! Did you know he wrote *We Are the World* to raise money for Africa? His music changed lives!"

I sighed. "Say you were successful. You managed to cast Michael's spirit into someone else's body. That person was alive, not an animated corpse..."

"I wouldn't do that! I was going to cast him into a corpse. I never finished, but..."

"But say his spirit somehow found its way to someone's body, a living person's body. What would happen if that spirit actually took hold and claimed the host?"

Cassidy shook her head. "That doesn't happen, you know, by accident. Not if the spirit was cast into a human, I mean. There are other races, I suppose, that are more susceptible to possession."

"Like ogres?"

"Well, yeah. I mean, if you could ever find one. But that wouldn't be good. When a spirit returns, they come back different. They remain their true selves, but they carry with them something from the beyond. They come with unique abilities."

"Like mind control, perhaps?"

Cassidy shrugged. "Maybe. I mean, I never let it go that far. My parents warned me against that. They had the same ability, you know."

"I wasn't aware of that. What happened to your parents?"

"They died in an accident. I tried to resurrect them, but they didn't want to come back. A spirit can't return if they aren't willing."

"Why wouldn't your parents want to come back to life?"

Cassidy sighed. "When a spirit is first revived, they live again as they were. Over time, though, they turn angry and vengeful. But that takes years! Before that happened, I could have released their spirits. I could send them back into the beyond. But my parents were stubborn. They didn't want to risk it."

A tear fell down Cassidy's cheek. I retrieved a handkerchief from my pocket and gave it to her. She dabbed her eyes. "I know this is painful for you to talk about. I've lost my parents, too."

Cassidy nodded. "I suppose you have. How do you go on? I mean, the whole idea of a world without my mom and dad…"

"It changes you. No matter how difficult your relationship might have been with your parents, and my relationship with mine was strained, it takes time to move on. But the wound of loss never leaves you. Not completely."

"But does it get any easier?"

"It does. But there's no timetable you can put on your grief."

"It's been almost two years. Still, it feels like if I move on, if I stop mourning, that I'll lose them completely. I know it sounds dumb."

"Not at all," I said. "It's really quite common. Many people who've lost people they love feel that way. But the people you love, you know, they never really leave you."

Cassidy sighed. "I guess that's true."

I cleared my throat. "I'm sorry, Cassidy. I really must ask you a few more questions. You said, before, that if you had cast a spirit into someone's body you could free the spirit?"

"I can," Cassidy said.

"In that case, I need your help. This is going to sound absurd. And before I ask you to do this, I feel like I owe you the truth."

Cassidy cocked her head. "What do you mean?"

I sighed. "It's been more than a decade since they expelled you from the Voodoo Academy, Cassidy."

Cassidy squinted. "What? No, that can't be. What have I been doing all that time?"

"I believe you were possessed by another spirit. Most likely, by whatever spirit it was they feared you might resurrect when you intended to revive the King of Pop."

Cassidy shook her head. "I don't understand how that could have happened. I already recovered Michael's spirit. I even had a body chosen for him to take. I tried to push his spirit into the body, but it wouldn't take. All I can figure is that the body I chose, the spirit of the deceased must've never moved on. She still haunted her grave. She must be the one they were afraid I was going to revive."

"Who was that woman? The one whose body you hoped to use as a vessel for Michael?"

"I chose it at random. She was buried in St. Louis Cemetery No. 1."

"What was her name, Cassidy?"

Cassidy sighed. "Delphine LaLaurie."

CHAPTER THIRTEEN

THIS WAS MY WORKING theory. When we put Cassidy into solitary, Legba's veve exorcised Delphine LaLaurie from her person. Somehow, somewhere, Delphine bound herself to another host. She must've used her connection to Cassidy to take the flambeau with her. Since Cassidy had done nothing since placed in solitary, I knew she hadn't used the flambeau there.

I suspected Delphine also played a role in what was going on with Trig. Most likely, it was little more than a distraction.

I buzzed Rutherford on the intercom. We had them in every room. It was a good way for us, or even for patients, to communicate with us if needed.

"Everything alright?" Rutherford's voice echoed, accompanied by static, through the small speaker on the wall.

"I need you to help us. I'll explain later. I think Cassidy can manage the flash mob situation."

"Flash mob situation?" Cassidy asked.

"The spirit of Michael Jackson got bound to an ogre. He's out there now, and somehow he has the whole asylum doing the *Thriller* dance."

Cassidy's eyes widened. "Holy crap! That's awesome!"

"Yeah, except for the fact that it's been going on for hours and he won't allow anyone to stop."

Cassidy scratched her head. "How long has this ogre been possessed?"

I shook my head. "The ogre, Trig, has been here in the asylum for about six months. But from what we were told when his family checked him in, he's claimed to be Michael Jackson for years."

"Delphine must have expelled him. Somehow, his spirit must've found the ogre."

I nodded. "That's the theory I'm working with. Do you really think he could control people like that?"

Cassidy shrugged. "Totally possible. Especially if Michael has been inside Trig all these years. His mind is probably warped and I assume he's gained some unusual abilities."

"And you're sure you can expel him, put his spirit at rest?"

"Absolutely. But I'll have to get out of here to do it."

"I could bring him here. Maybe the veve would exorcise Michael from him. If it exorcised Delphine LaLaurie out of you, it might do the same for Michael and the ogre."

Cassidy shook her head. "Except his spirit would then be left to wander, to roam, and probably find another host. If he is going to be put to rest, I have to do it somewhere else."

"Are you totally certain that Delphine is not inside of you, still? I'd hate to bring you out of this room only to have her take control again."

"Positively. She left me the moment I awakened. I'd know if she was here."

I bit my lip. I had to trust her. I didn't have any other option. There was the chance, of course, that I'd been talking to Delphine the whole time. That she'd been lying to me all the while. Still, I'm a pretty good judge of when someone is telling the truth. The way Cassidy spoke of her parents and the tears she shed were real.

"Follow me," I said.

Cassidy followed me out of the room. I walked beside her, keeping my eye on her just in case. So far, she hadn't changed. Nothing had suggested that Delphine had reemerged. That was good news and also bad news. Good news because it meant Cassidy was free. Her abilities could come in handy, not only to exorcise Michael Jackson from Trig, but to remove Delphine from whatever host she'd taken. She could also help with Abel, too, provided we could restrain him. I wouldn't allow Cassidy to be put into danger. Especially with my brother out there looking to create more wolves. The bad news was that this meant Delphine was, in fact, out there somewhere. She was planning something. She'd likely deceived Annabelle, or whoever reported Cassidy to the Voodoo Queen for a reason. She wanted to get inside. She had an agenda. The little I knew about Delphine LaLaurie, I feared the worst. She was a serial killer after all. She'd slaughtered dozens of slaves—to let her loose on Vilokan, populated largely by those descended from slaves, was probably what she'd intended all along.

Rutherford joined us in the hallway. "As soon as we do this, I need you to call ahead to Annabelle. Tell her that Delphine LaLaurie possessed Cassidy the whole time and that we think she's taken another host."

"About that," Rutherford said. "I didn't want to say anything earlier since you were dealing with other matters. But I think it might be too late."

I stopped in my tracks. "What are you talking about?"

"They found a body at the Voodoo Academy. Annabelle is trying to hunt down the culprit now. She said we should be ready for a new patient. Whenever they catch the killer."

I sighed. "This isn't good. Annabelle doesn't know what she's dealing with."

"I can help!" Cassidy interjected. "Please, allow me to come with you. This is all my fault. I have to stop her."

I nodded. "One more question before we begin. Are you familiar with your ancestor, Julie Brown?"

Cassidy nodded. "I've spoken to her. She lives in Manchac Swamp. She refuses to move on."

"Not anymore. She took a material body a while back. But then, she disappeared. She was in possession of a relic, something that courses with the power of hell itself. Do you know what I'm speaking of?"

Cassidy shook her head. "Not exactly. I knew there was some kind of power that bound her to that swamp before."

"Is it possible that Delphine LaLaurie could have used you, and your abilities, to take the relic from Julie? When she left in spirit, she likely took the item with her."

"If she could evoke Julie directly, if she somehow bound her to my body while she was in control of it, then yes. She could claim the item. But not without also binding Julie to the same host she's now inhabiting, presuming she has a host now."

"That's helpful. If Delphine is sharing a host, might it be possible to bring Julie out to take control instead?"

"In theory. But I don't know how powerful Delphine is. If she's been in my body this long, she's had quite a bit of time to practice. But Julie had my same powers. So, technically, if Julie is in the same body and Delphine is in control, she could continue evoking the dead and she could wield the same powers she had when she was in my body."

"But could Julie use those powers to expel Delphine also?"

"She could. If we can reach her. But if Delphine is dominant, in control, Julie will be there, but as asleep as I was for the last several years."

I turned to Rutherford. "Pass all that information along to Annabelle. Tell her I'll join her shortly. Once we've dealt with the situation here."

"Got it, Cain. I'm on it."

I smiled at Rutherford as she turned to leave.

"She's nice. You like her, don't you?" Cassidy asked.

I smiled. "Is it that obvious?"

"You look at her differently than you do me. Does she know how you feel?"

I nodded. "She does. But my relationship with Rutherford isn't important right now. We have to go deal with this flash mob."

Cassidy giggled. "I get to meet Michael! I mean, I had his spirit before. But now that he's in a host... I know he'll be pretty messed up now... but still!"

"Now isn't the time to be the fan girl," I said. "We just need to get Michael out of Trig, stop him from controlling the rest of the patients, and see that his spirit is properly put to rest."

Cassidy sighed. "I understand. Just know, the longer a spirit has dwelled in a host, the harder it will be to coax him out. I may need to speak with him. If he is willing to leave, it'll make the process less painful for him and for the ogre."

"Of course. Do what you have to do, Cassidy."

We walked together to the common room. The dance was still going on. It smelled like a gym. The gowns that the patients wore were soaked in sweat, pressed to their bodies as they danced, their clawed hands in the air, turning to their right and left.

Cassidy approached Trig and placed her hand on his back. When she did, everyone stopped dancing.

Trig did a spin. "Ow! Hee Hee!"

Then he grabbed his crotch.

"Michael?" Cassidy asked. "Do you remember me?"

"Yes... I remember the time..."

Cassidy smirked. "When we fell in love?"

Trig smiled. Or, I suppose I should say, Michael did. Considering the fact that, all the while, Trig wasn't suffering from a delusional disorder. "You're the one who saved me."

"You need to stop this, Michael. The people here, they need to rest."

Michael took two steps back. "I can't. We have to dance."

"Why do you have to dance, Michael?" Cassidy asked.

"It's who I am. It makes me feel alive, really alive again."

"Michael," I added, "If you keep this up, it will kill them. They need to rest, to get some water."

"I can't help myself. I don't want to hurt anyone, but..."

"Then you need to stop," Cassidy said.

Michael narrowed his eyes. "You think you're bad? Huh? Well, you ain't bad! You ain't nothin'!"

Michael took off down a corridor.

"I'm not sure he's going to go willingly, Cassidy."

Cassidy shook her head. "I suppose we'll have to do this the hard way."

"That hallway is a dead end. We'll catch him on the other side."

Cassidy and I ran after Michael, aka Trig. He had pressed his back against the wall at the end of the hall. "Beat it! Just, beat it!"

"We can't do that," Cassidy said. "You need to go, Michael. It's time to rest, to move on. Your music will live on forever. But your time has passed."

Cassidy took Michael's hand. I stepped toward him. "Back off, Doctor. The doggone girl is mine."

Cassidy giggled. "Thank you for everything, Michael. You'll always be loved. But you need to let go."

Michael shook his head. "Stop pressuring me... this makes me want to scream!"

Cassidy turned to me. "Cain, is that room open?"

"It's occupied. Though not at the moment. The patient staying there was dancing."

"Follow me, Michael," Cassidy said, opening the door. She led him to a small bathroom in the room.

"Michael, look at the man in the mirror."

"My nose is enormous... and my skin..."

"That face doesn't belong to you. This body isn't yours. You need to let him go."

Michael shed a tear. "I know. I've been avoiding mirrors for that reason. I can't do this anymore. You're right..."

"Then let go," Cassidy said, taking Michael's large ogre hand into both of hers.

Michael nodded. "I never can say goodbye, girl."

Cassidy released a pulse of red energies from her hand. Her power flowed into Trig's body. A translucent form that resembled the King of Pop in his prime stepped out of the body. He smiled, waved, and as a white light appeared behind him, he struck a pose, tipped the brim of his hat, and moonwalked into it.

Cassidy smiled. "That was pretty cool. Weird, but cool."

I laughed. "Just another day at the office."

CHAPTER FOURTEEN

THE NURSES WERE HELPING the patients rehydrate as Cassidy and I left the asylum. For now, at least, things were as normal as they could be at the Vilokan Asylum.

Annabelle was waiting for us just outside the gates.

Her eyes flickered green when she saw us, then returned to normal.

"Isabelle still with you?"

Annabelle nodded. "She is. That happens sometimes when she's upset. Who can blame her? We're all troubled by what's happening."

"Who was killed?" I asked.

"An elderly hougan. He saw Delphine take a host and tried to intervene."

"And Delphine killed him?"

Annabelle nodded. "But then she left. I saw it all on my surveillance cameras."

I narrowed my eyes. "I figured she'd want to attack Vilokan."

"I think she'll be back. Since she possesses one of our citizens, she'll be able to open the door to get back in."

I sighed. "Who did she possess?"

"A mambo. One of the more powerful vodouisants in all of Vilokan. I don't think her choice was random."

"Any idea where she went?"

Annabelle shook her head. "I'm uncertain. But when she left Vilokan, the cameras outside the doors saw a werewolf waiting for her."

"Did the wolf have a golden pelt?"

Annabelle nodded. "Was that..."

"My brother, yes. I'm pretty sure she's controlling him somehow. Able shot me with a gun. There's no way he'd know what a gun is if someone wasn't leading him."

"That makes sense," Cassidy said. "If your brother was raised from a corpse, a caplata could manipulate him the same way she might enslave and control any other zombie."

"Except, he's not a mindless zombie," Annabelle added.

"He is my brother. He looked like my brother. Even the way he spoke, there was an air of pride, of arrogance in the way he talked to me. It was my brother, even if Delphine has bound his will to hers."

"There weren't any other wolves in view of the camera. I can't say he has turned no one yet, but if he did, they weren't visible in the frame."

"Any reports of wolf attacks from the surface?" I asked.

"Nothing that I've heard. We might be lucky on that account."

"There's something else," I said. "I believe she also wields Julie's flambeau."

"The flambeau of the Witch of Endor?"

I nodded. "If she evokes it, when I'm near, she can force me to turn."

"But she can't control you, right?" Annabelle asked.

"I don't think so. When Julie used it to help me turn, though, she wasn't attempting to control me. It's still possible LaLaurie might manipulate me. We have to be careful."

Annabelle sighed. "She could also use it to turn and manipulate the rougarou."

"If she finds them. After last night's shift, they're free to return to their families."

Annabelle bit her lip. "Except they agreed to help renovate the new satellite of Vilokan Asylum. They're all at my family's old plantation right now."

"With Abel at her side, she'll be able to use him to track them. He's still a new wolf, and he's motivated by the seven-fold curse now more than anything else, but if she wants to use the flambeau to harness the rougarou, it's just a matter of time before she'll find them."

Annabelle nodded. "I'm afraid we might need some additional support. If she uses the flambeau to turn and enthrall the rougarou, and silver bullets aren't an option, it may take a small army of hougans and mambos to restrain them. Perhaps a few vampires could be of help. Cassidy, you may be able to convince them to join us."

"I realize that vampirism comes from Baron Samedi. When I was a student, I was a part of College Samedi, but that was a long time ago..."

"Because of your brother, Cassidy."

I shook my head. "Annabelle. You aren't thinking this through. She doesn't know. They expelled Cassidy from the Voodoo Academy and she doesn't have any memory of what Delphine LaLaurie did in her body after she took control of her mind. All that occurred before what happened to Nico."

Cassidy cocked her head. "What happened to my brother?"

"I– I don't know what to say," Annabelle's shoulders sank.

I put my hand on Annabelle's shoulder. "It's okay. I'll talk to her about it on the drive out. Perhaps we'll make a stop at Casa do Diabo and see if the vampires there will lend a hand. The flambeau won't impact them. Not to mention, they can move more quickly than Abel and the other wolves. Besides, if LaLaurie can manipulate me with the flambeau, you'll need all the help you can get."

"All fine points. Notably, Julie Brown spent the greater part of her existence, after she took a material form, living at Casa do Diabo with the vampires. If anyone knows how we might neutralize her power or counteract the flambeau, it's those vampires."

"Thankfully, most of them have been my patients at one time or another. And once they realize that Nico's sister is with us, they'll be doubly motivated to help. Provided, of course, that Delphine makes her move at night."

Annabelle nodded. "Yes, that is a problem. We can't count on that. I'll gather whoever I can throughout Vilokan, see if you can convince the vampires to join us after sunset, and I'll meet you at the plantation as soon as possible."

CHAPTER FIFTEEN

CASSIDY STARED BLANKLY OUT the passenger-side window of my truck. It was only a few blocks from St. Louis Cathedral in Jackson Square, where we emerged after leaving Vilokan, and it was a similar distance from Casa do Diabo, the "Devil's House." The old mansion had housed vampires for more than a century which, I suppose, bred more than a few rumors about what really went on behind the walls of the place. In New Orleans, though, strange isn't so strange. Do enough digging and you're bound to encounter something mysterious, something inexplicable to the common person. Leave it to the tourists, more often than not, to get involved in something they shouldn't. Most of the locals, well, they didn't know exactly what went on in places like Casa do Diabo, but they knew enough to stay away.

I parked in front of the old mansion, but Cassidy had said little since I filled her in on what had happened to Nico.

"So my baby brother ended up living thousands of years as a vampire? I'm sorry, I've been involved in some crazy stuff. But that's a little hard to swallow."

"And a few years back, he chose to die. He lived for thousands of years just to get back to the time he knew when he was born human, only to decide he'd lived long enough."

Cassidy shook her head. "If that's the case, I suppose he wouldn't be interested in coming back, would he?"

"I don't think he would. And more than that, Annabelle wouldn't approve."

"If the story you're telling me is true, Cain, Annabelle played a role in making him a vampire to begin with."

"It wasn't what she wanted. She tried, for quite some time, to bring him back. Before she could even figure it out, though, he was already back. He'd had his vampiric self staked when his human self was born. A person cannot exist twice at the same time. He was unstaked shortly after his grown-up human self went to Guinee. Annabelle had little chance to save him. All the time in the world, though, wouldn't have made a difference. We know vampires exist. We also know that your brother was the first of them. Any effort to change that, to remake the past, was doomed to fail. The existence of vampires proves it so. No matter who might have been responsible for what happened, sometimes fate dictates an unfolding of events beyond our control. In the end, Nico was no longer a monster. Even before he recovered his soul, he was more human than not."

"All those years, after Delphine possessed me, he did nothing to save me?"

I shook my head. "I wish I could tell you more. I didn't know Nico, personally. If anyone knows, it's Mercy Brown."

"You said Mercy *Brown?*"

"She and Julie Brown had the same father. She was also Nico's progeny. She inherited everything he owned during his vampiric life."

Cassidy sighed. "And she lives here?"

I nodded. "She does. I didn't know Nico, but I know Mercy well. In fact, she, too, was once possessed. That's what originally brought her to me at the asylum. I imagine you and she might have a lot in common."

"And she's probably the closest thing to family I have..."

"If she's here, I'll certainly introduce you. Be warned, though, she can be a little difficult to get to know. She's a little rough around the edges. At her core, though, she's the best of her kind. She has a good heart."

"A good-hearted vampire? I didn't even know such a thing existed."

I laughed. "Neither did she. But she's proven her own assumptions regarding the inevitable villainy of vampires inaccurate."

Cassidy opened the door and stepped out of my truck. "Alright, Cain. I'm ready."

I put my arm around Cassidy's shoulder and walked her to the door of Casa do Diabo.

"Getting Mercy's attention during the day might take some time. For obvious reasons."

I knocked on the door twice. Before my fist struck the door a third time, it swung open.

A young vampire, short with red hair that matched her eyes, greeted us, flashing her fangs. "Oh Goodie! Hey Mercy, did you order delivery?"

"What the hell, Mel!" Mercy's voice shouted from somewhere inside. "We don't open the door when the sun is up!"

"And I'm not a meal," Cassidy piped up.

"Could have fooled me?" the young vampire said, giggling. "You look tasty!"

With a blur, Mercy ran with enhanced speed, grabbed Mel, and tossed her across the foyer. The young vampire landed on her feet.

"Sorry," Mercy said. "Come in, Cain. And close the door behind you."

I stepped inside the door, Cassidy right behind me.

I closed the door. Two seconds later, Mercy had Cassidy pinned to the wall. "You brought *her* here?"

I cocked my head. "She isn't who you think."

"I know Cassidy. She tried to kill Nico. Twice!"

"I did not!" Cassidy said. "That wasn't me!"

"Mercy, the spirit of another possessed Cassidy all those years. The girl you knew wasn't Nico's sister."

Mercy huffed, released Cassidy, and took a step back. "For your sake, Cain, I'll trust that what you're saying is true."

"Who's the youngling?"

Mercy sighed. "That's Mel. She's a whole three days old. Excuse her eagerness to feed. Her bloodlust has yet to be tamed."

I looked past Mercy and saw Mel spinning around the living room, holding a grey tabby cat in her arms. "And you let her have a cat? I thought you hated cats."

"It calms her. Cats and penguins. And I wasn't about to bring a penguin here."

"Tough choice," I said, trying to suppress a laugh.

"Cats shit in a box. Penguins shit on everything. It wasn't much of a choice."

"Nice to meet you, Mercy!" Cassidy piped up. "We're family, I think."

"Sort of," Mercy huffed. "Pardon me for my rudeness. The last time I saw your face you had a stake in your hand."

"I'm sorry, I think," Cassidy said. "I really don't remember much of anything that Delphine did when she possessed me."

Mercy raised an eyebrow. "Delphine?"

"Delphine LaLaurie," I said.

Mercy shook her head. "Well, that explains a lot."

"Did you know Delphine?" Cassidy asked.

Mercy shook her head. "She died before I was turned. Nico knew her. He helped to see her banished from New Orleans."

"Holy crap," Cassidy said. "That makes sense!"

"How so?" I asked.

"Why she attacked Nico. Her spirit was looking for vengeance."

I nodded. "And she's still looking for revenge. She's taken a new host. And more than that, she's captured Julie's spirit along with her flambeau."

Mercy stared at me blankly. "You mean to tell me you treated Cassidy at the asylum, you exorcised Delphine LaLaurie, and you let her out?"

I sighed. "It wasn't intentional."

"Well, Cain. You really screwed the pooch on that one. Which, I guess, since you're a wolf probably isn't as unnatural as it sounds."

Cassidy giggled. "I like her. She's funny."

Mercy narrowed her eyes, shooting daggers in Cassidy's direction. "So, why are you here? You think Delphine came looking for Nico again? He's been gone for years, now."

I shook my head. "It gets worse. With Julie's spirit, and the flambeau, LaLaurie has also resurrected my brother."

"Are you serious? Cain, you're really losing your edge."

"Abel tried to kill me. I think it was under LaLaurie's influence. Still, he inherited my curse, so a part of him must've wanted to do it himself."

"And now he's terrorizing the city, making more werewolves?"

I shook my head. "I don't know. We know he's working with LaLaurie. Whatever she has planned, it's not good."

"Mercy! I'm hungry! Can you get me a tasty virgin or something?"

"Later, Mel. I'm busy."

"I need to feed!"

"You fed just hours ago," Mercy said. "Resist the cravings. It's a part of taming your bloodlust."

"Blah, blah, blah," Mel piped up. "I'm a vampire, now. I have new legs that work! My body needs sustenance!"

"New legs?" I asked.

Mercy nodded. "She was in a wheelchair. Fibromyalgia. Walking was too painful for her. So, I made her an offer. A cure. You'd think she'd be grateful!"

"I am!" Mel said. "I totally made the right choice. But now I'm starving!"

Mercy shook her head. "I'd love to help, Cain. But I can't do anything until nightfall. And even then, I obviously have my hands full. I need to supervise her feeds. There's a reason I never used to sire new vampires. But, you know, since I'm now in charge of the new Vampire Council, I have to set a good example. That means playing vampire mommy."

"She could feed from me," Cassidy said. "Provided she doesn't take too much. If it takes the edge off."

"Did you hear that?" Mel asked. "She offered! Come on, Mercy!"

Mercy sighed. "It's more than that. Even if I allowed her to have a taste, it might satiate her a couple hours, if that. If I left her here, well, I'm not sure I could trust her to not terrorize the French Quarter."

"Then bring her along," I suggested.

Mercy shook her head. "We're dealing with werewolves, Cain. I can handle myself with werewolves on the prowl, but if one bit her, you know what a werewolf's bite does to vampires."

"Chronic pain that lasts. I can see why you wouldn't want to subject her to that, especially given the condition she suffered from before."

Mercy nodded. "I won't do that to her. It's too risky, Cain. Besides, I'm still not entirely sure what you think I might do to help."

"You're fast. Faster than I am, even when I'm shifted. And if LaLaurie uses the flambeau, I need someone who is capable and I can trust to stop my brother. Annabelle is bringing some mambos and hougans to help, but given the situation, if Abel bit any of them..."

Mercy chuckled. "Yeah, that would suck. And no offense to Annabelle, but I don't think she has the gonads to take down a pack of werewolves."

"I'm pretty sure she doesn't have gonads!" Cassidy said, giggling.

Mercy smirked. "Look, Cain. I'd love to help. But Mel is a particularly challenging youngling."

I pressed my lips together. "Take her to the asylum. She wouldn't be the first youngling I've helped adjust to vampirism."

"You'd do that for me?" Mercy asked.

I nodded. "If you can help me stop my brother and LaLaurie, I'll owe you."

Mercy smiled widely. "We have an entire crop of younglings that could benefit from your services."

"We? And a crop?"

Mercy nodded. "The entire council has sired younglings. Four of them, in fact. I'll tell you what, Cain. Admit them all, the council will be free to resume business as usual until you've helped them gain control over their cravings, and I will come help you tonight. Once the sun has set and we can deliver the younglings to the asylum."

I nodded. "I'll tell Rutherford they're on the way. Annabelle will have to sign off on it, of course, since it will put us at maximum capacity. Either way, we're starting a satellite campus for the asylum. We'll have enough room soon enough. And you'd be doing us a service. Annabelle understands that. If you help us, she will owe you as much as I will."

Mercy grinned. "Alright. It's a deal."

"You're committing me to the loony bin?" Mel asked.

"We have plenty of donated blood," I said. "All you can drink!"

"Sweet! Sign me up!"

Mercy snickered, rolling her eyes as she turned her face away from Mel. "Bagged blood is delicious."

I smiled. Mercy's sarcasm was lost on the youngling. Mercy hated bagged blood. The soul that coheres in blood, which is what vampires really crave, fades after it's donated. I wasn't about to point that out, though. We'd deal with Mel's disappointment later. I was used to managing complaints about the meals served at the asylum.

"After you drop off the younglings, meet me at the Mulledy Plantation."

"Annabelle's place? Why?"

"That's where our new satellite campus is located. And I have a feeling that's where LaLaurie and Abel are headed."

"Why would they go there?" Mercy asked.

"Because my pack is there, the rougarou of Manchac Swamp. I suspect LaLaurie intends to use the flambeau to claim them. And even if she doesn't, I need to go there to warn them."

Mercy shrugged. "It's about three hours until sunset. We'll meet you there in four."

Chapter Sixteen

I WAS ANXIOUS THE entire drive from Casa do Diabo to the Mulledy plantation, soon-to-be the Vilokan Asylum extension. It assuaged my nerves when, upon arrival, I spotted Donald installing a new wrought-iron gate at the entrance to the property. It was a near-exact duplicate of the archway that guarded the entrance of the original asylum. The words "Vilokan Asylum" were welded into a decorated arch over the gate in iron letters.

Donald smiled at me as he pulled open his half-installed gate to let us inside. I rolled down my window.

"Everything alright, Doc?" Donald asked.

I shook my head. "Better than I feared it might be. Could you gather the pack? You've done a lot of work. I'm not even going to guess how you pulled all this off so quickly."

Donald laughed. "Werewolf strength. And Annabelle's money. It's a pretty potent combination."

I chuckled. "I suppose it is. I'll meet everyone on the steps of the mansion."

Donald nodded. "We'll be right there."

I pulled into the circular drive that led to the front doors of what used to be Annabelle's childhood home. Ever since she and her sister moved to Vilokan, though, the place was vacant. It was a large mansion, with several white stone pillars lining the front of the antebellum plantation home. I'd only been to the home a few times. Annabelle sometimes held holiday parties and random social events for the voodoo community there. It was an irony, of a sort, that an old plantation—complete with a red-brick building that used to serve as slave quarters about fifty meters to the rear of the mansion—was now an above-ground extension of Vilokan, a place where slaves used to find refuge from their oppressive owners. I suppose, given my journey, I had a special place in my heart for a redemption story. People, places, or even things once used for evil redeemed for a good and noble purpose.

Ryan was on his hands and knees just inside the front door, a bucket beside him and a large sponge in his hands, which he used to scrub the grime from the floors.

"You're still here?" I asked. "I figured you'd be off to Missouri by now for the holidays."

Ryan shook his head as he tossed his sponge in the bucket. "I've decided to stay here with the pack. My family isn't thrilled that I won't be home for Christmas, but they were excited when I told them I received a recommendation and scholarship to the psych program at LSU. They understood I needed the time to get settled here before the new semester."

I cocked my head. "A scholarship?"

"You all said that you'd cover my tuition!"

I laughed. "We said we'd pool our funds. I suppose a little white lie won't hurt. Your parents probably wouldn't get it if you told them the truth."

"That I joined a pack of werewolves who are going to help me through school? That I'm being counseled by *the* Cain from the Bible? I think if I told them the truth, they'd certainly agree that psych was in my future... just not as a career choice."

As Ryan talked, I noticed him making eyes at Cassidy. She was a few years older than him, technically, but emotionally, she was probably younger. Still, while I'm typically oblivious to such things, he had clearly noticed her.

"My apologies," I said. "Ryan, this is Cassidy. Cassidy, Ryan."

Ryan cleared his throat and extended his hand. "Nice to meet you, Cassidy."

Cassidy giggled. "Likewise! So, you're a werewolf?"

Ryan chuckled. "I guess I am. Still getting used to that. Look at us, here. Beauty and the Beast."

Cassidy smirked. "You calling me a beast?"

Ryan's eyes widened. "No. Not what I meant... the other way around."

"I wasn't sure. You are awfully pretty."

Ryan cocked his head. "Thanks. I think."

"I like pretty boys."

"Alright, well, you two can flirt as much as you'd like another time. We have important issues we need to talk about."

"We were flirting?" Cassidy asked, winking at Ryan. "I had no idea."

Ryan laughed nervously. "Yeah. Funny. Let me go dump this bucket and I'll be right out."

"I'll help!" Cassidy piped up.

I chuckled. "You're going to help him dump a bucket of water?"

Cassidy stared daggers at me. Clearly, helping him wasn't the point. Obviously, particularly now that Ryan was adjusting to his newfound strength, a bucket of water wouldn't be a problem to handle. But, you know, I've learned well enough that when young people take an interest in one another, it's best to get out of the way. Young romance is like a hurricane. There's no stopping it until it has run its course. Putting up walls, trying to impede it, won't do a thing to slow it down.

Of course, this wasn't a hurricane yet. Maybe a whirlwind, perhaps a tropical storm. So long as they didn't lose focus, given what we were about to face, it was harmless. Given that Ryan was away from home, and had nothing but the pack, and Cassidy had no friends and no family outside of Mercy Brown, connecting with another person, be it as a friend or something more, was healthy for both of them.

I stepped out onto the porch. Donald and the rest of the pack, apart from Ryan, were already waiting. It didn't take long before Ryan and Cassidy appeared behind me.

"First, I wanted to say I'm proud of all of you. Working together like this when you're all free to go back to your everyday lives. It shows real growth as a pack."

"This is our family," Donald said. "We have human families, too. But we've been together a lot longer. We need a place to gather, a place where it's safe, and less crowded."

"Besides," Christoper added. "The asylum in Vilokan smells like pee all the time."

Evie backhanded Christopher on the shoulder. "Rude, Chris!"

"Well, it does!"

I smiled. "You get used to it. But I agree, it comes with the territory. And we need the space. With all this land, we have plenty of room. We could even shift and run free here if we'd prefer to stay out of the swamps."

"A change in venue would be nice," Donald said. "We lived in that swamp a long time. It feels like home, sort of. But it was also something like a prison. That infernal object was like razor-wire, preventing us from leaving. I think it's time we move on."

"I couldn't agree more," I said. "Though the reason I wanted to speak to you, ironically, has to do with the flambeau."

"It's gone, right?" Yvette asked, shifting her weight from one foot to the other.

"Of course it's gone," Andrew piped up. "We have nothing to fear, right?"

I sighed. "Not exactly. You all realize that my brother has returned. He's likely on the prowl even as we speak, looking to establish a pack of his own."

Donald shook his head. "A territorial war might be brewing."

I nodded. "And more than that, the spirit who raised Abel now possesses a mambo. Who it is, exactly, I'm not sure. But she once possessed Cassidy, here. She is a descendent of Julie Brown. We believe the spirit used Cassidy's power as a necromancer and her connection to Julie to recover the flambeau."

My announcement hung in the air for a few seconds.

"We'll stop her," Donald said. "Somehow, we have to. I won't allow the pack to be enslaved, again."

"Is that smart?" Andrew asked. "I mean, if she has the flambeau, we aren't really the ones who should fight her. If she uses it on us, we'll be in her thrall."

"I think it's best if we split up," I said. "At least for now. Andrew is right. I understand your inclination to fight, Donald. But this isn't a battle you can win."

"But we can stop the new pack. If we can use the flambeau, if you can get it away from the witch who has it, we can shift and fight the new wolves while we still have the numeric advantage."

Evie raised her eyebrows. "How could we possibly steal the flambeau from the witch?"

"She has the spirit of Julie Brown," Cassidy said. "But I'm her family. If I can engage her, if I can reach Julie, I might be able to convince her to give the flambeau to me."

"So, you'd be able to control us, then?" Ryan asked.

"It wouldn't work that way," I said. "Whoever holds the flambeau *could* use it against the pack. But Julie used it in the past to help me shift when it was convenient. She never forced me to do anything contrary to my will."

"I would use it the same way," Cassidy said. "Though, I have to admit, holding that thing myself is a bit intimidating."

"It's an infernal relic," I said. "If it did not intimidate you, you wouldn't be suited to wield it."

"It's a weapon," Donald said. "A healthy fear, a respect of what it's capable of, is necessary if you're going to wield it responsibly."

I shook my head. "It can be a weapon, but it need not be. The flambeau was not originally forged to be used in such a way. The Witch of Endor made it to evoke the spirits of the dead."

"A hunting rifle is meant for exactly that," Andrew said. "In the hands of the wrong person, though, it is a weapon."

"Agreed," I said. "Which is why we have to trust Cassidy to do this. I'll protect her. The vampires are coming to aid me, in case the flambeau enthralls me. But the rest of you must leave."

Donald shook his head. "We'll keep our distance. We can hide in the swamp. But we aren't running away, Cain. No offense, but this is personal to us."

I nodded. "I can respect that. But please, be responsible. The woman who possesses the flambeau is not of a right mind. She was a serial killer when she was alive and now that she's been dead, inhabiting other bodies for years, she's even more warped than before. I must emphasize that her actions may be unpredictable. We need to exercise an abundance of caution. There's no telling what Delphine LaLaurie might do."

Christopher sighed. "Delphine LaLaurie? You can't be serious."

I nodded. "I'm not joking, Christopher. I take it you know of her?"

"Everyone knows who she is," Donald said. "At least, back before we became werewolves, her history wasn't so far in the past that it was yet forgotten."

Cassidy sighed. "I'm sorry. This is my fault. I didn't know who she was when I raised her. I didn't even mean to resurrect her spirit at all."

"Wait," Christopher said. "You are responsible for this?"

Cassidy's shoulders fell. "I am."

I raised my hand. "The past should remain in the past. Cassidy did not evoke LaLaurie intentionally. And we need Cassidy to stop her, now."

"Cain is right," Ryan said. "Assigning blame right now won't help anyone."

"I, too, agree with the young wolf," Donald said. "We follow Cain's lead. If we judged people based on their mistakes, we'd never have found ourselves after we became human again. If we didn't allow Cain to help us..."

"Then his brother wouldn't be here forming another pack to fight against us," Christopher said.

I nodded. "Again, it's a fair point, Christopher. I'd be wrong if I didn't accept some of the blame in this situation."

"It doesn't matter!" Yvette shouted. The rest of the wolves widened their eyes. They weren't used to her speaking up like this. I wasn't either. "If we judged people based on their mistakes, we'd all be damned for it. We're werewolves, for Christ's sake. We try not to hurt people, yes, but we all did awful things through the years. How many people died because of us while we were still wolves in the swamp?"

Donald smiled. "You're right. All of us have blood on our paws."

Cassidy giggled a little.

Donald chuckled. "Or, on our hands. Whatever. You know what I meant."

I nodded. "We've all made mistakes. Some of them, quite serious. But we have a choice. We can live in our past, allow our sins to define us, or we can strive to be better. We can rise, we can grow. Redemption is always within reach. What matters is not what any of us did in the past. It's what we do next that counts. The question is this: can we be better?"

"Of course we can!" Donald piped up.

Christopher nodded. "We must be."

A piercing howl echoed from somewhere behind the house. There was no mistaking it. It was a werewolf. And because the full moon had passed, and the sun was still setting on the horizon, we all knew exactly who it was.

"Your brother?" Donald asked.

I nodded. "He's here."

"We can't fight him like this," Andrew said. "We're strong. But we aren't any match for him in human form."

I nodded. "Abel is my responsibility. Remember what I said. Keep your distance. If he's here, LaLaurie won't be far behind."

CHAPTER SEVENTEEN

THE PACK TOOK OFF into the forests bordering the road that led up to the Mulledy plantation. They could navigate the trails through the woods behind the mansion and watch from afar.

Cassidy followed me around the side toward the back of the house. I stopped and turned. Cassidy was moving with such purpose she almost walked right into me.

"You should keep your distance. We don't know if LaLaurie is here. We know my brother is. Since he's in wolf form, I can't say if he's turned anyone but I know he hasn't filled out his seven-member pack."

"Wouldn't that be eight members?" Cassidy asked.

"It's a seven-fold curse. That's what it means."

"Yeah, but Abel counts too, right?"

I sighed. "Fine. He hasn't filled out his eight-member pack. The point is, he'll still be looking to turn more people. And if he got you, Cassidy, we'd lose our chance to exorcise LaLaurie from her host."

Cassidy sighed. "I get it. Be careful. Keep my distance."

I nodded. "Stay inside and watch from a window. He'll be able to move faster than either of us since I'm not shifted. If he comes after you, there's nothing I'll be able to do to stop him."

Cassidy gulped. "Yeah, okay. I guess that makes sense."

"But watch for us. If LaLaurie shows up, be ready. We might only have one chance to exorcise her from her host."

Cassidy nodded. "I'll find a window somewhere inside facing the back of the house."

Abel howled again. He was closer now. It sounded like he was near the back of the house.

"I have to go."

"You don't have to, Cain. He will kill you!"

I shook my head. "I killed him once. I have to face him again. He'll find me either way. This way, it's out in the open. And hopefully, the vampires will be here soon. All I have to do is distract him long enough."

Cassidy nodded and took off back around the front of the house. I took a deep breath and ran around back.

Abel stood there. He was roughly twice my size–which was comparable to the size I was when shifted. His golden coat caught the red hue of the setting sun. He saw me the moment I appeared.

Abel didn't charge me. He looked at me and took two cautious steps forward. He howled again. Two more wolves emerged from the treeline behind the plantation. Then four more appeared behind them. He's already turned six. Why not seven? There was only one reason. He was waiting until he could kill me while he still had the advantage.

I didn't see anyone else, no one who Delphine LaLaurie might have been possessing. That didn't mean she wasn't manipulating him, controlling him somehow from a distance. Without the flambeau, I had a chance to exert dominance over the pack.

I might have been in human form, but I was still the first-ever werewolf. They were children of my curse. I couldn't enthrall my pack when they weren't shifted. But these wolves were still susceptible.

The key was no hesitation. He was moving toward me carefully. He sensed my power, my control, already.

I walked toward my brother, holding my head high. I stared him straight in the eyes.

"Back down!" I shouted.

Abel snarled back at me as the other wolves formed a semi-circle behind him.

I took two more steps toward my brother. He stepped back, still growling.

So far, so good. If I could enthrall him, the rest of his pack would fall in line.

"We don't have to be enemies," I said. "I know I wronged you, brother. And for what I did, I've suffered for centuries. But now, we can run together. We can be brothers, we can be family again!"

Abel grunted and stomped his large clawed foot.

I was about to take another step toward him, to demand he bow and accept my dominance, when a golden light appeared between us.

I shielded my eyes as Annabelle stepped out of it, her soul-blade in her hand. Her eyes flickered green, then returned to their usual shade of brown.

She nodded at me, turned, and looked at Abel.

"Stop!" I said. "I've got this under control."

Anabelle raised her hand toward Abel. Then, he and the whole pack lowered their heads and bowed toward her.

I cocked my head. "How in the world did you just do that?"

Annabelle turned at me and grinned. Then, she released her soul blade and in its stead, the witch of Endor's flambeau formed in her hand.

"No!" I screamed, as the heat from the flambeau's infernal flames struck my body. My skin hardened. My bones popped.

"You!" I screamed.

LaLaurie laughed. "That's right, Cain. Annabelle is here, somewhere. But she's not in control right now."

Again, Annabelle's eyes flickered green for a moment. Then the flames shot up into the skies. My fur burst through my skin as my face lengthened.

I heard screams of pain in the distance. It was my pack, the rougarou. They were shifting, too.

"Combined with Annabelle's powers, this flambeau's power is magnified!"

"You can't do this!" I screamed, even as my mouth reshaped itself.

Delphine LaLaurie, in Annabelle's body, stepped toward me. "Oh, Cain, I certainly can."

"I can resist your control," I grunted, even as my words turned to growls.

"I don't intend to control you, Cain. And don't worry, Abel will not kill you. Not until I'm done with you. I have other ideas."

I tried to scream, but I'd fully shifted. I roared at her instead.

"Perhaps I'll command your pack to kill you. Imagine that. A whole pack, each inheriting the seven-fold curse. I'm not great with math. But let's see. There are six more rougarou in your pack. And if Abel's six also try to kill you. What's twelve times seven? No matter. That's a lot of wolves, each cursed to turn seven more themselves. I'll have a whole army, and with this host, I can lead them all into Vilokan. Once we're done there, the rest of New Orleans."

I snarled. I didn't know how this would pan out. Since Delphine LaLaurie planned to compel the wolves to kill me, my pack probably wouldn't be cursed. But Abel's pack might follow through willingly. Given the best-case scenario, they'd all be cursed and since it was Annabelle who LaLaurie possessed, she would be too. Worst-case scenario, the lot of them would be cursed. Once it was done, there'd be nothing to stop them from killing me. Or worse, enslave me so they could force others to do the same and grow their nightmare of a pack exponentially.

An ear-piercing scream startled my attention back toward the mansion. It was Cassidy.

I grunted at Annabelle before I took off running back to the mansion. If someone had attacked Cassidy, I had to save her. She was the last one who could exorcise LaLaurie from the Voodoo Queen.

I blasted through the door of the house, breaking the doorframe as I charged through it. I bounded up the stairs.

Ryan, fully shifted into wolf form, stood over Cassidy.

I snarled at him.

Ryan whimpered and backed down. LaLaurie had evoked the flambeau, but he still respected my authority. At least he did for now.

I was too late.

Blood soaked through Cassidy's pants. Ryan already bit her. Cassidy screamed as her body expanded. The flambeau was too close. She was changing. And there was nothing I could do to stop it.

CHAPTER EIGHTEEN

I TURNED AND RAN out of the house. There was nothing more I could do for Cassidy. And since it was only a matter of time before LaLaurie enthralled her, too, I only had one option left.

I hated it. If I bit Annabelle, she'd change. But it might force LaLaurie to lose focus, to release the flambeau long enough that Cassidy could exorcise her. Would Cassidy even be in the right mind, as a wolf, to know what needed to be done? She'd shift back after LaLaurie released the flambeau, but could she get to us fast enough to do it before LaLaurie summoned the flambeau again? It wasn't a great plan, but it was all I had.

The way I saw it, if LaLaurie had her way, Annabelle would end up becoming a wolf under the seven-fold curse. This wasn't ideal, and Annabelle would probably be pissed about it later, but I had no other choice.

I charged after LaLaurie. She raised her flambeau again and blasted me with infernal flames. They didn't consume me. I didn't burn at all. But the power she wielded slowed me down. She was trying to take control, to dominate me with her power. I lowered myself down on all fours and dug my paws into the ground, pressing forward with all my strength.

Anger. Resentment. Envy. It was the same mix of emotions I'd experienced thousands of years ago when I killed Able. No, the infernal power didn't burn my body. It did something worse. It brought the worst part of me to the surface.

The flambeau might not enthrall me like it did the rougarou, but this was just as dangerous.

It took every bit of focus I could muster to work through those thoughts. These weren't foreign emotions. I knew my darker side well. I'd spent thousands of years fighting it, burying my resentments. But then, I'd worked through them. Thank you, Dr. Freud. I was at peace with who I was. Or, was I? Mostly, but there was always a lingering part of my psyche that kept my resentments, my anger, my pain, and my guilt alive. Yes, my darkness was still a part of me, but it didn't have to control me.

I howled, releasing all my pain, all my rage, at once. Then, I focused on Annabelle's body, now possessed by Delphine LaLaurie. One bite, that's all I needed. I could only pray that Cassidy would know what to do. She wouldn't have much time. Once LaLaurie started to shift, and she released the flambeau, she'd shift back into her human form quickly. Cassidy would have seconds, if that, to act.

I dove toward her, the flames of the flambeau still blasting me in the face. Then, something like a streak, a blur, blasted out of the woods and stopped right behind Annabelle.

It was Mercy.

I roared and growled. I couldn't tell her to stop while shifted. There was nothing I could do. Before I could get to her, to bite Annabelle myself, Mercy's fangs were sunk deep into the Voodoo Queen's neck.

Mercy took off back through the woods, Abel and the wolves from his pack following her close behind.

Cassidy stumbled out of the house and tried to get to Annabelle.

Annabelle's eyes glowed green and bright as Isabelle, the spirit within her, healed her wounds with the magic she drew from the Tree of Life, itself.

I stopped Cassidy before she could reach the Voodoo Queen. "She's not LaLaurie anymore. The spirit is now within Mercy."

Ryan came up behind Cassidy, his head hung low. He knew what he'd done. Cassidy turned and hugged him.

"You don't hate me?"

Cassidy shook her hea d. "I guess I'll be one of you now. Worse things could happen, you know."

"I came back to protect her," Ryan said, clasping his hands together as if begging me for empathy. "I didn't think she should be alone. I can't believe I was so dumb."

"Nevermind that," I said. "What is done, is done. We'll talk about all that transpired later."

"I don't understand," Cassidy said. "How did the vampire's bite exorcise LaLaurie?"

Annabelle struggled to her feet. "Vampires don't consume blood because they have a taste for iron. It's the soul in the blood, they desire. When she bit me, LaLaurie saw her chance. She left me and went into Mercy."

I sighed. "This was what she wanted the whole time. Delphine LaLaurie spent years in Cassidy learning the ins and outs of the Voodoo world. She learned about Mercy and the rest of the vampires. She discovered the only way that, as a spirit, she could break into a vampire's mind was if the vampire sucked her spirit into her. She'd already possessed you when she suggested we get the vampires involved, didn't she?"

Annabelle nodded. "She had."

"I don't understand," Cassidy said. "You remember what happened? When she possessed me, I didn't have any memories of the incident."

"I had the advantage of Isabelle within me already. Together, we were fighting Delphine's control. Unfortunately, it wasn't enough. With the power of the flambeau, it was like hell itself was fighting against us, preventing us from taking my body back."

"What about her plan?" I asked. "It sounded like a pretty nasty one."

Annabelle shook her head. "Delphine is smart. She knew if she actually carried it out she'd be the one cursed."

I bit my lip. "I figured you'd be cursed, since you were the host she inhabited at the time."

Annabelle nodded. "That was a possibility. Still, Delphine has other ideas. She still intends to attack you with Abel and his pack. That much is true. She knew the rougarou wouldn't be cursed because they weren't willing to kill you of their own accord. But if she could masquerade as Mercy, leading the Vampire Council, and rally the bloodsuckers to do her bidding instead, along with Abel and his pack, she'd be able to do everything she said she intended to do before."

I sighed. "She still plans to attack Vilokan and the rest of New Orleans. Mercy has compulsion abilities. Not all vampires do. It works on other vampires. If LaLaurie knows this, and uses the ability, she could rally a lot of vampires against Vilokan and New Orleans. On the other hand, a compulsion has a scope limited to what is spoken. Unlike a wolf, bound to the will of the alpha, the most Mercy can do is issue one command at a time. Vampires can't be enthralled to her in the same way that a wolf might be to its alpha, or the wolves might be when under the influence of the flambeau."

"Of course they aren't," Annabelle said. "But there is a large contingency of vampires here in New Orleans who wouldn't think twice about slaughtering the city. They'd enjoy it. They wouldn't need Mercy's compulsion. All they'd require is her permission."

"But vampires have more control over their spawn," I said. "Mercy just took a bunch of brand new vampires to the asylum."

Annabelle nodded. "Even if she doesn't use them, or can't convince all the vampires to fight with her, all she has to do is start biting people herself. She can turn as many as she'd like, and form an army of younglings, all with untamed bloodlust."

"How can we help?" Donald asked as he and the rest of the pack assembled behind me.

I sighed. "I'm not sure. If LaLaurie still has the flambeau."

"About that," Annabelle said, snickering. "When LaLaurie left, Isabelle and I held on to something that you might find useful."

"You didn't!" I said, laughing.

"We did! I'd show it to you but, you know, it might cut our conversation short if I did."

"How in the world did you take the flambeau from her?"

"The only way that LaLaurie could wield it herself was through a partial bond to Julie Brown. It was enough that LaLaurie could access the flambeau, but not enough that Julie could get a foothold in the host LaLaurie possessed, herself. Let's just say that with Isabelle's power, the power of life itself, we could revive Julie fully. And what do you know? She was smart enough to realize what was happening and didn't leave with LaLaurie."

Donald grunted. "Once LaLaurie realizes she's lost the flambeau, she'll panic. She'll probably start attacking people and turning them into vampires."

"Can you use the flambeau to turn us back?" I asked. "We can track her and stop her before she hurts anyone."

Annabelle cocked her head. "Julie says no."

"What do you mean she says no?"

"She said it's too risky. You saw how powerful the flambeau was when she used it, enhanced by my power before. Julie said it's too volatile to use that way. If the hellfire were to blast out of the flambeau like that in the city, there's no telling what might happen."

"I can wage a guess," Cassidy said. "The Witch of Endor originally made the flambeau to evoke the spirits of the dead, correct?"

"That's right. That it forces us to shift is more like a side effect of the fact that it's a relic that's enchanted with infernal magic than a power particular to the flambeau itself."

"I'm guessing that the flambeau might awaken a lot of spirits if we allowed it to go off in the city."

"Exactly," Annabelle said. "But Julie said it might also consume and damn the souls of the living. The only way we can use it is if we can somehow revive Julie to wield it herself."

"That's simple enough," Cassidy said. "We just need a corpse. This is going to sound weird. But do you have any bodies in your backyard, Annabelle?"

"There's an old family graveyard on the property."

I shook my head. "Remember what happened the last time you tried to cast someone's spirit into a body, Cassidy."

"I know. It has to be someone at rest, someone we know whose soul has moved on. Otherwise, well, we may create a second version of Delphine LaLaurie."

Annabelle winced. "I hate to suggest this. I don't like it, but it's probably the best option."

"What are you thinking?" I asked.

"I never knew most of the people buried there. But my grandmother died peacefully when I was just a child. She was buried here. I can't imagine her ghost lingered. She told us, as she died, that she was ready to move on, to go be with Papa."

"This is your grandmother's body we're talking about, Annabelle. Are you sure you're okay with that?"

Annabelle nodded. "Like I said, a part of me doesn't like it. But if she moved on, it's just a body, right? It's not really my grandma. Not anymore."

I rested my hand on Cassidy's shoulder. "Are you sure you can do this? You were just bitten. Your mind isn't focused."

Cassidy shook her head. "My brother became the world's first vampire. So what if I'm going to be a werewolf now? This pack is pretty cool. And I need a family. I don't get the impression that Mercy will want to get together for Christmas meals or celebrate my birthdays. Don't get me wrong, Dr. Cain, I'm anxious as hell. The way it felt when I shifted, it was strange. But I've seen how this pack respects you, how much you've helped them. I'm trusting you can do the same for me. I have to believe I can get through this. Now, if LaLaurie is going to use vampires to kill hundreds or thousands of people I can't let that happen. That's a part of my brother's legacy. I will do what I have to do."

Chapter Nineteen

I couldn't blame Annabelle for not wanting to watch as the pack worked to dig up her grandmother's body. Unlike the people buried in New Orleans, who were entombed in mausoleums, where the Mulledy Plantation was located, common graves were feasible. Still, we weren't that far from the city. The elevation was still low. The graves were apparently shallower than those you might find elsewhere. It didn't take Donald and the others long at all to retrieve the casket from the ground.

Annabelle turned her head away as Cassidy, holding her hand, led her to the open coffin. I couldn't blame the Voodoo Queen for not wanting to see the decomposing corpse of her dead grandmother. That's not the sort of thing anyone should have to see.

Cassidy was unfazed by it. She placed both hands on Annabelle's chest, channeling a red power into her, before a translucent form, one that resembled Julie Brown as I remembered her, stepped out of the queen. Julie glanced at Cassidy. They'd never met before, but they were family. Julie and Cassidy exchanged resolute nods as Julie climbed into the coffin.

A red mist hovered over the casket, creating a crimson fog that spread over the ground. Annabelle stepped away and next to me before turning to look.

Cassidy held her hands out, guiding Julie's spirit into her new host.

Then, out of the mist, Julie's figure emerged. She appeared just as I remembered her. She was a light-skinned Black woman with an atypical but breathtaking beauty and grace about her. Her features were not delicate like the supermodels you might see featured in modern magazines, but bold and pronounced. She had an undeniable allure about her. It was as much the way she carried herself as it was her natural appearance that always caught my eye.

"Welcome back to the land of the living," I said.

"Hello Cain," Julie said, her voice airy and her cadence disjointed. She turned to Annabelle. "Thank you, to you and Isabelle alike, for pulling my spirit out of that... creature..."

Annabelle nodded. "It was our pleasure."

"You were aware of all that was happening?" I asked.

Julie nodded. "I saw it all. I could do nothing."

Cassidy stepped up toward us, looking at Julie with wide eyes. "Julie, I think I'm your great-great granddaughter."

Julie cracked a grin. "It is a privilege to know you, child."

"Unfortunately, we don't have time to get better acquainted. LaLaurie will not waste any time. And my brother and his pack are with her. If we don't stop them fast, many people could die."

Julie nodded. "Lead the way."

I smiled. "If we're going to take down Abel's pack, we need to shift. Can you help us out with that?"

Julie grinned, extended her hand, and her flambeau materialized in her grip.

I shifted into wolf form. The rest of the pack followed suit, Cassidy included. When the transformation was complete, Julie climbed onto my back. Donald nuzzled Annabelle, and she mounted him in the same way.

Donald ran beside me. The rest of the pack assembled in a staggered formation and followed us as we raced toward the city.

I sniffed the air. Abel's pack had its own scent, a pungent odor distinct from that emanated by the rougarou.

The waning moon illuminated our path. I resisted the urge to howl. We had a mission and we couldn't afford the delay.

We followed Abel's scent to Jackson Square. Then the odor dissipated. There was only one reason I could think of why that might happen.

Abel had entered Vilokan. His pack was with him. And if I were a betting man, I'd wager Delphine LaLaurie was, too. After all, Mercy was the only one among them who could access the voodoo underworld.

The steep stairwell leading into Vilokan was tight in wolf form. Julie hopped off my back. Annabelle left Donald's. I entered the stairwell first. The others followed behind me in single file.

Abel and his pack were waiting for us at the bottom of the stairs. He charged me. Our bodies tumbled through Vilokan's streets, crashing into the side wall of one of Vilokan's crumbling buildings, sending bricks flying.

The other wolves attacked the rest as they came through the doorway. They'd planned this. They were waiting, knowing we'd only be able to enter the underworld one at a time.

Abel landed on top of me and batted me in the face with his paw. I kicked him off of me. He was strong. Not as strong as me. I bounded on top of him and snarled.

I could have bitten him. If I wanted to eat his heart, or rip out his esophagus with my powerful jaws, there was nothing stopping me.

But that wasn't who I was anymore. I wasn't a killer. I couldn't do that to Abel. Not again.

I took a step back. I glanced off in the distance as Abel struggled to his feet.

The wolves from Abel's pack were too strong. We'd shifted back and forth too many times in succession. We weren't at full strength.

We couldn't make it much longer. If they killed us, though, the rest of Vilokan would be next.

I looked back at Abel, whimpering, as he tried to get back to his feet. I couldn't fight him. Not anymore. This wasn't the way. It wouldn't work.

I looked again into the distance. I saw LaLaurie, still in Mercy's body, dragging a person's bloodied body out of a building. If a vampire drains someone, they nearly always die. Unless they're healed. Unless, somehow, once their body is devoid of blood, some kind of spell or a once-in-a-million sort of medical miracle occurs and they survive. Then they're turned. Mercy knew enough magic she could do it. LaLaurie, so far as I knew, had never been a witch.

LaLaurie let the man she'd dragged out of the building die. She didn't heal him. But she had Cassidy's power. She'd been bound to her for more than a decade. She'd absorbed that ability, it seemed, since a red magic coursing from her fingers flowed into the corpse. The man stood up, his eyes red. A vampire.

I stared in horror as she went for another victim. Then, a giant paw struck me, tearing the flesh and fur from my chest.

I screamed in agony as I fell to my knees.

I'd never wept as a wolf before. All those years, I'd felt a lot while shifted. Anger. Rage. Hunger. Never sadness.

Abel howled at the blue magic, the firmament suspended above us, before he fixed his eyes back on me.

Then a flame struck him in the chest.

I turned. Julie had her flambeau extended, channeling a torrent of hellfire into his chest.

I knew what that felt like. It awakened the worst of me. It brought me to my lowest point. Why would she do that to Abel now, when he was just about to kill me?

Julie released her flames, and Abel charged her instead. He bit her. That was all it took. She didn't shift. She wouldn't. Not until the next full moon. Julie completed Abel's pack. She was the seventh.

Abel's body shrank, the fur fell from his body at his feet. He became human again. So did the rest of the wolves in his pack. The seven-fold curse had run its course.

And since Julie had released her flambeau, we changed back, too.

CHAPTER TWENTY

MY BROTHER LOOKED AT me with wide, tear-filled eyes. "Cain?"

I nodded. "Hello, brother."

"I'm sorry. At first, it was that flame, the one that Delphine used to control me. It brought out my anger. Then, even after she lost the flame, as a wolf I couldn't suppress it."

I shook my head. "I'm the one who should apologize. It is my fault that you harbor anger toward me at all. I deserve it."

Abel nodded. "I admit, a part of me is angry about what you did. But I'd be lying if I didn't admit I had regrets as well."

I cocked my head. "Abel, you did nothing wrong. Not really."

Abel sighed. "When your sacrifice was refused, I should have embraced you. Instead, I gloated."

"It was no excuse for me to do what I did, brother."

"No matter. The past is in the past. I forgive you, Cain."

My lip quivered as I tried to suppress my cry. I couldn't hold back the tears. I embraced Abel. He wrapped his arms around me. "I've lived for six thousand years thinking I had no way to truly atone for my sin. I never dreamed I'd have this chance to make amends."

Abel nodded as we pulled apart. "We still have a problem. She's making more vampires."

"Will you run with me, brother? Together, as one pack?"

Abel nodded and clasped my hand in his. "It would be an honor."

"Um, Cain," Christopher piped up. "We're standing here in the streets naked."

Cassidy giggled. "Watching two naked dudes hug... that's an image that I don't think I'll ever be able to erase from my mind."

I chuckled. "Julie. Can you turn us back?"

Julie nodded. "Gladly."

"Shall we take out the vampires?" Donald asked.

I shook my head. "Don't kill them. Take them to the asylum."

Abel stepped next to Donald. The two men shook hands. "We'll handle that together."

Annabelle extended her hand as her soul-blade materialized within it. This time, it took the shape of a stake.

"You can't stake them with that, Annabelle. It will kill them."

"It's just a precaution. I'll go to the asylum and help Rutherford get them processed. She'll have her hands full, otherwise."

"Thanks, Annabelle. Everyone ready?"

"We are," Donald said.

"So are we," Abel added.

I nodded at Julie. She called forth her flambeau, and we shifted back again. This time, two packs, united as one. Julie shifted, too. She held her flambeau between her enormous jaws.

I nodded at Abel. A part of me was anxious that the moment he became a wolf again, he'd rediscover his rage. It depended, I suppose, how genuine he was when he forgave me. That he nodded back, and didn't even snarl, suggested he genuinely loved me. His words were more than words. They came from the heart.

That's the secret to taming the wolf, to quelling the monster within us. We have to deal with our baggage, our defects, our resentments. We have to own up to what we've done wrong, and seek to make amends. Only then are we truly free to run.

Cassidy and I took off after LaLaurie. We couldn't bite her. If we did, Mercy would have to deal with a festering, painful wound for a hundred years or more. That's how long it took a vampire to heal from a werewolf's bite.

LaLaurie used Mercy's speed to run as we bounded after her. We had to get to her fast. The other werewolves, short of biting the younglings, couldn't do much more than prevent the vamps from hurting anyone. I'd be surprised if they got any of them to the asylum. Not until we saved Mercy and she could order them to go. She was their sire. They'd have to heed her demand. And, knowing Mercy, she wouldn't be interested in parenting a dozen or more baby vamps. She had her hands full with the youngling, Mel, already. It thrilled her to punt her away to my treatment program.

Provided we could catch her. Catching a vampire is sort of like trying to swat a fly. Just when you think you've got it cornered, it slips out of your grip.

I grunted at Cassidy and pointed with my snout down an alley that ran parallel to the Voodoo Academy. LaLaurie didn't know Vilokan well. Cassidy didn't either. But that didn't matter.

This particular alley wrapped around the back-side of the academy and hit a dead-end. Cassidy took the hint and took off down the alley. If I could circle around LaLaurie, and force her to double-back, she'd have no choice but to either go down that alley or walk right into the other packs as they surrounded the newly turned vamps.

To do that, though, I had to let LaLaurie out of my sight. If I could see her, she could see me. I needed to take her by surprise. I turned, racing down the road that led to the Ghede quarter of Vilokan.

The roads were narrow. Not even wide enough for a vehicle since, well, no one had cars or even carriages in Vilokan. That also worked to my advantage. There wasn't a lot of room for her to move around me.

When I turned, she kept running in the opposite direction. I knew where her road would lead. While she was faster, her path took a long way around and there weren't any other roads she could take except the alley where I hoped to herd her.

I still had to move fast. If she got past the intersection where I hoped to cut her off, my plan wouldn't work. She'd also have a straight shot to one of the more highly populated residential districts in the city.

It was a gamble. Especially since I wasn't sure how far from Julie I could run before I'd shift back.

Vilokan wasn't much larger than the area in Manchac Swamp where the rougarou dwelled before. If the flambeau kept the rougarou shifted within the swamp, before, I hoped it would have a similar radius of influence in the city.

I ran faster on all fours. My muscles burned as my legs churned beneath me, my paws forcing me across Vilokan's cobble-stone roads. I saw the intersection just ahead. I dug deep and used the last of my energy to leap into it.

LaLaurie wasn't twenty feet away when I landed in front of her. She took two steps back.

I heard a roar coming from the road I'd just traversed. Who was following me?

I looked at LaLaurie and snarled. She looked back at me with Mercy's eyes and smirked. Then she raised her hand. She had a pistol. Probably loaded with silver bullets.

She raised the gun, took aim, and fired just as the other wolf leaped over me. I recognized his golden fur immediately.

It was Abel. He shrieked as LaLaurie's bullet struck him in the gut.

With a last burst of energy, Abel dove at LaLaurie and swiped the gun out of her hand. Then he collapsed, shaking, as the silver spread through his body.

I howled. LaLaurie turned and ran.

She was moving the direction I hoped. But Abel... I couldn't just leave him there...

I nuzzled him with my snout. He turned, snarled, and waved his paw in the direction LaLaurie ran.

He'd sacrificed himself to save me... to give me this chance...

He wanted me to leave him there, to pursue her.

I had to make this quick. My only chance to save my brother was to end this, get Annabelle, and bring her back to Abel before the silver spread. A part of me wanted to stay with him. I couldn't. If I did, I'd lose him for sure. And I'd lose my chance to corner LaLaurie.

I nodded at Abel and took off after LaLaurie. The other wolves had several of the newly turned vampires cornered on the far end of the road. The flames from Julie's flambeau gave away her position as the hellfire cast a golden glow on the buildings and streets around them.

LaLaurie took the bait. She knew she couldn't run straight into the pack. She turned down the alley where Cassidy was waiting. I followed her to ensure she couldn't escape.

She stopped when she saw Cassidy, snarling at her, at the dead end of the alley.

I moved toward her, staring her down. She had no choice. She charged toward me. I swiped her down with my paw. Cassidy pounced, pinning LaLaurie to the ground. Then, a red magic flowed out of Cassidy's paw. A translucent form separated from Mercy's body. The vampire screamed as LaLaurie tried to hold on to her former host. Cassidy's magic intensified.

Then, the ghost disappeared. Delphine LaLaurie was gone.

CHAPTER
TWENTY-ONE

MERCY STOOD UP AND straightened her dress. She glared at me and poked me in my chest.

"I've half a mind to kick your furry ass, Cain. This wasn't what I agreed to."

I chuckled, which, as a wolf, sounded more like a series of huffs.

Mercy smirked. "You owe me. I'm not taking care of this litter of newbie vamps."

I shrugged and whimpered.

Mercy rolled her eyes and walked back down the alley and into the streets. Cassidy and I followed her.

"Alright, kids. Everyone follow me."

The other wolves released the vampires they'd pinned down. They obediently stood and followed Mercy as she led them to the asylum. Annabelle was waiting there, as she'd promised, to help check them in.

I looked at Julie and nodded. She released her flambeau. We all shifted back into our human forms.

Annabelle tossed me one of the asylum's hospital gowns.

It had Scooby Doo printed on it.

"Put that on," Annabelle said. "No one wants to see Cain's.... cane."

"Speak for yourself," Rutherford giggled. "I'll go get gowns for the rest."

"Annabelle, I need your help. LaLaurie shot my brother."

Annabelle nodded. "Take me to him."

Annabelle followed me back to Abel, now shifted back into his human shape. Black spider-webbed veins riddled his body, infected by the silver as it spread from the bullet.

Annabelle knelt beside him as she rolled him to his back. Abel was still awake, still alert, but just barely. Annabelle's eyes glowed. Then Abel grabbed her hand.

"No, don't."

"Abel, she's trying to heal you."

Abel shook his head. "I know what she's doing. Brother, I don't belong here. My life ended a long time ago. Now that we've made our peace, I have no other reason to live."

I knelt and took Abel's hand. "You can have a new life. We'll find a new reason, a new purpose. You deserve a chance to live out the years I stole from you."

Abel sighed. "If I stay like this, it will change me. I can sense it, the magic that revived me, eating away at my humanity. I'd prefer to depart, now, in good conscience. I'm not afraid to die, Cain. I've been dead a long time. I know where I'm going."

I pressed my lips together, trying to suppress my tears. "I don't want to lose you again."

Abel winced as he pushed himself up into a seated position. He grabbed me and pulled me close. "I love you, brother."

"I love you, too! I'm sorry, Abel. I really am."

"I know," Abel said. "And I'm sorry I can't stay. Perhaps, someday, you'll join me."

I nodded. "Maybe. Someday. This curse keeps me alive."

"You're forgiven already, brother. You aren't a curse. You've suffered enough for your sin. Now, you're a gift to the world. These people need you."

I nodded. "Just tell me one thing. Mom and Dad. They're there, too? In the beyond, in heaven?"

Abel nodded. "They are."

"Do they hate me?"

Abel shook his head. "You're their son. They could never hate you."

"And our other brother, Seth?"

"He's as insufferable in death as he ever was in life."

I chuckled. "In that case, give them my love."

Abel nodded. "I will. Take care, brother."

Abel squeezed me one more time before his arms went limp. I laid him down, closed his eyes with my hands, and took him into my arms.

Annabelle put her hand on my back. "At least you know he's at peace."

I nodded. "He isn't the only one. For the first time in my life, I'm at peace, too."

I sat in a chair on the opposite side of Annabelle's desk. Two stacks of folders sat in front of the Voodoo Queen.

"I've signed off on all of them. One stack includes the new vampires, including the ones Mercy sent to us before. The other stack are the wolves, your brother's pack."

"They're a part of Donald's pack, now. But it will take some time for them to adjust."

Annabelle nodded. "But they'll need guidance. So will Cassidy and Julie. There's plenty of space at the satellite campus for them. At least there will be once we finish the renovations. A few more patients will join you there as well. We need to make room for the vampires here in Vilokan. They'll be shielded from sunlight. Besides, most of the new vamps are also members of the voodoo community."

I nodded. "Even with the extra space, I'll probably have to treat the new wolves on an out-patient basis until we can get things in order. I suppose the expanded pack will be helpful in that regard. Thank you, Annabelle. For the asylum. For giving my brother a resting place with your ancestors on your plantation. For everything. "

Annabelle shook her head. "I should be the one thanking you, Cain. I sent Cassidy to the asylum, not knowing that she wasn't herself. I took an anonymous tip at face value and because of that, I allowed all this to happen."

I shook my head. "You can't blame yourself for how other people manipulate your good intentions, Annabelle."

Annabelle sighed. "I'm responsible for everyone here, Cain. Anything that happens and hurts the people of my city is on me."

"We deal with supernatural beings, powerful entities, witches, vampires, and necromancers. Bad things are bound to happen, Annabelle. If you beat yourself up over everything that goes wrong, any time someone gets hurt, you'll never be happy."

"My happiness is secondary to the safety and security of Vilokan."

"I disagree. The prosperity of the people here depends on your happiness. The actual test of a good queen isn't what tragedies might befall her domain. It's how she responds when such things occur. In my mind, you did everything you could."

"She possessed me, Cain. A lot of the evil LaLaurie did, she did through me."

"Did you invite her to possess you?"

"Of course not!"

"She possessed you because you are the most powerful person in this city. She didn't win in the end."

"She almost did. Several good people are now vampires as a result."

"Just because someone is turned into a vampire doesn't mean they have to be a monster. As a werewolf, trust me, I know. It's not what we are that defines us. It's what we choose to do with the lot in life we've been given."

Annabelle smiled slightly. "To make a blessing out of a curse?"

I nodded. "Precisely."

Annabelle smirked and pushed both stacks of folders across her desk toward me. "Well, in that case, you have a lot of curses to bless."

I grinned. "All in a day's work at the Vilokan Asylum for the Magically and Mentally Deranged."

The End of Book 1
Continued in *Razing Cain* (Keep reading...)

RAZING CAIN

THEOPHILUS MONROE

CHAPTER ONE

"Vampires are a pain in the butt," Rutherford remarked as she crammed more bags of donated blood into the refrigerator we'd designated for that purpose.

I chuckled as I leaned, arms crossed, against the door frame. "Not really. Technically, they're a pain in the neck!"

Rutherford froze for a moment, her head still halfway into the fridge, then turned and looked at me, smirking. "Was that supposed to be a joke, Cain?"

I smiled, trying my best to suppress the urge to laugh at my own joke. "It's pretty good, right? You know, since vampires bite necks, Not butts. I mean, most of them don't bite butts. Some might."

Rutherford laughed. "Cain, the joke doesn't become funnier after you explain it."

"I think it's clever!"

"You would," Rutherford snorted. "Classic 'Dad' joke. How many times have you been a father, anyway, over the last six-thousand years of your existence?"

"One hundred and thirty-five times, to the best of my knowledge. I mean, there may be a few more I don't know about. I had a promiscuous phase back in the Bronze Age."

Rutherford closed the refrigerator, pulled a chain around it, locked it, and shoved a few garlic cloves through the links. A necessary measure. The last time a youngling broke into the cafeteria, the young bloodsucker binged our entire supply.

"Do you remember all of your kids?" Rutherford asked.

"Each and every one," I said. "I could tell you their names in order. Chronological or alphabetical. I could tell you what they did with their lives, how many grandchildren each of them had, and how they died."

Rutherford bit her lip. "That must be hard. To outlive so many of your children."

I pressed my lips together. "I miss every one of them. The wound left behind when a parent loses a child never truly heals."

"I can't imagine what that must be like. Living with that kind of pain in your heart."

I smiled. "I've had my seasons in life when I allowed the losses I experienced to overwhelm me. Now, though, as much as it hurts, I'm more grateful than anything."

"For the time you had with your children?"

"That's right. Every child I've ever had was a blessing. When you lose a blessing, you have two options. You can focus on the loss, or you can be thankful that you'd been so blessed to begin with."

Rutherford nodded. "That's a nice way to look at it. Still, I don't know if I could do that, you know, if I lost a child. I mean, I'd need to have children first. I'm already past prime childbearing age. Who knows if it will ever happen."

I narrowed my eyes. "Is that some kind of hint, Rutherford? I know we're not exactly a conventional couple. Our relationship has always been complicated."

Rutherford waved her hand through the air. "Oh, heavens no. Like you said, you've had children before. I'm just running my mouth, blabbing away. I didn't mean to suggest..."

"If that's what you want, Rutherford. We should talk about it. Like I said, I've had children before."

Rutherford sighed. "That's not what I'm saying. Just forget I said anything, alright?"

I wanted to remind her she couldn't bullshit a psychotherapist. Of course, that's not strictly true. People do it all the time. But the longer people think you can't hide a lie from a shrink, the easier it makes my job. Instead of telling her that, since I *was* an experienced therapist, I knew better than to call her out on it. "Very well," I said instead. "I suppose we'll be back in here after dinner doing the same thing."

Rutherford sighed. "It's exacerbating. If we could just freeze it, it would make this a lot easier."

I shrugged my shoulders. "It doesn't matter if it's frozen or not. Refrigeration only buys us a little time."

"I know, I know. The soul is in the blood. Leviticus, or whatever. I just wish that taste of the soul lingered a little longer than a day. Recruiting donors, drawing their blood, storing it, and delivering it to the young vampires, is really a full-time job."

I nodded. "It should get better soon. The more the younglings curb their bloodlust, the less blood they'll demand."

Rutherford snorted. "That's true. But it could take weeks or even months before that happens. In the meantime, I guess I'm the blood bitch."

I raised one eyebrow. "That's a colorful way to put it."

Rutherford sighed. "I'm sorry. I know it's a part of the job. I know you have your hands full counseling all of them. I appreciate the help."

I chuckled. "I didn't do much, Rutherford. I stood here and talked to you while you shoved blood bags in a refrigerator."

Rutherford smiled. "It helps, Cain. Your company always makes even the most intolerable tasks somehow pleasant. Even if you do have a lot of bad dad jokes."

I smiled widely. "When does a dad joke become a dad joke, anyway?"

Rutherford rolled her eyes. "I don't know. Tell me, Cain."

"When it becomes apparent!"

Rutherford groaned even as the tension at the corners of her mouth proved she was trying her best to suppress her urge to laugh. "That's horrible. But it's funnier than the vampire joke before."

"Because I didn't explain the joke?"

Rutherford giggled. "Well, that certainly helped. I know that between the vampire younglings, the new werewolves, and the satellite campus, you're swamped right now. I just wanted you to know that I really appreciate the time you take just to brighten up my day a little."

I smiled. "It's my pleasure, Rutherford. Want to hear another vampire joke?"

Rutherford sighed. "Sure. Why the hell not?"

"Why did the Vampire CEO resign from the company?"

"I don't know. Why did he?"

"Because all the stakeholders were coming after him!"

Rutherford snorted through a laugh. "That's actually not half-bad."

"Thank you, thank you. I'll be here all week. And probably the week after that. And the one after that."

"I said it's not half bad because it's only half good. You know, because I'm an optimist. I wouldn't give up your career for stand-up comedy if I was you."

I chuckled. "I actually tried that once."

"Stand-up comedy? Are you serious?"

I nodded. "No one laughed. Someone threw their beer at me."

Rutherford grinned. "That must've been embarrassing."

I shrugged my shoulders. "I'm a werewolf, Rutherford. Do you know how many times during my existence I've woken up after a full moon and had to find my way home, totally naked?"

"Okay, I suppose that's a fair point. I imagine after that, getting heckled on stage is probably nothing at all."

"I wouldn't say it's nothing. I mean, my shirt was soaked in cheap beer. I was just so shocked that someone would waste a perfectly good glass of pilsner to get me off the stage."

Rutherford shrugged. "Pilsners are all right. If they showered you with a hefeweizen, you'd have a real enigma on your hands."

CHAPTER TWO

TECHNICALLY, ALL THE YOUNGLING vampires I was currently treating at the Vilokan Asylum were the progeny of Mercy Brown. However, most of them had been turned by force when the spirit of Delphine LaLaurie possessed the vampire. Mel, however, was different. She chose vampirism. And it was Mercy's choice to turn her. Since Mercy had already been working with her, albeit not for long, her blood cravings weren't initially as overwhelming as they were for the other younglings.

Why would anyone choose to become a vampire? Well, it's more common than you'd think. The prospect of living, potentially, forever, has an allure to it for many. There's also always been a sort of gothic subculture that has found vampirism intriguing. Sure, there's the goth culture, born in the United Kingdom during the early 1980s. Like many 20th century subcultures, it was connected to a particular genre of music. Goth rock, an offshoot of the post-punk movement, has had its fans ever since. Though, there's always been an underground, counter-cultural element in every human society I'd ever known. When vampirism was first born, courtesy of Baron Samedi and his bargain with Niccolo Freeman, also known as "Niccolo the Damned," members of such communities were a popular feeding ground for vampires. The rationale, from the vampires' perspective, was simple. Vampires have always been a marginalized, minority community. Their aversion to sunlight has necessarily forced them into the shadows. More than that, though, since they require human blood, human hunters and slayers have always pursued them. For many such hunters, hunting vampires is a sport. The best way to avoid the attention of those who'd like to stake vampires is to hunt people on the fringes of society, those already perceived as rebellious, anti-conformists, who weren't likely to turn to the establishment for help. Over time, among such communities, tales of vampires tended more toward the romantic than the horrific. Only in recent years, partly because of the now deceased Nico's efforts to rehabilitate the vampire's image in popular culture, has the "vampire romance" become a part of mainstream culture.

Nico's plans were, frankly, brilliant. In an age of smartphones and the Internet, the notion that vampires could keep their existence secret became less tenable than ever before. If the world were to finally discover the truth, it was advantageous to vampires that the world view them empathetically, as creatures whose angst was understandable and redeemable, rather than as bloodsucking monsters.

Despite being Nico's favored progeny, Mercy never bought into the idea. She believed it was a lie. In truth, I'd never met a vampire with a bigger heart than Mercy Brown. At every turn, although she was literally heartless for the better part of her existence, she put her life on the line to save others, to stand against evil, to do what was right. She still wouldn't admit that she was good at her core. She insisted that the darkness within her, and all vampires, was too pervasive to be countered by a few well-intentioned actions. Though, Mercy had more compassion than most humans I'd met. That was why she'd turned Mel.

Mel was a sweet girl. A redheaded firecracker with the sort of personality that could light up a room. As a human, though, she'd suffered from fibromyalgia. Her pain was so intense that it limited her to a wheelchair. Mercy gave her a gift. She gave her a chance to walk again. It came with a cost, of course. Becoming a vampire always did. Unfortunately, despite Mercy's many praiseworthy attributes, she lacked the patience to raise a youngling alone. So, when she agreed to help me deal with the Delphine LaLaurie situation, I agreed to take Mel under my wing. It wasn't a permanent arrangement. Once Mel's blood cravings were under control, she'd return to Mercy at Casa do Diabo, an old mansion where Mercy and a few other vampires lived in the French Quarter.

I found Mel pacing in front of my office. Her hair was frizzy. She tugged at the small, metal collar around her neck. It was a standard-issue for our vampire patients. If they acted out or tried to bite someone, we could activate the collar remotely. It emanated ultraviolet radiation, which, at the very least, was mildly painful. At worst, it could leave a scar that might take a century to heal. It was enough that, in most instances, it kept even the youngling vampires in check. Of course, it wasn't the most comfortable device imaginable.

"About time," Mel said. "I've been waiting forever."

"I'm only five minutes late, Mel."

"Yeah, five minutes going on forever."

I smiled, unlocked my office door, and allowed her to walk in ahead of me. I gestured to a red-velvet chaise, where my patients often reclined during our sessions, and she sat on the edge.

I closed the door behind me, pulled my chair out from behind my desk, and sat down. "What's going on, Mel? You seem stressed."

"You think? These other vampires are insufferable."

I crossed my legs and folded my hands over my knee. "In what way?"

Mel took a deep breath. "First, they're all hougans and mambos. It's all Baron Samedi this, and Maman Brigitte that."

I shrugged my shoulders. "Yes, they were all citizens of Vilokan and practitioners of voodoo before they were turned. It's no wonder they'd look to the Baron or the other Ghede Loa for help."

Mel grunted. "They're insufferable. They think that if they evoke Baron Samedi, they can convince him to change them back."

I raised an eyebrow. "Is that so?"

"Yeah. Can you believe it? There's been, what, one vampire ever who became human again?"

"Niccolo the Damned," I said.

"Right," Mel said. "He was Mercy's dad, or I guess sire is the right word. Whatever."

"And he was the first vampire. Originally, it was a bargain with the Baron that made him a vampire. It was with another bargain that he became human again, only that he might die."

"As I was saying, it's pretty presumptuous. They're all under the impression that because Mercy was possessed, it shouldn't count. They think the Baron should let them out of it on a technicality."

I chuckled. "Well, I'm no hougan. However, from my time living in Vilokan, I've never heard of Baron Samedi doing anything for anyone without a bargain. So far as I know, there aren't any rules about what counts or doesn't when someone is turned."

"That's what I'm saying!" Mel said, nodding her head. "I don't know much about voodoo or any of this stuff, either. But I think, you know, since you're the therapist here, you should know. I think they're holding onto false hope. That might get in the way with their progress, you know, taming the bloodlust. If they don't think they'll be vampires for long, why bother, right?"

I smirked. "So, you're telling me all of this, Mel, because you're concerned about the wellbeing of the voodoo vampires?"

Mel bit the inside of her cheek. "Not really. It just pisses me off that they're walking around the whole damn asylum like they own the place."

I shrugged my shoulders. "I get it. I'm something of an outsider here, too. But they originally established this facility for treating the voodoo community."

Mel snorted. "Yeah. Zuckerberg originally created Facebook for college students. Amazon originally sold only books. Bubble wrap was originally invented to be an innovative wallpaper."

"Wait, what?" I asked. "I thought it was created as a stress reliever."

"Nope. Google it. Did you know Lysol was initially marketed as vaginal contraception?"

"That's asinine. You were supposed to spray Lysol up your... you know..."

"My hoo-hah? Yeah. They thought it might kill sperm before it fertilizes the egg. I promise you, I'm not making this up."

I smiled. "I believe you. But what's the point you're trying to make here, Mel?"

Mel cocked her head and stared at the wall for a second. "Damn it. I forgot. Wait, oh yeah. The Vilokan Asylum may have been originally meant for the New Orleans voodoo community. Still, the fact that you're here and, hell, since you have a whole second campus now outside of Vilokan, I'm pretty sure what used to be doesn't matter. Just because those voodoo vampire bitches think they own the place, it doesn't mean they do."

I uncrossed my legs and recrossed them, the other leg on top. My left leg was falling asleep. "Why are you worried about them, Mel? Does their reluctance to accept their vampirism have any impact at all on your progress here?"

Mel sighed. "Not directly."

I narrowed my eyes. "But indirectly?"

"I don't know. I mean, strictly, I don't see why they'd have an influence at all on my ability to get past my cravings."

"But they still bother you. Tell me, Mel. Do you like being a vampire?"

"Are you kidding? I love it. I can walk. I don't have any pain. I don't even miss the sun that much because, well, I'm a redhead. The sun never treated me well, anyway."

I uncrossed my legs and leaned forward, resting my forearms on my thighs. "First, it's forbidden for any vodouisants to evoke a Loa within the asylum. Second, even if they pulled it off, the chances that they'd be able to convince Baron Samedi to give them their souls back are slim. Third, even if they did, there's no reason to believe that their arrangement would make you human again."

Mel took a deep breath. "But if it's possible to make vampires human again, say the Baron gives them some kind of antidote to vampirism or something. How long would it be before people started arguing that we should turn all vampires back?"

I pressed my lips together. "Tell me, Mel. What are some things that used to make you happy? When you were a child. When you were perfectly healthy, without your limitations?"

Mel shrugged. "I don't know. Before my fibromyalgia, I used to love exploring new places, experiencing new things."

"And you think your condition robbed you of that?"

Mel shrugged. "Not completely. But it made everything so much harder and more complicated. A lot of times, if my friends were going out, I couldn't. Not without someone who could help me, and a lot of things they liked to do I couldn't do."

"Your condition took a lot more from you than your legs. It took away things you enjoyed doing. I imagine it also impacted your friendships since you couldn't do everything with them you used to do."

Mel rubbed her eyes. "Yeah. I felt robbed."

"Are you happy now that you're a vampire?"

Mel shrugged. "I'm getting there. I have hope."

"But you're expecting the other shoe to drop, aren't you?"

"I guess. I mean, I guess a part of me is anxious that my condition will come back somehow."

"Or if the voodoo vampires convince the Baron to turn them back, that you'll have to go back to your life before."

Mel's lip quivered. "That thought has crossed my mind."

"How does that make you feel, Mel?"

"Anxious. Afraid. A bit angry."

"You realize, Mel, that the other vampires have done nothing wrong yet, right?"

"Of course not. But that doesn't mean they won't."

"You're afraid that they'll steal your newfound happiness, correct?"

Mel nodded. "I guess so."

"But you just admitted that you're nervous, fearful, and angry. The other vampires haven't done a thing yet, Mel. But you're already allowing them to steal your joy."

Mel fidgeted back and forth in the chaise. "I guess you have a point. But I still think the voodoo vamps are playing with something that could be dangerous."

I grinned. "And now I'm aware of what's going on. Allow me to worry about them, Mel. But you're here for yourself. Don't let anyone screw with your happiness. You deserve it. And if you put in the work, if you get your cravings under control, I promise you'll find what you're looking for."

Mel stood up and straightened her shirt. "Thanks, Cain. That helps. You are going to do something about all this, though, right?"

"Leave it to me, Mel. This isn't the first time I've dealt with vodouisants, or even vampires, who've had other ideas about how they're going to resolve their issues. I have one question, though, if you don't mind."

"Yeah, of course. Anything that will help."

"There are about a dozen voodoo vampires I'm treating currently. Which one do you suppose is most fixated on evoking Baron Samedi?"

Mel sighed. "I don't want to snitch. But if it helps…"

"I won't tell anyone what you've shared with me, Mel. Anything you share with me in this room stays in this room. Unless, of course, you're comfortable with me bringing the information to Annabelle Mulledy or Mercy Brown."

"You can tell either of them if it helps. I'm not totally sure which vampire came up with the idea. But if I were you, I'd keep an eye on Clairvius. That dude gives me the creeps. And the others all seem to listen to him."

I nodded. "Thank you for bringing this to my attention. Rest assured, I'll handle it."

CHAPTER THREE

I'VE BEEN WRITING A memoir of my life. I figure I'd sell it as historical fiction. Maybe something in the fantasy lane. Most people wouldn't believe that a tale about 'the' Cain from the bible, still alive in the 21st Century, was true. Of course, I wasn't trying to sell a bunch of copies. I didn't need the money. I'd accumulated enough wealth over time that I technically didn't *need* to work.

I was writing it for two reasons. First, I figured my story deserved more than what people knew of me from Genesis. Second, and more importantly, I was writing it because writing my history was cathartic whether people read it or not.

One of the many things I'd learned while studying under Freud was that all lives have a trajectory. The best way to know the direction your life is heading is to consider where you've been. If you ignore your past, your present is nothing but a single data point. Chart out your whole life, add as many data points as you can, and a picture emerges.

If your life is on an upward trajectory, the best advice is to stay the course. Don't give up. Things are improving. Things will get better. If, however, things are declining when you chart your history, it might mean it is time to change something.

It was a principle I used to evaluate my own life, to guide my personal decisions. It was also important when working with my patients.

Annabelle Mulledy, the Voodoo Queen, had yet to provide me with any files on the voodoo vampires. I'd conducted basic introductory interviews with all of them. Nothing struck me as unusual. They were predictably in shock. None of them were turned willingly. Their blood thirst was overwhelming, which was to be expected since they were younglings. Maslow's Hierarchy dictates that until someone's basic needs are met, there isn't much one can do to address their social needs, not to mention issues related to personal identity, which Maslow termed self-actualization. Thus, Clairvius didn't stand out from the rest in any way when I spoke to him. He was disturbed by his situation, which was quite understandable. He told me nothing about his past and shared little about his emotions. Like the rest, he begged me for blood. I complied. Older vampires can't stand blood bags. Younglings, though, who know little else, find them more palatable. The only thing about him that stood out at all was that he was older than the rest. I wasn't sure exactly how old he was, but among the new vampires, he was at least a couple of decades the senior of the others. Compared to me, of course, he was just a baby. But if I learned he was eighty, or even ninety, it wouldn't have surprised me.

I don't think I'd ever met a vampire so old. First, hardly anyone would choose to be turned at such an age. When one becomes a vampire, they keep the appearance of their human age. Mercy Brown, for instance, was turned at only nineteen. She was one of the oldest vampires, technically speaking, in New Orleans. Looking at her, though, no one would guess it by appearance alone.

I needed to catch up with Annabelle and see if she had any information that might be helpful regarding the voodoo vampires. Were Mel's fears warranted? Probably not. I'd treated my share of vodouisants who'd threatened to evoke various Loa before. Most of the time, it was a cry for help. Still, if Clairvius or any of the other voodoo vampires were looking to a Loa, willing to risk a bargain with the likes of Baron Samedi, rather than do the work to master their cravings, I needed whatever information I could get to help. Hopefully, they'd come around. Usually, they did. Even when I treated humans in my former private practice in New York, I'd often encountered people with problems who were looking for a way out, an escape, rather than the mental resilience and cognitive tools necessary to work through their issues.

I stopped by Rutherford's desk at reception on my way out of the asylum. I tapped my knuckles on her desk three times. Rutherford looked up from her computer screen, removed her set of earphones, and looked me in the eye, smiling slightly.

"Could you rearrange my schedule this afternoon?" I asked.

"Sure. What changes need to be made?"

"I don't think I had the new vampire, Clairvius, on my agenda. I'd like to speak with him this afternoon. Move around whatever you need to."

Rutherford raised her eyebrows. "I think you had the afternoon slated to work with the vampires who came in with Mel."

I nodded. "They can wait. They're all doing relatively well. This may be a more pressing matter."

Rutherford raised her left eyebrow. "How so?"

I pressed my lips together. "I'm not sure yet. Annabelle hasn't sent over those files on the voodoo vampires yet, has she?"

Rutherford shook her head. "Nope. Did you really think she would?"

I chuckled. As well-intentioned as Annabelle was, her organizational skills were lacking. When it came to paperwork, at least. Her shoe closet, well, I hadn't ever seen it, but it was legendary in Vilokan. I don't think I'd ever seen her wear the same pair twice. If she'd applied the same energy to organizing her files as she did to her shoe collection, things would move a lot smoother. This wasn't the first time I'd had to chase her down to get more information on a newly committed patient.

I stepped into the elevator at the Voodoo Academy that led to Annabelle's office. It was one of those walk-through elevators that you enter on one side but exit on the other. The elevator ascended to Annabelle's office and halted.

"Can I help you?" Annabelle asked across the crackling speaker mounted above the button panel on the elevator.

"It's me," I said. "I'm looking for the files on the new vampires."

Annabelle didn't respond. Instead, with a ding, the elevator doors parted directly into her office. Annabelle was behind her desk, her legs kicked up on the top, flashing her designer shoes. I wasn't sure what they were or who the designer was. That was a world I'd never engaged in. Hell, I'd spent most of my existence wearing sandals and walking dirt roads. My white Nike Air Monarchs weren't stylish, but they were certainly comfortable. Given the callouses I'd accumulated over the last few millennia, comfort was a higher priority than fashion. Still, I was reasonably sure that Annabelle's shoes were probably more expensive than some automobiles. She didn't need to finance them. She had money. Even more than I did, and I'd had a lot more time to save.

Annabelle glanced at me and nodded as she focused again on her computer monitor. She had one of those large Apple computers with massive screens, all self-contained. She was clicking her mouse furiously and tapping a few of the same keys on her keyboard repeatedly.

"Are you busy?" I asked.

Annabelle shrugged. "I'm in a raid."

I sat down in one of the wooden chairs in front of Annabelle's desk. "You're pillaging a village from your computer?"

Annabelle snorted. "Not that kind of raid, Cain. No raping or pillaging involved. I'm just trying to level up and get some new gear."

I raised one eyebrow. "It feels like you're speaking a different language right now."

"I just got Internet access down here. Fiber. It's super fast. And now I can play my MMORPGs!"

"Your lips are moving, but nonsense is coming out."

Annabelle giggled. "Sorry, just one second. We're taking down the boss."

I started twiddling my thumbs. "So, the files?"

"One second. Wait... yes! Take that, you piece of crap. How does my blade taste?"

My eyes shifted back and forth. "Don't you have anything more important to do?"

"Just a little more," Annabelle said, still clicking away as she ignored my question. "Almost... almost... *damn it!*"

I stared at Annabelle blankly. "Something wrong?"

Annabelle grabbed a pen off her desk and chucked it across the room. "We were so close! Our healers dropped the ball on that one. This boss drops a great tanking breastplate I really need."

"I'm sorry things didn't work out as you were hoping. As I was saying..."

"Yes, of course," Annabelle said, pulling open one of the side drawers on her side of the desk. "The files. I have most of them. They need a little work, but most of them are there."

"You don't have my files done, but you have time to play games?"

Annabelle stared at me blankly. "Everyone needs a hobby, Cain. And I can only handle so much paperwork at a time without losing my mind."

I nodded. "Never mind it. Do you at least have a file for a hougan turned vampire named Clairvius? He's an older man and speaks with a Haitian accent."

Annabelle smiled. "I have his file. It's in the stack. He's certainly an interesting character. I can't say I'm surprised you'd have a few questions about him, given his story."

"What story?" I asked. "He hasn't told me a thing apart from the fact that he was hungry. Kept going on about how he wanted his pudding. He meant blood. Kept on referring to blood as pudding."

Annabelle smiled. "That sounds like Clairvius."

I folded my hands and rested them on the edge of her desk. "Would you care to elaborate?"

Annabelle smiled, reached into her drawer, and flipped through a few files before she found the proper one. She opened the file and traced her finger down the first page. "They pronounced Clairvius Narcisse dead in a Haitian hospital in 1962. They buried him shortly thereafter."

I cocked my head. "He's certainly not dead now. Was a necromancer involved?"

Annabelle shrugged. "His family thought he was dead until he reappeared eighteen years later, claiming a bokor raised him from the grave and forced him to work as a zombie slave on a sugar plantation for two years."

"But he didn't reappear for sixteen more years after that?"

Annabelle folded her hands, resting them on her desk. "Apparently, the bokor who raised him died after those two years. Unaffected by the bokor's control, he gradually and mysteriously recovered. When his memories returned, he went home, much to his family's surprise. I mean, can you imagine something like that? Someone you loved and mourned suddenly showing up almost twenty years older?"

"Is that normal? I've never heard of a zombie who recovered before."

Annabelle shook her head. "Not at all. Zombies are similar to vampires. They're both considered undead. Both are vivified by the power of the Ghede. Vampires by the aspect of Baron Samedi. However, the biggest difference is that a zombie is raised from a corpse. A vampire is created when, after one is bitten and drained, they're healed before the brain begins to deteriorate. Neither zombies nor vampires have souls. For the zombie, their soul may have moved on. Whatever regularly happens to the soul at the time of death doesn't change. Baron Samedi acquires the soul of the vampire when they change and keeps possession of the soul indefinitely."

I raised an eyebrow. "Another of my patients has reported that some of the voodoo vampires, especially Clairvius, are hoping to appeal to Baron Samedi to turn them human again."

Annabelle pinched her chin. "It's technically possible, though I've only known of one instance ever when the Baron agreed to a bargain involving the return of a vampire's soul."

"You're speaking of Niccolo Freeman?"

Annabelle nodded. "And even his case was unique. A bargain made him the world's first vampire to begin with. You know the story, how all that happened, and my involvement in those events, so we need not rehash it here. But suffice it to say, while I imagine other vampires have appealed to the Baron before, he either refused to bargain with them or the terms he demands are too steep."

"So, even if it's unlikely that Clairvius could convince the Baron to restore his humanity, it is theoretically possible."

"Possible, but not likely. With Clairivius's story, the notion that he'd recovered his soul after becoming a zombie, well, I suppose I can't say it's impossible. Still, how one might go about doing something like that is beyond my knowledge. Even Marie Laveau, based on the records she kept after Clairvius came to Vilokan, noted that his case perplexed her. There aren't any spells, or practices, in voodoo that could restore a human soul to a zombie's corpse."

I scratched the back of my head. "That brings us back to what I suspected from the start. Only a necromancer, so far as I'm aware, can raise the dead and restore a soul to a person."

Annabelle leaned back in her chair, kicking her platform-heeled feet and crossing them atop her desk. "Perhaps you should talk to Cassidy. She's still at the Vilokan Asylum satellite, correct?"

I nodded. "She is. She and Ryan, along with the wolves that Abel turned while still under the sevenfold curse, are living there currently. I hoped we'd have more time to work together before the next full moon. I'd intended to hold daily therapy sessions with the pack. Unfortunately, because of this new vampire issue, I'm struggling to figure out how to squeeze that into my schedule."

"Tell me about it," Annabelle said. "There aren't enough hours in the day."

I smiled. "Plenty of time to play games, apparently."

Annabelle raised an eyebrow and smirked. "You're old Cain. You wouldn't get it."

"Try me," I said.

"Look, Cain. It doesn't matter how busy you are. Make room for a hobby, something relaxing that you enjoy. Maybe gaming isn't your thing. But everyone needs to blow off steam. Gaming gives me an escape. It clears my mind so I can focus again on my work."

I bit my lip. "I understand that. Sometimes, though, you just have to suck it up and press forward with your tasks. Take a break when things slow down again."

"As a therapist, Cain, certainly you know how damaging stress can be. Busy or not, you need to unwind. Otherwise, the stress will overwhelm you."

"For some people, that may be true. I've lived long enough, though, that I'm pretty sure I know my limits."

Annabelle smiled. "I didn't mean to suggest you don't. But you're the one who criticized me for spending time playing games."

I snorted. "Fair enough. I guess I just don't get it. Games seem like a colossal waste of time. To think, what if you spent all those hours playing games, learning a musical instrument, or learning another hobby like painting or sculpting?"

Annabelle narrowed her eyes. "Certainly, Cain, gaming is more profitable than using whatever time you don't have in your busy schedule to worry about someone else's hobbies."

"I didn't mean to judge, but–"

Annabelle raised her hand to cut me off. "Usually, when people say that, Cain, they immediately start judging people afterward. Mind your own business. Focus on this case."

I nodded, biting my tongue. It had been a while since anyone had tried to call me out on anything. Though, I suppose, since she was technically my boss, she had as much a right to do it as anyone. Anyone who wasn't a therapist, anyway.

Annabelle recovered a few more files from her drawer and stacked them up on her desk before pushing them toward me. "This is all I've managed to get together on the new voodoo vampires. Regarding Clairvius, I'd suggest that you consult with Cassidy but allow him to explain his story to you in his way. I'm not concerned about the likelihood that he'd convince Baron Samedi to help. Though, if he's overcome zombiism, which is even more challenging to reverse than vampirism, is it so hard to believe that he'd hold out hope for becoming human again longer than other new vampires might?"

I nodded. "I suppose you're right. Thanks, Annabelle. I'll do what you suggested."

"Good," Annabelle smiled, returning her eyes to her computer. "Now, if you don't mind, I have work to do."

I smiled. "It's always good to get back to work."

Annabelle nodded. "I just have to acquire a better sword. The attack points on this one aren't cutting it."

I snorted. "Your sword isn't cutting it? Good one."

Annabelle cocked her head. "Good one? I don't get it."

"It was a joke. A sword not cutting it. Surely you meant to..."

I stopped talking when I realized Annabelle wasn't listening. Her computer screen enthralled her. "Talk to you soon, Cain. Keep me posted on the situation with Clairvius and the voodoo vamps."

CHAPTER FOUR

THE ABOVE-GROUND VILOKAN ASYLUM satellite was in Annabelle Mulledy's old family plantation. She'd grown up there, but now she lived in Vilokan. Her sister, Ashley, had also attended the Voodoo Academy but didn't live in Vilokan. She didn't live at the Mulledy plantation, either. Most of the time, Ashely Mulledy stayed with her fiancée's family. Her intended, Roger Thundershield, was a Choctaw shaman on the reservation.

All things considered, it made sense that the plantation wasn't in use. To say the least, it was shocking that Annabelle agreed to dedicate her family's antebellum estate to the Vilokan Asylum.

Annabelle and I worked well together most of the time. We didn't always see eye-to-eye. No two people in a professional relationship do. Despite her youth, she was my boss. She had more weight on her shoulders than most people could handle. Still, she was an outstanding leader. Even if she had a few habits I didn't understand—like collecting shoes and playing online video games.

Most of the original rougarou in my pack were back with their families. Donald, the pack's natural alpha, was married. Christopher and Evie, a couple, had an apartment and jobs in the city. I'd expected Andrew and Yvette, who each had jobs and lives of their own, to be off doing whatever it was they did between full moons. It surprised me to find both of them painting the columns on the mansion as I pulled through the iron gates in the front of the plantation home and parked along the circle drive in front of the house.

The rest of the wolves were brand new. A random werewolf in Missouri had turned Ryan. We'd integrated him into the pack during the last full moon. Ryan bit Cassidy when Delphine LaLaurie, the ghost of a murderess who'd been exorcised from Cassidy and possessed Annabelle, evoked the infernal flambeau and forced the pack to shift. Ryan felt awful about it all, but Cassidy was oddly cool with what happened. After being possessed for several years, and awakening to discover that she had no human family left, becoming a part of the pack wasn't the worst thing that could have happened to her. Then there was Julie Brown. She was Cassidy's great-great-grandmother, but having been resurrected by Cassidy's power and given a new body, she now wielded the flambeau that could cause us to change at any moment. The problem? While trying to take down Delphine, Abel bit her. She was the seventh wolf, her turn fulfilling the seven-fold curse my brother garnered when he attempted to kill me under Delphine's influence. Delphine used the flambeau to bring out the worst of his desires, his wish for revenge, bringing it to the forefront. Abel died in the conflict, but not before he and I reconciled.

There were six more wolves, too, who'd been turned while Abel was shifted, fulfilling the sevenfold curse. Now, the wolves Abel led were a part of my pack. Technically, Donald's pack. He was the Alpha. But whenever I joined them, which was during most full moons, I assumed control.

The problem was that the entire pack, previously comprising five rougarou, now had nine new members. The youngling wolves, what you might call the werepups, outnumbered the original members of the pack. Without my help, they'd never be prepared for the next full moon. But how in the world was I going to give them the time they needed while trying to deal with all the new vampires at the original, underground asylum?

"The place is really coming along," I said, nodding at Andrew and Yevette as they stood atop tall step ladders, painting the columns.

"Cain!" Andrew said. "I was wondering when you were going to show up."

I smiled. "I've been busy. Someday I'll sleep, I suppose. My hands are full with the new vampires."

"I bet," Andrew said, nodding his head.

I looked over at Yvette, who'd only sent a few fleeting glances my way. Had it been anyone else, I would have thought she was hiding something. Yvette, though, was notoriously shy and soft-spoken. Every now and again, in our group therapy sessions, we'd coax her out of her shell. But mostly, getting her to talk or carry on a conversion was sort of like teaching a cat to bark. She was an introvert to the extreme.

I waved at her. "Hello, Yvette."

Yvette turned and flashed me a close-lipped grin. "Hi, Dr. Cain."

"I need to talk to Cassidy. Do you know where she's at?"

"I think she's working on the old slave quarters in the back."

I cocked my head. "Why?"

Andrew shrugged. "She has all kinds of ideas for renovating the place. I checked it out. I don't think they have done much to the place for a century or longer."

"Sounds like she's taken on a tall task. I'll head back there now. Thanks, Andrew."

"No problem, Cain," Andrew said.

"Keep up the good work, both of you," I said.

Andrew smiled. "Donald was here until about an hour ago. I think he went to get supplies at the hardware store."

"Was this his idea? To work on the renovations?"

Andrew nodded as he placed the final touches on the capstone of the column. "He said it would be good to spend some time here working on the place. He thinks it will be helpful if we can bond with the new wolves before the next full moon."

I smiled. "That's a wise move. I'll leave you to it. I'll try to get back here this evening for our group session."

"See you then," Andrew said.

I stepped off the porch and walked around to the back of the mansion. The old slave quarters were several yards removed from the house itself. It was a fairly large building, big enough to accommodate all the people who used to live there as slaves. Still, Cassidy was right. One thing we lacked in the new facility was living space. There were several bedrooms, but unless we divided them up into several smaller rooms, sufficient to house the numbers we needed for the asylum once it was fully operational, there wasn't nearly enough space in the mansion. There was no reason, provided we repaired and updated the place with essentials (like electricity, running water, and a bathroom) why the old slave quarters couldn't house a half-dozen patients. That was the plan, at least.

I approached the old quarters. The door was closed. I pushed it open.

A high-pitched yelp forced me to take a step back. Then, a glimpse of two naked bodies tangled up with one another forced me to cover my eyes.

"Oh Jesus! I'm sorry. I didn't realize..."

Cassidy giggled. "Maybe knock next time?"

I shook my head, my hand still firmly pressed over my eyes. "If I knew you two were... you know..."

"I'm sorry," Ryan piped up. "Are we in trouble?"

Pressing my eyelids closed, I lowered my head. "In trouble? You're two consenting adults. It's not encouraged for patients to... you know... but whatever. I just wish you'd given me a little warning."

"What did you want me to do, Cain? Send you a telegram or something, you know, since you don't text?"

"A telegram?" Ryan asked, laughing. "Like a message in song?"

"Not all telegrams are singing telegrams," I said, my eyes still shut. "But that would certainly be something."

"What would we say, anyway?" Cassidy asked. "Hey, Doc, just thought you should know. We're screwing!"

I shook my head. "Not like that. Just some kind of warning. No matter. I know, now."

"We're covered up now," Cassidy said. "You can open your eyes."

I slowly opened my eyes. It wasn't like I hadn't seen them naked before. Nudity is unavoidable when a werewolf returns to human form. Still, it was a bit jarring since I didn't expect it and because, well, they weren't just nude. They were mid-tryst. I was less upset than embarrassed by the situation.

"Sorry again. Andrew said you were back here working. I assumed there might be some screwing or nailing in here, but this wasn't what I expected."

Ryan cocked his head. "Was that a joke?"

I nodded. "Sorry. Rutherford says my jokes are more likely to merit groans than laughs. I'm working on it."

Cassidy giggled. "I think it's funny. Anyway, yes, we were working on the place. But you know, when a man is working. There's just something about it. He looked so hot..."

"And I wasn't exactly inclined to decline the opportunity," Ryan said.

I smiled. "Like I said, it's fine. But I am here for a reason."

"What's up?" Cassidy asked.

"One of the new vampires claims that years ago, a bokor turned him into a zombie and enslaved him to work his sugar plantation. I haven't spoken to him yet, but have you ever heard of a zombie recovering its soul?"

Cassidy shrugged. "I could make it happen. But my abilities aren't exactly conventional. Most bokors or caplatas can't do anything close to that."

"In addition, it took several years before this patient recovered his soul. He died and was raised as a zombie in the sixties. He didn't totally recover his mind and, presumably, his soul until nearly twenty years after the bokor who enslaved him died. Presuming the story he's told about his experience is true."

Cassidy cocked her head. "That's strange. For me, if I raise a soul and invest it with a body, it's a fairly quick process."

Ryan chuckled under his breath. "This stuff is all so weird."

I smiled. "Welcome to the world of supernaturals, Ryan. We're only scratching the surface."

Ryan shrugged. "In just a couple weeks, I've learned that I'm a werewolf, vampires exist, and magic is real. It shouldn't surprise me to learn that zombies are a thing, too."

"Zombies are nasty," Cassidy said. "Many hougans or mambos who work with the Ghede can raise zombies. I've done it myself, but I never would have if I couldn't also invest the corpse with a genuine soul. Otherwise, they're just rotted corpses. That the bokor forced this patient you're talking about to work as a slave isn't surprising. That's some standard bokor voodoo. Then again, there are some bokors who've devised other methods to raise zombies that don't involve the Loa."

I raised an eyebrow. "Really? Care to explain?"

Cassidy nodded. "There are potions, herbal concoctions that some bokors use to poison someone they hope to enslave. These days, I guess, it wouldn't work. Not with doctors who can better determine if someone's really dead. But I know there are some bokors and caplatas who've done it in the past. Whatever the poison is, it nearly kills the subject, but not completely. The bokor will wait until they bury the body, exhume the person before they totally die, and give them other drugs or potions that keep them in something of a zombie-like state. I'm not saying this happened to the patient you're talking about, but it might fit."

"Because in a case like that, the zombie wouldn't really be a zombie at all. He'd never lose his soul?"

"Right," Cassidy said. "But it might take a lot of time to heal, to recover, and to muster the courage to go back to your family when they all thought you were dead."

"Would someone who was a victim of something like that know what happened? Would they realize someone had drugged rather than zombified them?"

Cassidy shrugged. "I suppose there's no reason they'd know. In that state, they'd be quite pliable, their minds would be aloof. If they were continually being poisoned by the bokor, they'd be oblivious to everything. Then, once the bokor died, the person's body would slowly heal."

"Could it take almost twenty years?"

Cassidy shrugged. "I really don't know. But my parents warned me about this sort of thing. Since I had necromantic abilities, they were concerned that some folks in the voodoo world might associate me with that kind of practice."

I huffed. "Annabelle didn't seem to know anything about all that."

Cassidy shrugged. "As I understand it, Annabelle didn't grow up in Vilokan. She might be Voodoo Queen, but she's only studied the arts for a few years. Some hougans and mambos have studied voodoo their entire lives. I can't say it's shocking that this might be something she wasn't aware of. It's a part of the darker side of the history of voodoo, but it certainly happened, and it's very real."

CHAPTER FIVE

I STOPPED BY RUTHERFORD's desk on my way back to my office at the Vilokan Asylum.

"Did you get Clairvius on my schedule today?"

Rutherford nodded. "He's your last appointment of the day. I've informed him of the change."

I nodded. "Thanks, Rutherford. You're a gem."

Rutherford smirked. "I'm not. Not exactly. But if you'd like to buy me some gems, I won't protest."

I chuckled. "Maybe someday, you know, if whatever this is between us becomes, well, something more serious."

Rutherford smiled. "You want this to be something more than it is?"

I shrugged my shoulders. "Don't you? I mean, I know it's complicated since we work together, but..."

"That's not it, Cain. I'm sure we could make that work. It's complicated for other reasons."

I cocked my head to the side. "What kind of reasons? I'm not sure I understand."

Rutherford took a deep breath and held it a half-second, pressing her lips together before exhaling. "Earlier, you told me you've had more than a hundred and thirty children."

"A hundred and thirty-five," I said. "Each one matters."

Rutherford nodded. "I'm sure they do. But you haven't said a word about their mothers. How many women have you been in love with? How many of them gave you children?"

I cocked my head. "It's not that simple. I've loved before, yes. I've had one-night stands, temporary trysts, and even long-term marriages."

"And were you in love with any of those women?" Rutherford asked.

I nodded. "Of course."

Rutherford sighed. "If I were to be with you, Cain, and open my heart to you, I know that I'd fall hard. You'd be the love of my life. Could you really say the same about me?"

I pinched my chin. "I could certainly fall in love with you."

Rutherford shook her head. "But could I ever be *the* love of your life, Cain? After you've had so many wives and lovers, fathered so many children, and loved so much. If I'm going to fall for someone, if I'm going to find the love of my life, I deserve to be the same to him. I don't know if that's possible for you."

I snorted. "But I don't see why that's an issue, Rutherford. Sure, I've loved before. But it isn't like once I have given my heart to someone, I can't give it to another."

"I don't want a retread romance, Cain. If I'm going to be with you, I want to be your once-in-a-lifetime love. I won't settle for being one of twenty, or ten, or however many women you've loved over the last six thousand years."

"It's not my fault that I've lived so long and loved so often. Don't you think I deserve to have love now, too, even though I've loved before?"

Rutherford nodded. "I do, Cain. But I have high expectations for romance. I am looking for my one and only. Don't you think I also deserve to be loved as much as I love the one who holds my heart?"

I scratched my head. "But you've had relationships before, Rutherford. You took a chance on love before. Why not give this a shot and see where it leads?"

Rutherford reached up from where she was seated and took my hand. "I've never met a man like you, Cain. I can't be with you because I know how I feel. I know how hard I'll fall for you. For me, if I give in to that, it will be a once-in-a-lifetime kind of romance. It's because I can see how easy it would be to love you and because I know you could never fall for me in the same way that I'm not sure this can ever be anything more than it is."

I snorted. "If that's how you feel, and you're still looking for the love of your life, why flirt? Why hook up from time to time? Why lead me on like this?"

Rutherford shook her head. "Because I can't help myself with you, Cain. I want this, but I don't. I have feelings for you and, sometimes, I give in to my desires."

I bit my lip. "Rutherford, if you're going to string me along like this, if we're going to resist our desires ninety percent of the time but give in to our passions the other ten percent of the time, you'll never be able to open yourself up to anyone else."

Rutherford sighed as she placed both her hands flat on her desk. "Then, maybe, we need to stop."

"You can't be serious. You feel what I feel..."

"Which is why we can't keep doing this, Cain. You're right. If I keep giving in and leading you on, I won't ever be able to find what I'm looking for."

I nodded and turned to leave. Then I turned and looked back at Rutherford over her shoulder. "Sometimes, what you're looking for is right in front of you. You're right. I can't deny that I've been in love before. I can't say for certain that I'd ever love you more than those I've loved in the past. But I can say that my feelings were unique each time

I've loved. If I loved you, you'd hold a place in my heart no one ever has."

Rutherford nodded. "A place. One room in a mansion with enough room to love dozens, if not hundreds. But I don't want my own place in your heart, Cain. I want your whole heart."

CHAPTER SIX

I DRAGGED MY FEET back to my office. I understood why Rutherford was reluctant to move forward with our relationship. What could I really say to her to ease her concern? I couldn't deny that I'd loved before. I'd lived full lives with other women, had families with them, and adored some of them with all of my heart. I'd had briefer, thrilling romances that were cut short by death. I'd fallen in love and had my heart broken. After six thousand years, could she really expect that I'd still be waiting for one love, the love of my life? Of course, it wasn't about me. Rutherford didn't begrudge me for loving others in the past. But she only had one life to live. Her unwillingness to pursue our relationship further wasn't about me. It was about her. I just wished there was some way to change her mind. My heart wasn't some kind of hotel with rooms dedicated to others. My heart was and could be a home. Just because others lived there before, as many families often move into previously owned homes, didn't mean I couldn't love her with all of my heart.

I had a few appointments before Clairvius was scheduled to see me. While the new vampires and werewolves had claimed most of my attention as of late, other patients needed attending to.

I dedicated most of my afternoon to them. I had a session with a young Fomorian mermaid who had a fear of drowning. She was a challenging case for obvious reasons. A young mambo, one of Annabelle's former classmates, saw me on an outpatient basis. She possessed the aspect of Erzulie Freida, the Loa of Love. Ellie had cast a spell on a hougan, hoping to win his affections. The spell missed and struck a mirror. Now, Ellie thought she was in love with herself. We'd broken the spell, but the human heart is stubborn. Once it feels affection, even if magic was initially responsible, it's hard to tell it otherwise. My last patient, before I saw Clairvius, was a middle-aged hougan with obsessive-compulsive disorder. Not everyone's condition at the Vilokan Asylum was supernatural or magical. Magically gifted humans, and even supernatural creatures, suffer from common psychological conditions at rates comparable to the average population.

I dismissed the hougan and checked the clock. I had a bad habit of running a little late. Usually, when a patient was scheduled, they'd have to wait five minutes or so before the previous patient left and I was ready. Clairvius wasn't waiting outside my door.

I scanned the hallway. The common room was on the opposite side of the asylum. There wasn't usually any reason for anyone to be in my hall unless they had an appointment with me or had a visitor. The visitation room was just a little further down the hall from my office, near the secured exit to reception.

No one was heading in my direction. I could hear patients carrying on in other parts of the asylum. My hallway, though, was completely empty.

It wasn't entirely shocking. Patients often forgot about their appointments. A new vampire, like Clairvius, was probably so fixated on his blood cravings that it skipped his mind.

I locked my office door and made my way down the hall. The Vilokan Asylum had a unique floor plan. It was arranged like a wheel, several hallways leading off a central hub where the nurses' station was located. Some hallways led to a dead end. At the opposite end from the hub, other hallways joined at the common room, rec room, and cafeteria. The voodoo vampires were all assigned rooms in one of the isolated halls. We reserved those rooms for the more dangerous supernaturals in the asylum. If we had to, we could seal their halls from the rest of the facility. As I made my way around the hub, I found a crowd of the voodoo vampires gathered at the entrance to their designated hallway. Clairvius, however, wasn't among them.

I approached the vampires. "I'm looking for Clairvius. Have any of you seen him?"

One vampire, a broad-shouldered man named Latavius, stepped out from the group. "Clairvius isn't taking visitors."

"Excuse me? I think you're mistaken about how things work here. Clairvius has an appointment with me he's missed."

Latavius stepped toward me again and pushed me gently in the chest. "When he's ready, he'll come to see you. "

I narrowed my eyes. "You'd best mind yourself, son. Remember that I control your blood supply. And if you push me again, well, we could easily activate that sunlight collar around your neck."

Latavius narrowed his eyes as the other voodoo vampires snickered. "You aren't even a member of our community. We owe you no loyalty, Cain."

"I don't expect your loyalty, Latavius. I don't even demand your respect. What I require is compliance with your treatment program. I will not tolerate any effort to thwart another patient's progress. I'm not your enemy here. I'm only here to help you adjust to your new life."

"We don't need to adjust," Latavius snapped back. "This is only temporary."

"Unfortunately, it is not. Until you, all of you, cooperate with your treatment and get a handle on your cravings, the Voodoo Queen will not allow me to discharge you."

"She's not our queen," another of the voodoo vampires, a middle-aged woman named Regina, said. "She's an outsider, like you."

I snorted. I knew some vodouisants in Vilokan weren't thrilled that their former queen, Marie Laveau, had chosen Annabelle as her replacement. I understood their reluctance to a point. Annabelle was an outsider and, more than that, she wasn't exactly an accomplished mambo. Still, Marie Laveau believed Annabelle would grow into her role and had the unique characteristics needed to guide the citizens of Vilokan into the twenty-first century. If these voodoo vampires weren't opposed to Annabelle's rule before, they certainly were now that they'd become vampires.

"This isn't a political matter," I said, doing my best to keep a calm tone. "I do not pretend to be a part of the voodoo world. But I am here for a purpose and I was hired by Marie Laveau, not Annabelle Mulledy. My role here has not changed. I intend to help all of you, but you must cooperate with my efforts. Please, all of you, step aside. I need to see Clairvius."

"He made it clear that you, especially, were not to see him until he was ready," Latavius said.

I narrowed my eyes. "Clairvius is not in charge here. Step aside, or it will mean a day in solitary for all of you."

"First, you intimidate us with sunlight collars. Now you threaten us with punishment?"

I stepped up to Latavius. He was the sort of man, I guessed right away, who responded to a direct approach. "My point is not to threaten you. But trust me, son. I've handled creatures far more threatening than you. Do not underestimate my resolve."

Latavius and Regina exchanged glances.

"It's been long enough," Regina said. "Let Cain pass."

Latavius grunted and stepped aside. I nodded at Regina and pressed past the crowd. Clairvius was in the last room on the left. The crowd of voodoo vampires followed me as I approached his room. I opened the door.

I gasped. Clairvius was lying in his bed. They had torn a bar off his bed rail. It was protruding from Clairvius's chest.

I turned. As a werewolf, even in human form, I ran hot. My blood boiled, sending a wave of heat across my brow. "Who did this! Which one of you staked him!"

"He did it himself," Latavius said.

"He didn't break his bed frame alone. Vampires are strong, but he couldn't rip metal without assistance."

Latavius shrugged. "We worked together and pooled our strength."

"So he could stake himself? Why would he do that?"

Regina stepped up toward Clairvius, touched the make-shift stake, and gripped it. "He has no death wish, Cain. He simply went to where he might find someone who could help. As you know, Cain, when one dies, they go with the Ghede."

I shook my head. "When someone stakes a vampire, they go to vampire hell."

"And that, too, is a domain ruled by the Ghede, Dr. Cain. Clairvius went to hell so that he might appeal to Baron Samedi on our behalf."

Regina yanked the stake out of Clairvius's chest. The older vampire's eyes shot open, and he inhaled a quick breath.

"Did you do it?" Regina asked. "Did you consult with the Baron?"

A wide grin split Clairvius's face. "I've made the arrangements. The Baron will join us shortly."

CHAPTER SEVEN

CLAIRVIUS FOLLOWED ME TO my office without protest. I gestured toward my chaise.

"I'll stand, doctor, if it's all the same to you."

I nodded and, rather than sitting in my chair beside him as I normally would, I leaned my rear against my desk. "I have to say, Clairvius, this might be the first time I've brought a patient to my office, and I'm at a loss for words."

Clairvius cocked his head. "You wish to know why I approached Baron Samedi?"

I shook my head. "I know why you did it. You're hoping he'll make you human again."

Clairvius grinned, flashing his yellowed teeth. "Then you know, Dr. Cain, that our time here will be short. Once the others have recovered their mortality, they'll have no reason to remain in your care."

"How many vampires do you imagine have ever been staked, Clairvius?"

"Thousands. Why do you ask, doctor?"

"Do you imagine, over all that time, not a single one thought to approach Baron Samedi to bargain for their souls?"

Clairvius nodded. "I'm sure many have tried, doctor. But most vampires have very little that might interest the Baron. He already has their souls, after all. What else could they possibly offer?"

"What did you offer him, Clairvius, that no other vampire could?"

"Come now, doctor. I know you are no hougan, so I suppose I might excuse you for your ignorance. But one dare never speak of a bargain one makes with a Loa. It's considered rude."

I folded my hands at my waist. "I've never heard that. But you can confirm that you did, in fact, make a deal with Baron Samedi?"

Clairvius leaned against my door and crossed his legs. Then, with a flick of his wrist, a cigarette appeared in his hand. "Suppose I did."

"Where did you get that?" I asked. "I forbid smoking within the asylum."

Clairvius twirled the cigarette between his long, bony fingers. "Tell me, doctor, what do you know of my history?"

"I have a file on you, Clairvius. I know you claim to have died once before and were later raised as a zombie. Somehow, though, you recovered your mind in the years that followed."

"I did indeed," Clairvius said. "Do you believe my story is true?"

I shrugged my shoulders. "It doesn't matter what I believe. Do you believe it?"

"It is, I admit, strange that a zombie might recover its soul. I suppose some witches could help with that. What is it they are called?"

"Necromancers."

"Yes, necromancers. Funny thing, isn't it, that it was a necromancer who possessed the vampire who bit me? What was her name? Mercy, was it?"

I nodded. "Surely you know the name of the vampire who sired you, Clairvius. Where are you going with all of this?"

"Mercy didn't sire me. Not willingly, at least. I am, more properly, the creation of Delphine LaLaurie, correct?"

"Again, Clairvius, I'm not sure what your point might be. Certainly, LaLaurie was manipulating Mercy, but it was Mercy's bite that turned you into a vampire."

Clairvius chuckled. "How do you think I recovered my soul, doctor? After I was a zombie?"

"Does it matter what I think?"

"Would you flatter an old man's curiosity by wagering a guess? I'm curious what you think might have happened."

I sighed. "Well, there are some drugs I've heard about that some bokors used to use to make someone fall ill, to swoon near the point of death. They then recovered their victims after they were buried, returned them to health, then bound them to work their plantations with other mind-altering substances."

"This was certainly common among bokors of my day, doctor. And I admit, the facts of my case might give anyone other than myself the impression that's exactly what happened."

"What happened, Clairvius? How did you recover your soul?"

Clairvius laughed as he continued twirling his cigarette between his fingers. "It's funny, you know. They say these things will kill you."

"You're avoiding the question, Clairvius. Why is that?"

"I'm not avoiding it, doctor. On the contrary, I'm answering it."

"By discussing the health hazards of nicotine?" I asked, raising an eyebrow.

"Oh, this cigarette contains a lot more than that, doctor. I can assure you, it poses no risk that I do not accept."

"You still never told me how you got a cigarette in here, Clairvius."

"Isn't it obvious? Any hougan or mambo would realize from the start! Did you know that Baron Samedi keeps the souls of those he's collected, all those harvested by the spread of vampirism or taken through unmet bargains, as cigarettes that he carries within a small box on his person?"

"I didn't know that," I said. "That must be a lot of boxes."

Clairvius shrugged. "It's a mystical box of some sort. He can draw any soul he's ever taken from the box at any moment. Were he to agree to return someone their soul, all one would need to do is smoke the cigarette."

"And what you're holding now is your soul? Your cure for vampirism?"

Clairvius laughed. "Oh, he couldn't give me that, doctor. He never acquired my soul. Well, I shouldn't say never. He certainly didn't this time around."

"Would you mind explaining what you mean?"

"Certainly," Clairvius said. "I wasn't made a zombie by the bokor through herbs and spices. It was no potion that made it appear as though I'd died, and no hallucinogenic kept me in such a condition. It was not the bokor's death that allowed me to recover."

"Then enlighten me, Clairvius. Tell me what happened."

Clairvius smiled. "The bokor enslaved my body to work his plantation. This much is true. What the bokor did not know was that my sister had married into the sugar trade. Her husband recognized me on the bokor's plantation. You asked before if I'd entered a bargain with the Baron, correct?"

I nodded. "I did ask you that."

"Well, it was not I who entered a bargain with Baron Samedi, but my sister. He did not own my soul, not like he might if I were a vampire, so her terms to recover my soul and free me from my condition were not so steep as they might be otherwise. After all, the Baron is the guardian of the land of the dead. He recovered my soul and sold it to my sister at a price."

"And what price did she agree to pay?"

"A soul for a soul. If she could find a vampire willing to turn the bokor who enslaved me, the Baron agreed to give her my soul as this very cigarette."

"And you haven't smoked it?" I asked.

"I certainly have, but as is so often the case with the Baron, his bargain with my sister had a catch. He gave my sister my soul. That was what he promised. He did not promise, at all, that what he gave her would contain only my soul."

"So you smoked the cigarette, one puff at a time, gradually recovering your soul?"

"The first time, my sister had to force it to my lips until I inhaled. It worked. But I was not yet myself. I was a shell of who I once was. I was aware, but my thoughts were blurred and unclear. I could move my legs, arms, and the rest of my body. But my movements were sloppy. I had little balance. So, I smoked it again. I gained more control, more focus. But as I did, the cigarette did not disappear. It retained its length, even as it still appears full as if never smoked."

"Due to whatever else the Baron included in the cigarette?"

Clairvius nodded. "Each time I smoke it, something else, besides the soul I'm trying to recover, mingles with my spirit. Over time, I can master it and suppress the influence of the other spirit, the one that the Baron added to the cigarette. But until I finish it, I'll never recover my soul in total. Each time the cigarette restores, whatever is left of my soul that I've yet to require is diluted with the spirit of the other, the one whom the Baron wishes to possess my revived body."

"So you haven't totally recovered your soul?" I asked.

Clairvius shook his head. "The Baron believed that my natural drive, the urge to restore my soul completely, would lead me to finish the cigarette. But once I realized what was happening, I knew I could never finish it. Not if I wanted to keep sole control over my body."

"Sole control?" I asked, trying to suppress a laugh. "That's funny. You know. *Soul* control."

Clairivus furrowed his brow and bit his cheek. "I'm not sure I follow, doctor."

"Nevermind," I said, snorting. "Are you saying that when you became a vampire, the partial soul you'd recovered became the Baron's?"

Clairvius nodded. "But here's the rub, doctor. If I were to finish this cigarette, I'd still gain the spirit that the Baron once hoped to trick me into accepting from the start. There is little I can do for myself. My destiny is sealed. But when I went to the vampiric hell, and I confronted Baron Samedi, I knew I still had something he wanted."

"He wants you to smoke the cigarette and revive whatever spirit it was that he piggy-backed on the cigarette years ago?"

Clairvius nodded. "Which is why I needed to bring this to your attention, doctor. The Baron agreed to trade the souls of the rest of the hougans and mambos who were turned, provided I complete the smoke."

"And when you do that, you'll become someone else?"

Clairvius nodded. "That is why I am here, now, telling you these things. I've had a long life. Each time I regained more of my soul from the cigarette, it rejuvenated my body. I have no intention of remaining a vampire indefinitely. I am ready to move on. I will give my body to the one the Baron hopes to revive in exchange for the restoration of my friends."

"I'm not sure that's a great idea, Clairvius. If we do not know who the Baron hopes to revive in your body, it may be a risk."

"The other hougans and mambos have less faith in you and the Voodoo Queen than I do, doctor. But I believe whoever I should become, you can stop him. You must. This is the only way..."

"Clairvius, I..."

As I started to speak, Clairvius put the cigarette to his lips. The moment it touched his lips, a flame appeared on its tip. I reached for him, hoping to tear the cigarette from Clairvius's hand. When I did, he raised his free hand, and something like a wall of energy formed between him and me. He inhaled, drawing on the entire contents of the cigarette.

Clairvius lowered his hand. When he did, the magical force field he'd established before disappeared. Then Clairvius looked at me, his eyes glowing red.

A swirl of matching red magic spun around him like a tornado. When it dissipated, Clairvius was gone. His body changed. Even his hospital gown was now replaced with what looked like a black tuxedo, complete with a top hat. His face was white, like a skull.

"Well, hello. Fancy seeing you here."

"Who are you?" I asked. "What happened to Clairvius?"

"His soul is free, as agreed. And the rest, well, I suppose I owe them their souls as well. Though, poor Clairvius was not as precise in his verbiage as he should have been when he approached me with his proposal for a bargain."

I stared at the man blankly as his red, glowing eyes met mine. "You're Baron Samedi?"

The Baron smiled, revealing gold-capped teeth. "In the flesh!"

"What are your intentions here, Baron?"

The Baron laughed. "I'd tell you, but then I'd have to kill you."

I narrowed my eyes. "Trust me, you don't want to do that."

"Oh yes, that pesky curse of yours. I'm aware of it, Cain. You've been around long enough. All of us know of you, your curse, and the mark. I cannot say that I am not curious about how your curse might affect me. I'm not human, but this body, this host, certainly is. Alas, it's not worth the hassle. I have all I need, a vessel, a progeny of one of my kind. Ah yes. If Niccolo was my son, and his progeny was my granddaughter, I suppose this new vampire is my great-granddaughter. She shall suffice."

"Stay away from Mel!" I shouted.

The Baron looked at me, cocked his head, retrieved a flask from his cloak, and took a swig. "Make me."

Then, in a cloud of red mist, Baron Samedi disappeared.

Chapter Eight

I searched everywhere. The Baron was gone. Mel was, too. He'd taken her. I had to tell Mercy. Mel was her progeny. She'd engaged in a few dealings with Baron Samedi before. She might have some ideas. I also needed to tell Annabelle. She'd dealt with the Baron several times throughout the years.

This was the first time, in all my centuries, I'd ever encountered him face-to-face. Of course, they did not know him as "Baron Samedi" in every culture. The Hebrews knew him as Abaddon, the destroyer, the angel of the abyss. For the Greeks, he was Apollyon. In Chinese legend, he was Yanlua, ruler of the ten gods of the underworld Diyu. However, for the people of Vilokan and the rest of the voodoo community, he was Baron Samedi, chief among the Ghede Loa.

No matter the myth, or the story, or the name he's given, one truth, like a golden thread woven between every tradition, remains consistent: you don't want to screw with him.

You don't live six thousand years by making a habit out of battling demigods, certainly not one responsible for the realm of the dead.

True to the Baron's word, the other voodoo vampires were human again. Latavius was slapping five with the rest of his cohort as they pressed toward the exits of the asylum, even as I was trying to leave to find Annabelle and Mercy.

"We're leaving," Latavius said. "Let us out of here. We don't need to be here anymore."

I nodded, unclipped my janitor-sized keyring from my belt, and unlocked the heavy metal door that guarded the exits. "If anything happens, anything out of the ordinary, as you adjust, we're always here to help."

Latavius nodded. "Thanks, but we won't need it."

I nodded back. I'd never admit that there were patients in my asylum in the past who I was eager to get out of my hair. Latavius and the former voodoo vampires had tested my commitment to that principle. And really, I'd only spoken to each of them once or twice. I never give up on my patients, but these voodoo vampires weren't at all compliant with our efforts. They were as close to a lost cause as I'd ever treated. Clairvius might have saved them. But what had he unleashed on Vilokan and, perhaps, the rest of the world in exchange? Had he bargained for the lives of a few at the cost of many? It sure seemed that way. The little I know about the Loa, when they enter bargains, the terms tend to skew in their favor. Baron Samedi was like the used car salesman of the voodoo pantheon. What he sells you might look nice and shiny on the outside, but you'd better check under the hood before you sign the papers.

I made eye contact with Rutherford as I left. She'd seen the monitors. Her face was flush of color, her eyes wide when mine met hers. She knew what had happened. It takes a lot to rattle Rutherford. She'd been invested in the world of the magically and mentally deranged longer than me. I mean, aside from being something of a magically deranged individual myself for a good portion of my existence.

I ran to the Voodoo Academy and pressed the button on Annabelle's elevator about a dozen times. It didn't make the damned thing move any faster, but it made me feel like it did.

Usually, the elevator was on the ground floor already when I arrived. The only reason her elevator was ever, well, elevated was if she had a guest.

I wasn't the sort to barge in on a meeting, but this couldn't wait.

Eventually, the elevator made its way back to ground level. The doors parted with a ding. I stepped inside. Hit the "2" button five or six times. The stupid doors didn't get the message and took their time closing. Then, the elevator ascended at a pace comparable to sucking yogurt through a straw.

I heard shouting on the other side of the elevator doors from within Annabelle's office. The sound was too muffled to make out their words, but whoever Annabelle was talking to was pissed.

I banged on the doors.

"Cain, get in here," Annabelle said tersely through the elevator intercom.

The door dinged again and opened.

Mercy stood there, leaning over Annabelle's desk, digging her nails into the wood. Annabelle was in a similar posture on the opposite side.

"She's your progeny, Mercy. If you hadn't pawned her off on us, this never would have happened."

"And it was your hougans and mambos, your vampires, who evoked the Baron's bony ass to begin with!"

"Because you bit them, Mercy!"

"After I was possessed by the same bitch who possessed you first! When I came to save your pretty ass from the shit storm you unleashed on the rest of us."

"I had nothing to do with that!" Annabelle protested.

"You weren't the one who put Cassidy in the asylum, where that murderous ghost could be exorcised from her to begin with?"

"First, I didn't know Cassidy was possessed! Second, Cassidy is your relative, Mercy. And she's doing well now. Would you prefer she stayed possessed by that ghost indefinitely?"

I cleared my throat. "I presume you all figured out what happened already? I was coming to tell both of you..."

"Yeah, we know," Mercy said, glancing at me over her shoulder. "I came here, as soon as the sun set, to check on my progeny, only to be greeted at the door by the fucking Baron, who had Mel enthralled in his spell."

I cocked my head. "As a vampire, don't you revere the Baron?"

Mercy snorted. "I tolerate him. I have no choice in that matter. I revere him in the same sense someone might respect their dickhead of a boss. They do what he says, when they must, to get him out of their hair. But most of the time, they try to avoid him so they can do their job without dealing with all his bullshit."

"What color were his eyes?" Annabelle asked. "Were they red or green?"

"Red!" Mercy and I said in concert.

I nodded. "Bright red, the moment he took over Clairvius's body."

Annabelle contorted her face in disgust. "The Baron has two aspects. When he emerges in his green persona, he's a benevolent Loa. In the past, the Green Baron has taught here at the Voodoo Academy. He's a beloved figure. But when he's evoked in fear, or out of desperation, he emerges as the Red Baron."

Mercy chuckled. "Like cheap frozen pizza?"

Annabelle narrowed her eyes. "Like a fucking plague, Mercy. He might be red, but as the Red Baron, he's like the Black Death. His motive as the Red Baron is to acquire more power and to wield it to wreak havoc, to unleash death and destruction on a massive scale. The more who die at his hand, as he absorbs their souls, the stronger he'll become."

"Then we'd best kick his red cherry ass before he hurts anyone else," Mercy said.

Annabelle shook her head. "You can try, Mercy. But I don't think he's the sort who ever gets his ass kicked. He's the one who does all the ass kicking."

"Then how can we stop him?" I asked.

"I've faced the Red Baron before," Annabelle said. "If we can draw the Green Baron out of him, bring out his more benevolent side, then his darker, evil side will go dormant."

"Then what can we do to awaken his green aspect?" I asked.

Annabelle sighed. "The Red Baron is fueled by fear. He kills and collects souls because the more he does, the more he can draw on the fear of those he kills. He can use the fear he evokes in those he terrifies to gain strength. The only way to counter that is with courage and kindness."

Mercy snorted. "You want to kill him with kindness? You've got to be fucking kidding me."

"Language, ladies," I said. "Fighting amongst ourselves won't help."

"Shut up, Cain," Mercy said. "I will not tame my goddamn tongue for you or anyone else."

I pinched my chin, ignoring Mercy's chastisement. "When someone is looking for power, it isn't usually because they like the way it feels. People seek power so they can use it."

Annabelle nodded. "That's always been the Baron's goal. The Red Baron's, at least. For years, in fact, he tried to acquire Isabelle's soul so that he might use her power to lay claim over Guinee. To expand his rule beyond the realm of the dead."

"Why would he enthrall a youngling like Mel? So far as vampires go, she's hardly the most powerful one he might claim."

"But she's easily impressionable," Mercy said. "Older vampires, like me, are more resistant to the Baron's influence."

"The Baron will harm no one directly. He cannot. If he did, the other Loa would rally against him to bind him. So long as he works through a proxy, through a vampire like Mel, he can use her to strike fear in people's hearts, to kill and claim souls, and grow in power."

"Wait," I said. "Your boyfriend is a Loa, is he not, Annabelle?"

Annabelle nodded. "I will speak to Ogoun and see if he might help. But Oggie is the Loa of War. He can help battle the Baron, to fight against whoever he might use Mel to turn and enthrall, but he cannot bind the Baron alone. Nor will he be of much use to evoke the Green Baron."

"No one stakes Mel," Mercy said. "She's my progeny. I gave her my word I would protect her."

"I agree, we must save her."

Annabelle nodded. "Eliminating her would slow the Baron down. But that's all it would accomplish. He'd find another vampire to enthrall in her stead. Presuming, of course, he can find another youngling to claim. And if I were a betting girl, I'd gamble he's using her to create more younglings, even as we speak. It won't matter if we take one or two out when he does. He'll still have plenty of others to use."

Mercy sighed. "And he'll expose our existence to the world. Once humanity comes to terms with the reality of vampires, there's no telling how things will go for me and my kind."

"It will cause a wave of fear unprecedented in history," I said.

Annabelle nodded. "And he'll use that fear to grow more powerful. When he's reached his apex of power, he'll return to Guinee and attempt to lay siege to the Tree of Life, to the garden groves, to the power of life itself."

"He'll destroy Eden," I said. "If the Tree of Life falls, there will only be one tree left to influence humanity. The one that my parents were first tempted to eat from, the Tree of the Knowledge of Good and Evil."

Annabelle nodded. "In Voodoo we value balance. We respect the balance of light and dark, of good and evil. As a Catholic, too, I know that there is a tension between the corruption of evil, call it sin if you like, and goodness or righteousness."

I nodded. "If the balance is tipped away from the light, away from goodness and righteousness, darkness and evil will overwhelm all of mankind."

Mercy snorted. "Well, that sounds like some kind of shit show I'd rather not buy tickets to see."

Annabelle sighed. "What's at stake here is not just Mel, the reputation of vampires, or the safety of Vilokan and New Orleans. It's the future of all humanity that hangs in the balance."

CHAPTER NINE

OUR PRIORITY WAS TO survive the night. Once we did, we could try to track down the Baron and Annabelle could do whatever voodoo she needed to turn him green. We had to rally as many forces as we could. So far as we knew, the only weapon that Baron Samedi had claimed was Mel. We couldn't rule out the possibility that he'd found and claimed more younglings or that he'd used Mel to turn others.

One vampire who lived with Mercy at Casa do Diabo, Sarah, had gained over the years a vampiric gift that allowed her to track and communicate with other vampires. She was, perhaps, the only vampire in New Orleans who was older than Mercy. In fact, Sarah was there in Exter, Rhode Island, when Mercy was turned. She didn't do it herself. But she saw it when Mercy rose from her grave. After her family thought she'd died. Most older vampires had a few unique abilities. When they fed, drawing on the power latent in human souls, different powers sometimes manifested. Mercy could compel people—-a power she refused to use most of the time. Some vampires could shift into bats. Others could turn invisible.

According to our plan, Mercy was going to use Sarah's gift to track any vampire younglings in the city. She and a few other vampires would do what they could to prevent the Baron from claiming more younglings. More than that, though, if Sarah could track Mel, we could focus our efforts wherever she was located and hopefully prevent her from biting anyone else.

Annabelle planned to find Ogoun, the Loa of War, so they could also fend off the Baron. Ogoun couldn't bind the Baron or send him back to Guinee, but he could keep him distracted. If the Baron had to fight the Loa of War, well, that meant he couldn't terrorize the city.

Then, my plan was to rally the pack. Vampires are averse to werewolf bites. Julie could evoke the flambeau and force us to shift. She'd shift with us since she was one of us now. The problem was that we couldn't enter the city as wolves. We could chase any vampire younglings that Sarah identified within the city away.

There was one challenge to all of this. We had to communicate, and I didn't use a smartphone. Annabelle and Mercy could text back and forth. Mercy probably wouldn't text herself. Instead, she'd rely on Hailey, another young vampire, who was much more technologically savvy than Mercy, to handle her communications.

Ryan could handle the communications for the pack. We couldn't text back and forth. Wolf paws aren't great on touch screens. But Ryan could carry his phone with him and show me the messages.

That was the plan Annabelle, Mercy, and I cooked up on the fly. They garnished the plan with a few f-bombs and "screw you, Annabelles" coming from Mercy, but all in all, I was pleased we managed to come up with a viable strategy.

Since it was already after dark, we had little time to waste. Annabelle and Mercy went their respective ways. I left for the Mulledy plantation, aka the Vilokan Asylum satellite, to rally the pack.

I was supposed to meet the pack for a group therapy session. When I arrived, the pack was already gathered in what used to be Annabelle's living room. They had several rectangular tables set up with folding chairs all around. I could smell the cheap coffee roasting as I walked through the door.

I was late for our group therapy session. The situation with Clairvius, the Baron, and the subsequent meeting with Annabelle and Mercy set me behind schedule.

I was pleased to see Donald sitting at the head of the table leading the discussion when I showed up.

The new wolves were introducing themselves, sharing their histories with the group. Given all that had happened, I hadn't even learned all their names. I'd only had a few words with them. It was a problem I needed to correct. We only had a few weeks until the next full moon. Of course, if the Baron succeeded, there was no telling what the situation would be by that time. If he unleashed hell on the city, and we couldn't stop him, a pack of untamed wolves would be the least the citizens of New Orleans would have to worry about.

"Hello, everyone," I said, stepping up to the table. "Apologies for my tardiness, and I didn't mean to interrupt, but we have a situation."

"What's going on, Cain?" Donald asked.

"First, I'm glad you all started without me. We're going to have to shift tonight. I hope if anyone has any burdens that need to be addressed, that you've shared them with the pack."

"We're shifting tonight?" Christopher asked. "It's not a full moon."

"Julie," I said. "We'll need you to carry the flambeau."

"Certainly, doctor. But why?"

"One of the voodoo vampires has evoked Baron Samedi. For those of you who do not know, the Baron is a Loa. He governs the realm of the dead. He's emerged in his red form, his darker aspect, and he's claimed a youngling vampire who he hopes to use to unleash hell on the city."

Christopher smirked. "Vampire hunting. I'm down for that."

"Hell yeah!" Andrew added.

I shook my head. "We cannot harm the vampire. She's Mercy Brown's progeny and one of my patients. The Baron is manipulating her."

"Why is he doing that?" Cassidy asked.

"The Baron can only control younglings. He has an influence that older vampires are more likely to resist. The younglings, though, are vulnerable. I've spoken with Annabelle Mulledy, the Voodoo Queen, and Mercy Brown, the chief mistress of the Vampire Council. They're going to help us, but we all have to work together. We believe the Baron intends to use the youngling that he's enthralled to create more vampires he can easily manipulate."

"What's his endgame?" Donald asked.

"The Red Baron feeds on fear. The more fear he can spread, the stronger he becomes. And if he gains enough power, he has designs on corrupting the entire human race."

"Damn," Christopher said. "He sounds like a real dickhead."

"Christopher!" Evie said, backhanding Christopher on the shoulder.

"What? He does!"

I nodded. "It's true. Though I might choose a less colorful term to describe Baron Samedi's intentions, Christopher's assessment is not far off. Our goal is not to hunt any vampires but to find any younglings, even if it is Mel, Mercy's progeny, and prevent them from turning anyone. We don't have to hold them off forever. Just until sunrise."

"And then what?" Donald asked. "Take a break while the vampires are sleeping? Rinse and repeat tomorrow?"

I sighed. "I hope to stop the Baron, somehow, before tomorrow night. Once the Baron learns our strategy, he'll likely counter it somehow. I'd rather not play a game of chess with a demigod when lives are at stake."

Christopher grunted. "That word 'somehow' doesn't exactly represent a foolproof strategy."

I nodded. "You're right. But I'm not the only one working on this. Between Annabelle's efforts, Mercy's, and mine, I'm confident we will figure out a way to stop him before the next sunset."

CHAPTER TEN

THE WOLVES FROM ABEL'S pack said little. They were still adjusting to the fact that they were wolves. Their connection to the pack was still loose. It seemed they connected to Donald and the rest more thoroughly when I was there. They still hadn't totally submitted to Donald's leadership, though. Not like the rest. When a pack loses its alpha—and they'd all been turned and led by Abel—it can take some time for the orphaned wolves to forge a bond to another pack. Add to all those adjustments, now I was telling the new wolves that they needed to use their gift to thwart the nefarious plans of a voodoo demigod. If I were in their shoes—though they wouldn't be wearing shoes for much longer—I'd be speechless, as well.

I was anxious about how well I'd be able to keep control over a pack this large. The rougarou were a pack of only five. They had spent years together as wolves and were bonded. While integrated into the pack, these other wolves didn't have the same deep-seated connection to the pack or to one another. Still, I didn't think it was wise to leave them behind. It would be counterproductive to their progress and their assimilation into the pack. When the pack was on the prowl, we could leave no wolf behind.

We gathered outside to shift. After all the work the pack had done to renovate the place, well, if we shifted inside, chances were better than not we'd do a lot of damage to the place. The downside, of course, to shifting outside was that we had to strip down first. Provided we didn't want to ruin our clothes.

The original rougarou took off their clothes as if it was no big deal at all. The younger wolves—Cassidy, Ryan, Julie, and Abel's former pack—were a little more hesitant. A couple of them went and hid around the corner of the house. One of them ducked down behind my truck. Outdoor nudity was something that took some getting used to.

Even my parents, I remember, used to talk about how they once frolicked through Eden with no shame at all. The more they told that story, the more grateful I was that they'd agreed to the serpent's temptation. I mean, if I'd been raised in the garden, I'd have had to see my mom and dad naked constantly. My former mentor, Freud, would have had a field day with that experience if it had played out in my childhood. Siggy believed the Oedipus complex was an integral part of the developing mind. It was one of few components of his theory that I differed with. I don't know how many times I had to tell him that, despite his instance, I was never attracted to my mother. She was a pretty lady, but she was my mom, for Pete's sake! Yuck!

The long and the short of it—alright, I get that's not a great phrase to use when you're talking about naked dudes walking around outside—was that I understood why some of the new wolves were reluctant to strip in front of the pack. They'd get used to it, eventually. We all did.

Ryan grabbed his phone. I gave him Annabelle's and Mercy's numbers. He sent them each a text so they'd have his number. Then he removed one of his shoelaces and tied one end around his phone as tightly as he could. We tied it in a slipknot around his wrist. That way, the loop would expand when his body changed. It was preferable to trying to carry his phone with his mouth. A werewolf's rear paws are like standard but oversized canine paws. The front paws are something like a hybrid between a paw and a hand. We could do a few things with our front paws. We could turn a doorknob, for instance. We could pick up larger objects. Smaller items, well, it was a pain in the butt to grip smaller, delicate things. Still, our front hand-paws lacked the dexterity to effectively operate a smartphone, and our furry fingers couldn't operate touch screens. This was the best option we could come up with.

No sooner did we get the phone fastened to Ryan's wrist, and the device dinged.

"Looks like Mercy replied," Ryan said. "She has a GPS location."

I bit my lip. "On a map?"

Ryan nodded. "I could bring it up on a map and it would give us directions."

Ryan showed me his phone. He'd already clicked whatever link Mercy sent. Because it was a link, I imagined it was actually Hailey using Mercy's phone. I didn't know how to make links. Hell, I wasn't even sure how to turn one of those touch-screen contraptions on. Mercy was only marginally savvier than me when using new-fangled technologies.

I grunted when I noted the location. "This makes no sense," I announced.

"What's the deal?" Donald asked.

I shook my head. "She's at the edge of Manchac Swamp."

Donald snorted. "Why the hell would the Baron send the vampire there?"

I sighed. "Beats me. Vilokan empties into Jackson Square in the French Quarter. There are many people there. If the Baron wanted to unleash a youngling like Mel on large numbers of people and evoke palpable quantities of fear, he could have stayed there. Not to mention, there aren't very many people in the swamp at all."

Donald shrugged his shoulders. "Maybe that was too predictable? I mean, since it's close to Vilokan, it's also close to the voodoo population. Are there hougans or mambos who might control the Baron somehow?"

"I really don't know. That's not my expertise. Though, I suppose, it might make sense that he'd try to avoid Annabelle. She's faced him before. She insists she knows how to suppress the Red Baron and evoke the Green Baron."

Donald shook his head. "It's still strange that he'd choose our swamp, of all places. There won't be many people there if any, this time of night."

"It's impossible to know what the Baron is doing unless we go there and see for ourselves," I said. "Perhaps he's already forced Mel to bite and drain several people, and he's removed them from the city so he can revive them. We just don't know. Still, we need to go for her. If by chance she has bitten no one yet, if we can keep her in the swamp all night and hold the Baron at bay, we can regroup in the morning and try to sort out what happened."

"Wouldn't it be less risky to shift once we're closer to the swamp?" Christopher asked.

I bit the inside of my cheek. "Yes, and no. I mean, it would minimize the risk of being seen. But we aren't getting regular updates. Vampires can move fast, even younglings. By the time we arrive, we need to be ready."

"It's not too far from here anyway," Donald said. "And thankfully, we'll be able to avoid the busiest parts of the city to get there."

I nodded. "Alright, everyone. Remember to stay close. My influence should be able to keep your worst urges in check so long as you're close by. Do a few stretches to loosen up your joints. We don't have time for a full yoga routine to prepare."

Each of the young wolves nodded their agreement. A few bent over to touch their toes. Some of them stretched their quads, attempting to stand on one foot while holding the heels of their opposite feet to their corresponding butt cheeks. It wasn't the best pre-shift routine, but we didn't have time to loosen up the body. The shift would hurt, especially for the young wolves, but the pain would quickly pass once the thrill of the wolf set in.

I nodded at Julie. She took the hint and extended her hand. The Witch of Endor's flambeau formed in her hand, hellfire blasting from its apex. The heat of the flambeau radiated from the infernal relic as our bodies shifted. Our bones popped. Our skin burned as our fur grew from our pores. When the shift was complete, we howled at the waning moon.

We took off in a tight formation toward the location on the edge of Manchac Swamp, where Mercy had said we'd find Mel. If Mel fled into the swamp, we'd have a major advantage. The rougarou, the original part of the pack, had lived in that swamp for more than a century. They knew every rock and tree. They knew each spot where gators were likely hiding in the waters.

We ran as fast as we could. The younger wolves still weren't as fast as some of us, but they did better than I expected.

We arrived at the edge of Manchac Swamp. I could see Mel's eyes, glowing red, as we approached. Vampires have red irises. The glow, though, was new. It must've been on account of the Baron's thrall. Mel wasn't at the edge of the swamp any longer. When she spotted us, she turned and ran.

She wasn't acting of her own volition. The Baron controlled her every movement. Why would he send her directly into such a familiar place? The rougarou, at least, weren't afraid here. They were at home.

Even the new wolves appeared invigorated as we took off through the swamp, the waters splashing around us.

Could it really be this easy? The Baron had Mel running deeper into the swamp, further from the city than before. If this was all we had to do, keeping her in the swamp until morning wouldn't be a tremendous problem. We had the numbers that we could easily surround her and ensure she didn't escape.

She lured us to the small hill where the pack often gathered. It was where Julie Brown, now one of us, and the other wolves once guarded the Witch of Endor's flambeau.

Mel turned toward us and smirked. The glow from her eyes exploded into a blast of red energy that enveloped her body and the hill on which she stood.

Mel raised her arms over her head. When she did, the ground beneath her feet cracked. Then, figures emerged from under the surface. Figures of bone and rotted flesh.

The Baron was using Mel to raise zombies, corpses buried in the swamp for more than a century.

The Baron didn't waste any time. These weren't slow-moving, drag-your-withered-limb-behind-you zombies. The Baron's power invigorated them. No sooner did they take foot on the hill than they charged after us snarling.

I hadn't dealt with zombies before. They weren't candidates for my treatment program since they don't have souls or functioning brains at all—apart from those they eat. Still, I'd had more than a few patients through the years who *had* fought zombies. What I knew was that you didn't want to get bitten. Could their teeth penetrate our thick hides? I didn't know, and it did not incline me to find out.

We werewolves didn't speak in words. But as their alpha, I could exert my will over them. I could send them messages, and, usually, they'd pick up on the gist of it.

Don't let them bite you! Take off their heads!

All that came out was a growl. The pack appeared to respond. The zombies outnumbered us, probably three-to-one, but they weren't any match for werewolves.

A zombie dove at me. With a snarl, I bit its head clean off. The zombie's body collapsed, splashing in the water.

The rest of the rougarou were handling them just as effectively. It was a slaughter if you could call it that. These monsters were already dead, after all.

Cassidy, Ryan, and Julie also fought well at my side. Julie, holding her flambeau in her jaws, blasted one of them with hellfire. When the smoke cleared, the zombie was gone, burned up in a second.

Brilliant, I thought. *This shouldn't take long.*

The other young wolves, who belonged to Abel's pack before, were more reluctant to fight. They took a few steps back. They were afraid.

Don't show fear! It will give the Baron more power!

The young wolves didn't respond. Did they get the message at all?

Instead, they took a few steps back while the rest of us tore through the zombies. Something clenched down on my leg. A dull pain followed. I shook my leg. A zombie was trying to bite me. Would he inherit the sevenfold curse? Probably not. He didn't have a soul.

I shook my leg, sending the zombie flying, then I dove on him, holding him under the water as I grabbed its skull with my jaws and ripped it off its neck.

I checked my leg. He didn't draw any blood. If the Baron thought he'd use Mel to trap us in the swamp, to use these zombies to take us out, then I suppose Baron Samedi wasn't as smart as I'd assumed. The zombies didn't stand a chance.

There were only a few left. Donald and Christopher teamed up and tore them apart.

Then a red glow shone across the swamp. Mel was still standing atop the hill, but her eyes no longer glowed as before. The Baron had released her. Now, she was huddled over her knees, shaking in fear. So much fear. So much terror. Not just from Mel, but from the young wolves, too. We were giving the Baron exactly what he wanted.

I turned to find the source of the glow.

I heard a howl.

Baron Samedi approached us, walking across the swamp waters. Something like a chain of red energies formed a leash that he'd connected to a wolf.

Was it one of my own? One of the new wolves? I couldn't tell. I didn't notice any of the wolves missing. If it wasn't one of our wolves that the Baron had leashed... who could it be? Where on God's green earth had he found another werewolf that I didn't know about?

Then the wolf's eyes, glowing red as Mel's had before, roared.

The new wolves rallied around the Baron and his wolf. The Baron's red magic expanded, enveloping all of them. I snarled at them. I reared up on my hindquarters and roared as loud as I could, attempting to reassert my dominance. Why weren't the young wolves responding to me? I should have been able to rein them in...

Then the Baron's leashed wolf stepped into the light cast by Julie's flambeau. His fur was golden colored but caked in mud.

It was Abel. At least it had been. It was the body that Abel possessed before.

The Baron had raised my brother. He must've gone to the plantation after we left. We'd buried Abel there after he died. He raised my brother, then he followed us, using Mel as bait to lure us here to the swamp. The Baron enslaved Abel as a zombie.

I roared again. Could a zombified werewolf really exert control as alpha over a pack? In six thousand years, I'd seen nothing like it. The werewolf curse wouldn't affect a dead body alone. But Abel had died,

238

and the Baron could draw souls from the otherworld. He could infuse them into a corpse, enslaving them to his will. Now, the Baron was using Abel to take control of my brother's former pack.

I released a low-pitched growl. For more than six thousand years, my brother had rested in peace. Now, in the span of a single month, he'd been forcibly resurrected twice, enthralled by nefarious characters, and forced to kill. It wasn't right. I wouldn't stand for it.

We're going to have to fight. Be ready...

The rougarou, along with Ryan, Cassidy, and Julie, rallied around me. All of us snarled at the other wolves together. We were about to pounce, to do whatever we had to do to wrestle the wolves away from the Baron...

Then, the Baron tipped his hat. With a blast of red magic, he invigorated his wolves, and they took off together in a blur, running so fast we didn't stand a chance to keep up with them.

The Baron was leading the wolves into the city. His plan wasn't to use vampires to evoke fear in the French Quarter. He could only use *them* at night. But with werewolves, if he could use his power to bind them to their werewolf form, he wouldn't be dissuaded by the rising sun.

CHAPTER ELEVEN

I NUZZLED MEL WITH my snout. She was back to herself. She was still vulnerable, though. If the Baron needed to use her again, he'd certainly try. But now that we knew what he was up to, he wouldn't take us off guard again. I pawed at my neck, hoping my gesture would communicate my intentions. Mel nodded and climbed aboard my back. She took two fistfuls of fur to maintain her balance. While not as painful as you'd think, it's hard to describe having your hair pulled as anything close to comfortable.

I couldn't remember the last time I allowed someone to ride me. You can't domesticate werewolves. While I ran faster on all fours, given my druthers, I preferred to remain standing on my hindquarters while shifted. Annabelle never showed up with Ogoun. Mercy hadn't arrived yet with any vampire backup.

Not until *after* the Baron absconded with half of my pack and my brother's twice-resurrected corpse.

"You got her!" Mercy interjected as she approached, with Sarah and Hailey alongside her. Sarah was older than Mercy in vampiric years, and she was also turned at an older human age. She wasn't old, by any means. She was probably just shy of thirty when she became a vampire, though I'd never asked her. I'm not always the best judge of age. Hailey, however, hadn't been a vampire much longer than Annabelle had been the Voodoo Queen. She was also young when she was turned. She was a pretty girl with long blond curls. Hailey and Mercy were both witches, besides being vampires. While Mercy trumped Hailey in terms of her prowess as a vampire, Hailey was the superior witch.

I wasn't sure what either of them could do to help take down the Baron, but given how the situation had escalated, we needed all the help we could get.

I didn't have time to waste. I couldn't leave Mel there in the swamp, shivering and frightened. Now that Mercy was here, though, she could take care of her. At least for the night. The problem? If I asked Julie to extinguish the flambeau so I could explain to Mercy what had happened, we wouldn't be able to shift back with the same vigor. The shifting process takes a lot of energy. We couldn't risk losing any strength if we hoped to stop the Baron from manipulating Abel and his pack from terrorizing the city. Ryan's phone dinged. Mercy's did, too. Hailey grabbed Mercy's phone right out of her back pocket.

"It's Annabelle," Hailey said. "The Baron has wolves now?"

I nodded.

"Damn, Cain. I'd say you screwed the pooch, but I've already used that joke on you. I need to come up with some original way to say you fucked up."

I grunted. I didn't like it when she cussed, and she knew it. Not that I was some sort of pious prude or anything. I was just old-fashioned. Still, Mercy wasn't the sort to hold back or censor herself to spare someone offense. She was who she was. Love her or hate her.

"Annabelle has Oggie, Pauli, and Sauron," Hailey said. "They're hoping to stop him. They could use a little backup. Their goal is to stop them from getting into the French Quarter."

Mercy looked at me. "Go, Cain. We'll catch up with you."

I nodded, howled to rally the pack, and took off. Ogoun, aka "Og-gie," was a formidable counter to the Baron. He could best the Baron in a one-on-one combat situation, but he didn't have the power to banish the Baron or thwart him permanently. Pauli was a young hougan, one of Annabelle's former classmates at the Voodoo Academy. He had the aspect of Aida-Wedo, the Loa of snakes and rainbows. Pauli was a shapeshifter, and he could teleport. He also had a flair for style. Sauron was a mambo, also one of Annabelle's classmates. She held the aspect of Sogbo, the Loa of storms. Based on the dark cloud I saw situated right over the French Quarter, I suspected she was already doing her thing. The best way to prevent the Baron from terrorizing the people in the quarter was to rain them out. If the weather outside was frightful, well, a good storm wouldn't be as horrific as a pack of enslaved wolves doing their worst. It would drive people indoors. A brilliant move. It gave us a chance to pull this battle off without being seen.

We ran hard and fast. I'd never seen the pack move with such vigor. Even Cassidy, Ryan, and Julie, who were just pups, kept up as we zeroed in on the French Quarter.

Annabelle and her friends were already facing off with the Baron, Abel, and the rest of the wolves.

We united in a semi-circle behind them and had them surrounded.

Ogoun approached Baron Samedi. Many of the Loa had human hosts who'd given themselves to the Loa willingly. Usually, they were hougans or mambos on their deathbeds, who dedicated their bodies to the service of the Loa in death. It wasn't unlike how Clairvius had given his body to the Baron. The host that Oggie had claimed, while not the most intimidating vessel I'd ever seen the Loa of War inhabit, was still an imposing figure. He stood a full head taller than the Baron with long, chocolate hair cascading down his back.

"Back off, Samedi," Oggie said, staring down the Baron.

Baron Samedi laughed. "Oggie, how many times must we go through this charade? You may overpower me in the flesh, but your power pales compared to mine."

"Would you like to test that, Samedi? I'm not facing you alone this time. You have nowhere to run."

The Baron shrugged. "If you haven't noticed, I'm not facing you alone, either. Do you think Cain has what it takes to slay his brother a second time? Or is it a third time? From what I know, he's died in his brother's arms twice now."

I snarled at the Baron from behind his position. He snapped his fingers and Abel turned and stepped between us. His eyes, aglow with the Baron's red magic, showed me all I needed to know. He wasn't in control. He didn't want to hurt me or anyone else. But he couldn't stop himself, either. And it frightened him.

Fear...

Had the Baron raised Abel to frighten others? Perhaps the Baron's plan was to use my brother as well of power, a fear factory of a sort. The Baron could draw on my brother's fear and use it.

I narrowed my eyes. *Take courage, brother. Your fear is his strength...*

Abel wasn't a part of my pack. Even when I sent such messages to my pack, they didn't hear every word. They received impressions, urges that they'd follow. I could only hope that something of my message got through. But Abel's expression didn't change.

Oggie took two steps back. "I can restrain you. That's all I need to do. Annabelle will send you back to Guinee if that's what it takes. If you will not go willingly."

Baron Samedi straightened his top hat on his head. "I'll go when I'm ready."

Oggie retrieved a flask from his back pocket. He poured some of its contents, whiskey or rum, most likely, between his feet. Then, with a snap of his fingers, he lit the booze on fire. An impressive feat, especially since it was raining hard all around us. Whatever power fueled Oggie's fire magic must've been resistant to water. The flames blasted from the puddle of rum, tickling Oggie's thighs.

Oggie smirked. "My testicles were cold."

"Cain!" Annabelle shouted. "Hold him there! Make sure he doesn't run!"

I howled back at her.

"Pauli! Now!" Annabelle shouted.

A split second later, with a flash of rainbow-colored light, Pauli took the form of a snake, its scales matching the colors of his magic, and he wrapped himself around Abel. In another rainbow-colored flash, Pauli and Abel disappeared. Where Pauli had taken my brother, I wasn't sure.

But with Abel gone, I had an opportunity. I released a roar. The other young wolves from Abel's pack turned and lowered their heads in submission.

"No!" the Baron shouted.

Oggie swung his arms through the air. The flames he'd evoked blasted toward the Baron.

Baron Samedi laughed as the flames charred his skin. "Nice try, Oggie!!"

"Beli!" Annabelle shouted, green magic pulsing in her eyes as she charged the Baron. Annabelle's soul blade formed in her hand. She lunged at Baron Samedi.

With a single jab, she'd send him back to Guinee.

Annabelle's blade struck nothing but a red mist as the Baron disappeared.

"Damn it!" Annabelle shouted. "I thought your flames would hold him, Oggie!"

Oggie shook his head. "He's too powerful. He's siphoned too much fear."

Annabelle turned to Julie. "Release the flambeau."

I winced. When she did that, we'd become human again. And we'd be naked. But that was the least of our worries. It was raining over us, after all.

Present company excluded. No one else would likely see us.

Julie released the flambeau, and we returned to human form. The young wolves collapsed over their naked bodies, shaking in fright.

"That's the power he used. The fear he evoked in Abel and his pack. That's why he resisted your flames, Oggie."

The Loa nodded. "I think you're right."

"Wait," Annabelle said. "Look! He's moving toward the cathedral..."

"He's not going for the cathedral," I said. "The cathedral is to the southeast of the direction he's moving. He's heading for St. Louis Cemetery No. 1. He's going to raise the dead."

Annabelle shook her head. "There aren't a lot of things more frightening than a pack of wolves terrorizing the French Quarter. A zombie uprising just might be one of them."

Pauli returned in a flash of rainbow-colored magic.

"Did you take care of it?" Annabelle asked.

Pauli nodded and looked at me. "Your brother is back at the asylum. He's human again. Totally naked. But I didn't mind."

I chuckled, "I'm sure you didn't, Pauli."

"He's well hung! And from the looks of it, girth runs in the family."

I snorted. "I'm going to pretend I didn't hear you say that."

Annabelle shook her head. "This isn't the time, Pauli. We have bigger issues on our hands."

Pauli smirked. "How much bigger could it get?"

Cassidy giggled from behind me. I turned and narrowed my eyes.

"Sorry. It was pretty funny."

"Can we get to the cemetery in time to stop him?" I asked.

Annabelle shook her head. "He's too fast. We'll have to focus on containing it. Sauron, can you turn up the intensity a bit? We need to keep everyone inside as long as possible."

Sauron, who'd been channeling a sort of golden magic from her hands into the skies, nodded her head. "I can do that. Once I get the tempest raging, it'll keep going until I cancel it."

"Good," Annabelle said. "That's helpful. We're going to need more hougans and mambos, those trained in the ways of the Ghede, to harness the zombies that the Baron's raising as we speak."

"And you need to get inside. This is about to get pretty nasty," Sauron said.

"Pauli," Annabelle said. "Head back to the asylum and grab a bunch of gowns. For the wolves."

Pauli shook his head. "You're always trying to spoil all my fun!"

Annabelle rolled her eyes as Pauli disappeared again. "He'll meet us just inside Vilokan. We need to take cover. The storm should prevent the Baron from unleashing the zombies. But it might also work against us."

"If the storm frightens people?" I asked.

Annabelle nodded. "The intensity that Sauron will need to evoke to both scare people inside and to make it too difficult for the zombies to move through the quarter will probably make the Baron more powerful."

"No storm is more frightening than zombies," I said. "This is probably the best option."

Annabelle nodded. "The lesser of two evils. But it's what we have to work with right now."

CHAPTER TWELVE

I HURRIED BACK TO the asylum in Vilokan. Annabelle intended to meet up with Mercy and the other vampires. I wasn't sure if Mercy would bring Mel back to the asylum or not. Technically, Mel was only in my care as a favor to Mercy. Given the fact that Mel was temporarily possessed by Baron Samedi while in my care, I suppose I couldn't fault Mercy if she insisted on taking over Mel's bloodlust taming herself. In truth, it was better that way. I'd developed a method to help vampires adjust to situations similar to the one we'd faced with the voodoo vampires. Hailey's sire, for instance, was staked just moments after she was turned. It's not an altogether uncommon occurrence that a youngling might be orphaned by their sire. In the past, such younglings usually lost control and went on a tear that ended at the sharp end of a stake. A hunter or slayer might take down an untamed, feral youngling. More often, though, it was another vampire, concerned the youngling posed a liability to other vampires, who intervened to end the youngling's existence.

The rest of the wolves joined us as well. With the storm brewing and the Baron still out there, we didn't want to send them back to the satellite campus. So, they joined me at the asylum. With the recent discharge of the voodoo vampires, since they weren't vampires anymore, we had a little extra space. It wasn't a permanent arrangement, and we weren't committing them to my inpatient program. Still, I had been working with them already at the satellite campus. Until we had a plan, a strategy to take down the Baron, and Sauron quelled the storm, the least we could do was offer the wolves shelter.

Before I dealt with any of that, though, I had to see my brother.

"Where is he?" I asked Rutherford as I approached her desk.

"He's already waiting in your office. I figured you'd want to see him straight away."

I nodded. "Thanks, Rutherford."

"Cain, wait," Rutherford said.

"What is it?"

"Are you doing okay?"

I shrugged my shoulders. "I'm not sure. Baron Samedi traumatized the young wolves, resurrected my brother, and now has a brood of zombies ready to terrorize the French Quarter."

Rutherford shook her head. "You can't do everything, Cain. You can't stop the Baron and treat your patients with the care they deserve."

"I know. But if I don't stop the Baron, I'll have a lot worse to worry about than a few neglected patients."

"If you neglect these patients, you'll leave them vulnerable again to the Baron. If what I understand has happened is true, if what Pauli told me when he dropped off your brother really happened, the Baron fed off the fear of Abel's pack. If you'd had the time to work with them, maybe that could have been prevented."

I sighed. "I was dealing with the new vampires here. I was trying. While I might be a werewolf and seemingly unable to die of natural causes, I am still human in all the ways that matter."

Rutherford raised an eyebrow. "Do you really believe that?"

I narrowed my eyes. "Of course, you'd say that."

"What is that supposed to mean, Cain?"

I sighed. "Nothing. Forget I said it."

Rutherford pressed her lips together. "Mmhmm. You're trying to make this about what I told you earlier. About why we couldn't take things further in our relationship."

I stared at Rutherford for a second and counted to three in my head. It was a tool I sometimes gave to my patients. If you're afraid you're going to say something you might regret, count to three, then decide if what you're thinking is worth saying. If not, shut up or say something else.

"Abel's in my office, waiting?"

Rutherford nodded. "That's what I said."

I grunted and stood there for a half-second too long. Just long enough that made it awkward when I turned and left. Rutherford said nothing as I walked away, but I was pretty sure she sensed it, too.

I pressed open the door to my office. I found Abel seated on a chair in front of my desk, playing with a ball-point pen, clicking the button over and over. "What is this thing?"

"It's called a pen," I said. "It's for writing things down."

Abel cocked his head. "How does it do that?"

"There's ink inside. In a little tube. The ballpoint on the end draws it out of the tube just slowly enough to allow you to write your letters on a page."

Abel held the pen up to his face and, pressing his right eye shut, tried to peer into the tip with his left one.

I laughed and extended my hand. "Let me show you."

Abel set the pen in my hand. I twisted it apart and showed him the inner workings of the pen. He was most fascinated by the spring. It's funny how many things we take for granted in the world, things that someone who lived thousands of years ago never could have imagined.

"I bet the world seems strange to you," I said.

Abel nodded. "Looks like that snake was right after all."

I raised my left eyebrow. "What do you mean?"

"He told Mom that we'd become gods unto ourselves. All these devices, everything people make. It's sort of like imitating God, attempting to create things."

I tugged at the stubble of my beard. "Invention isn't exactly the same thing as creation. And it's not necessarily the result of the fall. After all, didn't our parents tell us that God told them to exercise dominion over the world? What could that mean if not to make the best use of everything in creation?"

Abel pressed his lips together. "That's an interesting thought."

I smiled. "I've had a lot of time to think about it."

Abel sighed. "It's not normal to die twice. Much less three times. I suppose that my third time is coming. Funny, you know, since no one would die at all if Mom and Dad hadn't messed up."

I shrugged my shoulders. "We don't know what might have happened if they never took the fruit. We might never have been born, either. The past is in the past, Abel."

"It certainly is," Abel said. "I meant it before, you know."

I cocked my head. "Before?"

"Before the last time I died, when I said I forgive you. I wasn't just saying that because I was about to die again."

I nodded. "I know. And I meant it, too, when I said I was sorry for what I did to you. I was being petty and jealous."

Abel shook his head. "I understand why you were angry. You sacrificed the fruit of your labors, the grain from your fields. I sacrificed the sheep from my flock. Why should my sacrifice have been acceptable, but yours wasn't?"

I took a deep breath and let it out. "That's another thing I've had a lot of time to think about. It wasn't about my offering, Abel. It was always about my heart. I made my sacrifice reluctantly, out of a sense of duty. You made your sacrifice out of gratitude and joy. Yours was a sacrifice of the heart, which is why God accepted it over mine. The proof of the pudding is in the eating, as they say."

"Excuse me? What does that mean? The pudding?"

I chuckled. "I'm just saying that the way I reacted after God rejected my sacrifice, revealed what was in my heart. It wasn't your fault that my sacrifice wasn't acceptable. It wasn't even God's fault. It was mine. I missed the point of the whole exercise."

Abel caught his image in a mirror on my wall and approached it, furrowing his brow. "Is that me?"

"It is. Strange, right? Looking at your own face."

Abel chuckled. "The best I'd ever seen of myself before was in the reflection of water."

I nodded. "I can assure you, you look as I remember you. When you're not a wolf, at least."

"I feel like we're wasting time here," Abel said. "When that thing, that demon or whatever he was, raised me, I could sense a darkness within him. He has to be stopped, brother."

"You're right. But until we know he won't be able to enthrall you again the moment he has the chance, you'll need to remain here."

"And what do you expect me to do? I can't just sit and do nothing, Cain."

I bit my lip. "Well, I don't know how it works when Baron Samedi resurrects someone. I'll have to ask Annabelle if Ogoun's flames totally freed you from his thrall or if they impacted you at all. But if you're here for the long haul, you're going to have a lot to learn. There's so much that's different about the world, as you've certainly noticed, it wouldn't be bad if you had someone who could help you. Ideally, someone who could also relate to what it's like to be an alpha of a pack."

Abel rubbed the back of his neck. "Everything is quite overwhelming. Frankly, it's terrifying. Not just Baron Samedi. He's frightening enough. But the rest of the world also intimidates me."

"I can't imagine how hard it must be for you. The very notion of assimilating into the world as it is, doing so as a werewolf, and trying to lead a pack at the same time, must be overwhelming."

Abel nodded. "I'm not sure if it's more overwhelming than it is just confusing."

"I'm going to hook you up with Donald. He's the alpha of the rougarou. He certainly doesn't know what it's like to emerge in a world after being absent for six thousand years, but the flambeau kept the rougarou in the swamp for more than a century. At the very least, he can relate to what it's like to step into a world that seemed to leave you behind. And he could teach you a thing or two about leading a pack."

"Don't you lead that pack?"

"I do, and I don't. Until now, I've taken control when they shifted. If so much insanity wasn't going on that could impact them adversely, though, Donald would be ready. The pack would be ready to run without me. I'm staying now largely for the sake of the newer wolves as they integrate into the pack. I must ensure their safety in the light of recent threats. Besides, while I might not run with the pack under the full moon forever, I expect I'll be working with them on an outpatient basis, at least for some time."

Abel chuckled. "I don't know what that means. Outpatient. But I think I'm getting the idea of what you do. Your gift is really incredible, brother."

I smiled. "It took me a long time to accept the wolf as anything other than a curse."

Abel shook his head. "That's not what I'm talking about. Maybe that's a gift of a sort too. But the way you help people, Cain. How you can see into their souls and help them find themselves, no matter how lost they might be. I don't know if your relationship with, you know, our Maker has evolved at all over the years. But while he may have cursed you, it seems he never really abandoned you."

I sighed. "Well, I appreciate you saying it. But I owe most of my skill as a therapist to a man named Sigmund Freud. His tutoring, and the school of experience, I suppose, are what have made me who I am today. I haven't really spoken to God at all, not in any meaningful way at least, since the day he placed the mark on me."

"I wasn't there for that," Abel said. "Maybe you don't give God credit for who you've become. But at the very least, I suppose, he's brought people into your life who have helped to make you into the man he always intended you to be."

I smiled. "I'm glad you and God have a good working relationship. I suppose being in heaven for all these years engenders that. I have nothing against God. Not anymore. Not after all these years. But I wouldn't say that he and I are on speaking terms."

Abel smiled. "Well, perhaps that's something I can offer you. While you help me adjust to the world, maybe I can help you mend that relationship."

I snorted. "I appreciate the sentiment, Abel. I'll think about it. But if it comes down to you and me offering a couple of sacrifices again to see whose he likes the best, I can't say I'm interested in competing for his affections again. The last time, well, it didn't go so well for me."

Abel laughed. "Don't take this the wrong way, but in the end, I'd say it didn't go too well for me either!"

I winced. "Okay, I suppose you have a point there."

Abel winked at me. "But you said it yourself. It was about your heart. You didn't make your offering out of love but out of duty."

I nodded. "Just because I understand now why God rejected my offering doesn't mean that I have the heart to attempt it again."

Abel shrugged his shoulders. "I don't know if that's right, Cain. I'm not talking about some ritual to earn his affections or appease his wrath. That was never what the whole offering thing was about. You've figured out a part of the puzzle. You know one reason your grain offering was unacceptable. But there's more to it than that."

"Oh, really?" I asked, raising an eyebrow. "Would you care to enlighten me?"

Abel pressed his lips together, forming a kind grin. "What do you think it means that, as our parents told us, God made us in his own image and likeness?"

I shrugged. "I suppose I just figured it meant, you know, that God is good looking like me."

Abel laughed. "I hope that was a joke."

I nodded, smiling. "It was. Honestly, I remember Mom and Dad saying that. It's even in the book about our story, what people call Genesis. But I've always figured it meant that we could reason, self-reflect, and create things with our hands."

"It's not so much about our capacities to work as it is about our unique ability, as a species, to love for love's sake."

I bit my lip. "I'm not sure I follow."

Abel pinched his chin. "Do you realize why God got so pissed when Mom and Dad ate from that tree?"

"I presume it's because they disobeyed. He told them not to do it and they did, anyway."

Abel chuckled. "They were like children, in a lot of ways. When children disobey, they aren't committing some sort of grievous sin worthy of death. It's just a part of growing up in the world, isn't it?"

I sighed. "I suppose so. I always thought that the whole, well, you took a cookie out of the cookie jar, so now you have to die, thing was on the extreme side."

"A cookie? It was fruit, Cain."

I smiled. "I know. I'm using a modern analogy to make sense of what happened."

"The essence of what Mom and Dad called sin isn't just disobedience, Cain. God never intended humans to be mindless children, following a bunch of arbitrary rules as if to place us under some kind of test of obedience."

I sighed. "Then what was the point of it all, Abel? You've hung out with the big guy for as long as I've been on earth, doing my thing."

Abel laughed. "I wouldn't say we've done a lot of what you call hanging out. Even if we don't have clothing in heaven."

I cocked my head. "Not the kind of hanging out I was referring to."

Abel grinned. "I know what you meant."

"Ah, you have jokes now!" I said.

Abel shrugged his shoulders. "I suppose I'm already adapting to this world well. This is the point I'm trying to make, Cain. God didn't up and create the world, and humanity, because he was bored and needed something to distract him from an eternity of the droll of perfection. He did so because it is his nature to love, selflessly, for love's sake."

"That still doesn't explain the extreme punishments. Death for a piece of fruit, for instance..."

"Or an eternity as a werewolf for killing your brother?" Abel asked, raising one eyebrow.

I pinched my chin. "I suppose I got off lightly on that one. But even that makes little sense. I know the mark protected me. People were supposed to know that if they ever attempted to kill me, they'd suffer a fate worse than what they exacted upon me. But I'm not sure becoming a werewolf is the dreadful fate that God intended it to be when he placed the curse upon me."

Abel narrowed his eyes. "How has the wolf changed you, Cain?"

"Well, when we shift, Abel, all our human emotions are amplified. If I don't want to be a killer anymore, I have to be honest with myself.

I have to take the task of self-examination seriously. I need to resolve all my harbored resentments, or buried emotions before I shift. We'll have to work on that together, as well."

Abel grinned widely. "Then, it sounds to me that the curse has done what God intended from the beginning. It didn't damn you, Cain. It saved you."

I bit the inside of my cheek. "That's an interesting take on it. I'll have to give it some thought."

"Remember what I said about why we were created to begin with?"

I nodded. "Of course."

"Our parents didn't exist for no reason at all. They had responsibilities. They were supposed to tend to Eden. When we were growing up, our parents gave us specific vocations, too. Different ways of exercising dominion over the creation. Not as lords, or tyrants, but as servants to all. You were placed over the fields to tend to grain, wheat, and various crops. They initially tasked me to become a shepherd. They gave us avenues, specific callings whereby we could reflect the generous, selfless love unto others, which Mom and Dad experienced in their bond of love before they fell. Love was supposed to bind them together, to be an icon of Divine love in the world. Our tasks, our vocations, were meant to be extensions of Divine care and generosity, preserving and tending to the needs of the world."

I tugged at the collar of my shirt. "Are you suggesting that you loved your sheep more than I loved my fields?"

Abel shook his head. "Not at all. But my sheep were not my own. You had a lot of pride in your work, Cain."

"Of course I did. Shouldn't one take pride in the fruits of one's efforts?"

Abel shrugged his shoulders. "To a point. But did you cause the wheat germ to grow? Did you create the sun or the water it needed to flourish?"

I chuckled. "Of course not. But my efforts were nonetheless integral to the harvest."

Abel nodded. "They were. But our labors were always meant to be done in love for others, not that we might become puffed up in the love of self, Cain."

"You're suggesting that my offering wasn't accepted because I took *too much* pride in my work?"

"Yes and no," Abel said. "You didn't realize that your calling, your vocation, and the fruits you produced were a gift. Your whole life was a gift. Your vocation was meant to be a way whereby you might take part in God's love. To provide wheat and grain for others that they might see the generosity of the Divine reflected in you."

I nodded. "I suppose my work really wasn't supposed to be all about me at all. Still, I was young. I was naïve."

Abel shrugged his shoulders. "So was I, Cain. No offense, brother. But I was never so bold as to imagine that my offering was purely the fruit of my efforts. I put a lot of work into my flocks, no doubt. But raising them was a privilege, an opportunity to participate in divine love. It did not pain me to make my offering. Love is always a sacrifice, brother. But it need not hurt."

I sighed. "I suppose burning up some of my grain that I'd worked so hard to grow was irksome. It seemed wasteful."

"When we consider the fruits of our labors, we imagine that what we have to give is limited. But when we recognize that we only are the stewards of our vocations, that our real labor is in love, and that what is produced has its origins in the Divine rather than our pride, we never run out of more to give. An offering need not be painful because there's always more to give since the generosity of the Divine knows no limits."

I smiled. "Well, that's an interesting way to look at it. Either way, though, it seems like I missed the point."

"The question is not what you might have messed up in the past, brother. You do not tend to grain fields any longer. But you have a new field, a place where you exercise love for love's sake. This asylum is your field. These people, and whatever sort of creature you help, are your crop, your new offering."

"I'm not sacrificing my patients if that's what you're suggesting."

Abel laughed. "That's not what was required. A true sacrifice is of the heart, not of grain or even of an animal. When the heart is right, the ritual is immaterial. That does not mean it is without its place. We are creatures of action. Our love is not just an emotion or a disposition of the heart. It is lived out in the world, in our interactions with all creatures. The ritual, in our case the sacrifices we offered, was simply taking what we were blessed with in Divine love and offering it in love, again, to the world. There will always be rituals of a kind. This truth is not genuine if it remains a mere idea and isn't put into action."

I snorted. "And you picked up on all of this insight in heaven over the last six thousand years?"

Abel shrugged. "In that place, a day is like a thousand years and a thousand years like a day. Still, I suppose I did. I won't say my offering, before, was perfect or pristine. But I know that when we make our offerings out of love, rather than out of pride or in some effort to prove our worth, then we're closer to the heart of the Divine."

I embraced Abel. "Good to have you back, brother. I thought I'd lost you a second time."

Abel nodded. "I suppose it's good to be back, though it is a bit strange. This whole place."

I grinned widely. "Well, it is an asylum for the magically and mentally deranged."

Abel chuckled. "Not what I meant. I'm talking about the rest of the world. This place doesn't seem all that weirder than anything else."

"I suppose it's time I formally introduced you to Donald. We have a lot of work to do. And, one way or another, we'll have to stop the Baron."

I opened the door. Abel stood up and exited first. I followed him out the door and closed it behind us. "I believe the other wolves are probably waiting for us in the common room."

Abel nodded. "Concerning the Baron, I think we're already making progress. He's fueled by fear, right?"

I nodded. "Indeed, he is."

"It's funny, Cain. But after our little talk, I don't feel as afraid of him as I did before. I think I pity him."

"I feel the same way. The problem is that now that he's raised a bunch of zombies, he won't need our fear as fuel. If we don't stop him soon, he'll have the entire city afraid. We're going to have to face him sooner rather than later."

Abel nodded. "Do what you have to do, brother."

Abel followed me to the common room. He and Donald had only met before as wolves. Now, though, they looked each other in the eye.

"Donald, this is my brother, Abel."

"Pleased to meet you," Donald said.

"Likewise," Abel concurred.

"I wondered, Donald, if you'd take my brother under your wing. Or your paw, at least."

Donald shook his head. "I know what you meant. Funny, doctor."

I smiled. "I know. I have a lot of jokes. Just talk to him about your experience when you returned to the world, and also about how you've grown as a leader of the rougarou."

Donald nodded and put one of his massive arms across Abel's shoulders. "It would be my pleasure."

CHAPTER THIRTEEN

I COULD HEAR THE screaming the moment the elevator reached Annabelle's office. The ding of the elevator doors suggested that the Voodoo Queen allowed me in, but, clearly, my arrival did not distract her at all.

"You've done this before, Mercy. You and a bunch of other vampires stopped the zombie uprising in Kansas City just recently! There's no reason you couldn't just handle this."

"If you told Sauron to quell the storm, and we went out there, we'd expose ourselves. I'm not giving up vampires forever to stop a few zombies that you could handle with a stab to the Baron's chest."

Annabelle shook her head. "We might have gotten away with that before. But if we do that, Mercy, we send him back to Guinee."

"Yeah. Back where his bony ass belongs, Annabelle."

"But if we send him back charged up on all this fear, if he takes his power there, he'll assault the Tree of Life. If he does that..."

Mercy narrowed her eyes. "I'm *not* exposing my kind to the world, Annabitch, just so I can clean up *your* mess."

"My mess? Clairvius evoked the Baron because he became a vampire, Mercy! I get that you were possessed, or whatever, when you bit him, but he was still your progeny. I even understand that you only got possessed because Delphine had seized me first. But you could have talked to the guy, tried to use some of your influence over him and the rest to settle them down."

Mercy huffed, turned around, and folded her arms. "I'm not some kind of fucking shrink, Annabelle."

"Hey!" I interjected. "I resemble that remark."

Mercy looked at me and rolled her eyes. "Sorry, Cain. No offense."

"You're insufferable, Mercy. Sometimes I wonder why I don't just stake you and be done with it all."

I snapped my head around and glared at Annabelle. "That's quite enough! I get that you two don't like each other, but we're on the same side. I will not stand for either of you threatening the other."

Annabelle took a step back, her eyes wide. "Cain, I..."

"You two have been at each other's throats as long as I've known the both of you!"

Mercy snickered.

"Not what I meant, Mercy. The point is you both share some of the blame for this situation. And you both deserve some of the credit for stopping Delphine before. Even if things didn't go as well as we'd hoped. From my recollection, you've each saved the other's life more than once."

I allowed my words to hang in the air for a few seconds, hoping one of them would take the first step to bridge the divide between them. No one took the bait.

"Follow me," I said.

"Where are we going?" Annabelle asked.

"Tell me, while you two were bickering about whose fault this is, did either of you come up with a viable solution?"

"I suggested the vampires handle it because zombie bites can't turn them," Annabelle said.

"That's a complicated solution that doesn't solve the primary problem."

"A potential zombie apocalypse isn't our primary problem?" Annabelle asked.

I shook my head. "If we removed the Baron from the equation, if we stopped *him,* what would happen to the zombies?"

Annabelle shrugged. "In this case, since they're totally controlled by the Baron, I think they'd all die. Or stop walking. You know, since they're already dead and people don't generally die twice."

I snorted. "Tell that to my brother."

"Fair point," Annabelle said.

Mercy grunted. "We didn't even think about what this must be like for you, Cain."

I shook my head. "Never mind that, for now. Both of you, come with me."

"Where are we going?" Mercy asked.

"We're going to solve this entire problem, once and for all."

"You have a plan to stop the Baron?" Annabelle asked.

I shrugged my shoulders. "Maybe. But I was talking about this little feud between the two of you. We're going to my office."

"We can talk here," Annabelle said.

I shook my head. "This is your office, Annabelle. Here, you speak from a position of power. I'd much prefer that we continue this discussion on neutral ground."

"Good idea," Mercy said. "That way, Annabelle can't hide behind all her pretentious Voodoo Queen bullshit."

I turned and glared at Mercy. "I've heard quite enough from you too, young lady."

Mercy's eyes widened as she opened her mouth to speak but couldn't find the words. She clearly wasn't used to being stood up to.

And, she probably wasn't accustomed to being called a "young" lady with nearly a century and a half of existence in her rearview mirror.

"He sure told you," Annabelle said, smirking.

I took a deep breath. "You can shut your mouth, too."

"Excuse me? I'm your—"

"Boss? Yeah, and I've got a job to do, which is exactly what I'm doing."

Annabelle and Mercy followed me, each separated by a good three paces since it did not incline them to be too near one another. I opened the heavy, wooden door at the Vilokan Asylum's entrance. I gestured inside, welcoming the Voodoo Queen and the Head Mistress of the Vampire Council to my little kingdom. Rutherford looked up at us from her position behind the receptionist's desk, her eyes wide.

"They'll be joining me in my office," I told Rutherford.

Rutherford chuckled. "To be a fly on the wall…"

I smiled as Rutherford unlocked the metal door that separated the reception area from the asylum itself. A metal door because, well, when Mercy was a patient there, she busted through the old one. Yeah, she was quite the handful in those days. In some ways, things hadn't changed. In other ways, though, she'd become quite the admirable lady, so far as vampires are concerned. I'd say the same for Annabelle. She'd really adapted well to her role as the Voodoo Queen. Two remarkable women, really. But when you put them together, while they're quite the force, they're as likely to destroy themselves as they are any supernatural threat they might be up against.

I opened the door to my office. "Ladies, first."

Annabelle sighed. "That's patriarchal bullshit."

Mercy rolled her eyes. "He's just trying to be respectful and nice, Annabelle."

"Whatever," Annabelle said, stepping into my office.

Once Mercy was inside, I closed the door. "Why don't you two get comfortable and take a seat?"

"This is a waste of time," Annabelle said, ignoring my invitation to sit down while Mercy relaxed on my chaise longue, kicking her black boots up and resting her arms behind her head.

"And arguing with one another about whose fault this was, and that was, and which one of you was to blame for the future extinction of humanity wasn't a waste of time?"

"I never said she was going to destroy humanity," Annabelle said.

"But that's what's at stake, isn't it? If we continue to fuel the Baron with fear and he returns to Eden?"

"It's true," Mercy said. "And if the humans lost their civility and killed each other, we'd have nothing to eat."

Annabelle rolled her eyes. "You see what I'm dealing with here?"

Mercy snorted, "Relax. It was just a joke."

"It wasn't funny," Annabelle snapped, crossing her arms in front of her chest as she reluctantly lowered her butt into a small couch I had on the wall perpendicular to the one where the chaise was located.

Mercy snorted. "Annabelle, I don't know what you've stuck up your ass. I think it would behoove you to remove it."

"I have nothing up my–"

"Stop it, the both of you," I said. "None of this is helpful. The Baron feeds off of fear, correct?"

Annabelle nodded. "That's right."

"You might have the soul blade that could send the Baron back to Eden or Guinee," I told Annabelle. "And Mercy, you might be able to take down the zombies with relative ease. But fear, what's fueling all of this, well, that's my expertise."

"No offense," Mercy said. "But I don't think talk therapy is going to convince the Baron to leave."

"But if we want to stop him, we have to make sure we're not giving him the very fuel he needs."

"I'm not afraid," Annabelle said. "I'm frustrated.'

"And I'm pissed at the whole situation!" Mercy added.

"Fear is never an independent emotion. But it is often foundational or fundamental. Anger, resentment, and even straightforward bitchiness can usually be traced to fear."

Mercy smirked. "Good thing none of that applies to us."

"Fear is a natural, primitive emotion. It's associated with a neurochemical response to external stimuli we perceive as a threat. Fear is a defense mechanism, meant to protect us when the things that give us security and safety in our lives are threatened."

"Cut to the chase, Cain," Annabelle said.

"I believe you two are resentful toward one another because you feel threatened by each other. At the core of your conflict…"

"Our bitchiness, you mean?" Mercy interrupted.

"Right," I said, grinning. "At the center of that is fear. By keeping up your little feud, you're giving the Baron exactly what he wants."

Annabelle rolled her eyes. "I'm not all that threatened by Mercy. She'd never bite me. Not under normal circumstances. The time I was possessed by Delphine LaLaurie, of course, the exception. She had good reason to try and stop me, then."

"And Annabelle knows better than to stake me," Mercy said. "Not that she'd ever succeed if she tried."

"Fear of death, which includes the fear of sickness and pain, is one of only five primal fears," I explained. "There is also the fear of abandonment, the loss of identity, the loss of meaning, and the loss of purpose. I'd suggest that behind the feud you two have been intent on maintaining now for several years is one of these core fears."

Annabelle looked at me blankly. "Don't tell me you're going to make us talk through this to figure out which kind of fear is to blame. We don't have time for that."

Mercy sighed. "I think the fear of abandonment is big in my life. I don't know if it has much to do with how I feel about Annabelle, but..."

Annabelle rolled her eyes as Mercy spoke. I ignored it. "Would you care to explain, Mercy?"

Mercy nodded. "My father never accepted me. He tried to cut out and burn my heart after I became a vampire. Then, you know, Nico was probably the closest thing I ever had to a real father..."

"And he left, too," I said. "When he made a deal with the Baron to recover his soul."

Mercy nodded. "Annabelle was there and played a role in all of that."

"I didn't kill Nico!" Annabelle protested.

Mercy sighed. "That's not what I'm saying..."

"No, this is good. Mercy, you think that Annabelle's role in Nico's death, a death he chose, is a part of the reason you don't get along with her?"

Mercy shrugged. "I don't get along with her because she's insufferable. But besides that, well, I don't blame her for Nico's death. That was his choice."

"But you have associated her, in some way, with your feelings of abandonment?"

Annabelle sighed. "Oh, this is rich..."

I glared at Annabelle. "We'll get to you soon enough, Annabelle."

Mercy narrowed her eyes. "Nico never got along with Annabelle, either. Even before he was a vampire, he didn't like her."

"Is this true, Annabelle?" I asked.

Annabelle nodded. "It is. And I didn't like Nico much, if you want to know the truth. That didn't mean I wanted to cast him into Guinee or leave him to the Baron so he could become a vampire."

Mercy shook her head. "I don't blame you for that, either. Nico did, sort of. The first time we met, Annabelle, it was under the pretense that Nico was hoping to get his revenge on you."

Annabelle sighed. "I remember that. Obviously."

"I don't know why," Mercy said. "A part of me feels like I owe it to Nico to hate her."

"Why would you think that?" I asked.

Mercy shrugged her shoulders. "For a century, all I ever heard about her, before she was even born, was how awful she was. I can practically hear Nico in my mind telling me all about how pretentious she is, how she showed up at the Academy, the descendent of slave owners, thinking she could insert herself into the world of voodoo."

Annabelle shook her head. "You might not believe me if I said it, but I had the same trepidation about coming to Vilokan. I didn't think I'd belong. I'm still not sure I do."

"Tell me, Mercy, do you miss Nico?"

"Of course I do. I mean, he could be a pain in my ass. He was probably the closest thing to a good father I ever had. But when he was around, I was safe. I had little to worry about."

"And you think that by keeping up his resentment toward Annabelle, maintaining this feud, you're keeping him alive somehow?"

Mercy scratched the back of her head. "It sounds dumb when you put it that way. But I guess that might be a part of it."

I crossed my legs as I leaned back in my chair. "It's not dumb at all. It makes perfect sense. The person who gave you a sense of safety and security also harbored centuries of resentment against Annabelle. If you let go of that resentment, or worse, allowed yourself to befriend

Annabelle, you'd feel you were letting go of a part of Nico. If you did that, it would threaten your safety and security."

Mercy wiped a tear from her cheek. It wasn't the first time I'd seen her cry, but it was certainly the first time I'd ever seen her show an ounce of vulnerability in front of Annabelle.

I half expected Annabelle to mock her for it. That sort of "jab" would have been in character with their ongoing feud. Instead, Annabelle stood up and put her hand on Mercy's back. I was a little surprised that Mercy didn't push her hand away.

"What about you, Annabelle? Any thoughts on what kind of fear you might have and how it might have fueled your part in all of this?"

Annabelle sighed. "Like I said, I've always struggled to find my place here. Yeah, I know I'm supposed to be the Voodoo Queen, but I'm not exactly the most advanced mambo in Vilokan. I wasn't raised here. Half the time, I'm like a fish out of water, floundering around, flopping across the dock, hoping to find the edge."

"What do you suppose Mercy has to do with all of that?" I asked.

"From the first time I met Mercy, I could see that there was good inside of her. Something that she tried to hide. I don't know. Even as she used me, abused me, or whatever, in Nico's name, I felt like I owed it to her to help her see that she wasn't as evil as she thought she was."

Mercy chuckled. "You thought I was a decent vampire, so you decided to hate me for it? How does that make any sense?"

"Let her finish, Mercy," I said.

"I'm not sure if I saw the goodness in her or if I just was hoping it was there, so I made myself see it. Either way, I've always felt guilty about what happened to Nico. The events that led him to become the first vampire. I've felt responsible for what happened. I think I thought if I could redeem Mercy at all, that it would mean that what I'd played a part in unleashing on the world wasn't so horrible after all."

"You were looking for something to exonerate you from some of the guilt you felt?" I asked.

Annabelle shook her head. "I don't think it's that. We've talked about this before, Cain. I know I didn't leave Nico in Guinee intentionally. I wasn't the one who entered the bargain with Baron Samedi. I did none of this on purpose. Even so, if it wasn't for me, there wouldn't be vampires in the world. I think a part of me was clinging to the idea that if they weren't as evil as I always thought, if Mercy could embrace her goodness, then I'd at least know that there was a little good to come with the bad of what I'd played a part in unleashing on the world."

"And she hasn't shown you that already?" I asked.

Annabelle sighed. "That's the thing. She has! She's done as much as I ever did to thwart evil, to protect the world from supernatural threats, and all of that. But maybe I've held up an impossible standard for what I wished she was. It's like I expected the goodness within her to grow and blossom until she became something that's just not realistic, like some kind of Mother Teresa."

Mercy laughed. "Yeah, that's not me. While I don't openly admit it, I know I will do the right thing when push comes to shove. But I will not pretend that I'm a good little girl or some kind of teacher's pet."

Annabelle sighed. "I think that, maybe, I just have to accept the fact that Mercy is who she is, not necessarily who I want her to be. It's not fair to use her as some kind of token vampire to assuage my anxiety over what I did to Nico."

I smiled. "That's certainly a positive development, Annabelle. But you started this whole conversation off by admitting that you didn't feel you belonged. It sounds to me like you have a lot of fear tied up in your sense of identity, or even your purpose and sense of belonging."

"I know not all of the hougans and mambos support me here," Annabelle said. "Some of those who'd become vampires, in fact, were among my most vocal detractors in Vilokan."

"Latavius, I presume?"

Annabelle nodded. "He's argued since day one that I don't belong here at all, much less in the role that Marie Laveau charged me to fill."

I grinned. "As someone who most of the world knows as the bad guy of the Bible, second only to Satan himself, I've had to come to grips with the fact that I'm not responsible for what other people think about me. I can only control my own actions and what I choose to do next. If my decisions don't convince them to change their minds, well, I suppose they're the ones to blame. I've always thought, you know, if they'd bothered to read the rest of their holy book, they'd learn about things like redemption and forgiveness. But you know, many people are bigoted and hateful but imagine that they're loving and refuse to see their own darkness. The only way to overcome the darkness in someone's heart is to bring it out into the light. But you have to be willing to do that. No one can coax the darkness out of another person. Not by lecturing them about their bigotry, and certainly not by judging them. Do that and, well, the most likely outcome is that all you've done is set up more walls around their darkness, making it even less likely that they'll ever even notice it, much less confront it."

Annabelle nodded. "I know I can't control what people like Latavius think about me. Still, so long as there are people out there who don't accept me, who think I'm an outsider who doesn't belong, it's hard to embrace my role. It makes me question, every day, if the Voodoo Queen really is who I am or if it's some kind of façade, a role I'm playing to cover up the truth about myself."

"I can totally relate to that," Mercy said. "I'm supposed to be in charge of Nico's Vampire Council, but there are vampires older than me, especially those in Europe, who refuse to accept my position. A lot of them don't recognize the authority of the Vampire Council at all now that it's me, not Nico, who is running things."

Annabelle chuckled. "Maybe that's a part of all this. I didn't realize that at all, Mercy. I thought you had this great position leading the vamps."

Mercy snorted. "Hailey mentioned none of that to you?"

Annabelle shook her head. "She and I might spend a fair amount of time together since she's also a witch and a friend of mine. But she doesn't discuss vampire business with me. I think she knows that when she mentions your name, I get a little bitchy."

I smiled. "I suppose both of you have a unique relationship with Hailey that bonds you. Annabelle, you were the one who healed Hailey after she was bitten, effectively turning her into a vampire, correct?"

Annabelle nodded. "That's right."

"But she's worked with me a lot more recently, as I've helped her learn how to navigate the world of vampires," Mercy said.

"I hate to draw any analogies between you two and a divorced couple," I said. "But there are parallels between this situation and what I've seen when counseling young people whose parents were separated or divorced in the past. Sometimes they allow their resentments and insecurities about each other to take over, to the detriment of their sons or daughters."

"I think Hailey is fine," Annabelle said. "She's not that dependent on either of us."

"I agree," I said. "But perhaps it is analogous to anything else that you two might have a shared interest in. Look past your differences for the sake of doing what's right."

"For the good of everyone else," Annabelle said, "we need to either resolve our issues or, at least, not let them take over every time we find ourselves in situations like this."

"If you don't resolve them, I doubt you'll be able to set them aside completely with the Baron. He'll see through it."

Mercy shrugged her shoulders. "I think I feel a lot better now. I understand where you're coming from, Anabelle. I'm not saying we're going to become besties soon, but I might hate you a little less now."

Annabelle nodded. "I agree. I didn't realize all this time that Mercy and I were so much alike. Maybe that's one reason I'm always so terse with her, too. She is a lot like me, but unlike me, she's more comfortable with who she is. She isn't trying to hide her truth or pretend she's something she isn't. I'm jealous of that. I can't do that. I'm struck by having to try to appease people who will never accept me."

I nodded along in agreement. "Trust me, I had many of the same feelings regarding my brother and his relationship with my parents long ago. You don't have to appease them. All you can do is the next right thing, Annabelle. If they don't come around, well, that's on them. You aren't responsible for other people's feelings. But you are responsible for your own. Otherwise, if we don't own our feelings, we allow other people to turn us into victims."

Annabelle chuckled. "Which brings us back to this whole fear thing. Safety and security. If we allow other people to control our emotions, if we let them turn us into victims, then we feel unsafe constantly."

"Right," Mercy said. "Because we live in a world where there will always be people who don't like us, who judge us unfairly. If we don't own our own emotions and constantly lament what other people do that we can't control, we'll never be happy. We'll always be afraid."

I nodded. "Exactly. This is how we stop the Baron."

"But he's drawing on more than our fear," Annabelle said.

"Is he?" I asked. "I'm not sure. I know he was drawing on Abel's anxieties. His and those of his pack. I've spoken to Abel already. I think we have that covered. And until the storm ends and people learn about the zombies that the Baron has raised, I'm not sure that the Baron is siphoning a lot of fear from there, either. Only what's naturally produced by a storm, and I doubt that kind of fear is strong enough to give the Baron the power he requires."

Annabelle extended her hand to Mercy. Mercy took it and stood up beside Annabelle.

"So this is what we do," Annabelle said. "We face the Baron together. I'll tell Sauron to calm the storms, and we'll stand together to take him down."

"But not just Annabelle and me, Cain. You and Abel, too. You said it yourself. Most resentments are rooted in fear. If you've really overcome that in your relationship with your brother, I think if you two stood side-by-side, we'd stand a chance."

"I was going to suggest the same thing," I said, smiling ear-to-ear.

"And if we confront him without fear, but with boldness, confidence, and compassion, we might suppress the Red Baron and bring out the Green Baron instead."

CHAPTER FOURTEEN

ANNABELLE CALLED PAULI AND asked him to grab a set of decent clothes for Abel. He was still wearing one of the Vilokan Asylum's standard-issue cartoon print hospital gowns. This one featured the cast of the Muppet Babies.

When Pauli showed up, teleporting into Annabelle's office in a flash of rainbow-colored light, he held a few articles of clothing I presumed must've come from his own wardrobe. Pauli wasn't a large man. Neither was Abel. Abel was maybe an inch or two shorter than Pauli, but they were both relatively thin and trim. Supplemented by a collection of multicolored stars in sequins, Pauli's designer jeans fit Abel well. Pauli's shirt was also form-fitting, black but semi-translucent, with a deep v-cut. It had lace around the arms. I think it was a woman's shirt, but I couldn't say that it didn't look good on my brother. Pauli had quite the sense of style. It was over-the-top and flamboyant, and I wasn't sure it fit Abel's personality. Still, it beat a hospital gown, and so long as Abel remained clueless about twenty-first-century clothing styles, he wouldn't have any reason to protest.

Annabelle asked Sauron to end the storm. We had to move fast before the Baron could unleash the zombies he'd raised from St. Louis Cemetery No. 1. If we could turn the Baron green, the link he had that allowed him to control the zombies would end. He raised them and ruled them.

We walked at a brisk pace, four in a row down Pere Antoine alley toward Jackson Square. We turned right on Chartres Street. From there, we followed Toulouse Street until it crossed Basin Street, leading to the cemetery. Abel was on my left. Annabelle and Mercy were on my right. We had a lot of history between the four of us, plenty of resentment linked to fear and insecurity that the Baron could use if we entertained it. But we were past that, now. If we confronted him, we could bring out his better nature. If the Green Baron emerged, and he could keep hold of his host body, he'd not only cease to be a threat, he might even be an ally or even a friend.

The storm cleansed the air. It was thick and humid but also fresh. You never know what odors might fill the air in the French Quarter.

We saw the Baron, still in the cemetery, his top hat dripping with rain. The zombies he'd raised were all around him. The Baron and the undead all shared glowing, red eyes. That was the magical bond that animated them. It was what the Baron used to manipulate the zombies. Turn Baron Samedi green, sever the connection, and rebury all the bodies in their proper graves. The storm raged long enough. I hoped that most of the folks who'd holed up in shops and bars in the French Quarter were more eager to get home than party. It was roughly four in the morning at this point.

Annabelle, with Isabelle's soul temporarily bouncing around inside of her, had green glowing eyes and her soul-blade in hand. Mercy was ready, too. If the Baron sent his zombies after us, we'd be ready. Still, we were confident. All we had to do was approach the Baron with confidence, with all our fears and resentments set aside. We did the work. We talked through our differences. We were ready.

"We're not afraid of you!" Annabelle pronounced as we entered the cemetery grounds. The Baron looked at us, scanning all four of us with his glowing eyes.

"We approach you as one! No anger, no resentment, no fear!"

The Baron's eyes flickered green. Then they returned steadily red.

"Keep it up," Annabelle said. "He may need to hear it from all of us. We're giving the Green Baron more power. To overtake the Red Baron, he needs more."

"I stand here, side-by-side with my brother, Cain," Abel declared. "I've forgiven him. I am not afraid of death, nor do I fear you, Baron!"

"And I'm not afraid of shit!" Mercy piped up.

The Baron's eyes flickered again. They went green for a moment, flickered red, then back to green.

"This is not how it seems!" the Green Baron announced. "You cannot suppress him now, not even with your courage!"

"I don't understand," Annabelle said. "Why can't we?"

"The Red Baron was used to raise the dead, but he is not the one who manipulates them. The one who controls him controls them. He is the one you must stop!"

The Baron's eyes flashed Red again. Annabelle and I exchanged glances.

"A bokor is behind this?" I asked.

Annabelle sighed. "A hougan gone bad, apparently. If someone else is manipulating the Baron, he must've arranged it before the Baron took over Clairvius. It had to be a hougan or mambo who was in the asylum when the Baron took over Clairvius. I'd guess one of the former vampires."

I sighed. "Latavius."

Annabelle nodded as she gripped her soul blade tight. "He wants to get rid of me. This was his plan. Latavius never intended to allow the Baron to overtake the Tree of Life. But he knew if we thought he was unleashed, free to do that, we couldn't resist confronting him. This is his shot, his best effort to take me out once and for all."

Mercy grunted. "I won't allow that to happen."

"Stay close," Annabelle said as the zombies started emerging from between the above-ground tombs and surrounded our position. "We can try to fight, but if push comes to shove, I can carve us a gate out of here."

I nodded. "We need to have each other's backs. If we stand with our backs together, we can focus on what's in front of us."

Mercy grinned. "You three do that. I'm faster than the rest of you. Let me do my thing."

I nodded as Abel, Annabelle, and I turned our backs to one another and braced ourselves. I didn't have a weapon. Neither did Abel. As werewolves, though, we had a lot of strength and speed, even in human form. I wasn't sure how we'd go about decapitating the zombies with our bare hands, but at least we could play defense and allow Mercy to take them out one by one. That was the best we could do.

The Baron perched himself, again, atop one of the tombs. His eyes still glowed, but the Green Baron told us he wasn't the one pulling the strings. He wasn't acting independently. It must've been Latavius. He had to be in the cemetery somewhere.

"If you can find Latavius, Mercy, do what you have to do."

"You got it, Cain."

The zombies started coming at us. In a blur, Mercy took them down. With her speed, she tore through them, grabbing and twisting their heads off of their bodies like the cap on a bottle of cola.

"If they get close," Annabelle said, "we can keep our backs together. We'll rotate so I can take them out. My soul blade should send them straight into the land of the dead."

It didn't take long before that situation presented itself. We moved clockwise to make sure Annabelle had a shot. She jabbed her soul blade under the chin and into the skull of a snarling zombie. Its entire form disappeared in a flash of green and golden energies.

"Here comes another one!" Abel shouted.

We repeated the process, rotating to get Annabelle in position. This time, Mercy intercepted the zombie, dropping its body while still holding a skull by a tuft of its hair in her hand. Mercy shrugged. "I've got this."

I snickered. "I think she's just trying to get ahead."

Annabelle groaned. "Dad jokes now, Cain? Seriously?"

Abel laughed. "Some things never change."

"We need to find Latavius," Annabelle said. "If we can stop him, we'll still have the Baron to deal with. But it's Latavius who has the Red Baron evoked and under his control."

"How do we stop him?" I asked. "I won't kill him."

Annabelle sighed. "I don't want to do it, but if I have to, I can use my blade to banish him to the void. Or you could try to talk him out of it. You know, do your psychotherapy mumbo jumbo on him and convince him to let Baron Samedi go."

I chuckled. "Alright, you do your voodoo. I'll do my mumbo jumbo. Annabelle, six o'clock!"

We rotated our circle until Annabelle was facing where I envisioned six o'clock would be. With a jab of her blade, she eliminated another zombie.

"If we keep this up, Latavius will have to try something else," Annabelle said. "I'm the one he wants dead."

"He knows better than to target me directly," I said. "He's aware of the seven-fold curse. If you move, he'll focus on you. That might give me the freedom to track him down."

"You'd better be right, Cain. You don't have any weapons. If you're wrong..."

"Then Latavius will become a werewolf. I don't think he'll be able to maintain his focus to keep the Baron and the zombies under his influence if that happens."

"Let me come with you," Abel said.

I shook my head. "I'll be fine. Latavius knows better than to attack me directly. He won't want to assume the curse. Annabelle needs you here so you can watch her back."

Abel nodded. "Alright, brother. Be careful."

CHAPTER FIFTEEN

MERCY WAS STILL WHIZZING around the place, dropping zombies faster than she dropped f-bombs in casual conversation.

As I stepped away from Abel and Annabelle, I glanced atop the tomb where Baron Samedi sat before. No one was there. Where had he gone?

Latavius had to be here, somewhere. If he was using bokor magic to control the Red Baron, his eyes would be aglow, matching the Baron's. From what I understood about how this kind of magic worked, when channeling zombie slaves, the bokor behind it could see through the eyes of the corpses he manipulated. That meant, while he might not see me coming directly if I spotted him, since he'd be so distracted by so many visions in his mind, he'd probably see me coming at the same time. There weren't a lot of zombies left. Mercy was relentless. But there were still enough, many of them wandering around between the tombs, that he must've known I was coming.

A flash of red caught my eye just outside the cemetery gates. There was no mistaking him. It was Latavius. He was moving northwest on Conti Street, toward St. Louis Cemetery No. 2. There was only one reason I could figure he headed that direction. He was going for more bodies, more zombies.

Using my enhanced werewolf strength, I jumped as high as possible, grabbed the wrought iron bars on the cemetery fence, and pulled myself over. My flip would not earn me a spot on the U.S. Men's gymnastics team, but for a man of my age, I had to say I was marginally impressed with myself.

I didn't have time to bask in the imaginary glory of my aerial somersault and landing. With a clear view down Conti Street, now with Latavius running in the opposite direction, I took off, my feet smashing the pavement, splashing through the puddles left behind by Sauron's storm.

Baron Samedi was with Latavius as the former vampire turned bokor commanded the Loa to resurrect the bodies.

"Latavius!" I shouted. "Stop!"

Latavius turned, narrowing his eyes. "This isn't your concern, Cain. My issue is with the pretender queen."

"I can't let you do this. Come with me, Latavius. There are other ways to make a difference than to murder the Voodoo Queen."

Latavius chuckled. "I have no intention of killing her, Cain. Not unless she forces my hand."

I cocked my head. "You sent a whole cemetery of zombies after her just moments ago."

Latavius shrugged. "Like I said, Cain. Step aside. My quarrel is not with you."

"You're still my patient, Latavius. I've been in Vilokan long enough that you surely know I advocate for my patients. If you have an issue you'd like to address with Annabelle Mulledy, I can see that she gives you an audience."

Latavius shook his head. "Unless you think she'll be open to resigning and leaving Vilokan forever, I don't think chatting with Annabelle Mulledy will do much to advance my goals, Cain."

"What is your problem with her, Latavius? Is it that she's an outsider? I realize she's not as experienced as some mambos. But she was the successor Marie Laveau chose."

"In due respect to Queen Laveau, she made a mistake. It has nothing to do with Annabelle being an outsider, Cain. It has even less to do with the fact that she's inexperienced. It is who she is, who she comes from."

I scratched my head. "You're speaking of her ancestry?"

"The Mulledys weren't just slave owners, Cain. They were the worst of the worst. My own ancestors labored on the Mulledy plantation, Cain. If you had their journals, if you read about the horrors they endured under the Mulledy thumb, you'd think twice about a Mulledy governing Vilokan."

I sighed. "I wasn't aware of that connection, Latavius. I remember well what it was like for people who look like us in these parts back in those days."

"Then you should agree with me, Cain. She's not fit to be our queen!"

I sighed. "Annabelle is more than her last name, Latavius. We cannot blame her for her ancestors' sins. And you do not need to be enslaved to the rage that now consumes you on account of your ancestors' suffering."

Latavius shook his head. "Surely you, of all people, understand the power of a generational curse, Cain. Annabelle was born into generational wealth and privilege. I was born into generational poverty. Do you really think the fact that her ancestors owned and abused mine as slaves has nothing to do with that?"

"I agree with you, Latavius. It's hard to break the cycle, to escape the shadow of our past and our ancestors. But that does not mean we should be judged by their virtues or vices, by their sins, or their acts of charity. Those things belong to us as individuals."

Latavius shook his head. "You don't understand, Cain. Slaves built Vilokan with nothing but their own determination and the support of a few abolitionists. My ancestors, suffering at the hand of the Mulledys by day, often snuck away and took refuge in Vilokan by night. There, they learned to read and write. They built all this without a single advantage, with little money to support their efforts. They established Vilokan despite the world's best efforts to keep them in chains. For a young lady, born into privilege, to come to Vilokan now and presume she can govern our world isn't just absurd. It's insulting."

I took a deep breath. "I understand where you're coming from. You might be surprised to know that Annabelle shared the same trepidation about accepting the role that Marie Laveau willed to her."

"Then why did she agree to it?"

"Allow me to pose another question. Latavius, why do you suppose that Marie Laveau chose an outsider, someone like Annabelle, as her successor?"

Latavius huffed. "Perhaps Annabelle bewitched her. We know she had access to another kind of magic before she ever came to Vilokan. Or maybe the good Queen Laveau lost her edge during her last days."

"Again, Latavius. I think if you spoke to Annabelle about these things, it might surprise you to discover that you and she are not as different as you think."

Latavius huffed. "I doubt that very much."

"Brokenness comes in many forms, Latavius. Do you truly think that Annabelle is more the product of her ancestors, who died decades ago, than the events that have befallen her own life? Do you not know that she and her family were attacked by a Caplata when she was just a child, that the attack she suffered resulted in the very powers you say she might have used to 'bewitch' Queen Laveau?"

Latavius shook his head. "I wasn't aware of that."

"The Caplata raised zombies, even as you are now, and assaulted her family. Her parents were bitten and never completely recovered. They left Annabelle and her sister to grow up with very little parental guidance."

Latavius shrugged. "A tragedy, for sure. But despite that, they had advantages. They had money and opportunity. Annabelle even attended a private school, if I'm not mistaken."

I nodded. "She did. But do you truly think that money, or privilege, heals the wounds of the heart? I've been a psychotherapist for a long time, Latavius. I've lived even longer. I've enjoyed the wealth of kings and the company of paupers. One thing is common to all of us, Latavius. We all experience pain. We all have scars. It doesn't matter where one comes from or what their means might be. Those scars can have a paralyzing and lasting impact. Loss feels the same, betrayal feels the same, and resentment enslaves us all the same no matter what we look like, what the rest of the world thinks about us, or what advantages we're given. Sometimes, in fact, the more we're puffed up by distractions, by comforts in this world, the more likely we are to retreat into such things. At the same time, we allow our emotional wounds to fester."

Latavius sighed. "I get it, Cain. But you don't understand. Vilokan is our safe place. We need to protect it."

"And you think Annabelle poses a danger?" I asked.

"Look at the facts! She brought the vampire into Vilokan who bit me and the others!"

I shook my head. "Mercy was the progeny of a hougan, Niccolo Freeman. I realize Nico was also a vampire, but Nico introduced Mercy to the voodoo world long before Annabelle arrived. Annabelle did not resurrect Delphine LaLaurie, either. A young mambo who lacked the support of the voodoo community and the Voodoo Academy did that by mistake. Annabelle played a role in eliminating the threat."

"And what was I? What were Clairvius, Regina, and the rest of us? Collateral damage?"

"I welcomed you as patients, Latavius, because I knew you needed help to adjust to your new condition."

Latavius shrugged his shoulders. "It's too late for that, now, Cain. If you haven't noticed, Clairvius's bargain cured me."

"And what was your bargain, Latavius? You must've engaged in a deal with the Baron yourself, since you are the one pulling his strings."

"I didn't exact a bargain with him at all. We marked Clairvius's body with the Baron's veve. It acts like a trap to bind him within his host. As a result, I have control over him. It's a basic voodoo evocation."

I stared at Latavius blankly. "We're not talking about a lesser Loa, Latavius. I'm no hougan, but I've had my experience treating patients who've underestimated the Loa they attempted to bind in the past. Are you certain you are the one in control here?"

"Stay in your lane, Cain. I have this handled."

"And if killing Annabelle isn't your purpose, what are you hoping to do with these zombies?"

"I'm bringing them to Vilokan, Cain."

I stared at Latavius blankly. "You can't do that, Latavius. Do you really think that assaulting Vilokan with zombies is going to help your case to replace Annabelle?"

"When Regina is the one who defeats them, Cain, I should think we'll have a fine rival to challenge Annabelle's claim over Vilokan. They'll have a new hero, and when this entire problem is traced back to what Annabelle did when she released Delphine on the city through the vampire, Mercy, I will easily convince the citizens of Vilokan to exile Annabelle. Regina will be the obvious candidate to take her place. She comes from a long line of vodouisants. She's an accomplished and proven mambo."

"If you unleash these zombies on Vilokan, how long do you really think you'll be able to maintain control? Once the city is consumed by fear and the Baron gains control, will you be able to keep him restrained?"

"Step aside, Cain. There is nothing you can do to stop us."

"I know what you're doing. I'll do everything I can to prevent it!"

"Will you?" Latavius asked, reaching into his pocket. He held in his hand a small doll. He was dressed in slacks, a button-up shirt, and had dark skin and a short beard.

"Is that supposed to be me, Latavius?"

"When you shifted back into wolf form before, after you pursued the Baron, along with Able and the wolves, back to the French Quarter, you shed some of your fur as you changed. I used your fur to create this."

"You can't kill me, Latavius. If you have any deadly intent at all..."

"I have no intention of killing you, Cain. Only to see to it you're out of the picture until I've completed my task."

Latavius held the doll with his left hand and started manipulating its limbs with his right. My legs moved like the doll's. With gigantic steps, a longer gait than was natural, Latavius forced me on the grounds of St. Louis Cemetery No. 2. Two zombies stood beside a tomb, their eyes ablaze with red magic. They pulled a giant stone slab away from the entrance.

"This isn't necessary!" I shouted. "I'm not your enemy, Latavius!"

Latavius didn't respond. Instead, he forced me into the tomb. Then, the zombies closed it and sealed it behind me.

CHAPTER SIXTEEN

I SLAMMED MY FIST against the stone slab that formed the door of my tomb and immediately regretted it. Punching stone hurts, especially when your jab has an extra oomph of wolf strength behind it.

I sat on the edge of what must've been the crypt of someone who was now a zombie under Latavius's control. Just long enough to regain a little strength and confidence. I stood up again and faced the slab that kept me imprisoned in the tomb.

I pressed my shoulder against the door and, pushing as hard as I could with my legs, tried to move the slab out of the way. The thing didn't budge. It wasn't the first time I'd been buried alive. In the past, I did it to myself. It was one of a series of futile attempts I made early in my existence to restrain the wolf. Who would have thought that a wolf would have the strength to blast through six feet of earth?

If only I could evoke the wolf now...

I coughed. The air in the tomb was stale and uncomfortably humid. It smelled of zombie rot which, might very well be the most repulsive odor on earth. I'd smelled a doozy or two in my day. I mean, I'd briefly hitched a ride on Noah's ark and hid among the animals. It's hard to imagine anything more repugnant than that. Zombie rot, though, gave the ark a run for its money.

Most of these zombies were skeletons, with only a few lingering hunks of withered flesh still stuck to their bones. When animated, though, something black, like tar, moistens whatever flesh remains. It gives them an odor comparable to dead vermin stuck in the furnace. Roasted death, I suppose, is the best term I could use to describe the odor of zombie rot. I wasn't sure where the roasted part came from, probably from the magic that animated the zombies to begin with.

Worst-case scenario, I'd linger in the tomb until the next full moon. If that happened, I'd be so hungry and thirsty the chances of keeping my wolfish urges under control would be slim.

It would be dangerous if I allowed that to happen. And I couldn't wait that long. Annabelle didn't know what Latavius was up to. If he got the zombies into Vilokan, I wasn't sure he'd be able to keep control over the Baron. The vampire attack on Vilokan by Delphine was frightening enough. It was nothing compared to this, though. Zombies are unpredictable, and their condition spreads more easily. A single bite and the victim would turn. Turning a vampire was more complex. As terrifying as hungry vampires could be, Vilokan had often welcomed vampires in the past on the condition that they behaved and only fed on the willing. There'd probably been a few zombies in Vilokan before, too. I knew that Cassidy, for instance, had raised a zombie when she was a student at the Voodoo Academy. She invested the body of a dead mambo with her own soul and commanded the zombie to do her homework. It wasn't what got her expelled, but it certainly raised red flags to the faculty about her unique necromantic abilities.

It was dark in the tomb. I couldn't see much, and, as a werewolf, I had great night vision, even when in human form. Like the residual strength and speed that my human form retained on account of the wolf, my senses were also more acute than average. I don't know what I was hoping to find. How many items, typically buried with someone in a tomb, could be useful to break out of the thing? It wasn't like people frequently took jackhammers to the grave.

I reached into the abandoned crypt, which I presumed belonged to one of the zombified bodies. There was a book. Probably a bible. Other than that, a lot of dust.

I almost threw the bible against the door on a wing and a prayer. Then, I realized it was a dumb idea. I'm not a religious man, despite my intimate involvement with the Divine during the early part of my life. Still, I had enough working against me at the moment that committing an act of what some might deem sacrilege with no chance at success wasn't wise.

I couldn't act angry or irrational. Was I supposed to be afraid here? Was the Baron using *me* like a battery, siphoning my fear as I tried to break out, afraid of what the zombies might do when freed in Vilokan? In this situation, any act of anger or desperation would *unequivocally* come from fear.

Instead, I had to focus. I had to clear my mind. Maybe do a little werewolf-style yoga if that's what it took. The only thing I could do in this situation was not do anything that might give the Baron more power, that might exacerbate the risk that the Baron would escape Latavius's control.

It's hard to focus, meditate, and take deep breaths in a place that's so rank. I wanted to gag every time I inhaled. After a while, though, my olfactory senses adjusted to the odor. It was still there but, somehow, less noticeable, more tolerable than before.

Cain... where are you?

I wasn't sure if I imagined the words or truly heard them. As a wolf, I could communicate on something like a psychic level. They couldn't understand my words, though. It wasn't like that. I thought in human words, but as the wolf, my brainwaves translated them into general urges and directions. Wolves don't have a complex language. Was that what was happening now? I'd never communicated with a pack while in my human form. But I did still have the semblance of some of my wolf abilities. Was this one of them? The voice I heard was airy, distant, and muffled. I couldn't identify the tone. It must've been someone who belonged to my pack. Was it Donald? Ryan or Cassidy, perhaps?

"Can you hear me?" I asked.

I waited. I didn't receive a response. Then, a few moments later.

Where are you?

I sighed. The voice was a little clearer that time but still indiscernible. I tried to visualize the tomb Latavius sealed me within. Sometimes, a visual image was more powerful than words when I spoke to the pack as a wolf. I imagined it was because visual images didn't have to be filtered through the language barrier separating human thoughts from the wolf's mind.

"In St. Louis Cemetery No. 2," I said, adding more direction for safe measure. "Latavius sealed me inside a tomb."

It was just as likely as not that I was speaking to myself, that the voice I thought I heard was my subconscious mind speaking to me from the depths of my inner anxiety. If that was the case, entertaining it would bring my deep-seated fears to the surface. But if I was speaking to Donald or someone else in my pack, I might also be able to warn them. It wasn't so important that they got me out of here as it was that whoever was speaking to me told Annabelle what was happening.

"Whoever is out there, if you can hear me, Latavius intends to lead the zombies into Vilokan. He's hoping to frighten the place, create enough havoc to convince them to depose Annabelle."

The voice didn't reply. I was probably speaking into thin air, conversing with myself, with no real benefit at all, beyond attempting to navigate my own emotions, to resolve my own subconscious fears. If I really was speaking to myself out of fear, I could manage it. I could use the tools I had, the same ones I used with my patents, to resolve my fears. First, I'd challenge my cognitive distortions. What irrational thoughts were at the center of my fear? Then, I could examine my past, history, and lineage and attempt to understand and uncover the source of my fear.

Losing one's identity and purpose. That was one of the sources of fear. I wasn't afraid of death. That wasn't really on the table. I was afraid of what might happen if I lingered in the tomb too long. It scared me that Latavius might succeed, that he might remove Annabelle, that Regina might take over and remove me from the Vilokan Asylum. I was an outsider, and the one thing that Latavius made clear when I talked to him before was that he had little tolerance for outsiders in Vilokan.

While I know it sounds trite, I'd done nothing more fulfilling in six thousand years than treat my patients at the Vilokan Asylum. I worked with troubled populations who didn't have access to mental health services. I was saving lives. Vampire younglings, for instance, like Mel, who struggled to tame their cravings, or young werewolves like Ryan or Cassidy, rarely lived beyond their first year before being met with a stake or a silver bullet, respectively. But those who came to the Vilokan Asylum had great outcomes. Most of them, better than nine out of ten, would live long and fulfilling existences devoid of excessive bloodshed, free of guilt or self-loathing.

I recalled my conversation with Abel. Our purpose, as humans, was to find a calling, a vocation, whereby we could communicate divine love, selfless love to the world. We were to be like gods, not in the way the serpent tempted my parents, not by acquiring knowledge or power, but by sacrificing ourselves, by giving of our lives for the betterment of others. The reason my sacrifice wasn't acceptable, the one I made of grain, and Abel's was, was because love had nothing to do with my offering. It was painful because I was giving up something that I'd worked to produce, something that fueled my pride of purpose.

Now, though, my work at the Vilokan Asylum was different. Just as I used to tend the fields but could only water the seed and tend to my crops, but couldn't invest the seeds with the power to grow, my work at the Asylum was like watering, like tending to the health of the soul. I couldn't make anyone grow. After entering my treatment program, who my patients became wasn't of my making. I simply gave them the life-giving water they needed. I helped point out the weeds that had grown around them and threatened to choke the life out of them. I didn't even pull those weeds myself. My patients had to do that themselves. I certainly wouldn't sacrifice any of my patients on an altar. But I could offer them back to the world as a contribution to make the world a better place as a token of love. I couldn't claim credit for anything that any of my patients accomplished. They had to do the work themselves. But I could show them the path. I could help them forge a better future for themselves.

I was never much of a theologian. My experiences with the Divine were too personal, too intimate, to be codified into any kind of dogmatic system or creed. But I realized this was probably the closest I'd been to the heart of God in all my life. I had various gifts, even what I'd always thought to be a curse, that I was using to help others realize their callings, their purposes, in the world. I was giving others a chance to live freely, be happy, and love others. That was all I needed to be free and happy myself.

I took a deep breath. My eyes remained closed. Something constricted around my body.

I opened my eyes. A vibrant, glowing creature radiating all the colors of the rainbow had wrapped itself around me.

"Pauli?" I asked.

In snake form, Pauli turned and looked at me. "Damn, Cain, you smell like shit."

I sighed. "That's not me. It's this place. The smell of the rot when Latavius raised the body here as a zombie."

"Sure it is. Do you want to get out of here or what?"

I nodded. "Of course! How did you find me?"

"Your brother," Pauli said. "He told Annabelle where you were. She sent me to bust you out of here. We need your help."

"What's going on?" I asked.

Pauli sighed. "Abel tried to warn us. But it was too late. Latavius led a horde of zombies into Vilokan. People freaked out like bitches. I figured, what's the fuss? It could have been worse. It wasn't like corduroy was coming back in the spring catalog or anything dreadful like that."

"Cut to the chase, Pauli."

"Annabelle and Mercy were trying to confront the Baron, to bring out the Green Baron, but they couldn't pull it off. Not alone. They need you and Able to confront him together. If you two really worked through all your shit, then I guess it makes sense."

I nodded. "Alright, Pauli, take me back. I'll do what I can."

CHAPTER SEVENTEEN

WE APPEARED IN ANNABELLE'S office. Mercy was there. So was Abel.

"Welcome back," Annabelle said.

Abel hugged me. I hugged him back. "What's the deal, now?"

Annabelle shook her head. "Mercy took out most of the zombies from St. Louis Cemetery No. 1. By the time we finished, Latavius was already in Vilokan. Your message came through Abel about five minutes too late."

I sighed. "I didn't even know I was speaking to him. That was the first time I communicated, like a wolf, while in human form."

"I believe we share a bond, brother. I don't know how. But I heard your voice."

I shook my head. "We aren't of the same pack. You have your own pack. I'm not sure how this works."

"Are we not?" Abel asked. "You aren't technically the alpha of the rougarou, are you?"

I shook my head. "I'm not. That privilege belongs to Donald."

"Blood binds us, brother. But blood isn't enough. We've opened our hearts to each other. That must have something to do with it."

I sighed. "I suppose we might be a pack of two if that's even a thing. But you're still the alpha of your own pack at the same time."

Abel shrugged. "Maybe there's nothing magical at all about pack membership, Cain. Perhaps it's just the bond of trust that unites us. We've forged that bond. The rougarou have the same trust in you. That's why we can speak to each other."

"You may be right," I said. "Whatever the case, we're united now. We're connected. We almost turned the Baron green once already. I have to believe we can do it again."

Mercy sighed. "That might be more difficult now than before. Back in the cemetery, after you went after the Baron, I continued fighting. I'd nearly finished off the zombies from St. Louis Cemetery No. 1 when Abel heard your message. By the time we got back to Vilokan, Latavius was already inside with the Baron and a hundred zombies, give or take, from the other cemetery."

"You had little difficulty with the first batch of zombies. Can't you take them out?"

"I started doing exactly that," Mercy said. "But then, as people saw what was happening, the Baron gained power. Latavius lost control of the Baron, and then, well, he let the zombies loose. Free of Latavius's control and with more power at his disposal, I'm afraid if I get too close to him, he'll be able to manipulate me like any youngling. He's too powerful right now."

"Which is why Mercy and I can't turn him Green,' Annabelle said. "We tried, but Mercy felt his compulsions and had to turn back."

I looked at Abel. "We've got this. It's our only chance. But once we draw out the Green Baron, we may still need to do something about Latavius. He may attempt to re-exert control over the zombies, if not the Baron as well."

"We expect he will," Annabelle said. "We'll do what we have to do."

"Bring him back to the asylum," I said. "I spoke to him before. I really think I can help him if I have more time."

"He's trying to usurp my position, Cain."

I nodded. "And I've known many unjust queens through the centuries who would behead the originator of any such conspiracy against her. That's not you, Annabelle. You're not that kind of queen."

Annabelle nodded. "I'm not. I'm just not as sure as you are that he's open-minded enough to reconsider."

"Like I said, do what you can to bind him. Take him to the asylum. Rutherford will get him situated, and I'll do what I can. Right now, we need to go. The longer the Baron unleashes his horror on the city, the less likely it is we'll be able to break through the fear and evoke the Green Baron."

"It will be difficult to bring out the Green Baron permanently. So long as the zombies are in the city, I don't think we'll be able to totally clear the air of people's fears."

"If we can't bring the Green Baron out permanently," Mercy said. "You know what you'll have to do, Annabelle."

Annabelle nodded. "I may have to open a gate to Guinee. If we can turn him green just long enough to send him through it, he'll stay green when he arrives. There's no fear in Guinee."

"What about Latavius?" I asked.

Mercy smirked. "Leave him to me."

"Don't bite him," I said. "He still remembers you as the vampire who turned him before. We don't want to give him any reason to fuel the Baron further."

"We have a zombie uprising," Mercy said. "I think one bokor afraid of a vampire is just a drop in the bucket."

"That may be," I said. "But we're already facing an uphill battle. Able and I are only two men. For us to counteract an entire city, terrified by zombies, to give the green baron a chance to emerge is going to be difficult as it is."

Mercy nodded. "I'll try to keep my distance until Annabelle establishes the portal to Guinee. After that, I'll do what I can to stop him before he re-exerts control over the zombies."

I looked at Abel. "Alright, brother. Ready to confront death together?"

Abel chuckled. "I suppose he is something of an angel of death, isn't he?"

I nodded. "This isn't the first time I've crossed paths with him. Under different names, he's shown himself at various times in history. Now, though, we must face him together."

"I've faced death before," Abel said. "I'm not afraid."

I nodded. "We do this together. No matter what he says, no matter how he tries to drive a wedge between us, we stand as one."

Abel nodded. "After everything we've overcome, I don't think that God himself could come between us now, brother."

"I'll be just behind you," Annabelle said. "Pauli, I may need your help to put me into position. We can't let the Baron realize what we're doing. We'll have to forge the gate quickly. Then, if you can cast a rainbow into the gate, it should hold it open long enough to ensure that we get him inside."

"Can't you just stab him with your blade?" Mercy asked. "Your soul-blade sends vampires straight to hell when you do that."

Annabelle shook her head. "The goal is to send the Green Baron into Guinee. If we stab him, he may turn red before he arrives. I don't think he has the power siphoned he needs to threaten the Tree of Life, but the best way to ensure he doesn't is to send him there green. I'll forge a portal. If the Green Baron is in charge, he'll know what's at stake. I have to believe that he'll go through willingly."

Chapter Eighteen

Abel and I left Annabelle's office and exited the Voodoo Academy. The firmament above Vilokan had changed. The blue magic, magic that was supposedly established by the Fomorian merfolk and their Loa, Met Agwe, had now turned red. If the zombie uprising wasn't evoking enough fear, compromising the firmament above Vilokan would do it. The last time the firmament was broken, the entire city flooded. Hundreds of people died. Now, whatever the nature of the magic was that kept the water table from flooding the city, it was infused with the power of the Ghede.

Abel and I walked side-by-side through the streets. There wasn't a single living soul outside. Everyone was holed up in their homes, avoiding the threat that lurked on the streets.

We walked past several zombies as we searched for the Baron. We didn't attract them at all. Did they feed on fear, even as the Baron did? Was it fear that drew them in, that the Baron seized upon through them, or was there something about my curse that dissuaded them from biting me? They ate people's brains. That was always my understanding. Were my brains not good enough for them? How insulting! More likely, it was because Able and I were werewolves.

Whatever the case, we continued to march through the streets.

Latavius was out here, somewhere, too. When the Baron overpowered him, there was no telling what might have happened. Was Latavius even still alive? Had he been turned already?

We found him on the steps of the Vilokan Asylum. He was beating on the door, trying to get inside. Rutherford must've thought better than to open the doors to anyone in the middle of a zombie outbreak.

"What are you doing here, Latavius?" I asked.

The hougan turned to me, tears falling down his cheeks. "Cain, please help me."

I nodded. "I told you before, I'd help you."

"How did you get out? I mean, I'm sorry I did that... I..."

"Time will tell if your regrets are genuine, son. It appears that the Baron overpowered you. I warned you of this, Latavius. I may not know voodoo well, but I've treated my share of hougans and mambos who thought they could harness a Loa and found themselves in over their heads."

Latavius nodded. "You were right, Cain. I thought I could manage him, but he was too strong."

"You need to quell your fears, Latavius."

Latavius sighed. "I'm trying. It's hard to just turn it off."

"I'm surprised none of the zombies bit you yet," I said.

Latavius shook his head. "The Baron can't hurt me. Not directly. That was a part of Clairvius's bargain that he made with the Baron before when he gave the Baron his body."

"Then why are you afraid?" Abel asked.

Latavius shook his head. "I led zombies into the city I thought I was trying to save. I'm not afraid for my safety, doctor. I'm afraid for the people! What have I done?"

"You could help us stop the Baron," I said. "If you can face your fear, if you can take responsibility for your errors, it's not too late to do the right thing."

Latavius sighed. "I don't know, Cain. I want to, but I have so much anger, so much resentment, I don't even know where to start."

I glanced at Able and smiled. "There's no shame in admitting we might be wrong. I've told many clients, including my fellow were-wolves, that we sometimes have to decide whether it's more important to be right than to be happy. "

Latavius shook his head. "I can't change my views just because of my regrets, Cain. But I suppose I could do as you suggested before. I could talk to Annabelle about my concerns."

"That's a great start, Latavius. Even when we find people who don't see the world as we do, believe different things, and come from different worlds, we aren't as different at the core as it appears on the surface. If we take the time to get to know one another, if we listen to them rather than think it's our job to convert them to our point of view, we'll find that there's a lot more that unites us than all the things in this world that divide us."

Latavius nodded. "What can I do to help, Cain?"

"Do you know where Baron Samedi is?" I asked.

Latavius nodded. "I do. I can show you."

"You don't have to, Latavius. If you're not ready to confront him, to face your fears, you can stay behind."

Latavius shook his head. "No, you're right. I need to do this. I have to set things right."

Abel nodded. "When we're united, when we embrace what we share in common and face our fears together, there isn't a force in the universe that can overcome us."

Latavius sniffed and wiped his eyes with the sleeve of his shirt. "I'm ready. And, thank you."

"For what?" I asked.

"For believing in me and not treating me like an enemy."

"I told you, Latavius. You're my patient. I'll always be your advocate."

Latavius led us through the Rada quarter of Vilokan to the Ghede quarter. I checked my shoulder. Annabelle and Pauli weren't far behind. They were lurking in the distance. She wasn't close enough to hear my conversation with Latavius. I meant what I told him, however. I would advocate for him. If he agreed to join me at the asylum, I was reasonably certain Annabelle would sign off on it. She'd already agreed to the plan before that Mercy would take him as soon as we seized the Baron and deliver him to the asylum. I didn't know where Mercy was. She was around somewhere. Perhaps she was taking out zombies and looking for Latavius. She couldn't get too close, not until the Baron turned green. Hopefully, by the time we did that, she'd figure out that Latavius wasn't a threat. He was with us, anyway, so worst-case scenario, I figured I could bring her up to speed once we handled the Baron.

Latavius led us to the door of a small house, one of many such structures in the residential districts of Vilokan. It wasn't a fancy building. When the founders of Vilokan built it, they fashioned the place out of stone and brick.

"This is my house," Latavius said. "The Baron is inside. He's using my place as a base, a place to hide while he controls the zombies and gains power."

"Surely he knows we're here," I said. "If he can see through the eyes of the undead, vampires and zombies alike, he has to know what we're up to."

Latavius nodded. "I suspect he does. But he's arrogant. He has about as much faith in humanity to conquer their fears as one might have in a politician, to tell the truth."

I chuckled. "That's not a lot of faith."

"Tell me about it," Latavius said.

Abel scratched his head. The metaphor was lost on him. He had a lot to learn about the world. Politics was on the shortlist of things I least looked forward to explaining. Still, he got the idea. The Baron knew we were coming. The Baron didn't think we had what it would take to stop him. Not with so much fear already flowing through the city. So much that it even infected the firmament over Vilokan.

Latavius unlocked his door, and we stepped inside. The Baron had three shot glasses arranged on a table in front of him.

"Welcome, friends!" the Baron said, his eyes still glowing red. "Come, let us have a drink."

I bit my lip. "We aren't here for drinks, Samedi."

The Baron cocked his head. "Come now, Doctor Cain. It's Baron Samedi. If I call you doctor, surely you can do me the courtesy of referring to me by my honorary rank as well."

I snorted. "My title isn't honorary. I earned my doctorate from the University of Vienna."

The Baron rolled his eyes as he poured his shots. "Yes, yes, yes. Everyone knows, Cain. The prized student of the renowned Sigmund Freud. Color me almost impressed."

"What is this about?" Abel asked. "Surely you know why we're here."

The Baron chuckled. "I know what you intend. I have another bargain I'd like to propose. Surely, you might attempt your plan. But do you really think you three have the strength to suppress my better side and bring back my... weaker nature?"

"We aren't interested in your bargains," I said.

"I didn't expect you would be," the Baron said. "Though I'm certain my proposal would appeal to at least one of you."

"What do you want?" Latavius asked.

I raised my hand. "There's no sense in telling us, Baron. We're not here to make bargains."

Baron Samedi smiled. He took one of the three shot glasses and pushed it toward Latavius. "Give me the Voodoo Queen, along with the spirit that dwells within her, and I will leave Vilokan unharmed. I will leave and return to Guinee of my own accord."

I glanced at Latavius. He furrowed his brow. "I don't understand. How could we give you the Voodoo Queen? We don't control her."

"She trusts the lot of you," Baron Samedi said. "Send her into Guinee with me. Surely, once she creates the portal that you intend to use to cast me out of your world, the three of you can force her inside."

I cocked my head. "She still has her blade. She'll use it again to escape. How would that even work?"

The Baron chuckled as he drew a cigarette from a pouch that dangled from his waist. "With a single touch, I can extract Isabelle from her and capture her within this cigarette. Provided, of course, we're already in Guinee when I do it. All you need to do, Latavius, is make sure she follows me through her own portal. I will do the rest."

Latavius cocked his head. "This spirit, inside of Annabelle, is named Isabelle?"

Baron Samedi snickered. "Nauseatingly cute, isn't it? Annabelle and Isabelle?"

Latavius nudged me. "This sounds crazy, but was Isabelle once a slave, born on the Mulledy Plantation?"

I nodded. "She was."

"I know my family history," Latavius said. "There was a girl, two of them, in fact, who were orphaned on the same plantation where my parents worked. My great-great-grandmother was a slave on that plantation. The girls were her nieces. Isabelle is family."

Baron Samedi grunted. "What is she to you, Latavius? One girl, whose spirit has long been dead, in exchange for all of Vilokan?"

Latavius reached for his glass and pushed it back toward the Baron. "I'll pass."

The Baron grunted. "Then, I suppose, I cannot convince Cain or Abel to assist me in this endeavor?"

"Not a chance," I said.

"What if I could see that your curse was removed? In fact, I could remove it from both of you. You could leave the wolves behind."

I shook my head. "There would still be other wolves who'd need my help."

"And if it were not for the werewolf gift, my brother and I never would have reconciled."

The Baron's eyes flickered green. The Baron clenched his fists, trying to hold on to his red aspect. There was no division between the three of us. There was no fear left defining the terms of our relationship. Being both werewolves and siblings, my brother and I finally shared a bond. We'd each discovered a new purpose, a place in the world. Latavius learned Annabelle wasn't just the descendent of slave owners, but that the spirit who'd dwelled within her, who gave her power, was a slave, herself, and one of his ancestors. The revelation, based on the resolve with which Latavius rejected Baron Samedi's proposal, suggested that it was a revolutionary discovery. He'd never again be able to see Annabelle the way he had before. Now, he knew a deeper truth about who she was and the source of the power that she could access that Marie Laveau also considered when she'd appointed Annabelle Mulledy as her successor.

The Baron's countenance changed. His grimace turned to a kind grin as a green glow emanated from his eyes.

The Green Baron removed his top hat and ran his fingers through the few strands of hair that remained on his bony scalp. He stood up and returned his hat to his head. "Apologies for my other half. He can be quite the knoblicker."

Abel cleared his throat. "What's a knoblicker?"

I snorted. "I'll explain it to you later."

"There is much fear in Vilokan," the Green Baron said. "I cannot guarantee how long your influence will prevail and keep my red aspect suppressed. I must return to Guinee now before it's too late."

"Annabelle, the Voodoo Queen, prepares to forge a gate to Guinee. I believe she's just outside."

"Then I must depart in haste," the Green Baron said. "My apologies for the inconvenience. I've set everything right. I have restored your firmament. The bodies raised are again at rest. Still, someone will have to return them to their graves."

The Green Baron opened the door and stepped outside. Annabelle stood there, Pauli in his boa constrictor form draped over her neck.

"Beli!" Annabelle shouted, causing her soul-blade to form in her hand. Then, Annabelle cut an oblong semicircle in the air. When her blade met the location where she started, a golden glow burst from the center. Then, through it, I saw what looked like green grasses, fields, and groves littered with blossoms of various hues. It must've been Eden itself. It was a gateway to Guinee. I'd never seen the place. My parents were kicked out of the garden groves before Abel or I were born, and they told us we should never attempt to return. For extra measure, the Creator severed the entire place from the earth's fabric of space and time and set Eden on a plane of its own. From what I understood, many of the Loa dwelled there when they weren't on earth in human hosts. If the Baron went there while in his green aspect, he'd remain in that form.

The Baron stepped toward the gate and turned to tip his hat at us.

In a blur, Mercy came around the corner and grabbed Latavius. That was all it took. A surge of fear.

The Baron blinked, and when he opened his eyes, they were red again.

"Mercy!" I shouted. "Let Latavius go!"

Mercy stopped and released Latavius. "I don't understand. I was supposed to..."

Before Mercy could finish, Latavius charged Baron Samedi, tackling the Loa and forcing him into the portal."

"Pauli, release the rainbow!" Annabelle screamed.

"No!" I shouted. "Latavius is in there with him!"

"We have no choice! We can't allow the Red Baron to return!"

"Annabelle, you don't want to do this. Not again!"

Annabelle winced. She knew what she was doing. I didn't need to remind her how she'd left Nico in Guinee once before. That Nico had been abandoned, also in the company of Baron Samedi. The result? Years, if not decades, fighting the Baron in Guinee. Then, eventually, a bargain sent Nico back to earth, centuries before he was born, as the first-ever vampire. "Fine. Cain, you can go after him. But if the Baron so much as approaches the gate on the other side, I'm closing it."

I nodded. "Very well. I'll be back."

"I'm coming with you," Abel said. "I'm not about to let my brother go back to Eden without me."

I nodded, grabbed my brother's hand, and dove into the gate.

CHAPTER NINETEEN

THE AIR HIT MY lungs as if I was taking my first breath. By comparison, I'd suffocated my entire existence. Eden's air vivified my mind and body alike. Every breath made me feel more alive than ever before. I looked around. I was there for a reason.

Abel stood beside me. His wide eyes and dropped jaw suggested he was every bit as in awe of this place as I was. The colors on the grass, the flowers, and the trees were vibrant. It was inspiring. The sky was bright, pure, and clear. There was no sun there. Eden wasn't a part of a solar system. Was it God himself who provided the light? Was it a magical glow that permeated the atmosphere? I didn't know. As much as I'd have liked to, I couldn't stay long enough to examine the treasure trove of mysteries that surrounded Abel and me. This was the world our parents abandoned, all for the sake of a piece of forbidden fruit and a serpent's lie.

"Where is Latavius?" I asked my brother. "Do you see the Baron anywhere?"

Abel shook his head. "They couldn't have gone far."

BANG!

A bolt of lightning struck not five feet in front of where we stood. A cloud of smoke burst from the grass in front of us.

A man stood there, his face shining like the sun. His skin had a golden hue. He wore a gown of pure white. When my eyes readjusted after the flash of light, I saw he had two wings growing out of his back.

"Sons of Adam, your presence is forbidden here."

Abel and I exchanged glances. "We're here to bring back a man who came through before. His name is Latavius."

"We will deal with the man. But you must depart in haste."

I snorted. "Who are you, anyway? Why do you get to tell us if we can stay or go?"

"I am Michael."

"The archangel?" Abel asked.

Michael nodded. "I was charged to prevent reentry into the garden by Adam, Eve, or their children."

"But our friend Latavius doesn't count?"

"I told you, he'll be handled his own way. But you two are not so far removed from your parents' sin that you have an excuse."

I sighed. "It's been six thousand years."

"And I've been in heaven for most of that time," Abel added.

Michael cocked his head. "I see. I sense it. You already have the curse, do you not, Cain?"

I nodded. "I do. What did you think? That we came here before... you know..."

"Before he killed me," Abel said, finishing my sentence.

"I assumed as much. As you know, this world exists on a plane of space and time separate from your own. A single breach into our realm could come from any time in your world. And if you were to forge a new gate back to the earth, it might engage your world at any time in your world's history."

"Which is why we must recover our friend. If we come again later, there's no telling if we'll be able to even find him, much less bring him back to the proper time."

"Why should I heed your request? Your very presence here is an abomination."

"I forgave my brother for his sin against me," Abel said. "Isn't that close to the heart of the Divine?"

Michael narrowed his eyes. "You still bear the mark, do you not, Cain?"

I nodded. "I do. But I no longer tend to fields. I care for the souls of the troubled. The man here is my patient. He is committed to my care. I beg of you, Michael, to return him to me."

"Listen to him," Annabelle's voice echoed behind me.

I turned. Annabelle was there and her eyes were aglow. "I am Isabelle. I wield power drawn from the Tree of Life itself. As a guardian of this realm and life itself, I petition you, Archangel, to deliver the man Latavius to us. You must also purge Baron Samedi, the Angel of Death, from the host he inhabits. He came to Guinee with designs to assault the garden groves and destroy the Tree of Life."

Michael nodded. "Very well, Isabelle. I know who you are. I know you've been chosen to one day ascend as a Dryad, to inhabit the Tree of Life itself. But I'd made my decision, already, before you arrived. For these brothers to make amends after so much time, after such a mortal sin committed by one against the other, is a remarkable occurrence. These men are closer to the heart of God now than their parents were the day they were exiled from these groves. And should you wish it, Cain, I shall petition the Almighty that your curse be removed."

I took a deep breath. "I will continue to bear it. I no longer see it as a curse but as a gift. There are others who've inherited my condition. Were I to accept that, and I was no longer a werewolf, there would be others that need me who I could no longer help."

Michael nodded. "It is good and noble to sacrifice oneself for the benefit of others. This is the substance of divine love."

"Then please," Isabelle said. "Send us Latavius. He needs our help."

"I will do as you wish," Michael said. Then, the angel extended his hand. A scepter materialized in his grip, and Latavius appeared in front of him.

Latavius looked around. "What happened? I was just fighting with the Baron... and now I'm..."

I rested my hand on Latavius' shoulder. "We're going home, son."

"Hello, Latavius," Isabelle said.

"Latavius, it is Isabelle, not Annabelle, who now speaks through Annabelle's body."

Latavius cocked his head and, looking at her with wide eyes, reached up to touch Annabelle's face. "I believe we are family, Isabelle."

"We are," Isabelle said. "I know your reasons to oppose the Voodoo Queen. But her heart is good. While I am not always within her, like I used to be, I am a part of her often. For my sake, Latavius, let go of your hate. If Annabelle and I can live together, having shared a body for many years, surely you can accept her as well. She is good and noble, and you must give her a chance."

Latavius nodded. "I will stand down. But Cain, I think I might like to spend a little more time with you if that's alright."

I smiled. "We already have a room for you at the Vilokan Asylum of the Magically and Mentally Deranged."

CHAPTER TWENTY

ANNABELLE RESUMED CONTROL OF her body after we arrived back in Vilokan.

"I'm proud of you, Annabelle."

Annabelle sighed. "I knew Isabelle would have the Archangel's ear. I could see what was happening through the gate, and I couldn't allow history to repeat itself. I couldn't allow Latavius to suffer the same fate as Nico."

"All worked out well and, besides that, I think it was good for Latavius to speak to Isabelle, even if only briefly."

"Do you think he'll really come around?" Annabelle asked.

I nodded. "I believe he will. Many of his assumptions about the world blew up in his face after he lost control of the Baron. He sacrificed himself willingly to push the Baron into the gateway after the Red Baron reemerged. If he didn't truly wish for the best for Vilokan, he'd never have done that. And Isabelle said some nice things about you, so that couldn't hurt, either."

Annabelle laughed. "She did, didn't she? She and I didn't always get along so well, you know."

I smiled. "You've told me."

"But we aren't the same people we were when the caplata, Messalina, first bound Isabelle's soul to mine when I was a child. In fact, I don't think any of us are the same people today that we were yesterday. That's why I'm willing to give Latavius a chance to atone for his error. If he wishes to change, there is no reason he should continue to suffer from his mistakes. Justice does not prevail through punishment but in restoration."

I nodded. "I believe that's wise."

"We'll need to make space at the asylum. Cain and Abel. Your packs are overtaking the place. You need to move them to the satellite as soon as possible."

I smiled. "Gladly."

"You do have a room for me?" Latavius asked.

I nodded. "We will. Don't worry about that."

We walked together back to the asylum. I approached Rutherford's desk. "Latavius intends to rejoin us for a while."

"Inpatient or outpatient?" Rutherford asked.

"Inpatient," Latavius said, approaching Rutherford's desk himself. "I need a little time to process things. If that's okay, I mean."

"It's certainly more than okay," Annabelle added.

Rutherford grabbed a stack of paperwork, an introductory packet, from beneath her desk. She handed it to Latavius. "I know you didn't fill this out the last time, but since you're committing yourself willingly, it would be easier if you just answered all the questions. None of it is especially personal. It's mostly your medical history, dietary concerns, and things of that nature."

"Thank you," Latavius said. "Should I fill it out here?"

"We need to clear a room for you," Rutherford said. "We have to get the wolves transferred back out of here first."

"How long will that take?" Latavius asked.

"It shouldn't take long at all," Rutherford said. "Cain, would you mind helping me prepare the room for Latavius while the other nurses discharge the wolves?"

I nodded. "I'd be happy to help."

"I'll stay out here with Latavius," Annabelle said. "It'll give us a little time to talk."

"I think that's a great idea," I said.

"I agree," Latavius added. "It's something I should have done a long time ago before I allowed my assumptions to get the best of me."

"All is forgiven, Latavius. Thankfully, despite the zombie incursion, I don't think anyone was bitten, so we averted what could have been a real disaster and tragedy."

Latavius nodded. "I'm glad to hear that."

"We'll let you know when the room is ready," I said. "It shouldn't take long."

I followed Rutherford down the hall as she retrieved a new set of sheets, a stack of cartoon-patterned hospital gowns, and a supply kit. The kits included all the necessities like a toothbrush, toothpaste, soap, shampoo, and deodorant.

Rutherford grabbed her chart from the nurse's station and chose one of the rooms from her list. She traced her finger down the list and stopped at one of them. "I think this room will work."

"Fine with me," I said as I followed Rutherford to the room she identified.

We stepped inside the room. Rutherford handed me one corner of the fitted sheet for the bed. "Just tuck it in around the corner."

I smiled. "I know how to make a bed, Rutherford."

Rutherford smiled. "I know. I'm sorry. After that last conversation we had, I'm just a little off."

"Why is that?" I asked.

Rutherford sighed. "I can't deny that I have feelings for you, Cain. My head tells me I shouldn't move faster with you, that I should let you go. That I should look for someone else, someone mortal, someone who can see me as the love of his life. But seeing you come around with your brother really touched me. Then, you risked everything to save a man who you could have easily judged a villain. I mean, Latavius might have destroyed Vilokan. He could have murdered people, but you still helped him. Now, he's here, ready to do the work necessary to change his life. It's remarkable, Cain."

I smiled. "I know you said you were afraid I couldn't give you all of my heart, Rutherford. But you know what? I'm not the same man I used to be. My heart has changed. My life has changed. I don't have the same heart I had before. This heart, the one I have now, if I gave it to you, it would be yours. Totally. Completely."

Rutherford grinned, tossed the sheet on the bed, and took my hands in hers. "I believe you."

I brushed a stray, red curl away from Rutherford's face. She ran one hand up my arm, across my shoulder, and to the back of my head. Then she pulled me into a kiss.

The End of Book 2

Continued in *Cain and Angel* (Keep reading...)

CAIN AND ANGEL

THEOPHILUS MONROE

CHAPTER ONE

ANOTHER FULL MOON. IN just a few hours, we'd run together. Two packs as one. My pack or, perhaps I should say Donald's pack, along with Abel's. I'd say it was a bonding exercise but over the last few weeks the wolves of both packs really came together to put the finishing touches on the old Mulledy plantation—now the satellite extension of the Vilokan Asylum of the Magically and Mentally Deranged.

We had a clear path from the back of the property to Manchac Swamp. It was perfect. While the area of the swamp where the rougarou roamed for the last century-plus was only a few square miles, the swamp itself spanned hundreds of acres. The freshwater marshes were populated mostly by alligators, cypress trees, and more creepy crawlies than I could count. Most locals knew the swamp for two reasons. The first being the Manchac Swamp Bridge, one of the longest bridges in the world over water with a length of about twenty-three miles. The other reason locals knew about Manchac Swamp is because they believed certain portions of the wetlands to be haunted. Thus, many referred to the place as the ghost swamp of Louisiana.

They weren't wrong. At least they didn't use to be. Julie Brown had haunted the swamp and, along with the rougarou, guarded the flambeau of the Witch of Endor which was buried in a gravesite in the middle of the swamp. Since then, though, the flambeau was removed from the swamp. Julie Brown took a body, got bitten by a werewolf, and was now a part of the pack of rougarou. After that, Julie could evoke the flambeau at will and cause the pack to shift. They didn't have to wait for a full moon.

I'd considered allowing Julie's gift, the flambeau, to accelerate our treatment plan. The goal of the plan, after all, was to help the wolves resolve any issues buried in their subconscious minds that might manifest while in wolf form. A buried resentment, a minor insecurity, could turn a wolf ravenous if not handled.

Most people can deal well enough for most of their lives without addressing all of their flaws, defects, or resentments. That's not the case for werewolves. If we hope to live long, productive lives without murdering people, we simply cannot neglect our mental health. For that reason, if you ever meet a werewolf who's lived more than a few years, chances are that they'll either be one of the most healthy and well-balanced individuals you've ever met, or they'll be sociopaths, so used to killing, so addicted to being the wolf, that they've lost touch with their humanity.

My goal was to ensure that my wolves, and Abel's, were of the well-balanced sort. The other kind of wolf, well, they were everything you'd ever seen in any werewolf horror film and more.

A part of that process, of embracing the nobler path, meant *enjoying* being a wolf. It required experiencing more than anger and rage while the wolf, but also elation and joy. This full moon was all about having fun.

It was Pack Donald versus Pack Abel. I was supposed to be the neutral party, the referee. I even found an oversized black-and-white spandex shirt that I hoped would stretch enough for me to wear after shifting. The other wolves were wearing similar oversized spandex. Donald's pack was in red. Abel's pack was in blue.

"I'm still not sure I understand the rules," Abel said.

"It's simple," I said. "Work together with your team to move the ball across the swamp. You can only touch it, though, with your snout. You're not allowed to bite the ball. You can't pick it up. That's a penalty. If you get the ball to the opponents' goal, the cypress tree marked by a ribbon of the other team's color, the goal is to hit the tree with the ball."

"It's like soccer," Donald said.

"Abel isn't from around here. He probably calls it football," Christopher said.

Abel cleared his throat. "I'm from a few thousand years B.C. We didn't have any of those games back then. But I think I get the gist of it. I'm supposed to slam my balls into the other team's wood."

Christopher started giggling. Evie slapped him on the shoulder. "Grow up, Christopher."

I bit the inside of my cheek. "That's basically it. But you only have one ball, Abel."

"Ouch," Christopher said. "Abel's a uniball!"

I cleared my throat. "The game is played with a single ball."

"Then how do we score if the other pack has the ball?"

"They'll bounce it around on their noses just the same way you have to, Abel. The idea is, when they have it, to intercept the ball and take control of it. You can move it yourself or you can use your snout to pass the ball to one of your pack mates."

"How do we know who wins?" Abel asked.

"Whoever has the most goals when the sun rises, when we shift back, prevails."

"We're doing this all night long?" Abel asked.

"Trust me," Donald interjected. "It's a blast. The time will pass like nobody's business. Plus, since we have a lot of young wolves in both of our packs, this will be a good way to keep ourselves distracted so that the wolf's more carnivorous side remains at bay."

Abel nodded. "I think I understand. It doesn't sound like a fair match. How many times have you played this game before, Donald?"

Donald shrugged. "We played similar games for years when we lived in the swamp as rougarou. Now, though, since we've been human and seen human sports, we've refined the game. With these rules, this is only our fourth time playing and the first time with another pack."

"Either way, you guys have an enormous advantage. You haven't only played this before, but you basically invented the game."

"I'd say we adapted it from other sports. But you're right. What do you say we spot you five goals?"

"What do we get if we win?" Abel asked.

"The pride in knowing you bested your opponent," I said. "And an appreciation of a night's worth of fun."

"No offense, Cain," Christopher said. "But that's lame as shit. I say we make a friendly little wager."

"What do you have in mind?" Abel asked.

"The loser buys the beer for both packs until the next full moon."

Abel cocked his head. "I haven't been alive very long. I don't have any money to buy beer."

"We've got this," Luka, one of Abel's wolves, said. "I'm a lawyer. At least I used to be before all of this happened. And I'm single with nothing to do with my stacks and stacks of cash. How about the winning pack has first dibs on rooms. That means some of the losing pack will have to sleep in the old slave quarters out back."

Donald shrugged. "We don't all stay at the asylum, anyway. We have families. Well, the older of our wolves do. Only Ryan, Cassidy, and Julie, who is really a part of both packs, are staying at the asylum."

"If we win," Luka said, "they move into the old slave quarters where half our pack is staying and the rest of our pack stays inside for the month. Next month, the winner gets the same privileges."

"What do you three say?" Donald asked. "This affects you more than it does them."

"I think there should be something more in it for us if we win," Ryan said. "With these terms, all that's at stake apart from the beer wager is the possibility that Cassidy, Julie, and I will have to move out of our rooms."

"Anything you can offer them if they win?" Abel asked Luka. "I have little to give."

Luka ran his fingers through his short, salt-and-pepper hair. He wasn't old. Maybe thirty years old. But he was prematurely gray. From my conversations with him, life as a lawyer wasn't as stress-free as he'd imagined it might be when he went to law school. "If we lose," Luka said, "I'll pay for professional massages for all of us."

"Not a poor deal," Cassidy added. "I'm always sore after a shift."

"We all are," Donald said. "Sounds like a wager I can get on board with."

"What if there's a tie?" Ryan asked. "Once we shift back, it's not like we can just shift back for overtime."

"That's not technically true," Julie said. "We could shift back. With the flambeau."

I snorted. "We're not having overtime periods. It's too risky to shift back again so soon after a full moon's shift. It just takes too much out of us. We'd all be worthless for a week until we recovered. If there's a tie, I'll tell you what. You guys can split the cost of the beer and the masseuses. And I'll see what I can do about getting air conditioning in the slave quarters so that whoever has to stay out there is more comfortable."

Cassidy chuckled. "You're seriously not going to get us air conditioning out there unless we tie?"

I bit my lip. In fact, I'd already planned on it. The HVAC guy was coming to give me an estimate the next week. "You don't know what I have planned."

"That's dumb," Ryan said. "If we tie on purpose, we can force Cain to buy us air conditioning for the spare quarters out back. Why would we even try to win?"

"To make the other team pay for all the beer," Christopher said. "And to get the free massages."

"Alright, fair point. I'm betting Cain is just bluffing, anyway. He's probably already arranged for air conditioning in the spare quarters."

I smiled. "Maybe I have. Maybe I haven't."

"You have," Abel said, laughing. "You do a little thing with your lip when you tell a lie, Cain."

"I do not!"

Abel shook his head. "He's done it since we were children. Look at him right now! He's lying about the fact that he does the lip thing. See how it curls up like that? To think that a tick like that would persist for, what, six thousand years now?"

I narrowed my eyes. "You shouldn't give away my tells, Abel."

Abel chuckled. "You shouldn't tell lies, either. But here we are."

I grinned back at Abel. "Touché. Yes, you're right, the lot of you. I am getting an estimate on the air conditioning next week."

"Still, if we win, we get to move inside in the meantime," Abel added.

"Better get ready to pay up, Luka," Christopher said. "I'm looking forward to that massage."

Luka grinned. "We'll see about that, Christopher."

I cleared my throat. "The sun is setting and the moon will soon ascend. If we've settled all of that, we should begin our preparations."

Donald popped his knuckles. "Alright. y'all. It's yoga time."

Abel narrowed his eyes and elbowed me in the side. "What's yoga?"

I grinned. "It's a kind of exercise, great for warming up the muscles and joints. It makes the shift more tolerable."

"How do I play?" Abel asked.

I chuckled. "You don't play yoga. It's just something you do. It's pretty simple. Donald will lead the group. He's gotten quite good at it. Granted, he doesn't look the part. No one imagines a three-hundred pound man going through vinyasas and performing balance postures, but if you follow his lead and do your best, you'll be fine."

Abel nodded. "Alright. But you aren't getting out of this, Cain."

I cocked my head. "I've shifted thousands of times. I don't need to do yoga to prepare anymore."

"I agree with Abel," Cassidy piped up. "If we're going to do this, I say the doctor joins us."

"Doctor Cain!" Ryan started chanting. Then the rest of the wolves from both packs joined in. "Doctor Cain! Doctor Cain! Doctor Cain!"

I laughed, shaking my head. "Okay, okay, okay! I'll do it. But don't laugh. Even if I make an ass out of myself, don't forget I'm still a wolf. I roar. I don't bray."

I knew I *would* make an ass out of myself. I knew yoga helped young wolves shift, but I was long past the more difficult phase of shifting before I ever heard about yoga, much less attempted it. And I only tried it once. For reasons that I assumed were about to become obvious to the rest of the wolves, I'd never dared to do it again.

I took a deep breath and stood next to Abel. Cassidy looked over her shoulder and winked at me. I smiled and nodded back at her.

"Alright, everyone inhale," Donald said, raising both arms overhead as he drew in a breath, lowering them again as he exhaled. I did my best to mimic his actions. "Good. And, again."

Another inhale. Another exhale.

"Arms forward," Donald said. "Feet just greater than shoulder-width apart as you lean forward into flat back."

The back of my legs burned. With my emotions, and my tolerance for dealing with people's nonsense, I was as flexible as they came. With my body, well, that was another issue. I had the flexibility of a brick.

I winced as I tried my best to hold what I imagined was an introductory warm-up pose. I began to think I was overestimating the flexibility of bricks. My hamstrings were as tight as a camel's arse in a sandstorm.

"Feet together," Donald directed. "To flat back, reach down, and step or jump back into your first vinyasa."

I did my best to mimic Donald's movements. The man was about a hundred pounds larger than me, and he made these motions seem natural and graceful. I followed the motion of the vinyasa into a posture he called "upward dog."

Ironic, I know. But then, a few seconds later we were in downward dog and, well, I wasn't sure how wise it was for a dog to stick his butt in the air like that. Especially in the company of other dogs.

"Step up, stand slowly, returning to flat back. Now step back and, with your feet pointing forward, raise your hands into crescent pose."

I did what Donald suggested, then I topped over, my face hitting in the grass.

Abel chuckled even as he stood there in perfect balance. "I guess you can't be good at everything."

"Shut up," I said.

Christopher turned and snickered. Yeah, I was their therapist. They were used to seeing me speak in a more refined way. But when you're a sibling, it doesn't matter how old you get; you don't pull any punches. We were brothers. We were mean to each other out of love. Most of the time. Barring the story about my brother and I that most of the world already knew about. But that was a long time ago. We were past that.

I did my best to keep up. Donald noticed and walked over to me while the rest of the wolves were holding something he called "tree pose."

"I have another pose for you, doctor."

"What's that?" I asked.

"It's called shavasana."

"Say what?"

"Lay down on your back," Donald said.

I laid down. "Now what?"

"Extend your arms, palms up. Just breathe. Clear your mind."

I snorted. "That's it? This isn't yoga, it's just lying down."

"Some say it's the hardest pose in all of yoga."

"Why is that?" I asked.

"Focus on your toes as you breathe. Relax your toes. Then, pull your focus up your body to your shins. As you move your focus up your body, relax each part. Then, when you're done, check the rest. Have you tightened up again? Has the tension returned anywhere you'd already relaxed? That's why it's so hard. We're so accustomed to working, to pushing our bodies and minds to the limit, that we don't know how to relax."

"You're seriously going to leave me on my back while the rest of you go through the rest of your routine?"

"Do you want to try crane pose, or royal dancer?"

"Those things sound a lot more fun than the hell they probably are."

Donald chuckled. "I'll take that as a no. Just focus on your body, relaxing and breathing like I told you before. We're going to shift soon, anyway. Then, it's game on."

CHAPTER TWO

I COULDN'T DO MOST of Donald's yoga moves. Still, while I didn't want to admit it, trying yoga again was a good thing. Especially since I'd encouraged the rest of the pack to do these routines before their shifts. Donald was right about shavasana, too. In a sense, it was easy. I just laid there on my back. When I tried to do what he suggested, though, and relaxed my body while releasing all my tension, it was crazy to discover how difficult relaxing actually was. Taking it easy is awfully hard.

Even though I only did a few of the moves, and less than half the routine, it made a noticeable difference when we shifted. I didn't think it would. My body had shifted so many times that I was used to it. But even so, while I didn't experience the same pain that younger wolves did, there was a pressure and a tension when I changed. It wasn't unbearable, but it was uncomfortable. This time, though, a lightness came over me as I became the wolf. In fact, I had to look down at my body just to double check to be sure I had changed.

Thankfully, I'd guessed my werewolf size right for my spandex referee shirt. From the looks of it, the red and blue shirts fit the other werewolves just as well. It was also important we select a ball that could withstand our abuse. Not any ball could do. We'd probably pop an inflatable ball before the night's end. When we played werewolf swamp polo—the name of our game is still a work in progress—we used a foam-filled soccer ball. It was the same foam that you could use to fill tractor tires to prevent leaks. Here, though, it helped prevent our incisors from spoiling the night's fun.

Donald and Abel faced off in the middle of the swamp at a location roughly four-hundred wolf's paces from each goal. We knew the spot. We'd measured it all out months ago. The trees were already marked, too. This was just the first time we'd played with enough wolves to form two full teams.

I'd say I blew the whistle to start the game. I tried using one of those the first time we did this. I couldn't get my big, hairy lips around the damned thing. So, instead, I howled at the moon to inaugurate the game.

The rougarou spotted Abel's pack five points to make up for the younger pack's lack of experience. I doubted it would be enough. Donald's pack, aside from the recent additions, was more than significantly older than Abel's bunch. They'd spent most of their time during the last century-plus *as* wolves. Competing like this was as second nature to them as going for a jog through a park might be for a regular human.

I tossed the ball into the air between the two alphas. Donald jumped a few inches higher than Abel and, jabbing the ball with his snout, Christopher took it and bounced the ball across the waters until Luka snuck up, stole the ball, and blasted the opposite direction. Diving under the water, he emerged, shooting the ball into the air, before head-butting it right into the red packs' goal.

I howled. The score was now six to zero, blue pack. If Luka was really this good, I was beginning to wonder if it was a mistake for Donald to spot Abel's pack with the extra points.

Then they faced off again. This time, it was Ryan on one side, Luka on the other. Luka won the ball initially but Cassidy intercepted his pass to Abel and, with a hard upward face-thrust, sent the ball back to Ryan who bounced it up and down off his snout until he reached the blue goal and scored.

Red pack, one. Blue pack, six.

Luka was good. Better than expected. Ryan was apparently pretty skilled with a ball, too. They'd surely never played werewolf swamp polo before, but they'd clearly had experience playing a similar sport. Soccer, perhaps. Maybe rugby. No wonder they were so eager to place bets. They each thought they'd buffalo the other team by pretending they didn't know what they were doing.

The score evened out eventually at eight to eight. Then, Luka went on a tear, scoring three straight goals, giving the blue pack a healthy lead. Until Donald, Ryan, and the rest of the red pack responded with four more straight goals their own.

When the sun rose, and we shifted back, it was red pack, twelve; blue pack, eleven. Most of the scoring happened between Ryan and Luka, though Christopher and Cassidy each scored a goal for the red pack. Abel didn't score a single one. No one else in Abel's pack scored aside from Luka. That ended up being the difference.

Ryan laughed and gave Luka a high five after putting on his pair of pants. Because, you know, slapping five in the nude is kind of weird.

"Good game, dude," Luke said. "I didn't know you had such skills."

Ryan chuckled. "I grew up playing soccer. Even had a small scholarship to my school back in Missouri."

Luka nodded. "Believe it or not, I was an alternate for the U.S. men's team, the summer Olympics before last."

"Really?" Ryan asked. "Impressive."

Luka nodded. "What's impressive is that you better than matched me point-for-point. Maybe we'll have a rematch. This time, regular soccer. In this shape."

"Sounds like a deal," Ryan said. "But you still have to pay up."

"Bring on the hot masseuses!" Christopher declared. "And a month's worth of beer!"

Luka laughed. "I'm a man and, apparently, a wolf of his word now. You've got it, fellas. I'll make a few calls. Plan on massages later this afternoon."

"Do you think they'll be hot?" Christopher asked, kicking his feet up on the ottoman in front of the couch where he sat in the common room, formerly Annabelle's living room, at the Vilokan Asylum extension site.

"The masseuses?" Ryan asked, even as I noticed Evie rolling her eyes.

Christopher nodded. "I've heard that most of the girls who give massages are good looking."

"Why does it even matter?" Evie asked. "It's a massage. That's it."

Christopher shrugged. "You don't have to act jealous about it, Evie. It's just a massage."

Evie rolled her eyes. "Exactly my point. It's just a massage."

Luka chuckled. "They should be here any minute now. I don't know how hot they are, but you can trust me. They're the best at what they do."

"I've never had a massage," Abel said. "I take it it's a pleasurable experience?"

I nodded. "It really helps. I don't know about you, but sometimes after a shift, my back muscles are pretty tense."

Abel nodded. "Yeah, I feel it. I'm excited to experience it. Like everything else. It's crazy how many things mankind has created in the world that now I have to experience for the first time."

"Hey Abel," Christopher said. "Be sure to ask your masseuse for a happy ending."

Evie backhanded Christopher on the arm. "Don't do that, Abel. He's messing with you."

Christopher chuckled. "What?"

Abel cocked his head. "Why wouldn't I want a happy ending? That sounds quite nice."

I snorted. "It's a euphemism. It means that, when they're done, they give you pleasure, you know, in your personal parts."

Abel furrowed his brow. "I'm not sure I understand what you mean."

"It means that the masseuse will finish you off with a handy!" Christopher piped up.

Evie sat there, shaking her head.

"A handy?" Abel asked.

"Never mind that," Evie said. "Christopher is trying... and failing... to be funny."

"I just assumed that if you got a massage, they used their hands," Abel said. "Or are you saying they massage our hands?"

Abel lifted his hands in front of his face, turned them, and examined them carefully.

"Not what it means," Christopher said.

"I do have some tension in my palms," Abel said. "I could definitely use a handy. I will bring it up."

"Don't do that," I said. "Christopher is trying to get you into trouble."

"I'm just messing with you, dude," Christopher said. "Don't ask the masseuse for anything like that. Just lay there and do what she tells you. Which basically means doing nothing at all."

I stood up and threw on my jacket. "Well, I hope you all enjoy your massages."

"What?" Luka asked. "You aren't saying? I'm paying for it."

I shook my head. "I'd love to stay, but I really can't. My schedule back at the asylum in Vilokan is pretty tight."

I started walking to the door when someone knocked on it four times.

"That must be them!" Luka said, standing up and hurrying to the front door. He opened it and four men with insanely large muscles walked through.

"Who are they?" Christopher asked.

"These are your *masseuses*!" Luka said, smirking.

Evie started giggling. "I can't wait!"

"No way," Christopher said. "A dude who looks like that can't massage you!"

Evie chuckled. "So when you thought they were going to be female masseuses you were excited, but now that we find out that we're being massaged by hot guys, you don't want me to do it?"

"Right," Christopher said. "It's different!"

"No it's not!" Evie protested.

"They're all quite professional, Christopher," Luka said. "You have nothing to worry about."

Christopher sighed. "How am I supposed to relax with a dude putting his hands all over me, anyway?"

The grin splitting Evie's face was so wide I was afraid she was going to crack her head in two. "Come on, Christopher. You said it yourself. It's *just* a massage."

Donald shrugged and removed his shirt. "Alright, if you all are going to bicker about it, I'll go first. I'm secure enough in my manhood to let another guy touch me."

One masseur followed Donald back to one of the rooms. They had portable tables that each of them carried at their sides, folded up so that they looked like suitcases.

"Any other volunteers to go first?" a masseur asked. "After we do this round, we can do four more at a time."

Cassidy, Julie, and Evie quickly raised their hands. They clearly didn't have any qualms about being massaged by guys.

Christopher grunted and gave the massage therapist, who followed Evie, a death-stare. I don't think the man noticed.

"You really should give them a shot, Christopher," I said. "It's not gay, to get a massage by a guy, if that's what you're worried about. No more than you'd be cheating on Evie if you had a female masseuse. It's therapy. It's no different than counseling with me. I massage your mind. They massage your body."

Christopher grunted. "That's very different, Cain."

Luka rolled his eyes. "It's not like he's going to touch your wiener, man. Relax."

Christopher rested his face in his hands. "I'll think about it."

I shrugged my shoulders. "Well, enjoy your massages. I'll see everyone back here for our evening group session."

Abel waved at me. "See you soon, brother."

CHAPTER THREE

I STOPPED AT RUTHERFORD'S desk on my way to my office. She was at reception and since no one was waiting for an appointment, and no one inside the asylum could see us, I leaned over her desk and gave her a quick peck on the cheek.

Rutherford winked at me. "Have a good shift?"

"We did! The two packs are doing well together. And since we didn't have any incidents, I'd call it a success."

"That's good to hear. You've got someone waiting for you."

"A patient?"

Rutherford bit her lip. "Not officially. He just showed up. He said he was looking for you. Annabelle doesn't have a clue who he is. She didn't refer him."

"And he's waiting for me? You just let him past the security door because he asked nicely?"

Rutherford shook her head. "I didn't just *let* him in, Cain. He walked right through the damn door like it wasn't even there."

I snorted. "What kind of supernatural creature could do something like that?"

Rutherford shrugged. "Hell if I know. Maybe an elemental? He doesn't seem to have much respect for rules at all. You'll figure that out soon enough. All I know was that he insisted he speak to you."

I sighed. "I wonder how he even got into Vilokan?"

"My guess is the same way he got through the security door. Whatever this guy is, doors and walls aren't much of an impediment to him."

I placed my key card to the reader next to the security door and waited for it to click. Then I pulled it open and stepped into the hallway. "Never a dull day at the Vilokan Asylum," I said to myself as I walked down the hall toward my office.

My door was locked. Was the mysterious visitor inside? I unclipped my key-chain from my belt, inserted the proper key, and unlocked my door. I turned the knob, opened the door, and stepped inside.

My unwelcome guest was already relaxed on my red-velvet chaise. He was wearing a three-piece black suit and was smoking a cigar.

"Excuse me, sir," I said as the visitor puffed three donuts of smoke into the air. "We do not permit smoking in the asylum."

"Apologies," the visitor said, tapping his cigar, dropping ash on the floor.

I cleared my throat. "I'm Dr. Cain."

The man smiled at me. His teeth were white as Chicklets and perfectly straight. His skin was olive in tone and his hair was a pasta bowl of golden curls. "I know who you are! The question is, do you remember me?"

I scrunched my brow. "Sir, I'm not sure I do."

The visitor stood up from my chaise and approached the bookshelf from behind my desk. He grabbed a King James bible from my shelf and started flipping through the first several pages. "My story isn't that far removed from yours. Well, the part of the story that the boss man saw fit to commission in his book. Yes, here it is. 'The sons of God saw the daughters of men that they *were* fair; and they took them wives of all which they chose.'"

I cocked my head. "You're one of the sons of God? My apologies. I was distracted with my own affairs when these events occurred."

"The name's Samyaza," the visitor said, extending his hand for me to shake. "But you can call me Sam."

I shook Sam's hand. "But we met before?"

"Of course we did, Cain. You didn't know who I was, I suppose. But I was the first of the Watchers."

"You're an angel, then? You were among those first tasked to protect the earliest generations of man?"

Sam nodded. "But when we chose human women as wives for ourselves, when we loved these marvelous creatures, God sent the archangels Gabriel and Michael to punish us."

"And our paths crossed in those days?"

"Certainly," Sam said. "Though, I suppose, you were not in this form the first time we met."

"I was a werewolf?" I asked.

Sam nodded. "My children, the Nephilim, intended to track you down and hunt you. As an angel myself, I knew of your curse. I intervened before they found you. I did not wish for them to fall under your curse."

"How noble of you," I said.

"Along with the rest of the watchers, on account of our lust for women, the Almighty disowned us. Surely you can relate. A single act, what we were told was a sin, and it excluded us from divine favor. After that, you'd think we'd be permitted to raise our new families without interference. But Gabriel, at the behest of the Divine, instigated a war between the factions of the Watchers, including our offspring. That war provided a distraction. That was all the archangel needed. Michael came at us from behind while focused on the battle ahead. He bound me. He did the same to many of my brothers. Then, shortly after that, there was the great flood which destroyed our children. Imprisoned by Michael, there was nothing I could do to stop it. My children were wiped off the face of the earth. And worse, bound by chains, the angels forced me to watch it happen."

I winced. "I cannot imagine how difficult that must've been for you."

"I was no demon, Cain. I was an angel who made the grave mistake of appreciating the beauty of human women, who dared to marry and have children. This was my great sin. Gabriel and Michael told me that my children were an abomination. After all of that, it shouldn't have surprised me when Lucifer approached. He offered me, and the rest of the surviving Watchers, a chance to join him, to pursue vengeance on behalf of our children."

"This was a low point in your life, I presume. You were vulnerable and took Lucifer up on his offer."

Sam nodded. "Thus, for thousands of years, we were demons. But my intention was never to overthrow the Almighty. I had no desire to deceive and destroy mankind. I loved humanity. I could not accept Lucifer's agenda. So, I left his courts."

I raised an eyebrow. "You're a repentant fallen angel? A remorseful demon?"

Sam scratched his head. "That's one way to put it. I'd say that I'm an unfallen angel. I'm what humans these days might deem a free agent, though I have no intention of re-joining either of my former teams. Before the Almighty commissioned the Watchers to earth, I lived in the celestial realm. I don't know that I could atone enough to regain my place there. Even if I could, I probably wouldn't desire it. I don't have the stomach to sing praises, for all eternity, to the Almighty. I'm still more than a little distraught over the loss of my children. But Lucifer is a real prick. I have no desire to return to hell, to take part in the evil he'd like us to inflict upon the earth."

I leaned against my desk and tapped my fingernails on the edge. "I have to admit, your story is intriguing. It certainly explains, I suppose, why you look familiar, but I don't know you. Your history also explains how you could get into Vilokan and even my office. I'm still not sure why you're here."

"You're a wanderer, Cain. You, too, have survived while walking the lonely way between the celestial and the infernal, between holiness and wickedness. But you have something I never did. A mark protects you. Unlike you, I'm now hunted by legions of angels and hordes of demons alike. Both sides wish to punish me for what they believe to be my betrayal of their respective causes."

"You said you're one of the Watchers. Are there more like you? Are there other unfallen angels?"

Sam shook his head. "Some of them remain with Lucifer. Others have fled, but I cannot say if they live. I am certain that many have died. If not slain by the angels, then by the demons. I'm running out of places to run and I can't hide forever."

"What are you looking for from me, Sam? I'm not sure I can protect you, either. I can't fight off angels and demons."

"I'm not looking for you to fight, Cain. You committed a grievous sin. You broke one of the commandments. Yet you, still, were given a mark of grace. A sign of protection. I know what is written of these affairs. I simply wish to ask if you might intercede on my behalf to the Divine, that he might also grant me such a provision, a protection, from those who'd see me, one of the last of the Watchers, eliminated forever."

I pressed my lips together. "Do you realize, Sam, I haven't spoken to God in nearly six thousand years?"

"I suspected you hadn't."

"Then why do you believe I'd have any success at all as your intercessor? Wouldn't you be better off finding a priest, or a saint of some sort?"

Sam shook his head. "I've tried. The problem, of course, is that they simply assume I'm a demon. Demons lie, right? When I tell my story, they don't empathize with my struggle. They cast me off as a devil, as if I tempted them to reject the Creator."

I snorted. "Well, to be fair, the way you presented your story to me clearly sets you at odds with God. You blamed him for killing your children. Now, I'm not saying you're wrong. But surely you can see why a religious person might not be inclined to accept your version of these events."

"Which brings me back to why I've come to see you, Cain. You were punished by God but also given his grace and protection. While exiled from your family and clan you were nonetheless granted a mark that warned any who might harm you to flee. You became a werewolf, but with that curse you were also granted a gift that no humans possess. Your years of life are seemingly unlimited, almost as if because of being cursed, it excused you from the curse placed upon your parents."

"That's an interesting way to look at it," I said, folding my hands in my lap. "I'll tell you what, Sam. Give me a little more time to get to know you. I'll see what I can do about securing a room for you here. We'll work together to sort through your issues, your resentments, and the like. If I'm satisfied with your progress, I know how I can reach the Archangel Michael. I'll see what I can do about securing a pardon, or at least a mark of protection."

Sam smiled. "Thank you, Cain. I knew I could count on you. Well, I hoped I could, anyway."

I cleared my throat, grabbed a metal waste paper basket from behind my desk, and extended it toward Sam. "Just remember, no smoking in the facility."

Sam sighed, took a draw from his cigar, and flicked his ash into my basket.

"The whole thing, Sam."

Sam took a deep breath and dropped the rest of his cigar in my trash can. Thankfully, it was empty. I didn't have to worry about it catching on fire. "Fine. So what's next?"

I smiled. "I have to do some paperwork. I'll send in a nurse to put you through processing."

"Processing?" Sam asked.

"It's standard practice. You know, we have to get your medical history, your condition, your basic goals, and we have to issue you a gown."

"A gown? I'm not a proper angel, Cain. I don't wear gowns."

"Not that kind of gown," I said, smiling. "Remember, Sam, if you want my help, you'll have to follow my rules."

Sam shook his head as he ran his fingers through his golden curls. "Rules. I've never had a great relationship with rules."

I grinned. "Of course you haven't. Which is precisely why that's where we'll have to start."

CHAPTER FOUR

WHEN YOU TREAT THE magically and mentally deranged, you never know what kinds of danger you might introduce to the population of the asylum when you bring in a new patient. Most of the time, the danger comes from a creature's innate abilities or disposition. A werewolf, for instance, poses a certain risk to other patients. Especially on a full moon. Vampires, especially the younglings we usually admitted, could be a threat on account of their bloodlust. In either case, mitigating efforts had to be made. We now treated werewolves at the extension site where, if they got loose on a full moon, I could track them down on the free range. We still treated vampires at the original campus, but we had sunlight collars that we could remotely activate to blast the vampires with a dose of ultraviolet radiation if they stepped out of line. Only on rare occasions did we need to use the collars. We did not zap most vampires in our care at all and I could count on one hand the number of times a vampire tested their collar more than once. In my experience, the collars were both necessary to prevent bloodshed and also important for teaching vampires that, despite their new nature, they still had rules to follow.

I had to teach Sam a similar lesson. But that wasn't the danger I was most worried about. It wasn't his own abilities, in fact, that had me most on edge. Granted, I was reasonably certain he had a healthy dose of power. Did he wield celestial power? Infernal power? A bit of both or a mixture of the two? I didn't know. We'd get there. What worried me the most was that two of the most dangerous and powerful entities in existence were after him. If the angels or demons learned he'd sought asylum at my asylum, well, I wasn't sure how I could effectively protect him. I mean, if he could walk right through the security doors to get in, chances were that the angels and demons who were hunting him could do the same.

I was in something of a pickle. I couldn't turn Sam away. He needed help. I wasn't sure exactly what I could do for him. But I had to try. Still, if his presence put the entire asylum in danger, well, I wasn't sure Annabelle would sign off on his petition for admittance.

All those things considered, I needed Annabelle for more than her permission to admit Sam to my program. The only time I'd engaged an angel at all in recent memory was just weeks earlier, after I'd taken a portal she'd made into Eden. Michael appeared the moment I arrived, intent on reminding me that my family wasn't welcome in the gardens. If I was ever going to fulfill my promise to Sam to advocate on his behalf, that was probably the place to start.

I stopped by Rutherford's desk on my way over. "Could you give Annabelle a call? Let her know I'm on my way over to get her approval for a new patient."

"What is he, anyway?" Rutherford asked.

I sighed. "His name is Sam. He calls himself an unfallen angel."

"Unfallen?" Rutherford asked, raising her left eyebrow.

"He was an angel. He fell. Apparently, he lost patience with the devil's antics and has disavowed the dark side of the force as well."

Rutherford chuckled. "So, he's not a Jedi. He's not aligned with the Sith or the Intergalactic Empire. Is there really room in the Star Wars universe for anyone in between?"

I shook my head. "Not really. Not in Star Wars. As much as I love the films, though, the supernatural world isn't as black and white as the dark and light sides of the force. It's rare that we meet anyone who's clearly a good guy or a bad guy. There are no heroes and villains. Everyone, it seems, is a bit of both and something of neither. Our visitor, Sam, is something of a lone ranger. An angel who doesn't belong in either the celestial or infernal realms, who doesn't buy into either side's agenda. As is often the case, those who refuse to choose a side become the enemy of both."

Rutherford nodded and picked up her phone. We were behind the times when it came to phones in Vilokan. While many vodouisants owned cell phones, they didn't work within the city. To communicate inside of Vilokan, or from Vilokan to the outside world, land lines were required.

Rutherford hit a button on the top of her phone's cradle, a pre-programmed speed-dial setting. Holding the phone between her ear and her shoulder, Rutherford got up and walked from her desk to a small refrigerator on the opposite side of her reception office. Her long, coiled cord stretched from the phone base all the way across the room.

"Come on, pick up your damn phone," Rutherford said as she grabbed a small dish out of our office refrigerator. Then she stepped out the door to the break room. The cord clicked against the wall as the coils stretched around the corner. Rutherford put her dish in the microwave and set it for two minutes.

"No answer?" I asked.

"Would you mind hanging up and dialing again?" Rutherford asked. "She's bad about picking up. Sometimes it takes a couple of attempts."

I stepped over to the base of the phone. I pressed the little flap that hangs up a phone call. Then I pushed the speed dial button labeled "AM." I presumed it referred to Annabelle Mulledy.

Rutherford was still waiting by the microwave. Since she wasn't talking, I presumed that Annabelle still hadn't picked up.

It wasn't the end of the world. Sure, she was the Voodoo Queen, but it wasn't like she lived in her office. If she was in Vilokan, I'd track her down. If she wasn't in Vilokan, well, she had a cell phone. I could get Rutherford, or maybe a wolf at the extension site, to call her up. I was reasonably certain that Ryan had her phone number.

Rutherford came back to her desk, a steaming dish of something that looked orange, red and mysterious but smelled savory, in her hands. I didn't bother asking what was in it. Knowing Rutherford, it was a lot of vegetables. I'm a werewolf. As much as I understand the health benefits of veganism and vegetarianism, I couldn't forego meat. Besides, as a werewolf, if the only thing that could kill me was silver (or perhaps a beheading) I doubted that trans-saturated fats or red meat was going to do me in. There were a few benefits to being a werewolf—the ability to eat whatever the hell I wanted without too much to worry about other than indigestion and maybe a little weight gain was certainly one of them.

Rutherford set her lunch down and handed me the phone.

I shrugged. "Why are you giving it to me?"

"Just wait," Rutherford said. "You can leave a message in a minute. Eventually, her machine will pick up."

I nodded and waited while the phone continued to ring. Then I heard a click.

"Hello," Annabelle said.

"Annabelle! I thought I'd missed you."

"Hello?"

"I can hear you, Annabelle. Can you hear me? It's Cain."

Annabelle laughed. "Fooled you! I'm not here right now. You're talking to a machine! Leave a message at the beep and give me a good reason to call you back."

I grunted. I heard the beep. "Annabelle, it's Cain. We need to talk. We have a new patient. He walked right into the asylum. I believe he's an angel. Other angels, and probably some demons, are after him. So, we need to discuss admitting him and how to better ward the place against angels. Call Rutherford if you get this message. I'm going to touch base with the wolves and see if I can reach you above ground."

I hung up the phone. "If she calls you, can you call Ryan's cell phone from here and let me know?"

"We have another phone line at the extension site now, Cain."

"We do?" I cocked my head.

Rutherford nodded. "The mansion already had a line, Cain. Annabelle called the phone company to have it activated last week."

"And I'm just hearing about this now?"

Rutherford shrugged. "You know how it is. She's constantly modernizing things. You never really use the new technologies."

I snorted. "A land line at the extension site isn't exactly innovative."

"Agreed," Rutherford said. "Annabelle thought it was a good idea to have a permanent line there just in case cell service goes down."

"Alright. Well, either way, call me if you hear from her. Or better, have her call me."

CHAPTER FIVE

I PULLED MY TRUCK through the iron gates at the extension site of Vilokan Asylum. I had a handy little remote that unlocked and opened the gates for me. It only had one button on it. It still might have been the most complex piece of technology I regularly used. Hell, I didn't even own a television. I read books. I rarely listened to music, but when I did, I played records. It took me a while to embrace that technology. By the time I did, everyone else was on to eight-track cartridges and, later, cassettes. When compact discs came out, well, they looked like alien technology. I'd try streaming music. I've heard they have little speakers with women inside of them, or maybe they're robotic women who will play music when you ask them. Simple enough, I suppose. But since streaming services don't function in Vilokan, there wasn't much reason to get one. I still had my records, and I was happy. I rarely went to my apartment. It was really little more than a bed in a room on the upper floor of one of Vilokan's shops. So, I kept my records in my office.

What did I listen to? It depended on the mood. I enjoyed Baroque music. You know what they say. If it ain't Baroque, don't fix it. I wasn't sure why the music scene ever changed. Still, I enjoyed some turn-of-the-century jazz and blues. The last century, I mean. The music at the dawn of the 2000s was hardly tolerable.

Cornetist Buddy Bolden was one of my favorites. In the early 1900s, his fusion of blues and ragtime was unprecedented. He played mostly in New Orleans. Unfortunately, he was committed to a mental institution in the first decade of the century and recorded no music himself. That was well before I'd studied psychoanalysis. I would have tried to help him if I'd known then what I know now. Still, despite his problems, Buddy's jazzy style set the stage for a new movement of music and, if I wanted something a little funkier than my Baroque favorites, early jazz was my go-to.

I made sure that the gates shut all the way, watching them slowly swing together as I drove up the circle drive in front of the white columns that were a staple for most antebellum plantation homes. Most everyone else parked in the grass at the side of the home.

When I left before, the masseurs were parked in the circle drive. Now they were gone. It had been a few hours, so that wasn't surprising. There was an old, rusted jeep, however, parked just in front of the doors, that I didn't recognize.

I stepped out of my truck, retrieved my keys, and made my way up the marble steps in front of the house and through two of the freshly painted white columns.

I was about to unlock the front door to go inside when I noticed someone left the door cracked open. I pressed the door open with my left hand.

"Hello?" I asked, looking through the foyer to the living room, aka common room, where the wolves usually gathered and we had most of our group sessions. We were due to start a session in about fifteen minutes. Where had everyone gone?

I looked out the back window. I didn't see anyone behind the house. There wasn't any evidence that anyone was inside the spare quarters, what used to be the slave quarters, either.

I turned around and gasped as a young, blond female and a tall, dark-haired Native American man stood there smiling at me.

I placed my hand on my chest. "You two scared the crap out of me."

"Sorry!" the blond girl said. "Do you remember me, Cain?"

I gave the girl a closer look. "You're Annabelle's sister, correct? Ashley Mulledy?"

Ashley nodded. "And this is my fiancée. Roger Thundershield."

I nodded. "Ah, yes. The Choctaw shaman. I've heard good things about you."

Roger nodded. "Likewise. I have to say, it's surreal to meet you in the flesh."

I chuckled. "I get that a lot. Ashley, any idea where everyone went? Why are you two here, anyway?"

Ashely shook her head, pulled her phone out from her pocket. "I received this text from Annabelle about an hour ago."

I looked at the text. "S.O.S. at our house."

Ashley nodded. "I don't know what brought her here or what the issue was. I tried to call her after I got the text but she didn't answer. I got here and, well, everyone was gone."

I shook my head. "All their cars are out front."

Ashley nodded. "Annabelle's Camaro is out there, too. She wouldn't go somewhere without it. Not unless..."

"You think she has Isabelle with her and they might have left through a gate to Eden?"

Ashley shrugged. "It's possible. But if that was the case, I'd think they were running from something. I don't see any evidence of anything here that's remotely threatening."

Roger bit his lip. "Someone is here. I can sense a spirit. A powerful spirit. An ancient spirit."

"A ghost?" I asked.

Roger squinted a little. "I don't think so. It's more pronounced than that."

I bit my lip. "Like an angel?"

Roger opened up a satchel, retrieved a bundle of sage, and split it between Ashley and himself. Then, he took a butane torch and lit Ashley's bunch and his. "If it's a spiritual entity, this should dispel its energies. If it's a corporeal being, even an angel or god, the sage shouldn't affect it."

I nodded and followed Ashley and Roger around the house. We searched the downstairs first, then we ascended to the second floor. Ashely grew up in the place. She knew her way around better than I did, despite the time I'd spent there recently. The wolves did most of the renovations. I was too busy with patients to help as much as I would have liked.

It completely shocked me when, entering a closet, Ashely pressed against the edge of what I thought was a clothing shelf in the back and it opened to another room entirely. From the looks of it, not even the wolves had discovered it.

"A safe room?" I asked.

Ashely nodded. "After our family was attacked by the caplata and her zombies, I had it built for Annabelle and me. We needed a place we could hide if something like that ever happened again. I have more wards on this room than anywhere else in the house. It's totally hidden, not only from the likes of you or I, but even those who inhabit the spiritual plane couldn't find it."

"Obviously, that's not where the entity is that you all are sensing is hiding," I said.

Ashley smiled. "It's not here. But I thought Annabelle might be."

I nodded. "I wish you'd been right."

"The sage isn't making a difference," Roger said. "Whatever presence I'm sensing here, something cursed, something very much alive, has a body. We must remain on our guard."

"If this room was warded, why not the rest of the plantation?" I asked.

Ashley chuckled. "It used to be. But it's hard to run an asylum for supernaturals with a bunch of wards preventing people from coming and going."

"Fair point. We have some wards at the original location in Vilokan. A few that suppress the use of magic. They work well, outside of the witching hour, of course."

Ashley chuckled. "I know. I set those up several years ago."

"Really?" I asked.

"Ashely isn't just a vodouisant, Cain," Roger said. "She's more than my fiancée, too. Ashley is also my apprentice, an accomplished shaman."

"Sha-woman," Ashley said, smirking.

Roger rolled his eyes. "The term isn't gender specific, Ashely."

Ashley snickered. "You keep telling me that. I'm not so sure." Ashley continued examining the place. She sensed someone, or something, but couldn't identify its location. "Whoever is here has to be hiding. "

Roger nodded. "But my guess is whoever it is knows where your sister and the wolves went."

CRASH!

"What was that?" Ashely asked.

I took off running down the stairs, skipping half of them. Somehow, I reached the bottom, still on my feet. I heard another bang. I followed it through the common area to what used to be the master bedroom—now divided into three patient rooms.

Abel was on the floor next to the bed in one of the rooms. He'd pulled a small table over which must've been the source of the crash. He was breathing heavily.

I placed my hand on my brother's back as Ashley and Roger entered the room behind me. Abel was shaking. He didn't feel cold. He must've been frightened.

"Abel, what happened?"

"I– We were–" Between his breaths, Abel struggled to get his words out. He was hyperventilating.

"Take a deep breath," I said. "Control it. Breathe in. Breathe out."

Abel nodded and tried to sync his breath with my words.

"In... and out. Good. Again. In... and out."

"They took them. All of them."

"Who took them, Abel?"

Abel winced. "Michael. And another angel. I think his name was Gabriel. They showed up with giant, flaming swords. They demanded we turn over some angel. They took us all to some kind of prison. I don't know how to explain the place. It wasn't heaven. It wasn't hell. But the angels were there, and they were terrifying. There was screaming. So much screaming. They said if you gave them the one they were seeking they'd return Annabelle and the rest."

I sighed. "Samyaza. They're looking for Samyaza."

Abel nodded. "That's right. That's the name they were using."

I scratched the back of my head. "He came to the asylum in Vilokan looking for help. He needed protection. He wanted me to intercede for him. Samyaza used to be a fallen angel. I suppose you could say he became a demon. But then he rejected hell, too. He called himself an unfallen angel. And it's not just the other angels looking for him, the legions of Lucifer are also hunting him down."

"We've warded the asylum in Vilokan against celestial or infernal magic. Angels and demons, both, can't get in. This Samyaza must've known that."

I narrowed my eyes. "That makes little sense. Samyaza got in just fine. If anything, he's wielded celestial and infernal magic. If he's something in between, both angel and demon, but also neither, wouldn't the wards exclude him also?"

"Not necessarily," Roger said. "I'm not an angelologist or a demonologist. But celestial and infernal power aren't on a continuum, as if the same source became celestial or infernal based on the goodness of the angel who wields it. They are different kinds of power. When you wield one of them, it overrules your access to any other magic or ability. If these angels and the demons are hunting someone, it isn't because they're so pissed that he hasn't chosen a side. Would archangels come and abduct all these people as hostages, Cain, just so they could get their vengeance on a fallen angel?"

"I don't think so," I said. "If they could take Samyaza alone, in fact, it seems like it would be easier to just go after him than try to manipulate me this way. Unless they can't take him."

"Well, they can't get into Vilokan Asylum," Ashely said. "I already mentioned that I set up wards there at Annabelle's request a while back."

"We're talking about angels and demons," Roger said. "If they wanted to, and he was relatively powerless, they should have been able to seize him before he could make it to Vilokan."

"They're afraid of him," Abel said. "I don't know why, but it's clear that they think he's a threat."

"Whatever power he has," I said. "It must be something that has both angels and demons anxious."

"That's my theory," Roger said. "But I must remind you, this is all outside my wheelhouse."

"No, it makes sense," I said. "He's looking for protection. That's why he came to me. He knows that the only way he can survive the onslaught of both the angels and also the demons is if he's given something akin to my mark, a guarantee of protection from the Almighty."

"I don't know," Abel said. "That place, wherever it is the angels took them, isn't good. We have to get them out of there."

"I agree," Ashley said. "We can't leave Annabelle there."

"And the wolves, they're making a lot of progress. But if they're too traumatized by whatever it is they're going through, it won't be good in a month the next time they shift."

"I just don't know how we could get there to rescue them," Abel said. "They sent me back to carry this message. To tell you to hand over the fallen angel."

"He calls himself an unfallen angel. Perhaps the next step is for us to go pay Sam a visit, together. I'd bet he knows where the angels took our friends. And more than that, if he wants my help, as he said he did, he'll need to come clean about exactly why angels and demons both view him as a threat."

CHAPTER SIX

WE NEEDED TO TALK to Sam. I rarely bring other people with me to confront a patient. Technically, though, since Annabelle was missing and couldn't sign off on it, Sam wasn't a patient. Even so, I intended to stick to my word. If I could help him and get our friends back, I would. I didn't want to turn him over to the angels. I wasn't the sort who responded well to intimidation. But my pack, along with Abel's, was in some kind of angelic prison. The way Abel described it, it wasn't all puffy clouds and rainbows. Angels could be beautiful. They could also be terrifying.

Abel was still visibly disturbed by what he'd seen. He'd only been in the angel's prison a short time before they sent him back with their ultimatum. His face was devoid of expression. Before, whenever we drove somewhere, he watched the world with wide-eyed wonder. He was one of those people who smiled a bit too much. So much so, in fact, that it probably made some people uncomfortable. Those who didn't know his story, didn't know his past, and didn't appreciate the fact that he was living a second-chance at life six thousand years' post-mortem wouldn't understand.

Now, though, it was as if Abel was a different person. Whatever he'd seen was traumatic. I knew the look. We didn't have a lot of folks in

Vilokan who served in the military, but we had our share of PTSD cases at the asylum. Magical mishaps and unintended encounters with insidious semi-divine entities could be disturbing.

"Would you like to talk about what you saw?" I asked.

Abel shook his head. "Not really. Words can't really describe... I mean, these are angels. They're supposed to be agents of God's will. What I saw..."

I sighed. "It doesn't align with your experience with God? When you were in heaven, I mean?"

Abel shook his head. "Not at all. Whatever it is they're after, whatever threat Sam poses, it has them downright terrified."

"I'm not saying we should turn Sam over to them. I really don't know what choice we have, however. We're dealing with angels, Abel. I'm not sure we stand a chance if we defy their demands."

Abel grunted. "Still, something feels wrong about all of this. I agree with you. We need to at least speak to this Samyaza before handing him over."

I checked my rearview mirror. Roger and Ashley were still behind us.

"Cain!" Abel shouted. "Stop!"

I looked back through the windshield and slammed on my brakes. A tall figure, probably twice the height of most humans, stood in the middle of the highway. He wore a black cloak. I stopped just inches before striking... whatever it was. The figure didn't even flinch.

I glanced at Abel. He gulped.

"Do you know who that is?" I asked.

Abel shook his head. "No. But I feel like I should. I don't know why. He looks familiar."

I stepped out of my truck. Generally, it's not a great idea to confront a supernatural entity when you don't know what it is. But in this case, well, he was blocking us on the highway. If he could find us, driving in excess of fifty miles per hour, and intercept us with no semblance of hesitation or fear, whoever this was wasn't someone I could avoid forever. He'd catch up with me, eventually.

"Who are you," I said. "What do you want?"

The man lowered the hood from his head. Green scales covered his face. Where his nose should have been were two holes. He more closely resembled a snake than a man.

"I am Belial. You have something that belongs to me."

I narrowed my eyes. "Belial the demon?"

Belial nodded. "Return it to me and I will refrain from destroying this city."

I bit my lip. "Return what to you?"

"You know that of which I speak, Cain…"

"There is one who has come to me. The archangels seek him as well. They've kidnapped my friends under the threat that if I do not give him to them, they will not return my friends to our world."

Belial hissed. "Would you choose your friends over an entire city, Cain? My threats are not hollow. I've destroyed villages, cities, kingdoms and even empires. I will not hesitate if you do not comply with my simple request."

"Don't agree with anything he says," Ashley said, stepping up from behind me. "Any agreement with a demon cannot be undone."

"Not without grave consequences," Roger added.

"What is the name of the one you seek?" I asked.

"You know his name because he's already come to you, Cain, son of the defiler."

I cocked my head. "The defiler?"

"Yes. The honorific is reserved for the one who cast all the world into our care."

"You are looking for Samyaza?" I asked.

"Yes," Belial said. "Give him to me and I shall leave your city unharmed."

"Why do you want him so badly? Why are the angels so desperate we should give him to them as well?"

Belial hissed. "It is of no concern to you! Do as I demand, or these people, all who live here, will taste the fires of hell. You have a single day to acquiesce to my demands."

"Where are we supposed to bring him?" I asked.

"Lead him beyond your wards. I will find him and you."

I stared at the demon for a second before responding. "I'll think about it."

"One day, defiler!"

I furrowed my brow. "Now, I'm the defiler?"

"The sins of the father are accounted to the third and the fourth generation."

Abel and I exchanged glances. I shrugged my shoulders. "Like I said, we'll think about it, Belial."

"You already know the consequences of resistance, defiler. When the sun reaches the same height in tomorrow's sky, I will unleash a legion upon this city should you not deliver the fallen one before that time."

"Understood," I said, nodding my head.

Belial hissed again. Presumably for dramatic effect. Then, a cloud of smoke enveloped his body, beginning at his feet and spreading to his head. With a gust of wind, the cloud dissipated, and the demon was gone.

"So what's the plan?" Abel asked.

I shook my head. "I can't give Sam to the angels without risking the city. But if I give him to the demon, I'll put our friends in peril."

"Then perhaps you shouldn't give him over to either side," Roger said

I took a deep breath. "I don't want to. But how could we possibly stop a demon? Do we stand a chance if we resist archangels?"

"Talk to the angel in your care," Ashley said. "Maybe he'll know a way. He's the one who put us in this predicament to begin with. If he wants you to help him, he needs to give us something we can use."

"I agree," Roger said. "But if he has no answer, Cain, are you prepared to make a choice?"

I shook my head. "I can't. I won't give up the wolves."

"And I won't let you abandon my sister," Ashley said.

"I wouldn't dare," I said. "But I can't put the entire city in danger, either. Would Annabelle want us to save her if it meant endangering all of New Orleans?"

Ashley sighed. "She wouldn't."

"It's an impossible choice," Abel said. "There isn't a noble or righteous way to proceed."

"That may be," I said. "We need to get out of the road. We'll talk about it after we've had a chance to discuss this predicament with Sam."

CHAPTER SEVEN

I SMILED AND NODDED at Rutherford as I passed her desk, unlocked the security door, and led Abel, Ashley, and Roger into the asylum. I looked back at Rutherford. "Do you have a room number for our new visitor?"

Rutherford nodded. "He's in the north wing, room 3."

I raised an eyebrow. "The north wing? Do you have any reason to believe he's dangerous?"

Rutherford shrugged her shoulders. "He can walk through walls. We don't know what he can do. I figured we'd best be safe rather than risk being sorry."

"Thanks, Rutherford," I said, shaking my head.

"What's wrong, Cain?"

I grunted. She didn't know. How would she? "Annabelle went to the extension campus. Angels abducted her and the rest of the wolves."

Rutherford furrowed her brow. "Angels?"

I nodded. "They want us to turn over our new patient."

"Strange," Rutherford said. "Angels who abduct people?"

"Trust me," Abel piped up. "They aren't as pleasant and gentle as you'd think."

Rutherford shook her head. "I suppose it's never a good idea to trust stereotypes. You aren't turning him in, I presume."

I shook my head. "I don't know. There's a demon looking for him, too. He's threatening to destroy the entire city if we don't turn Sam over to him."

"Why is this one, unaffiliated, angel so important to them?"

"I don't know. That's what we're hoping to find out."

"Well, Cain. All I can say is that you've never once betrayed a patient. Don't tell me you're considering doing so now."

I sighed. "I don't know, Rutherford. I'm not sure we have much of a choice. We can't fight angels and demons. If Annabelle was here, if she had Isabelle with her, we might stand a chance to at least thwart them for a while. Even Julie is gone. Without her here, with her flambeau, I can't even shift into wolf form to fight the demon. Not like I'd be able to defeat him that way, either. I really don't know what we're going to do."

"Stick to your principles, Cain. I know a lot is at stake, but you must do what's best for your patient."

"Even if it means sacrificing my friends or all of New Orleans?"

Rutherford pressed her lips together. "I think you have to save them all."

I snorted. "Yeah, well, if I knew how to do that, I would. I don't know why people think that just because my name is in the Bible that I have some kind of inside track on how to deal with angels and demons."

"Cain, I said nothing to that effect. That's not my point."

"Then what's the point, Rutherford? Because I really don't know what to do in this scenario."

Rutherford pressed her lips together, stood up from her desk, and took my hand. "I only meant to tell you, Cain, that I believe in you. I have confidence that you can navigate this situation the right way. You always do the right thing."

I sighed and pulled my hands away from Rutherford. "I'm sorry. I'm not trying to be a... well..."

"An ass?" Rutherford asked.

I chuckled. "Right."

"You're not being an ass, Cain. You're under pressure. I just want you to know that I have all the faith in the world that you'll find a way through this. Don't doubt yourself and don't you dare compromise your convictions just because some angels and demons showed up and are trying to bully you into submission."

I bit my lip. "Thanks, Rutherford. I suppose I'm not used to having such a burden on my shoulders."

Rutherford nodded, then glanced at Ashley. "Nice to see you again, Miss Mulledy."

Ashley smiled. "You too, Rutherford. This is my fiancé, Roger."

Rutherford raised an eyebrow. "Well, you certainly could do a lot worse."

Ashley grinned. "I know. He's a hottie, right?"

"Oh, I wasn't talking to you, honey. I was talking to your fiancé. You've got a good one here, young man. Treat her right."

Roger laughed. "Trust me, ma'am. I know. I'm a lucky man."

Rutherford smiled and returned to her desk.

"This way," I said.

"She's certainly nice," Roger said.

I nodded. "Ashley, I didn't know you and Rutherford knew each other so well."

Ashley shrugged. "I don't know her that well, to be honest. But, you know, since I'm a shaman, Annabelle asked me to keep the wards here fresh. She introduced me to Rutherford, and she showed me around. We had a few conversations about boys, love, things like that."

"She talked to you about boys?"

Ashley giggled. "She talked to me about men, Cain. More specifically, a man. I think you know who I'm talking about."

I chuckled nervously. "Of course."

"All I can say, Cain, is that she's genuine about how she feels about you. You realize that when I attended the Voodoo Academy, I was in College Erzulie, correct?"

I nodded. "Annabelle has told me."

"That means I have the aspect of the Loa of love within me. I can sense genuine affection or love and discern it well from lesser emotions like lust or infatuation. I'll just say that her feelings for you run deep. When she says she believes in you, she's not just trying to talk you up and encourage you. She really believes it."

I sighed. "Well, let's hope that what she believes in her heart is true. I'm not so sure. I'm just praying that Sam will have an answer, something that tells us why the angels and demons are going to such extreme efforts to claim him. And more than that, I hope he'll give us a good reason to stand up for him. There's an awful lot at stake here. It feels like there's not a good answer. No matter what we do, people will die."

CHAPTER EIGHT

SAM WASN'T IN HIS room. We found him, instead, in the common room playing table tennis with a patient named Nedley.

Nedley Mandico was a stink ape. Though, don't tell him I called him that. He prefers the term "malodorous primate." The stink ape is often mistaken for the sasquatch. It's on average a few feet shorter–usually of comparable height to humans–and only has three toes compared to a sasquatch's five. While a sasquatch, aka BigFoot, doesn't smell great, the stink ape got its name because it emits a foul odor that could make a skunk blush. The odor, however, isn't emitted from a gland, or anything of the sort. Stink apes are magical creatures and their odor is their chief ability. Yes, they are magically rank. And they have no control over their ability. The effect is constant. The wards at the asylum, though, silence the stink ape's mystical stench.

What does a stink ape smell like, exactly? Well, that depends on you. It will take on the odor that you, personally, find the most detestable. For one person, it may smell like cat urine, for another, it might stink like a decomposing corpse. For me, stink apes smell of asparagus. After you eat it. The first time you use the toilet afterwards. You know what I'm talking about.

Nedley wasn't exactly unstable. He simply had an interest in the finer things of life. He found high society desirable. Expensive wines. Classical music. Three-piece suits. And, of course, although he was born in the backwoods of Kentucky, he spoke with a fake British accent.

Why was he at the asylum? Well, when something that resembles a sasquatch attempts to purchase a Country Club membership, it causes something of an uproar. Stink apes are reclusive by nature. But they don't take well to insults. The poor fellow at the front desk at the Country Club apparently told him he was an animal, he needed to shave, and required a bath. Nedley took it personally. The insult unleashed his vicious side, and the man took the place of the escargots as his evening's hors d'oeuvre. I wasn't sure what, or who, became his main course, but when hunters received word of what had happened, Annabelle intervened and had him committed to the asylum. He'd been in my care for more than a year. Since he didn't stink within the confines of the facility, well, he found it was one of few places where he could engage in civilized conversation. Given the population of the asylum, I'm not sure that "civilized" is the word I'd typically use to describe much of anything that went on in the facility. Still, given his usual options, I suppose since the folks at the asylum weren't repulsed by him, they were the best conversation partners he could find. We couldn't keep him forever, but until we came up with a solution—to either convince him to give up his affinity for high society or discovered a viable way to suppress his magical stink—we simply couldn't let him loose. It would only be a matter of time before some highfalutin' gentleman insulted him and found himself on Nedley's menu for the night.

I suppose it made sense that of all the people Nedley might want to talk to, he'd zeroed in on the informally admitted unfallen angel.

"Three serving one," Nedley announced, rolling the "r" of "three." Sam was holding back. He was an angel, after all. He could move a lot faster than he was showing. Still, I suppose he was humoring the stink ape.

I cleared my throat. "I hate to interrupt, gentlemen. I need to visit with Sam, if you'd excuse us a moment, Nedley."

Nedley bowed his head. "Certainly, good sir! It has been a pleasure to defeat you, my friend."

Sam grinned and nodded. "The pleasure of defeat was all mine."

Nedley placed his hand to his breast and chuckled. "Bravo, bravo. I'm sure it was."

Sam made eye contact with Abel. He cocked his head. "Is this who I think it is?"

"It is my brother."

"How is this possible?" Sam asked.

"It's a long story," I said. "How do you recognize him anyway?"

Sam 's eyes widened. "I suppose that's a reasonable inquiry. Remember, Cain, I was one of the Watchers. We were what many today call guardian angels. We were commissioned to guard and protect mankind from the most insidious spiritual threats. I'll simply say that, in your day, when few humans walked the earth, I was pretty well acquainted with most everyone."

"There were more people in the world back then than most people realize," I said. "I've read academic theology journals, pondering the question of how I could have possibly found a wife who wasn't my sister. They fail to realize that the book of Genesis was never meant to be the story of the origin of all mankind, but the origin of a particular people, of a family of priests originally charged to represent mankind in a garden temple."

"Of course, our parents screwed that up before we were born," Abel said.

Sam smiled. "Indeed, they did."

"So, we've run into a bit of a problem, Sam. First, I'd like to introduce you to Ashley and Roger."

Sam nodded. "I know who you are. It's a pleasure to meet you personally."

Ashley cocked her head. "You know us? How?"

Sam laughed. "Again, it's a part of my original nature. My mind is essentially an encyclopedia of every human who is presently walking the earth. I cannot tell you, at any given moment, what someone is doing. But if I meet someone, I know, immediately, their entire past and history."

"That's a fascinating gift," Roger said.

"Indeed, it is, my friend. You, yourself, are quite the distinguished shaman, are you not?"

Roger nodded. "I don't know how distinguished I am. But my skills are widely recognized in my tribe."

"Follow me," I said. "What we have to discuss is not for curious ears."

"I'm not listening to you!" Nedley piped up. "I'm no church mouse!"

I smiled. "Then how did you know I'd just mentioned that curious ears might be listening in?"

Nedley laughed. "Ah, brilliant, doctor. You're a sharp-witted man. That's why I appreciate your distinguished company."

"Likewise," I said, nodding at Nedley. It was always important to acknowledge his attempts at civility. If I didn't, well, it wouldn't take much to trigger his rage.

Sam followed me and the rest of us to my office. He immediately plopped down on my chaise, rested his hands behind his head, and crossed his legs. "So, what did you need to speak to me about?"

I sighed. "The angels and the demons are both quite intent on convincing us to turn you over."

Sam stared at the ceiling for a moment, narrowing his eyes. "What has happened, Cain?"

"The angels kidnapped my sister," Ashley said.

"And two packs of werewolves," Abel added.

"Which angels?" Sam asked.

"I believe it was Michael and Gabriel," Abel said. "Those are the names they used."

Sam sigh ed. "Archangels. It is unusual they'd resort to human hostages, though I cannot say I blame them."

"And a demon named Belial approached us in the streets," I said. "He told us if we don't turn you over, he'll destroy New Orleans."

Sam uncrossed his legs and sat up on the edge of the chaise. He rested his elbows on his knees and planted his face in his hands. "That sounds like Belial. Demons don't often assault humans that way. Their attempts to do so usually come with consequences from the man upstairs. But if he wanted to, I'm sure he could find a way to do it."

"What do they want with you?" I asked. "If you're just an unaffiliated angel, someone disloyal to both heaven and hell, I can't imagine that they'd go to such lengths to seize you."

Sam shook his head. "It's because of my original nature. Again, as I've told you, I was a Watcher."

"Right," I said. "Like a guardian angel."

"And I am the last of our kind. At least, the last of the original legion of Watchers. I believe there are others today, but these angels were created with limited volition. They might as well be marionettes of the Divine."

"So as a Watcher, you had the power to defend humanity from spiritual attacks?" I asked.

Sam scratched his head. "It's more complicated than that. The new angels, the new Watchers, that's the limit of what they can do. Suppose someone inadvertently contacts a demon via an Ouija Board, in that case the Watcher can prevent the demon from afflicting the person. Someone falls asleep at the wheel and the guardian angel can startle them awake just in time. The original Watchers, myself included, could effectively wield the power of the Divine to thwart Lucifer's legions in their attempt to oppress and possess humans."

"How did that work when you were fallen, when you were aligned with the demons?"

"I had little power to do anything more than any demon might. I could tempt. I could oppress. I could lead humans down the wrong path."

"Then why would the celestial angels, Michael or Gabriel, be so anxious about your current status now that you've disavowed Lucifer and hell?"

Sam shook his head. "They fear that I'll once again copulate with women. They do not want to see the Nephilim reborn."

"Is that your intention?" I asked.

Sam shook his head. "I don't have any plans. I only wish to live independent of either the demands of heaven or hell. Should that mean that I might love a woman, perhaps giving her children, then so be it."

"Why would the angels be so worried about the rebirth of the Nephilim?" Abel asked.

Sam shook his head. "Even the Bible refers to my children as mighty and of great renown in their time. Yet, still, there was a sense from the start that they were an abomination to the Divine. A new species, not created in the beginning."

"Wouldn't the same thing apply to creatures like vampires, or even werewolves?"

"I suppose it would," Sam said. "Again, I cannot say why the Divine despised my children. Perhaps it is so simple as the fact that they inherited, through their human mothers, the place of humanity to exercise dominion on the earth, but, from me, angelic abilities to do so with enhanced abilities. In time, it is likely that the Nephilim would overtake humanity. If the notion that the fittest ultimately survives while the unfit die, the Nephilim would eventually become the dominant race on earth."

"And Belial would be anxious about this for other reasons?" I asked.

"The Nephilim could slay demons. They inherited my power, the power of the Watchers, to overpower and thwart demons. But they wielded it as men, in the material world. If demons were to engage the world, there was no creature that walked the earth more suited to fight them and thwart their efforts."

"Excuse me for asking," Ashley said. "But wouldn't the angels welcome that? If they had half-angel, half-human allies, who could fight the demons on earth?"

"You would think," Sam said. "But again, the angels and demons have been at war with one another since before humanity first walked the earth. If there were a race, like the Nephilim, who could fight demons directly in the material world, well, it risked bringing the war between angels to the earth. And if that happened, well, it might not bode well for the future of humanity."

"So both the angels and demons are concerned, now that you're free and uncommitted to either side of that war, that you might have children who could slay both angels and demons?"

Sam nodded. "This is the most likely reason they wish you to hand me over. I am gravely troubled by these developments. I never intended to put anyone at risk, certainly not your friends and not the innocent people who live in the city at the surface."

I scratched my head. "Well, be that as it may, we have less than a day to do something. If we do not turn you over, or somehow end this debacle before then, Belial intends to send legions of demons into the city."

Sam nodded. "He isn't bluffing. He will do what he said, one way or another. Probably in a way you wouldn't expect in an effort to thwart or avoid angelic interference. Even among the demons, his brutality is renowned."

"Here's the problem, Sam. I said, before, I'd attempt to intercede on your behalf. But the only way I knew to reach the archangels before was by leveraging an ability that one of my friends, the Voodoo Queen, could use."

Sam nodded. "I'm aware of Annabelle Mulledy's history and abilities. If she were to send you into Eden, it is likely that Michael would greet you."

"He's done so before," I said. "But I don't know now what choice we have. If we bring you out of the city at all, Belial said he'd know and will come for you."

Abel cleared his throat. "I'm not sure, either. I mean, the archangels seized us all and sent me back. They told me to find Sam and lead him back to them, but they didn't tell me how to do that or where I could find them."

Sam stood up from his chaise. "I don't know how to do it. But if you must turn me over to one side or the other, it should be to the celestials. If they free your friends, perhaps you can use them to fight against Belial."

"My friends include the Voodoo Queen and two packs of werewolves. How could we fight a demon's legions?"

"Gabriel and Michael, while they can be terrifying, I'm sure, ultimately have the protection of humanity at their heart. They are not evil. If they can be convinced that I will not bear children with the daughters of man, that I simply wish to live my existence peacefully, they may relent and allow me to fight at your side. Two packs of wolves and Annabelle Mulledy might not thwart Belial alone. But if I am your Watcher, if I guard you in battle, you should be able to slay them as if you were my children, as if you were the Nephilim."

"How could we possibly convince the angels of that? I told you I'd be your advocate, Sam. I will not give you up to anyone who wishes to imprison you or punish you for something you did thousands of years ago. Hell, you said it yourself. You came to me because I suffered from a curse on account of a single act done ages ago."

Abel chuckled. "To be fair, Cain. You didn't kill me out of love, and certainly not out of lust."

"That's the point, though, isn't it? What I did was infinitely worse."

"But werewolves do not pose a threat to angels and demons," Sam said. "You may be right. My only sin was that I was too much like the creatures that our Maker favored the most. So much so that I loved them, and fathered children with them."

Abel pinched his chin. "After my experience with these archangels, after they abducted me, I don't think they're going to be pacified by a mere promise. You can tell them you won't copulate with human women again and you can even mean it genuinely. I'm not sure they'll believe you. I mean, until recently, you were a demon, right? Aren't a demon's legions under the one known as the Father of Lies?"

"I agree. I think we need something to show the angels. Something that proves you've rejected Lucifer. And more, something that proves your promise not to bear more children is genuine."

"There's only one thing I can think of that I might offer the angels in exchange for my freedom and that of your friends. Acquiring it though, well, many have tried. Our chances of success are slim to none, especially with Belial on my tail and other demons likely hunting me as well."

"What is it?" I asked.

"Lucifer's name means 'morning star' or 'light-bringer.' His name is not immaterial. He carries a torch that, when lit, channels infernal flames. Flames once stoked in the heavens, that now fuel hell itself."

I snorted. "If Lucifer carries this torch, I don't think we stand much of a chance of acquiring it."

"That's the thing," Sam said. "The torch itself is both material and immaterial. There are a series of manifestations of it on earth. Six torches, together channeling the hellfire of Lucifer into the world, granting him and the demons access to the world. Lucifer, after all, is more than a light bearer. He is a light bringer. This is how he brought his light to the world. A light that gives him power and control over this world's affairs."

"Cain," Abel said. "Those sound like infernal objects. Not unlike Julie's flambeau. If we were exposed to it..."

"We'd become wolves," I said, scratching my head. "Sam, is the flambeau of the Witch of Endor one of Lucifer's six torches?"

Sam nodded. "It certainly is."

"But it's not always manifested in material form," I said. "She sometimes dispels it."

"It remains in her person, even as it once did for the witch who originally made it at Lucifer's behest. The other five torches are hidden in various, though similar, ways."

Abel sighed. "She's already in the angels' custody. Wouldn't that mean that they already have one of the six torches?"

"Not necessarily," Sam said. "Lucifer designed each of these torches to be hidden in ways imperceptible to other angels. Only the demons know how to find them and call them forth. Thankfully, you are in the company of an ex-demon. I know all the tricks."

CHAPTER NINE

"How does one break into a prison, much less an angelic prison?" I asked.

Sam chuckled. "Well, it's still news to me that the angels have prisons at all. I suppose a lot has changed since I was one of them. Still, Abel, you were there before, correct?"

"I was," my brother confirmed.

"Where did you emerge when they sent you away?"

"Back at the plantation. Why?"

"When a breach between realms is created, it leaves a mark. Think of it like a wound in the fabric of space and time that will take time to heal. I should be able to locate it and force it open again."

"How are we going to get you there, though, if Belial will know it the moment you leave Vilokan?"

"We might be able to help with that," Ashley said.

Roger winced. "Ashley, I know what you're thinking. I'm not saying it won't work, but we have not done it on an angel before. It might leave Sam vulnerable."

"What are you proposing?" Sam asked.

"A personal ward," Ashley said. "So long as it's in place, it would function much like the wards over Vilokan do that prevent demons from entering."

Sam smiled. "But not unfallen angels. Since my power is no longer purely celestial or infernal."

"Right," Ashley said. "We should be able to place a similar ward on you that would hide you from both angels and demons while we move you across the city to the plantation."

"But it would also leave you vulnerable," Roger said. "It's a risk. For all intents and purposes, you'd be as mortal as a human while under the ward."

Sam cocked his head. "Does that mean I'm vulnerable here, even now?"

Ashley shook her head. "Not at all. You said it yourself. Your power is neither celestial nor infernal. The wards here are not impacting you directly. But if we placed a ward on your person, well, the only way to prevent angels or demons from detecting you would be to silence the power that's uniquely yours."

"Can you do that?" I asked. "It sounds to me like his essential nature is unique. At least I've never known an unaffiliated angel before. How do we know it would work?"

"The ward Ashley is proposing would silence anything, any power, that has supernatural or mystical origins. It's quite dangerous. There is a mystical component, in fact, to all humans that cannot endure under such a ward."

"Their soul, or spirit?" I asked.

Roger nodded. "Under the ward, if someone was to die, it would erase their spirit from existence. Not even a necromancer could bring them back."

"And it would do the same to me?" Sam asked.

"Temporarily," Ashley said. "Only until we got you to the plantation."

I sighed. "It's too risky. Belial found us before, even when Sam wasn't with us. If we're on the move, he'll know it. He might not sense Sam's essence if he's warded, but the demon will surely recognize him with us if he tracks us down."

"Then we provide a distraction," Abel said. "Cain, you and I can go one direction while Roger and Ashley take Sam to the plantation."

"They won't be able to find you two?" I asked, looking at Ashley and then Roger.

"Choctaw blood is impervious to any sort of magic influence or detection," Roger said. "You all go together. Our best shot is if I go with Sam alone. Once we arrive, I'll ensure that the place is properly warded so that once you all get there, the place will be protected against any demons who might follow you."

I nodded. "That may be the best plan we have. At least it gives us a shot to appease the angels, save our friends, and then put up a fight against Belial and his legions."

"What if Julie doesn't want to give up the flambeau?" Abel asked.

Sam winced. "If she possesses it we cannot draw it out of her against her will. If she will not do it, well, then there are five more we might attempt to find. None of them are nearby, though, and I don't know if we'd be able to secure one within the timeframe that Belial dictated."

"Julie will help." I said. "She's sacrificed herself before, to save Vilokan. Surely she'd give up the flambeau if it's the only chance we have to save both packs and the entire city of New Orleans."

Abel nodded, biting his lip. Then he took a deep breath and released it.

"You don't like this plan?" I asked.

"Not that," Abel said. "I told you before, the things I saw there... I never thought I'd have to go back there again."

"Could we go without Abel?" I asked.

Sam nodded. "We might go there, but I won't be able to find the portal that brought him to this world from that place without his help. At the very least, he needs to come with us so I can open the gateway again."

Abel nodded. "It's okay, Cain. I'll do what I have to do. Besides, if the entire experience troubles me too much, if I do have to go back there, I have a brother who's supposed to be a pretty good therapist. I mean, that's what people say. I hear he's really some kind of quack."

I smirked. "Yeah, I've heard the same. But you know, wolves don't quack. Not most of the time, anyway."

"You ready to do this?" Ashley asked. "We can apply the ward on Sam now. But we'll have to move fast. His essence is stronger than most supernatural creatures. We might only be able to mask his true nature from the demons for an hour or so."

"I'm ready," Sam said. "Do what you have to do."

Ashley and Roger exchanged glances. Then Roger retrieved some herbs, a vial, and a mortar and pestle from his satchel. Ashley took the mortar and pestle, set it on my desk, and started grinding up some kind of paste.

"What exactly is it?" I asked.

"The herbs aren't all that uncommon. The solution in the vial, well, it's probably best that you don't know."

"How bad could it be?" I asked. "Goat's blood? Horse semen? What are we talking about here?"

Sam raised his hand. "That's enough. If it's worse than any of those things, I'd rather not know. I mean, you're putting it on my skin, right?"

"You have to swallow it," Roger said.

Sam gulped. "Please tell me someone has a glass of water so I can wash this stuff down."

CHAPTER TEN

WE LEFT VILOKAN AND stepped into Pere Antoine alley. No demons yet. So far, so good. Roger was driving with Sam in his jeep. I had Abel and Ashley in my truck. Yes, I had a crew cab. Plenty of space. The primary reason I drove a truck was to handle some of the remote unpaved roads around the swamp. I couldn't take the direct route to the plantation. If I did, and Belial followed me, I'd lead him right to Sam. I needed to take my time, give Roger the chance to ward the mansion before we arrived, then show up and hope that Sam could work with Able to re-open the portal that the angels sent him through before.

"How long will it take Roger to set up the wards?" I asked, pulling onto Interstate 10. Ashley shrugged. "Not long. Especially since he knows the place. He's set up wards there before. Any time you've warded a place once before, it's a lot easier to do the next time. Wards have to be placed perfectly, respecting the energy of a place. All things considered, it shouldn't take him more than half an hour."

I nodded. "Alright. I'll take us across the Manchac Bridge and come around Lake Maurepas."

"That should give him plenty of time," Ashley said.

"Keep an eye out, both of you. While I'm focusing on the road, let me know if you see anything that looks like it might be Belial or anything else out of the ordinary."

Every car that tapped its brakes ahead of me. Every flash of sunlight on the pavement. Every little noise, be it the engine of an approaching motorcycle in the fast lane or the squeal of someone's brakes, arrested my attention.

I'd dealt with a lot of dangerous supernaturals through the years. I was one myself, frankly. I'd handled werewolves whose murderous rage couldn't be easily tamed. I'd counseled ancient vampires and those newly turned. I'd confronted witches, necromancers, bokors, and caplatas. I'd dealt with religious zealots, the Order of the Morning Dawn, whose acolytes wielded magic they claimed was given to them by angels.

I'd never defied a demon directly. I'd never attempted to break into a domain governed by angels and I'd certainly never attempted to change an angel's mind. Though, given my profession, perhaps I had as great a chance as any mortal to at least give an angel a reason to pause and reconsider his positions. Could I do so now? Could we convince them that Sam wasn't a threat? Did I even believe that he was genuine about his intention not to have children again, to revive the Nephilim? If I didn't believe him, what were the chances that the angels would, even if we gave them the location of Lucifer's six torches or turned over the Witch of Endor's flambeau?

The strangest thing about all of this, though, might have been the fact that despite taking the scenic route and giving Belial ample time to catch up to us, that the demon didn't show his face at all.

My stomach turned. Did the ward on Sam work? If it hadn't, that would explain why Belial didn't bother hassling me. He probably had Sam already.

I clenched my steering wheel with both hands. "Any word from Roger?"

"Let me check," Ashley said, pulling her phone from her pocket. She tapped at the screen a few times. "I texted him. He's not great at texting back. Never has been. Especially if he's busy."

I pushed my foot on the accelerator. "I have a bad feeling about all of this. Are you certain that the ward you gave Sam worked?"

Ashely nodded. "As sure as I could be. I mean, it isn't every day that someone gets a chance to ward an angel. I'm not even sure if Roger has ever done anything comparable."

I snorted. "This doesn't make me feel any better. Any response yet?"

Ashley glanced at her phone. "Nothing yet. But that means nothing, Cain. Try not to assume the worst."

I sighed. "When you're dealing with demons, assuming the worst comes with the territory."

"I'll try to call, but again, if he's busy with his wards, he will ignore it. He needs to focus."

I shook my head. "Don't bother. We're only ten minutes out. I don't want to distract him if he's busy with the wards. Getting those set up properly is far more important than assuaging my temporary anxieties."

I didn't even realize I'd been holding my breath until I exhaled the moment I saw Roger's jeep parked in the circle drive just in front of the new asylum extension, the former Mulledy home. I'd given him my gate remote before we left the city. He left the gate unlocked but not open, which, again, was according to plan.

I parked just behind Roger's jeep. Abel got out of the passenger side door and Ashley exited on the same side from the back.

The front doors were unlocked. Again, that wasn't a surprise.

My wing-tipped shoes clicked on the tile floor as I stepped inside. "Hello?"

No answer. "We're here. Sam, Roger, where are you?"

Abel and Ashley stepped through the doors behind me.

"The wards are all set," Ashley said. "They were here for sure."

I bit my lip. "Then where did they go? If the wards are set, and you're certain the demons couldn't get through, they must be here somewhere."

Ashley pursed her lips. "I have an idea. Abel, do you know where you appeared here before? Where the portal opened?"

"Yes. It was just–"

"Don't tell me," Ashley said, raising her hand to silence Abel. "I just want to make sure you know. I have a theory that I'd like to test out."

Ashley reached into her purse. Really, it was similar to Roger's satchel, only with a few more decorative frills. She pulled out two l-shaped rods.

"Dowsing rods?" I asked.

Ashley nodded. "I should be able to find their energy. I know Roger intimately, so finding his signature, his trail, should be simple. And since Sam is basically an angel, that shouldn't be any problem either."

I shrugged my shoulders. "I suppose it's worth a shot."

Ashley moved through the living room. The dowsing rods pivoted through her hands. The tips drew closer. As they did, she followed them as the rods led her into the kitchen.

I glanced at Abel. He knew what I did. This was where he'd appeared. It was where the gate dropped him off, before.

When Ashley stopped over the location where Abel appeared, the rods crossed. "This is the last place they were. Roger and Sam both."

"That is where the portal was that sent me here before," Abel said.

Ashley sighed. "I don't know why they didn't wait. But they must've found the portal before we arrived. They've already left."

I shook my head. "Why would they do that? The werewolves there don't know Roger or Sam. If they want Julie's help, if they want me to try and intercede on Sam's behalf, it doesn't make sense they'd leave without us."

Ashley sighed. "That presumes that they left willingly. I can't believe we didn't think about this before."

"Think about what?" I asked.

"The wards prevent angels or demons alike from crossing. It wouldn't prevent them from using a breach, or a portal, already forged that might lead them directly into the house. The angels must've sensed Sam was here and come for him."

"And what about Roger?" I asked.

Ashley shook her head. "He either went after him himself or they took him, hoping we wouldn't be able to figure out where they went."

CHAPTER ELEVEN

HITTING THINGS WASN'T REALLY my style. When I was angry or frustrated, I tried to process my feelings, to examine where they were coming from. At this moment, though, it didn't take a shrink to figure out why it felt like someone had taken a rusty spoon to my heart.

If we didn't deliver Sam to Belial, he'd destroy this city. If the angels got him, well, where were the wolves? Where was Roger? I had to remind myself that they hadn't been gone long. Perhaps Sam and Roger were negotiating with the angels. I doubted it. They wouldn't have left without us unless the angels seized them. And if they did that, how likely was it they were interested in discussing the terms of Sam's freedom?

"If Roger tells them what Belial is planning, it may convince them to intervene," Ashley suggested.

"I'm not sure," Abel said. "When I was there, the angels who held us spoke little at all. I hardly saw them. They were behind a veil most of the time. When they spoke, I didn't even see their faces."

I sighed. "I don't have a good feeling about any of this. If only there was a way to break into the celestial realm. I've spoken to Michael before. He's not an altogether unreasonable archangel."

Ashley shook her head. "If Annabelle was here, we could do it. She could bind herself to Isabelle and use their soul-blade to make it happen. Unfortunately, I don't know if there's any other way to open this portal again."

Abel bit his lip. "I don't know how to open this portal. But we can open a channel to the celestial plane."

I cocked my head. "What do you mean?"

Abel bit the inside of his cheek. "We did it before. It's not a portal, exactly. But the very word 'angel' means 'messenger.' They are messengers of the Divine."

"I'm not sure I'm following you, brother."

"It's not something we did recently," Abel said. "I mean, we did it back in the day. When we made our offerings, our sacrifices. It was a part of our ritual."

I pinched my chin. "The prayers we were supposed to say over our offerings. I don't know if I even remember those prayers."

"It's been six thousand years on earth for you, Cain. But I've spent most of that time on the celestial plane myself. In my mind, it's almost like we'd said those prayers and made our offerings just months, or maybe weeks ago."

"I'm not entirely sure that will work again, Abel. I'm not a farmer anymore. I don't have any crops to offer. It's not like you have any herds of sheep wandering around, either. I doubt you will any time soon, you know, since wolves and sheep don't especially mix."

"You know it's not about what you offer, Cain. It's about the heart. Wasn't that what you were told after your offering was refused? That if you did what was right, you'd be accepted?"

I nodded. "I know. But we're not talking about earning Divine favor, Abel. We're talking about reaching out to the angels, trying to break through to our friends' captors."

Ashley cleared her throat. "Forgive me if I'm speaking out of turn. Annabelle is far more devout a Catholic than I ever was. She went to the girls' school and all of that. But check this out, on my phone..."

Ashley handed me her phone. She had the book of Hosea up in one of her apps. I read the highlighted verse aloud. "For I desire mercy, and not sacrifice; and the knowledge of God more than burnt offerings. But they, like Adam, have transgressed the covenant: they have dealt treacherously against me."

"Can I see that?" Abel asked.

I passed Ashley's phone to Abel. "Can you read?"

Abel nodded. "I guess I can. I think it had something to do with how the necromancer resurrected me, the first time I was brought back from the dead. Somehow, I suppose, her language skills were infused in my mind when I was revived."

I raised an eyebrow. "Fascinating."

A slight grin curled up at the corner of Abel's mouth as he examined the verses displayed on Ashley's phone. "This is fascinating. I wish we knew this stuff before we made our offerings back in the day. It could have saved us a lot of heart ache."

I bit my lip. "Or, in your case, a headache. You know, since I smashed your cranium with a stone."

Abel cocked his head, pressed his lips together hard, and stared at me blankly.

I winced. "Sorry. Too soon?"

Abel's shoulders bounced as the laugh he was holding back forced its way out. "Not at all. I was just surprised you said it! And it was quite entertaining, brother, to see you squirm when you thought you'd crossed a line."

I added a half-hearted laugh to Abel's. "I certainly thought I'd just put my foot in my mouth."

"No offense, brother. But I've seen you attempt yoga. I don't think that's something you could possibly do. And why would you want to? Feet are gross."

Ashley giggled as she looked at the verse on her phone again. "I'm not sure who this verse was written to or about, but things have changed little. If the people here who apparently ticked off the Divine were giving the wrong kind of sacrifice, well, it says, here, exactly what's needed."

Abel snorted. "The Divine desires mercy more than our sacrifices..."

Ashley snickered. "I don't think Mercy Brown would take kindly to being sacrificed."

I chuckled. "I don't think that scripture is talking about Mercy the vampire. It's about the attitude of the heart. I've learned that much over several thousand years, pondering why my initial offering was rejected. After all, I knew at the time that my offering wasn't given out of joy or gratitude, but from obligation and duty. Be that as it may, it's one thing to take some crops or the corpse of a lamb and put it on a stone altar, say a few prayers, and wait for some kind of celestial message to let you know how you grade. I don't know how I might sacrifice something like an attitude. It's immaterial."

Ashley shrugged. "Again, I don't know if you're thinking about it the right way. I mean, there's another passage somewhere that says whatever you do for the least of these, I guess the needy, the poor, the destitute, you also do to God. Because you've dedicated yourself, already, to caring for people who most everyone else would rather see eliminated than helped, I think you're well on your way."

I nodded. "I appreciate you saying that, Ashley. But again, I need something practical. If we're going to get the attention of angels and bust ourselves into their celestial prison, I don't think I can just say a brief prayer and say, 'Hey, look at me! I'm a great guy now. I help people.'"

"Abel, hand me back my phone," Ashley said.

Abel gave Ashley her phone. She navigated her finger across the screen. First, one direction. Then another. I wasn't sure what she was doing, mostly because I didn't have a clue how those darned devices worked. "Here, check this one out."

Ashley handed me her phone again. I read aloud another scripture she'd highlighted. "Do not forget to entertain strangers: for thereby some have entertained angels unawares."

Abel pressed his lips together. "That's interesting, isn't it?

I shrugged my shoulders. "I'm not sure what to make of it or how it would be helpful right now. I mean, there are a lot of people in the French Quarter at this very moment entertaining a lot of strangers. Some of them are playing instruments on street corners. Others are telling jokes on stages. Still others are taking their clothes off in bars."

Ashley smirked. "I don't think that's the kind of entertainment it's talking about, Cain."

I handed Ashley her phone back. "I'm aware of that. I'm given to sarcasm when I feel helpless. It's a defense mechanism, I suppose."

Abel cleared his throat. "Can I see that verse you found, Ashley?"

"Certainly," Ashley said, handing Abel her phone.

Abel stared at it a moment, a wide grin forming across his face. "The verse before the one you highlighted. It says what entertaining strangers is all about. It says, 'let brotherly love continue.' Maybe, Cain, all we have to do is join ourselves together. We need to let our love, for each other, show. In our love, we've shown mercy to one another. I forgave you. You refused to kill me a second time when I tried to kill you, you know, when I shot you in the back."

I chuckled. "You weren't acting entirely of your own volition at the time."

"Cain, I wouldn't have inherited your curse if a part of me wasn't blinded by vengeance. Delphine LaLaurie, even wielding the flambeau, couldn't have made me do it if there wasn't a dark part in my heart that wanted to kill you."

I snorted. "Well, I'd be lying if I said I couldn't relate to that. When we become wolves, it brings out our deepest motives, our instincts, our suppressed pains and resentments. The flambeau does something similar. I suppose it makes sense now that we know that the infernal item is one of six channels that Lucifer uses to maintain his influence in the world."

"I know this is going to sound corny. I don't mean it to. But if brotherly love, if a sacrifice of the heart and an act of mercy, is the sacrifice that elicits a favorable response. Well, I think the best way for us to make contact, to reach out through the messengers, the angels, and intercede for Sam and our friends, is to speak as one."

I sighed. "If we have to hold hands and sing Kumbaya to save our friends, well, I suppose it's worth a shot. I'm short of any other ideas at the moment."

CHAPTER TWELVE

WE TRIED PRAYER. I prayed by myself. Abel prayed by himself. We held hands and prayed together. Ashley even tried praying over us.

"I'm finding more scriptures about praises being a sacrifice," Ashley said. "Maybe we need to sing."

I grunted. "You don't want to hear me sing."

Ashley shrugged. "I don't know a lot of hymns. Just a bunch of songs we had to learn in Vacation Bible School."

"What's that?" Abel asked.

Ashley shrugged. "Free Summer babysitting, really. Churches run these programs for kids. They spend most of the day doing activities, crafts, or singing songs. Then the parents get to pick them up later."

I smiled. "Sounds more like a vacation for the parents. A temporary respite during the part of the year when their kids aren't in school for half of the day."

"I know, right? I mean, when I was little, my parents used to send Annabelle and me to a program that they actually called 'Mother's Day Out.'"

I laughed. "Now that sounds like genuine mercy! Don't get me wrong, I've raised a lot of kids through the years. I loved every one of them. But sometimes, well, you just need a little time for yourself."

Abel grinned. "You know, I never thought about that. Having kids. Starting a family. I've been so focused on trying to figure out how this new, complicated world works, it never occurred to me to consider what I might want for my future, for this second chance at living."

"We have plenty of time to think about that, Abel. Trust me, you don't have to decide tomorrow."

"It's true," Ashley added. "I thought when I graduated High School I wanted to be a nurse. Then, well, I realized it meant having to deal with a lot of bodily fluids."

I snorted. "And that little concoction you all worked up earlier, the one you made Sam drink, didn't have any bodily fluids in it?"

Ashley smirked. "I won't say it didn't. But I will say that I leave the retrieval of all our wares to Roger for good reason."

"Didn't you say there was horse semen in that? Are you telling me that Roger had to extract..."

"No!" Ashley interrupted, laughing through her words. "First, there's not actually horse semen in it. Cain suggested there might be, and we let it roll. But it's nothing like that. Nothing you have to extract in that... way... at least."

Abel wiped a little sweat from his forehead. "Well, that's good to know. This is a strange world, you know. Nothing would surprise me."

I laughed. "Well, I won't say that the world of dating and intimacy doesn't have a side to it these days that might leave you raising your eyebrows. But even today, there are some things that have always been weird, are still weird, and will always be weird."

"But some people are into freaky," Ashley said.

I snorted. "Yes, some people are."

Abel shrugged. "As you said, some things never change."

We all laughed together over it all, but it was forced. I'd turned from sarcasm to humor. I was still as anxious as ever, if not more than before.

"This is useless," I said. "We will not evoke angels like this. If that worked, people would call on angels all the time."

Abel shrugged. "Maybe they do. I mean, just because we can't see them doesn't mean they aren't there."

I shook my head. "None of that is going to help us right now. We don't need a bunch of angels looking over our shoulders. They are the ones who kidnapped our friends. We need to confront them."

"I hate to say this, brother, but we're running out of time for that."

I nodded. "I know. If we don't bring Sam to Belial soon, he's going to unleash his legions. We might not have any choice but to confront the demon head-on."

"I'm not sure how smart that is," Abel said.

"I can concoct a few protections," Ashley said. "A few wards that should prevent them from trying to possess you or anything like that."

I bit my lip. "Is there any way that you could ward the whole city? I realize it's probably a huge undertaking compared to warding a house. But is it possible?"

Ashley scratched her head. "Theoretically, yes. But I'm not sure if anything on that scale has ever been attempted. A city isn't like a house or a home. A home is protected, already, by the familial bond of those who dwell within it. It's why vampires, for instance, can't enter someone's home without an invitation. There are already wards of a kind over homes. But over a city, well, there's very little connection or bond. There are borders but there aren't visible walls that help define the boundaries of the ward."

"Walls actually keep vampires out of people's houses?" Abel asked.

Ashley shook her head. "It's not the brick and mortar that does it. Vampires or, in our situation now, demons, could easily break through a wall. It's the same energy that families create through their bond of love that defines the boundaries. Since people, naturally, think of the walls of a house as the walls of their home, the wards naturally contour alongside the walls, doors, and windows of a place."

"Trying to get everyone in New Orleans to bond with each other like family would be a bigger miracle than anything mystical we might be attempting as it is."

Ashley pressed her lips together. "This might sound dumb. I mean, I'm mixing a lot of my shamanism with the religion I was raised with to sort this out. But there is precedent for interceding on behalf of a city that was about to be destroyed."

I bit my lip. "Sodom and Gomorrah?"

Ashley nodded. "I don't think an angel, or even a demon, can just destroy a city without some kind of permission from the Almighty. I'm not saying that New Orleans is Sodom or Gomorrah, but it isn't exactly a city well known for its family-friendly atmosphere. Not the French Quarter, anyway."

"You're suggesting that if Belial wants to destroy the city, he'll have to get permission to do it?"

Ashley shrugged. "I don't know. I mean, I'm grasping at straws here. I probably know a lot less about angels and all this stuff than either of you two do. But it's a thought. In that story, when Abraham tries to intercede for Sodom and Gomorrah, he's told that if even a single righteous person was found within the city, it would not be destroyed. What if we don't have to unite the entire city and get everyone singing Kumbaya? What if you two, you brothers, stood at the heart of the city and were in the way of Belial's assault?"

Abel shrugged his shoulders. "If the Almighty won't allow the city to be destroyed on our account, he'd send angels to stop them. I can't say we'd be able to see them do it, but they'd be there."

"Are we really righteous enough to stop this from happening? I'm Cain. I'm not exactly a saint."

"You didn't used to be," Abel said. "But given how you live your life, today, you're as close as they come."

I shook my head. "I don't know. I still have my issues."

Ashley snorted. "Doesn't everybody? I mean, not even St. Peter was perfect. From my recollection, he's fumbling around and screwing up more than he's doing anything noble or righteous in most of the New Testament."

I smiled. "He's not the only one. No one in that book is as noble and righteous as a lot of church-goers these days would like to believe."

"This brings us back to our offerings, brother," Abel said. "It's a matter of the heart. I know you aren't religious or anything, but your heart is genuine."

"As is yours," I said. "I don't know how much I like this idea. But perhaps it's the only way. We have to go back to the city and stand up to Belial. We can only pray that the angels show up before we're turned into fire-roasted werewolves."

CHAPTER THIRTEEN

IT MIGHT HAVE BEEN the least confident I'd ever been when confronting something insidious. It wasn't just because I was facing off with a demon, but because our entire plan was based on a lot of theory, amateur biblical exegesis, and a sizable dose of desperation. It wasn't exactly a trifecta that inspired certainty.

At this point, though, we had no other option beyond sitting on our butts and hoping that Sam and Roger would come back, they'd have good news, and they'd lead a legion of archangels with them to stop Belial. The chances of that working out were slim to none. We didn't know for sure what had happened to them. Not exactly. We knew they'd gone into the portal which indicated they were back in the celestial prison that traumatized Abel before.

One thing I knew about demons was that if you shouted their name, they'd hear you. Demons are narcissists to the extreme. Belial hadn't confronted us when we were driving, before. Perhaps he knew that the angels already had Sam. That didn't mean he wouldn't show up to fulfill his threat to march his devilish legions on the city.

We left the asylum extension and drove back to the French Quarter. I parked the car and stepped into the middle of Bourbon Street. There wasn't any hiding this. If the demon attacked, well, there wasn't any sense in being secretive about it. The best thing I could do is call him out in public, give people a chance to high-tail it out of the area before Belial and his legions unleashed their fury on the quarter.

"You two are free to leave," I said. "I don't want either of you to put yourselves at risk."

"A three-stranded rope is unbreakable," Ashley said. "And the angels have my man. I'm standing with you, Cain."

"And we stand together, always, brother," Abel said, nodding at me and smiling at me kindly.

I extended my hands. Abel took one of them. Ashley grabbed the other. People were buzzing all around us. Some of them were partying. Others were there to grab a meal. A few were panhandling. But it had been a day. Belial was undoubtedly on his way. My only chance to stop him was to confront him and pray that the Almighty would intervene, that the angels would arrive to stop Belial before he devastated the city. If Abel, Ashley, and I weren't righteous enough to save, if we weren't worthy to stand up for the city, then so be it. We had to try. We had to stand against the forces of hell, even if it meant our end. If New Orleans would fall, it would be over our dead bodies—literally.

"Belial!" I shouted.

My heart raced as the demon appeared about fifty feet from where we stood, surrounded by a black cloud. A hint of sulfur caught the breeze, carrying the demon's scent with him as he moved toward us with steady determination.

I'd always heard that it's not wise to provoke a demon. In this case, that's exactly what I needed to do. If our theory was correct, if the demons couldn't just level cities without the permission of the Divine, then the best way to bring archangels into the scene was to egg the demon on. If I could mess with his head, poke at his ego, I might convince him to carry out his threat against New Orleans.

It was a high-stakes gamble. The way I saw it, though, was that if I was wrong and demons could assault cities at will without penalty, well, he was going to carry out his threat anyway the moment he learned I wasn't able to give him Sam. If, however, the theory we'd come up with was correct, I'd need to provoke him to attack. That might be the only way to get the attention of the angels.

I'd probably get a good idea of the truth right away. Once he learned about Sam, well, he'd either carry out his threat immediately and I'd never have been able to stop him anyway, or he'd try to back-pedal, issue another threat, extend my deadline, or do virtually anything other than attack New Orleans. Then, I'd know. I'd have to provoke him. It wasn't the way I usually worked. I knew psychology. I'd never used my skills as a psychotherapist to try to manipulate someone. I'd never do that to a patient. I'd never imagined doing so with a demon. But Sam was my patient. So were the wolves who were captured by the angels.

I was confronting a demon so I could negotiate with angels. And now that Belial was approaching me, it was too late to turn back. This was the plan. I'd have to see it through, even if it meant the end of me.

"Son of Adam. Tell me, what have you done with Samyaza? You did not deliver him as I demanded."

I shook my head. "I couldn't hand over an angel to you, Belial. Not even an unfallen angel."

Belial hissed. "Unfallen? Is that what he has told you he is? He remains every bit as vile as me. Only he is a fool."

"You cannot have him," I said.

Belial cocked his head, paused a moment, then turned around. "Very well. Do not think I will not find him, still."

I suppressed the urge to grin. He was confirming Ashley's theory. His threat on the city was hollow. "You're just going to walk away?"

Belial turned and narrowed his eyes. "This city is well steeped in sin, Cain. There are temptations here beyond all measure. Why would I wish to see this city destroyed?"

I grunted. I hadn't expected this complication. He'd threatened the city because he wanted to pressure me to turn over Sam. But he didn't want to bring demonic legions here at all. Sometimes, I suppose, when you're dealing with a high-stakes gambler, and Belial certainly qualified, it couldn't hurt to tip him off, to show him a bit of your hand hoping he'll raise the stakes even higher.

"I don't think you could destroy the city even if you wanted to."

Belial cocked his head. "Is that what you think, son of Adam?"

I nodded. "You demons have no authority over humanity. You harass and terrorize, but you can't kill people, much less destroy cities, without getting the stamp of approval from the big guy upstairs, can you?"

Belial hissed. "You don't know about that of which you speak, son of Adam."

I shrugged. "Maybe you're too weak to do it. More likely, though, you're afraid. You think if you overstep the boundaries, if you attack an entire city, that the Almighty will send his legions after you. And heaven forbid that an angel might bend you over his leg, smack your scaly bottom, and reveal how powerless you really are."

Belial shook his head. "It's a shame, you know. You showed such potential back in the day. Your parents took the fruit with which we tempted them. You, however, took that fruit and planted it, your sin taking root in the earth. You introduced murder to the world, Cain. Have you ever considered, every war, every violent death ever committed was born of you and your sin?"

I bit my lip. Abel put his hand on my shoulder. I narrowed my eyes. "I know what you're trying to do, Belial. You're trying to anger me."

"Anger is one option, Cain. Guilt would work just as well. And Abel, surely you still have a few seeds of resentment in your soul ready to sprout."

"I do not," Abel said. "I've forgiven my brother."

Belial laughed. "I am not speaking of your brother. Angels abducted you, faithful Abel. To think of it! Angels, of all creatures! The things they did, the things they made you see, it must've felt like an awful betrayal to witness the emissaries of God behave so cruelly. In fact, I'd imagine that it would be enough to bring the monster out of anyone. I've primed you both. I do not need to destroy the city. I can use the both of you."

I cocked my head. "What are you saying, demon?"

Belial laughed then, extending his hand, a torch formed in his grip. It must've been one of the six. Flames burst forth from it, just as they did when Julie evoked the flambeau. Belial was right. He'd stoked so much anger, so much fear, so much resentment that neither Abel nor I were ready to shift. But we didn't have a choice.

Abel screamed as his bones popped. I winced. I'd shifted enough that it wasn't so painful. But my heart raced more than it usually did. The wolf was coming out and, drawing on all the vile emotions that the demon had stoked within me, it was emerging with a rage I hadn't known in centuries.

"Run!" I shouted at Ashley. "Tell Rutherford. She'll know what to do. We have to be stopped..."

I howled at the moon, and Abel did the same. Belial laughed as he waved his torch through the air. "Who needs legions of demons when you have a couple of dogs who can do your dirty work?"

CHAPTER FOURTEEN

WHEN THE WOLF IS enraged, it's something similar to what a binge drinker might experience in a blackout. Everything I did as the wolf had its origins in my subconscious mind, but I lacked restraint. It felt like something else was in control. Belial may or may not be able to manipulate us with his infernal torch, but he didn't need to. Belial said he didn't want to destroy the city. As wolves, we wouldn't do that. But we'd terrorize the place. We'd leave a trail of bodies in our path. And more than that, our rage would probably draw the attention of werewolf hunters to the region.

I heard screams. I saw flashes of terror-stricken faces. With every flash of consciousness, my mind receded again into a blackout.

Belial must've been there somewhere. If he left, and his torch went with him when he did, we'd shift back again. I thought I heard him cackling between flashes. That might have been it. It could have been my own snarls, or the shrieks of the people I could only hope we weren't ripping apart. I'd find out soon enough. Once we awakened and could see the death toll all around us, the horror of what we'd done. If it was as grim as I feared, it might take a century before I could process those emotions and deal with the guilt well enough that I could shift free again. Before I'd recover a semblance of the mastery over the wolf that I'd had before. And what about Abel? He was still a young wolf. He was fragile, as it was. Could he ever come back from something like this?

The flashes I saw before changed. Bright lights. That's all I could see. The screams, the demon's laughter, all replaced by a constant, high-pitched ring.

My senses were out of whack. Had the wolf taken over? Had I done something so horrific that my mind suppressed my consciousness once and for all?

The ringing in my head went on for what felt like a century. Then it ended. I wiggled my toes. I was human again. When the bright light cleared, I saw Rutherford looking me in the eye.

"He's back," Rutherford said. "How is his brother?"

"Abel is also awake," Ashley said.

"I need to speak to them both," another voice said. It was a male voice. A smooth voice. Everything had an echo to it. Who was speaking?

Rutherford put her hand behind my head. Another hand grabbed mine. It was warm to the touch. He pulled. I clenched my arm and allowed the man, the one whose voice I heard before, to help me up.

I looked at him curiously. He had golden-flecked eyes. His hair was dark, his skin pure and golden.

"Michael?" I asked.

The archangel smiled at me. "Yes, Cain."

I winced. "I remember little. How many people did we hurt..."

"We intervened before you or Abel could bite anyone."

I looked over at my brother, who was on a hospital bed next to me. He was pulling himself up by the rails, rubbing his eyes. He looked all around the room with narrow eyes, attempting to focus. Then he stared at Michael, and his countenance changed. His lips quivered. His nostrils flared.

"No!" Abel said, springing to his feet, pressing his back against the wall. We were in a room at the Vilokan Asylum. It was a room we often used for processing. The walls were stainless steel. All I could think was that Ashley must've lowered the usual wards in the place to allow Michael entry. Or, maybe, they were never effective against angels at all.

Michael turned from me and approached Abel. "Calm down, Abel. You're safe. I have vanquished the demon for now."

Abel shook his head rapidly, panting. "I saw what you did! I know what you did to us!"

Michael cocked his head. "What are you talking about?"

I rubbed my eyes. "Samyaza. You kidnapped our friends. Annabelle Mulledy, the Voodoo Queen. Both of our packs. You or one of your friends demanded we turn him over to you in exchange for our friends."

"Samyaza, you say?" Michael chuckled. "We are not concerned about Samyaza."

I scratched my head. "But he said that since he disavowed Lucifer and was free, that if he mated with human women again, the Nephilim would be reborn. He said the angels fear the Nephilim because they might slay angels and demons alike."

Michael laughed. "The guy we work for could revive us in an instant, Cain."

I snorted. "I didn't think about that. Are you saying these Nephilim aren't really a threat to you, but they are to the demons?"

"The demons, alone, have reason to fear Nephilim. Lucifer cannot revive his demons. He is not the author of life."

"Samyaza also said that the Nephilim would eventually overtake humanity as the earth's dominant race. You know, survival of the fittest and such."

Michael shook his head. "First, no one knew of Darwin in those days. Second, do you think the Divine is not in charge of who survives? And still third, these days, the principles that governed what you call natural selection are not prominent in modern civilization. There are laws that protect the weak. I say all of that to say this. We were not the ones who kidnapped your friends or the Voodoo Queen."

"Then who did it?" Abel asked. "I didn't see your face, but I heard you speaking. You and Gabriel both."

Michael approached Abel and rested his hand on my brother's shoulder. "It is written that Lucifer often masquerades as an angel of light. It should not be a shock that his demons would do the same so as to deceive you."

"So it was demons, all the while, who captured and imprisoned us?"

Michael nodded. "This is certain."

I scratched my head. "But what about when the flood happened? Samyaza said that you bound him. He specifically mentioned you by name, Michael. He said you forced him to watch as his children drowned."

Michael folded his hands in front of his lap. "Again, though I'm sure the demon who bound him took my form and wished him to believe it was me, it was not. What better way to lead Samyaza to reject heaven once and for all and to join their legion than to present us as such? The flood, I regret to say, was a troubling time. I cannot tell you how much it troubled all of us, even the Almighty, that things came to that. But the souls of those whose lives ended, even the Nephilim, were preserved and judged according to righteousness."

I pressed my lips together, considering the archangel's words. It made sense, I suppose. I didn't need to understand everything. We still had a job to do. Now, it was clear that our friends were in genuine danger. The demons wouldn't release them, no matter what. They'd keep them out of spite, if for no other reason.

"How can we save our friends?" I asked. "We have to find them wherever they might be. The demons have Samyaza. He is my patient. I must rescue him, as well."

"They also took Roger Thundershield, my fiancée," Ashley added.

"I know the place where the demons likely took them," Michael says. "It is neither heaven nor hell. But it is outside of space and time. Like Eden, I suppose, but much less paradisiacal."

"Then you can go there," Abel said. "You and other angels can break them out of that prison and bring them home, right?"

Michael shook his head. "Unfortunately, we cannot. Not until the appointed time."

I stared at Michael blankly for a good three seconds. "The appointed time?"

"As much as I would love to rescue your friends, the larger war between our realms is not yet destined to end. There will come a time when we storm the infernal gates, when we demolish the intermediate realms such as the one where the demons hold your friends, but we cannot do so until all is ready to be fulfilled."

I bit my lip. "You can't just do a little preemptive strike? Just a rescue mission? You don't have to assault the place. Just help us get our friends out of there."

"I can help you, Cain, even if I cannot go with you. I can give you entry to their realm and, again, provide your way home again."

I glanced at Abel and back again at Michael. "I'm not sure we stand much of a chance against the demons on our own merits. After what Belial did to us, how can we possibly stand against however many demons might inhabit that place?"

Michael smirked. "The demon forced you to shift, before, through infernal power. What if I told you that celestial flames could do the same thing, with a few fringe benefits?"

I scratched my head. "I didn't even know that celestial flames were a thing. What benefits are you talking about?"

"A human frame cannot wholly harness celestial power. Infernal power, the light brought by Lucifer, channeled his essence. Since he'd fallen, his flames were also corrupted. But every angel has a flame. I will give you mine. It will not burn forever. I am not willing to divide my flame as Lucifer did with his. But I should be able to invigorate you long enough to rescue your friends, provided you act fast."

"What if we don't make it out of there in time?" Abel asked.

"Then you will again be subjected to the power of Lucifer's infernal flames. And if you're trapped in their realm, in the intermediate domain where they've imprisoned your friends, I will not be able to rescue you. Not until the appointed time, the end of the age."

I nodded. "We don't have a choice. Are you sure you can do this, Abel?"

Abel sighed. "I have to. I have to face my fear. It's the only way. I can't allow those fears to remain with me the next time we shift. If you go alone, even if you succeed, I don't know that I'll be able to get past this trauma unless I overcome it with you now."

I nodded. "I'm not willing to waste any more time. As troubling as this place was to Abel, I cannot imagine what the rest are going through. The longer we wait, the more they'll suffer."

"Very well," Michael said, retrieving two necklaces from the inside of his white robe. Each of them consisted of a single crystal sphere dangling from a golden chain. He placed one over my neck, the other one over Abel's.

I cocked my head. "You just happened to have these on you? That's awfully convenient."

Michael laughed. "Nothing happens by accident, Cain. Still, I cannot say I was ill-prepared for this moment."

"Are you suggesting that this moment was predestined to happen?" I asked.

Michael cocked his head. "Why are you humans so concerned with the tension between destiny and free will? Cannot all things be destined and foreknown, even if the means by which such things are accomplished are by agency or free choice?"

"I don't know. It always seemed a contradiction to me. The whole free will versus predestination thing."

"It's only confusing because, as humans, you imagine you can comprehend the mysteries of the Divine. The principle of destiny, or predestination, is not meant to minimize your responsibility as a moral agent. It is not at all in conflict with your free will and choice. However, when all seems doubtful and you are tempted to despair, you can take comfort in this—your future is secure, you've been chosen, even though you were cursed, for a higher purpose. After all, my boss has great foresight. Though you were cursed, he knew your curse would eventually drive you to redemption. It is not a mistake that today, though you assume the form of the wolf, you shall storm one of hell's prisons as though you were angels of light."

"As angels of light?" Abel asked. "I thought the appointed time had not yet arrived."

"Consider yourselves heralds of our coming victory. Should you succeed, the demons will never be more distraught or certain that their end draws near."

CHAPTER FIFTEEN

MICHAEL TOUCHED MY NECKLACE and also Abel's. When he did, a blue flame swirled in the crystal sphere that dangled from my neck. Abel and I shifted again—this time, though, we were inside Vilokan Asylum. I looked at Abel. He was a magnificent creature. Surely, I was as well. But the stainless-steel walls in the room weren't reflective. He was always an impressive-looking wolf, large of stature, with golden fur. Now, though, his eyes emanated a blue glow that mimicked Michael's celestial fires. It wasn't unlike the blue, magical, firmament that protected Vilokan.

Animated by Michael's celestial flames, I had more control than ever. My mind was clear. My senses were always acute in wolf form, but now it was more profound, almost like these weren't human senses at all. My vision was perfect. My sense of smell was enhanced. Even though the wards in Vilokan Asylum minimized Nedley Mandico's stink ape capabilities, it was immediately clear that our wards were only ninety-nine percent effective. I smelled him straight away, even through the walls.

Then there was my sense of touch. Ashley walked across the room to get a better look at us. I could feel the pressure in the air shift as she moved.

Michael extended his hand, and with his index finger, traced a semi-circle in the air. His finger carved a bright blue portal. It was like how Annabelle, when possessed by Isabelle, could cut gates into the fabric of space and time.

"So long as my power within you endures and the flames are not extinguished, I will keep the gate open. If, however, you take too long and the infernal flames take over, I will have no choice but to cut off the portal."

I nodded at Michael. Abel and I glanced at each other. I grunted. Abel licked his teeth. I dove into the gate and Abel followed close behind.

The place was light and bright. I could see why Abel would have mistaken the demonic prison for an angelic one. Nothing about the place suggested hellfire or brimstone. There weren't any horned goat-man statues. No inverted pentagrams. No pitchforks. The only thing about the place that was remotely hellish were the screams. Whatever these demons were doing to our friends wasn't good.

I glanced at Abel. We each nodded at each other. He'd been here before. He led the way, following the screams to a large, stone slab.

We can charge it together, I said, communicating through our connection as wolves and as brothers.

Abel nodded. We each took three paces back. With a roar, we both ran on all fours toward the door and threw our bodies into it. The slab cracked. I pressed through it with my snout, forcing my body through the cracks. Then, Abel blasted through the door, shattering it into pieces.

A demon, one I'd never seen, stood in the room with a torch aflame with infernal power. The wolves were all chained to a wall, completely wolfed-out. The demon released his flame. They became human again. Then the demon looked at us. While Belial resembled a serpent, this one was almost like a man, but his face had no features at all. It was blank. He wore white, presumably to give the impression he was an angel.

The demon cocked its head. It turned and ran the moment it saw the celestial flames in our eyes and in the globes hanging from our necks.

I tore the chains from the wall that bound our wolves. Their bodies collapsed on the ground. They were exhausted from the torture, from being forced to shift between forms repeatedly. But they were alive. Rutherford was a trained nurse. Sure, she'd specialized in psychotherapy, but she could help them.

I still needed to find Annabelle, Roger, and Sam. I looked at Abel.

Take the wolves home. One at a time, if necessary. I need to find the others. Do you know where they might be?

I do not, Abel said. My brain translated his wolf's language into something I could understand. Or, perhaps, under celestial power, even our ability to communicate was enhanced.

I relied on my enhanced hearing. I could have heard a pin drop in an automotive factory.

An exhale.

That was all I heard.

I took off down a corridor just outside the room where we found the wolves. Were we outside or inside? I couldn't tell. This wasn't on earth. There wasn't a sky, or a sun, above us. The light came from above, from an expanse of some sort that was pale and bright, like fluorescent lighting.

The walls on either side of me were white and smooth, as if they were hewn from bleached bone.

I paused. I listened. The breathing was shallow. As I got closer, I could hear a heartbeat. Two heartbeats. Annabelle and Roger? I wasn't sure if Sam had a heart, technically. What organs do angels have? I'd never cut one open and didn't intend to anytime soon.

I followed the breaths until I found another doorway. This time the slab that guarded the room was already cracked. I thrust my claw into the crack and pulled the slab apart. The stone didn't crack like the one we burst through before. It broke apart like slate. In this room there was a single cell, a sphere consisting something like crystal or plexiglass. It was in the center of the room.

Annabelle was inside. I tapped on the glass with my claws.

Annabelle rolled over. Her eyes met mine. I nodded at her. I didn't know, if I broke this globe, if the glass would shatter around her. Could I even penetrate it?

I reared back to charge the globe. I paused for a moment. I still heard two heartbeats. Where was the other one coming from? I ran at the globe. Somehow I had to get Annabelle out of there. She was alive. She was barely conscious. I dove at the glass sphere then passed right through it. My body hit the other side, the internal side of the globe.

What was this prison? I got in with no problem at all. But I couldn't get out. The convex surface was penetrable. The opposite concave side wasn't.

"I don't think..." Annabelle muttered, trying to speak. "I don't think there's any way out."

I threw myself at the globe again. This time, the whole thing moved. It rolled like we were inside a hamster ball.

"This way!" a voice shouted.

I turned and looked around the globe. The curvature of the glass distorted everything outside the globe. But there was no mistaking the man on the other side of the translucent shell. It was Roger.

I barked at him. It was the best I could do.

Roger nodded. "They couldn't hurt me. Not with their power. My Choctaw blood resisted all their power. I think they're just trying to get rid of me. Still, they have Sam. He's the next cell over."

I looked around myself, at the globe that surrounded me. I whimpered.

"Do you have a way out of here?" Roger asked.

I nodded and huffed, pointing my snout in the direction where Michael's portal was at.

"I don't know if you can get through the door in this globe. But if you get a running start, it may break through. Or it could shatter. Either way, it might work."

I used one of my clawed hands to touch the globe of celestial power around my neck. It was what kept me in wolf form. It also gave me the power I needed to face the demons. It was like a miniature version of the sphere Annabelle and I were caught inside.

"What is that?" Roger asked. "Fomorian magic?"

I shook my head. Then, I did my best to flap my arms to suggest angel wings. I was never good at charades. Trying to do it as a wolf was even more ridiculous. But I didn't know how else to communicate with Roger.

"Celestial magic?" Roger asked.

I howled and nodded my head. I couldn't believe he'd guessed it right.

"Can you use it? If you can, if you can wield that power to charge your sphere somehow you might be able to blast through the walls."

I grunted. It was an idea. How could I possibly draw on the magic? Besides, I only had a limited amount of it. Once it expired, Michael said he had to close the portal. I couldn't leave Sam behind. But I couldn't get out of here and save Annabelle, too.

I didn't know if it would work. But it was all I had. I grabbed the chain around my neck, hooking one of my claws behind it, and pulled. I dangled it in front of my face a moment before I slammed it to the ground.

The orb shattered, its magic filling the globe we were within. The power was even more intense now. Annabelle gasped. It was as if the celestial magic healed her in an instant.

"Come on," Annabelle said. "We can run. Let's hope it's enough."

I nodded. I ran. Annabelle ran beside me.

"There you go!" Roger shouted, running just in front of us. He crawled through the opening I'd made to enter the room. Seconds later, we barreled through it like a wrecking ball.

The sphere cracked when we hit the door, but it didn't shatter. We keep rolling. The corridor was just wide enough that we continued moving as if we were heading down a lane preparing to strike a set of pins.

The crack spread. Whatever this orb was, the magic was weakening it. I wasn't sure I could maintain it. If it broke, I'd shift back. More than that, if Abel was already gone and had the other wolves out of here, once my celestial power was spent, Michael would close the gate.

The globe shattered around us as we rolled toward the gate. Roger helped Annabelle to her feet as the energy from the sphere dispersed.

I shifted back as the power that maintained my wolf form dissipated. Roger didn't need to wait for me. He didn't know that the gate would disappear once my magic failed. I didn't see Abel. All I could figure was that in the time it took me to find Annabelle, he'd got the wolves home.

Roger helped Annabelle through the gate. I got to my feet again in human form. I had a moment. I could have dived into the gate, but Sam was still here. I couldn't leave him behind. I turned and ran. Sam was an angel once. He had powers, even if they weren't celestial or infernal in orientation. Could he get me out of here if I saved him? I wasn't sure. But I'd made him a promise. I'd be his advocate.

I turned and looked over my shoulder as I ran just in time to see Michael's gate disappear.

CHAPTER SIXTEEN

I WAS NAKED. IN a demonic prison. It sounded like a premise to a movie I'd never want to see, much less star in. If you find yourself in a situation like this, there aren't a lot of happy endings. I don't mean that, either, in the way Christopher did when referring to massages before. I mean it in the literal sense. I had one chance. I had to find Sam, save him somehow, and hope that he had some kind of power to bust us out of this place. If I didn't do that, well, I was likely to end up chained to the wall like the other wolves were before. I didn't have a crystal ball anymore, but I didn't need one to see an eternity of torture in our future. I narrowed my eyes and looked down the hall. Roger said he was here. In the next cell over from where Annabelle was held. If he was in a similar sphere, though, I wasn't sure what I could do. I didn't have access to celestial power. Sam didn't wield it, either. He had power, but it was neither infernal nor celestial. It wasn't a hybrid of both, either. It was something unique. Something unmorphed by his loyalties to either heaven or hell.

So far, I had seen no demons except for the blank-faced demon who was torturing the wolves. I ran past the cell where Annabelle was held before and found the next one. Again, a stone slab blocked my entry. I was still strong, stronger than most humans, but it was nothing compared to the power I had as a wolf.

I thrust my shoulder into the door. It didn't budge. Punching it wouldn't do much, so there wasn't any sense breaking my knuckles to confirm what I already knew was certain to fail. I kicked the door. Front kicks. Back kicks. Side kicks. I was no Chuck Norris, but I'd taken a few martial arts classes through the centuries. I knew how to kick. If the door was a pine board, I could have busted through it. Instead, it was some kind of stone, or maybe bone, and it wasn't likely to crack, much less break, with my diminished strength.

I knew there was a demon here. He held an infernal torch. Last time, Belial took me off guard. He'd stoked my anger, fear, and resentment. But now I'd already saved most of my friends. I wasn't blaming the angels anymore for what I thought was an uncharacteristic betrayal. I was at peace with my brother, as I was before, and I was here for one reason. I was here to save my patient.

If only I knew the demon's name, I could call him. Then again, he ran from me before when he sensed the celestial power within me. Now, I wasn't that different from any of the other wolves he'd tortured. I'd lived longer. There was the whole seven-fold curse thing which, surely, the demon knew about. But I didn't know if it would impact a demon and, frankly, he probably wasn't interested in killing me, anyway. From what I'd seen, he got his jollies from torture. And he'd done it to my friends by forcing them to shift.

"Hello!" I shouted. "I know you're here, somewhere."

Silence. I walked down the hall, my bare feet sticking to the cold floor as I made my way past the cell where they'd imprisoned Sam.

Surely, the faceless devil was around. He was probably watching me. Waiting for an opportunity to jump out, evoke his torch, and force me to shift. I didn't know how he'd bound the rest of the wolves. They were chained to the walls. I imagined he did it while they were shifting.

He could try to do that to me, but I shifted faster than they did. With my mind right, I could maintain my focus.

A familiar tingle settled on my brow. It was what I often felt for a split-second when I shifted. I turned around. The faceless demon was there, his torch in hand. I was half-way through my transformation. The demon wiped his hand across his face.

Sam's face stared back at me, smirking as I changed.

The children of Lucifer masquerade as angels of light.

Was it Samyaza? Had he been manipulating me all this time, just to lure me into this prison? Or was it a demon only pretending to look like Sam? There wasn't any way to know for sure. But if I allowed myself to believe Sam betrayed me, if that was the last thing that occurred to me before my shift completed, the wolf would emerge enraged.

I focused my mind. A part of it made sense. It would have been the ultimate charade for a demon to pretend he was remorseful, to do all of that to lure me into their realm. But why did they want me? I couldn't believe it. If Sam was a demon, if he held infernal power, he wouldn't have been able to get past our wards. This was a demon. Michael said he'd vanquished Belial, but it very well might have been him. Michael didn't tell me where he'd sent the demon. I knew little about how easily the demons navigated between realms. This wasn't hell. It wasn't the earth. It was some kind of in-between, a sort of purgatory.

The demon looked at me, still wearing Sam's face. I wouldn't be fooled. I was shifted again. I was the wolf. I couldn't hear Sam in the room where Roger said he was being held. But I would not allow this demon's infernal flame to warp my mind. Not this time.

When my eyes met his, the smirk on his face disappeared. He took two steps back.

The power from the torch, the demon's flambeau, was more palpable than before. Maybe it was because I was calm of mind. Perhaps it was because I'd acquired celestial magic before. But Michael had told me that Lucifer's villainy had warmed his light. His light wasn't unlike that of any other archangels. Not essentially. It was how he wielded it, and the lesser demons in his care carried it, that gave it infernal power.

I drew on the power, approaching the demon.

"Step back, son of Adam."

I laughed as the demon's face changed again. It was Belial, after all. At least, he was wearing the snake-like face he'd worn when he appeared to me on earth, before. My laugh came out like a series of cackles. I shook my head.

Then, I dove on the demon, grabbed the torch with my jaws, and took off. The torch flame, now in my possession, turned from red to blue. I didn't do it on purpose. It just happened. My senses awakened, as they had before. Then, I turned back around, and pursued Belial.

A black cloud formed around his feet. He was trying to flee. I was faster than he'd expected. I dove at him, sank my teeth into his chest, and ripped into his infernal flesh. Another black cloud emerged from the wound. I took the torch, swiping through the demon's essence. The flames consumed the demon's spirit.

Belial was gone.

I returned to the door I couldn't break through before. I blasted through it this time as if it were made of gelatin.

Sam was there, bound to a chair, situated over a sigil.

"Cain, is that you?"

I nodded.

"That flame... how did you get that?"

I shrugged. I couldn't answer him easily in this form. Then I glanced at the sigil beneath Sam's feet.

"It's a spiritual prison of a sort. But if that flame is what I think it is, it should be able to dispel it."

Holding the torch in front of my face, Sam ducked down and covered his face. I huffed, and I puffed because, you know, that's what wolves do. Then I blew the flames through the sigil that had imprisoned the unfallen angel.

Sam uncovered his face. "It worked! I can't believe it worked!"

I looked around. I whimpered a few times. I wasn't sure if he'd get the message.

"There is only one demon here, so far as I know. I can't say there weren't more before."

I nodded and snorted.

"Then we'd better get out of here fast. I know how we can leave. We should be able to get through the portal that leads to the mansion. The one that the demons used to bring Roger and I here before. If you just use some of that power you've acquired."

I nodded, followed Sam past the lump of flesh that used to be Belial, to a spot in the wall. There was a small crack in it.

"Just cast some of your power here. It should take us back."

I touched the crack with the torch and the crack expanded into a blue portal, one that resembled the one Michael had made before. Sam patted me on the back. "Thank you, Cain. For saving me. For believing in me."

I nodded, and once Sam went into the portal, I followed him through.

CHAPTER SEVENTEEN

SAM TOUCHED THE TORCH I was holding and, when he did, the flames dissipated. I shifted back into human form.

"Welcome back," Sam said.

I nodded. "What did you do with that flame?"

Sam shrugged. "I don't know. But I think it might have turned me into an angel again."

I cocked my head. "Is that what you want?"

Sam bit his lip. "I really don't know. I mean, when I first came to you in Vilokan, I thought it was angels who were after me. They weren't. They must've known I'd disavowed Lucifer and seemed content to let me live how I wished."

"I don't think you have to stay as an angel if you'd prefer to remain, you know, unfallen. This flame, it was infernal. I took it from Belial."

Sam cocked his head. "You stole one of Lucifer's flames and restored it to light?"

I nodded. "I suppose I did."

"That's... incredible. I never heard of anyone, much less a mortal..."

"I don't know how I did it. But it seemed to work. Michael might still be back at the Vilokan Asylum. He was there when we left, at least. I think some of the others left their cars out back."

Sam nodded. "We can go back. I'd suggest putting on some clothes first, though."

I looked down at my bare body. I chuckled. "Sorry about that. I have a set of clothes in my office here. I figured I'd need a spare for when I shift here on a full moon."

I quickly changed into a pair of athletic pants and a t-shirt. It wasn't my usual slacks and button-up shirt I wore when I was working. We'd been through enough, though, that I figured if there was ever a time I could get away with going casual, this was it.

I didn't have keys to any of the vehicles parked outside. I could only hope that one of the wolves had left their keys in their car. We were in a fairly remote area, after all, and the gates in front of the asylum extension site were secure

I checked a few of the vehicles. They were locked. I approached Annabelle's Camaro. It was custom painted with a glittery purple. The door opened. Her keys were in the cup holder. I laughed to myself.

"Well, Sam. It looks like we'll be delivering the Voodoo Queen's ride back to her in the city."

"We could fly, you know."

"Say what?"

Sam laughed, and two wings spread out from behind his back. They probably spanned twenty feet or more. They were white and feathered.

"Did you have those before?"

Sam shook his head. "Something about that flame... like I said, it feels like it restored me to my former angelic status."

I laughed. "You know, you've presented me with a dilemma. A once-in-a-lifetime chance to drive Annabelle's car, or to soar on the wings of an angel."

"Oh, come on, Cain. Is it really a choice?"

I shook my head. "I suppose it's not."

"But you can't really soar on my wings. I will have to carry you. I mean, on top of my wings would be a pretty bumpy ride."

I laughed. "Alright, I get it. Just try to remain inconspicuous. I'd rather we not be seen. An angel flying with a dude over the city is likely to garner some unnecessary attention."

Sam chuckled. "Well, if this works like it used to, we should be able to go invisible. But it's been nearly as long as since before you were cursed that I've been a proper, celestial angel. So, don't quote me on that."

"Just don't drop me, alright?"

"I'll do my best," Sam said, spreading his wings. Then, he hooked his arms under mine and took off into the skies like a jet.

Clearly, there was more to his propulsion than what his wings provided. Still, once we were in the skies, we glided across the city. The air struck my face. It was refreshing.

Then, as we approached Jackson Square, Sam circled the cathedral a few times before lowering us into Pere Antoine Alley.

"What a rush!" I said.

Sam laughed. "Yeah, it really was. I forgot how much fun that was."

"You couldn't fly as a demon, I take it?"

Sam shook his head. "I usually manifested like a goat. No fun at all. I ate a few t-shirts, though."

I grinned. "Well, your form now is far more appealing. Even when you were unaffiliated; unfallen, I found you quite likable."

"I might go back to that. I don't know. We'll see what Michael says."

I nodded. "Let's hope he's still here."

We entered Vilokan and made our way to the Asylum. Rutherford was checking out Annabelle when we arrived. The wolves were all gathered in the asylum, dressed in our standard cartoon-patterned gowns. Abel was laughing and talking to Donald. They were probably traumatized, but we'd work through it. When you're dedicated, when

you have a supportive family or a pack, you can work through anything. We'd just have to put in the work.

Michael was still there. He was talking to Nedley when I walked in.
I wasn't sure what Nedley was saying. He was probably drawling on
about something he thought made himself sound intelligent. From
the look on Michael's face, he was smiling and nodding, but wasn't
listening.

"Nedley, mind if I borrow Michael for a minute?"

"Certainly!" Nedley said. "It has been an honor, Sir Michael."

Michael nodded. "It's just Michael. I'm an angel, not a knight."

Nedley nodded, bowed slightly, and departed with one hand tucked
into his hospital gown, sort of like that famous painting of Napoleon
Bonaparte, but with a much less distinguished feel to it.

"Would you like to join me in my office?" I asked.

"I'd be happy to," Michael said before glancing and nodding at Sam.
"Samyaza."

Sam nodded. "Hello, old friend."

I opened the door to my office and let the two angels in ahead of
me. I closed the door. "When I welcomed Sam here at the asylum and
agreed to take him on as a patient, I promised him I'd intercede on his
behalf."

"How did you ever re-acquire your celestial power?" Michael asked,
looking at Sam.

Sam looked at me and grinned. "From Cain. He took Belial's torch.
When he did, Lucifer's flame was replaced with celestial fire."

Michael furrowed his brow. "You took one of the six torches of
Lucifer?"

I sighed. "Apparently, so. Between this one, which I think now
empowers Sam, and the one Julie Brown carries, we have access to two
of them that Lucifer can no longer access."

"Ah yes," Michael said. "The Witch of Endor's flambeau."

I nodded. "Only, I'm not sure why her flambeau still manifests with infernal magic while this one changed when I took it."

Michael placed a hand on my shoulder. "You've been cursed, Cain, but it was through your curse that you found redemption. I offered before, and I shall make the offer again if you like, to petition to see your curse removed. Though I suspect you'd prefer to maintain it."

I nodded. "I don't see it as a curse. Not anymore."

"All things, even a curse, can become a blessing. You can help her, Cain. You need not claim the flambeau from her, but if you wish, you can transform her flames. It would mean that we've weakened Lucifer's influence on the world by nearly a third of what it once was."

I nodded. "Here's the thing, Michael. Sam's power is restored. I'm not sure he's totally ready to go back into the service of the Almighty, though. And I think it would be best for him to make that choice when he's ready."

Michael grinned and put a hand on Sam's back. "Samyaza, take your time. There is no compulsion in the service of the Divine. Just make sure, you know, not to spread your seed too far and wide."

Samyaza laughed. "I'm not so sure that I even want to do that again, Michael. I just don't know what my future holds. But I know, now, that I will one day wish to help dismantle Lucifer's legions. I'm just not sure I'm ready for that yet."

"The appointed time is still far off on the horizon, Samyaza. But your story, your tale of redemption, is one that should be told."

"As should doctor Cain's," Sam said.

"I agree," Michael said. "In a world where guilt runs amok, where guilt breeds resentment and resentment leads many onto numerous unsavory paths, it's important to know that no one is too far beyond redemption. All it takes is an honest assessment of one's errors, to accept responsibility, and to commit oneself to a new path forward.

You've both done exactly that, even if your path, Sam, is not yet clear or defined."

Sam extended his hand to shake mine. I hugged him instead. I know it's not professional to hug your patients, but we'd been through a lot in a short amount of time. Then Michael embraced us both. "Well, brothers. I should depart. You are doing wonderful things here, the both of you. I don't know when we'll cross paths again, Cain. But Samyaza, when you're ready to rejoin our ranks, we'll be here. You'll always be welcome."

The wolves, along with Abel, returned to the extension site. I drove Annabelle there so she could recover her Camaro. I didn't address the possibility of morphing Julie's flambeau into one that wields celestial power. We'd talk about it later. The demon had forced the wolves to shift so many times, and I'd shifted more than I was accustomed to. We needed to rest a little while before Julie brought out her infernal relic again.

I left, following Annabelle back to Vilokan. Of course, she took off at something in excess of a hundred miles per hour down the highway. I shook my head as she left me in her dust. She was a wily one, that Annabelle Mulledy.

I went back to my office in Vilokan. I had other patients whose needs still needed to be addressed. There were many among the magically and mentally deranged who deserved another chance at life. I didn't know if I'd see Samyaza again. I hoped I would. But even if I didn't, well, at least I knew he had a chance to forge a new life without being beholden to anyone else. If he wanted to, some day, maybe he'd rejoin Michael.

Or, perhaps, he'd re-create the Nephilim. Michael didn't seem too bothered by that prospect if that was the choice he made. There was no telling what the future would hold. But at least now, Sam had a future that was his own.

I started sorting through the files on my desk. I still needed to do some work with Nedley. There were a few mambos who'd mistakenly evoked a trickster spirit by using the wrong herbs in their attempt to evoke Papa Legba for a blessing. The spirit was still on the loose, but he'd warped their minds and somehow their memories were swapped. Each mambo thought she was the other. This was going to be a challenge. Were their minds truly swapped or had the trickster only led them to believe that's what happened? I had my work cut out for me.

I'd probably sleep on my chaise longue. Yes, technically, I had a small apartment in Vilokan. It was little more than a bed, four walls, a toilet and a newly installed electrical outlet that I had a microwave plugged into. It was all I asked for when Marie Laveau first offered me the job at Vilokan Asylum. I'd lived lavishly in the past. I'd lived in large abodes where I'd raised children. The best parts of my life, though, were spent in smaller, more intimate communities. I found, through the years, that the more stuff I'd accumulated, the less content I was. So I lived something of a minimalist lifestyle. My little apartment was nothing more than a place to sleep and, as often as not, I rested in my office.

Someone knocked on my door.

"Come in," I said.

Rutherford stepped inside. "How's everything going? Sounds like it's been a busy day or two."

I sighed. "You could say that."

"Why don't you come home with me?"

I shrugged. "I don't know, Rutherford. I have a lot on my plate for the morning."

"Cain, I'm not asking you to spend the night. You need rest and relaxation. You need time to recharge and recover. And you need that every night."

"Every night?" I asked.

"I'm asking you if you'd like to move in with me, Cain."

I bit my lip. "Rutherford, I don't know. I'd love to, but..."

"But what? You have work to do?"

I laughed to myself, shaking my head. "I suppose I've become something of a workaholic."

Rutherford leaned over and kissed me on the cheek. "It's not your work that I think you're addicted to, Cain. It's your drive to help people that keeps you here, burning the candle at both ends."

"These people really need me, Rutherford."

"And if you're well rested, if you're happy, and you have a life outside of this place, I'm pretty sure you'll be a better therapist. Sometimes, when it comes to the kind of work you do with your patients, less is more. You need time for yourself. You deserve to be happy. And you know what, Cain? So do I. I'm putting myself out there. Don't you dare turn me down. I might never ask you again. And I sure as hell won't be moving into your place... ever!"

I laughed. "Well, I suppose you leave me with no choice. I have one question though. It's important to know in advance if we're going to move in together."

Rutherford smiled widely and took my hand. "What is it, Cain?"

"Do you hang your toilet paper on the roll 'over' or 'under'?"

Rutherford laughed. "It goes 'over.' Always. This is non-negotiable."

I smiled. "Good. Right answer. I knew we were meant for each other."

Rutherford snorted. "You realize, 'over' versus 'under' is one of only two options. The world is pretty split on that. I should hope that who you think you're meant for is based on a lot more than which way someone hangs her toilet paper."

I kissed Rutherford on the cheek. "Oh trust me, my feelings for you are based on a lot more than your bathroom habits."

Rutherford nodded. "Good to know. Because, you know, too much interest in my bathroom behaviors is usually a red flag for me when it comes to relationships."

"Understandable," I said, laughing. "I promise you, there's nothing all that freaky about my desires or preferences."

"Nothing at all?" Rutherford asked. "Well, in that case, I might actually have a few things to teach you."

I raised an eyebrow. "Is that so?"

Rutherford bit her lip and, taking my hand, led me out of my office. "I suppose you'll just have to find out."

The End of Book 3

To be continued in THE MARK OF CAIN

Also By Theophilus Monroe

Gates of Eden Universe

The Druid Legacy

Druid's Dance

Bard's Tale

Ovate's Call

Rise of the Morrigan

The Fomorian Wyrmriders

Wyrmrider Ascending

Wyrmrider Vengeance

Wyrmrider Justice

Wyrmrider Academy (Exclusive to Omnibus Edition)

The Voodoo Legacy

Voodoo Academy

Grim Tidings

Death Rites

Watery Graves

Voodoo Queen

The Legacy of a Vampire Witch
Bloody Hell
Bloody Mad
Bloody Wicked
Bloody Devils
Bloody Gods

The Legend of Nyx
Scared Shiftless
Bat Shift Crazy
No Shift, Sherlock
Shift for Brains
Shift Happens
Shift on a Shingle

The Vilokan Asylum of the Magically and Mentally Deranged
The Curse of Cain
The Mark of Cain
Cain and the Cauldron
Cain's Cobras
Crazy Cain
The Wrath of Cain

The Blood Witch Saga
Voodoo and Vampires
Witches and Wolves
Devils and Dragons
Ghouls and Grimoires
Faeries and Fangs
Monsters and Mambos

Wraiths and Warlocks
Shifters and Shenanigans

The Fury of a Vampire Witch
Bloody Queen
Bloody Underground
Bloody Retribution
Bloody Bastards
Bloody Brilliance
Bloody Merry
More to come!

The Druid Detective Agency
Merlin's Mantle
Roundtable Nights
Grail of Power
Midsummer Monsters
More to come!

Sebastian Winter
Death to All Monsters
More to come!

Other Theophilus Monroe Series

Nanoverse

The Elven Prophecy

Chronicles of Zoey Grimm

The Daywalker Chronicles

Go Ask Your Mother
The Hedge Witch Diaries

AS T.R. MAGNUS

Kataklysm
Blightmage
Ember
Radiant
Dreadlord
Deluge

ABOUT THE AUTHOR

Theophilus Monroe is a fantasy author with a knack for real-life characters whose supernatural experiences speak to the pangs of ordinary life. After earning his Ph.D. in Theology, he decided that academic treatises that no one will read (beyond other academics) was a dull way to spend his life. So, he began using his background in religious studies to create new worlds and forms of magic–informed by religious myths, ancient and modern–that would intrigue readers, inspire imaginations, and speak to real-world problems in fantastical ways.

When Theophilus isn't exploring one of his fantasy lands, he is probably playing with one of his three sons, or pumping iron in his home gym, which is currently located in a 40-foot shipping container.

He makes his online home at www.theophilusmonroe.com. He loves answering reader questions—feel free to e-mail him at theophilus@t heophilusmonroe.com if the mood strikes you!

ND - #0291 - 090924 - C0 - 229/152/25 - PB - 9781804675816 - Matt Lamination